Choice

Book Three of The Traveller's Path

L.A. Smith

CarpetPage Press

Cover design by ebboklaunch.com

ISBN: 978-1-9990140-6-3 (e-book)

ISBN: 978-1-9990140-7-0 (paperback)

www.lasmithwriter.com

Published by CarpetPage Press

Extra Content

A list of *"Who's Who"* is at the back of the book.

For more on the world of *The Traveller's Path,* and to get a FREE bundle of two novellas featuring characters from *The Traveller's Path,* scan the QR code below by using your phone's camera.

For more on L.A. Smith and her books, visit her website at lasmithwriter.com.

To Lesley, Miles, Vanessa and Cheryl
More than family, you are friends.

PROLOGUE: THE SCOP WHO PLAYS

Godric drifted in and out of himself, lost in the shadows. Most days, he barely remembered his own name. Trying to puzzle it out was too difficult, and he would succumb to the waiting mists again; sinking down, unresisting, into their depths.

Occasionally, the mists would part, giving him freedom. Often music was the hook that pulled him out, especially when he was performing. He welcomed those moments when he awoke with his fingers on the strings, the melody a sweet siren that called him back to life.

Which is what happened one night. Notes danced through the mist, teasing him, growing louder, and then he suddenly felt the lyre under his fingers. Awareness crashed over him in the blink of an eye, bringing with it a cacophony of sensations: a riotous crowd; the smell of ale, smoke, and sweat; a hard stool supporting him.

He faced a crowded hall. The audience, flushed with ale and pleasure, applauded loudly. He blinked and momentarily lost his grip on the lyre. Only his lightning quick reflexes kept it from hitting the ground, and as he clutched the instrument to his chest and straightened up, he heard the uproarious laughter from the men in the front.

"Ay, *scop*, mayhap you've drunk too deeply from our lord's ale!" Chortling, a young man with curly black hair and a stained tunic raised his own mug to his mouth and upturned it, ale running in rivulets down his chin.

Godric ignored him. These moments of sudden clarity brought with them a flood of impressions and memories, along with the sickening realization of what

Wulfram had done to him. Memories that lay quiet under the mist's suffocating influence.

His performer's instincts kicked in. "My lords, I beg your indulgence," he managed, bowing with a flourish of his cloak. As he straightened up, the room swayed around him, causing him to stagger a half step and steady himself on the stool, to yet more laughter from the crowd. He pasted a grin on his face and shrugged. "Even the *scop* who plays must play!" He winked at a young, buxom woman, who screeched with mock outrage and clutched at her husband's arm.

He threw her a kiss as he hurried off the platform and towards the door, ignoring the slaps on the back and the ribald comments. *Gotta get out, gotta get out.*

But as he reached the door, he couldn't keep himself from stopping and turning to scan the crowd. Self-loathing filled him as his gaze met Wulfram's.

Wait outside, Wulfram Spoke into his mind.

Godric's head dipped in acknowledgement—*like a damned puppet on a string*—and he pulled the door open in disgust, slamming it behind him.

He leaned up against the wall and sucked in the fresh night air, trying to pull himself together. How long had it been since the last time he had roused from his dark dreams? It was too difficult to judge. Time spent in the shadows had no meaning, no duration. It left behind only jumbled scenes and impressions, and he strained at them, trying to remember.

He rode a horse beside Wulfram through the rain, the surrounding forest sodden and dripping. Then he sat by a fire, conversation murmuring around him, the words sliding off his befuddled brain like the raindrops off the trees. Faces lit by the jumping flames flickered in and out of darkness: other Unseelies that Wulfram had gathered to him after his flight from Raegenold.

He remembered their furtive glances towards him, their faces filled with mingled pity and fear. *Cowards.* He clutched the lyre to him and strummed a discordant chord, chasing the memories away with the harsh sound.

He looked around, trying to discern where he was. A vague thought of escape wormed its way to the surface of his tattered mind and sudden hope seized him. *Find a Crossing. Get home.*

He pushed himself away from the door, but a raven's cackling call from above stopped him in his tracks. He looked up and saw the black bird lifting off the roof, melting into the night as it flapped into the darkness.

Rage boiled up. He stooped and picked up a stone, hurling it after the bird's retreating form. He missed, but the minor act of defiance made him feel more like himself than he had in a long time.

Wulfram stepped out, the raucous sounds from inside increasing and then muffling again as he shut the door behind him.

At the sight of the other Traveller, a blaze of anger seized him. In one quicksilver motion, he had Wulfram pressed up against the wall with his knife at his throat. "Damn you to hell," he hissed. Even as he spoke, a part of his brain wondered why he had not just rammed the blade home. Pierced the Fey's black heart and escaped into the night.

"Let me go," Wulfram said, his voice icy cold.

Godric's knife fell from nerveless fingers. He pushed off Wulfram with a strangled cry, ending up with his own back against the wall. His legs gave out, and he slid down. The rage and sense of purpose evaporated, replaced by despair.

Wulfram crouched in front of him, his head cocked to the side like one of his bloody crows examining a shiny trinket. But before he spoke, one of Wulfram's Unseelie followers stepped out.

"My lord?" He looked between Godric and Wulfram.

Wulfram looked up at him. "Never mind. I need to speak to our *scop* alone. See that we are not disturbed."

The Unseelie nodded and stepped back inside.

Wulfram hauled on Godric's arm, forcing him to stand. Godric didn't resist. The suffocating mists of the Undying had fled, but the Bond between him and Wulfram was as strong as ever. He had no choice but to follow, clutching the lyre in one hand.

Wulfram pulled him into the shadows behind another hut and shoved him against the wall, pinning him there as Godric had pinned him a moment before. His eyes glowed with Fey power as his gaze swept over Godric. Disgust twisted his features. He pulled at Godric's arm holding the lyre and pressed it to Godric's chest. "Play it."

Godric blinked at him, startled out of his stupor. "What?"

"Play it like you want to, like a *Fey*."

Godric's fingers twitched, and he held the lyre to him like a lover, caressing the strings. He tried to resist, but music's familiar siren call captured him. Wulfram's suggestion was unnecessary to prompt him to play. He sang the first thing that came to mind, closing his eyes to block out Wulfram's shining form, drowning out the rustle of feathers as the raven came back to rest on top of the hut above him. Grim appreciation filled him at his unconscious song choice. A song about a blackbird seemed a good fit. His voice strengthened as he crooned the words, revelling in the music that gave him as much energy as the dawning of the sun.

As the last notes faded away, Godric opened his eyes. The song had washed the fog from his mind. "What do you want from me, man?"

Wulfram made an impatient gesture. "What I have always wanted. Your cooperation."

Godric snorted, strumming a quick discordant chord. The raven squawked and hopped back from the roof's edge. "My cooperation," he muttered, stifling the urge to batter Wulfram over the head with the lyre. That would lead to the return of the Undying, who gloried in violence and rage. He needed this moment of freedom from its influence more than that short-lived revenge.

"Of course. This would be unnecessary if you would just cooperate!" Anger glittered in Wulfram's eyes. "You alone know the pathetic state of the Fey in our time. We could change that! Together we can turn the tide—here, now."

Godric scowled. "You mean using the Undying to Bind me to you? A minor inconvenience to you, is it?" Rage choked off his words.

Wulfram flinched. The sudden harsh cry of the raven on the roof confirmed what the other Traveller was trying to hide—the fear that pulsed through their Bond.

Interesting. "So how's it going, this plan of yours?" He played a few more notes and hummed the song to anchor himself. The music had jolted the Undying out of him, but he sensed it swirling around, looking to return. He didn't have long. His mouth stretched in a humourless grin. "As you may have noticed, I've been occupied as of late." He strummed a discordant chord. "I haven't been paying attention."

Wulfram's eyes narrowed. "If you would just join me, of your own free will, I would—"

Godric strummed again, interrupting him. The raven squawked. "You would what? Tell it to disappear? Use your words of power on it? Do you think that's why it came in the first place? Because *you* commanded it?"

He saw the flicker of uncertainty in Wulfram's eyes. *Aha. So that's it.* This *tête-à-tête* was not for Godric's benefit. Seeing him stumbling around in the thrall of the Undying had sounded an alarm in the other Fey, a dawning realization that he might have hooked his horse to the wrong wagon, so to speak.

Once this little game that Wulfram was playing was over, then what? The Undying would use Godric up and discard him like a shell from a nut. But he'd bet his bottom dollar that the Undying wouldn't just slink away into the night once Wulfram had finished with it. It would look with eager eyes at Wulfram and the other Unseelies. Wulfram had to understand that the game had bigger stakes than he realized.

The other Unseelies were not comfortable with Godric. He reminded them all that Wulfram had Bound him using the Undying. Almost certainly they were questioning the other Traveller about it.

He played another harsh chord. "You're a fool. You think this is *your* plan? It's using you, man. You're next. Once you've accomplished your little mission, it's coming for you and the rest of the Unseelies. And do you think the Seelies will just sit back and let that happen? Open your eyes! You think what you are doing is going to *save* the Fey?" A giggle escaped him. He tried to pluck at the strings, but his fingers were going numb.

You're going to destroy us, he wanted to say, but he couldn't. The mist rose around him, the raven's cries becoming muffled. *You're destroying yourself.*

Wulfram bowed. Mirth speared through him, snuffed out by the realization that the other Traveller was not bowing to him, but to the Undying, and he wanted to scream, *See? See what I mean?*

But he couldn't. He tried to resist the black mist, but it was like punching at a cloud. At the edge of his mind, the part that was still free, a chiming melody ran through his mind. He grasped at it, but it faded, suffocated under the mists, his feeble resistance coming to nothing.

As it always did.

CHAPTER 1

ALONE

*April 26, near
Bebbanburg*

The pelting rain almost soaked through Thomas' cloak before he spotted a well-worn trail leading off the main road and knew that he had found the holding he had been looking for.

He urged Missy down the track and soon saw a timber wall surrounding buildings that huddled together in the gloomy half-light of twilight. The leader of the last holding he had stayed at had told him about this place. Thomas hoped they would be friendly. He and Odda would both value a night under a roof, out of the rain.

The weather had been pleasant since he parted from Nectan and Brorda at Eoforwic almost a week ago. But soon after they woke this morning, the rain began. A steady drizzle at first, which turned into a downpour that showed no signs of letting up.

A man stood at the gate, watching him approach. Thomas pulled back his hood a bit to reveal his face. "Greetings. I am Master Thomas of Bebbanburg, seeking shelter for the night."

The man looked him over, silent. "Thomas of Bebbanburg, ye say? I've heard tales, I 'ave, of one such named. A sorcerer, they say, bringing the Devil and his Hounds of hell with him and twisting our king to his purpose." He made no move to allow Thomas to pass.

An icy hand touched Thomas' heart. Rumours similar to this had followed him throughout his journey back from Eoforwic, but this was the first one with his name attached. He shrugged, hiding his alarm. "There are others with that name at the king's fortress. None are as you describe, nor am I. I claim the Christ, and have been staying at Lindisfarne with Bishop Aidan at the monastery for the past few months. I've heard the tales, too. There's no truth to them."

At the mention of Aidan, the man relaxed. He looked him over once more and then moved to open the gate. "Aye, well, we cannot be too careful. There seems an ill wind blowing through the land, so there does." He stood aside to let Thomas pass. "Master Eldred is in the hall, as are most of the rest. I was just about to join 'em when I saw ye. Have ye heard the news of our king, God bless 'im?"

"News?" He kept his face blank with an effort. Had Wulfram made a move against Oswy so soon?

The man's grin lightened his face. "Aye. He and 'is men came through this morn. He's gone and brought back 'is brother's arm and head, so he has."

Arm and head? Thomas frowned. Penda, the pagan king of Mercia, had killed Oswald, the previous king and the brother of Oswy, in battle. To add insult to injury, he had left Oswald's arms and head on the battlefield, staked as an offering to Penda's god.

Or something like that. Thomas had never been quite clear on that point. But he knew the matter had been one of anger among the Bernicians. "Brought them back? How?"

"Bold as you please, our king took 'is brave men and snuck out on the battlefield in the night and stole 'em, right out from under Penda's nose." The man slapped his thigh, delight wreathing his face. "God bless 'im!" he repeated, shaking his head. "We celebrate the news in the hall."

"Ah, that is good news. May I put my horse in the stable, then?"

The man waved a hand and closed the gate. His previous caution had evaporated in the telling of Oswy's victory. "Oh, aye. Plenty o' room."

Thomas nodded in thanks at the man as he urged Missy through the gate. Through the drumming rain, music floated in the air, the sound of the celebration.

His gut tightened. At the same time Odda stiffened in his arms and looked up at Thomas, his eyes wide. Thomas forced himself to relax, seeking to calm both the boy's fear and his own. The chances of finding Godric here were slim. "Don't worry, Odda. I'm sure they're not here." He projected confidence in his voice. "We'll eat well tonight and be warm and dry."

As if to confirm his words, the smell of roasting meat reached them. His stomach growled. He urged Missy on to the stable, setting his thoughts of Godric and Wulfram aside. Tomorrow, they would arrive back in Bebbanburg. Unease seized him at the thought, but he pushed that aside, too. Let tomorrow take care of itself. A piece of wisdom from the monks, and one he was happy to apply now.

The rain abated the next day, but not entirely. It spat down at them in intervals throughout the day. The landscape faded into a wet wash of green and brown. Thomas kept his hood up and his head down against the rain, glad that they would be at Bebbanburg by nightfall.

Around mid-afternoon, a sudden tingle of Fey power caused his head to snap up. He drew Missy to a halt, looking around for what had alerted him. It wasn't the sense of another Fey but a slight tug that focussed his attention on a small clump of trees that huddled on a ridge by a stream that flowed nearby. He frowned. A worn path broke off from the one he was on, leading towards the trees. He looked around, orienting himself. He had travelled along this path a few times before in his explorations of the area. A man named Merton had a small farm here, if he remembered correctly.

He studied the trees. What was that elusive feeling? He was sure he had felt something similar before. He frowned, chasing it down, and suddenly he had it: this small tug held an echo of that same sense of invitation he had felt when Celyn took him to the oak grove where he had Crossed on Halloween. He turned Missy's head and urged her down the path. In a few moments, they found another path that broke off again, and following it, soon broke into a small clearing.

Odda had been dozing, but he roused as Thomas' excitement reached him through their Bond. He straightened up, rubbing his eyes. "Master?"

"Stay here. I need to check this out," Thomas said as he slid off Missy's back. He took a few steps as he looked around, allowing a small trickle of Fey power to fill him. He sucked in a breath as the sense of the power lurking in the clearing strengthened. A Crossing. He shook his head, bemused. When he had first arrived, he spent much time riding around Lindisfarne and Bebbanburg, searching for a Crossing. In fact, he had ridden down the main path that went past this spot more than once. How had he missed it?

You weren't ready, Tommo, Matthew's voice whispered through his mind. Thomas exhaled, acknowledging the truth of it. After the Crossing, when he first understood what he was, he struggled to come to terms with his Fey nature. In fact, he had been afraid of it. His father had showed him how to let it be a part of him without overwhelming him. With practice, he had become more sensitive to Fey power. Which is why he sensed the Crossing spot now. He shook his head. All this time, and a Crossing had been so close. Not that it did him much good. He couldn't Cross while being Bound to Odda. And Wulfram had to be dealt with before he could even think about going home.

He mounted Missy, leaving the Crossing without a backwards glance.

As evening drew near and they spotted King Oswy's fortress in the distance, the steady rain and the sea breeze coming off the ocean strengthened into a chill wind, driving the rain against them in hard, cold needles.

A sudden pang went through him at the sight of Bebbanburg perched on its rocky outcrop, and he pulled Missy to a halt. She snorted and tossed her head, impatient at the delay now that they were so close to home. He patted her neck in reassurance.

"My lord?" Odda pressed up against his back as the wind whipped against them, his voice a thin quaver.

"I know. I just need a minute." He took a deep breath, trying to corral the butterflies that swooped through his gut with wild abandon. His arrival would prompt questions he didn't want to answer. The first being Odda's presence. The second was how to answer the questions about how he was faring and how Fee had coped with the news of his father's death.

Another pang pierced him, and he shut his eyes against the wave of grief that swept through him. Going back to Bebbanburg would bring Matthew's absence back. The last time he had ridden back to the fortress on this very road, he had not known his father was dead. A sudden longing seized him to wake up from this nightmare and find his father, whole and unharmed, when he returned.

Wulfram's voice floated through his mind. *If you could change events so that your father didn't die, would you?* It wasn't just an idle question. As a Traveller, it was possible.

He sucked in a trembling breath. If he did so, his father would not thank him. The Rule forbids Travellers to change the future while they were in the past. Matthew had told him that more than once. It was why they had to stop Wulfram.

The questions that plagued him throughout the journey back to Bebbanburg reared up again. What could he do by himself, without his father? It was only Nectan's timely arrival at the Unseelie Gathering that had saved him from becoming the other Traveller's puppet.

And then there was Odda. He planned to tell the others that Fee's uncle had bought Odda from someone who had been mistreating him and that her uncle wished for Thomas to take him to the monks to be liberated, as a type of almsgiving. But that tale seemed inadequate as the time came nearer to tell it.

It wouldn't work with the Fey, nor with Celyn. He would have to tell him and Nona the truth. That he had Bound the boy to himself through his own ignorance.

He cringed at the thought. A wave of homesickness rushed over him. He wished he could be back in his old life, in his own time, where everything was familiar and his mistakes only affected him, not others. Would he ever get back to where he belonged?

Missy stamped her foot as the wind whipped against them again, bringing Thomas out of his reverie. He heaved another sigh, his jaw clenching as he urged the mare to a walk again, fighting the impulse to turn her head away from the fortress and all that awaited him there. *God, help me.* He wasn't sure of the usefulness of his prayer, but it couldn't hurt. Judging by the rumours he heard last night about Thomas the sorcerer, they would not welcome him back with open arms.

Far above, the thin cry of a gull pierced through the sound of the rain and waves. The high, lonely call pierced through him. *Alone*, it seemed to say.

And despite Odda's presence, he couldn't disagree.

CHAPTER 2

TALES OF THE TYLWYTH TEG

Celyn left the king's hall, stumbling on the steps as he walked down them. The heady celebration of the return of Oswald's remains continued unabated in the hall, but he was happy to leave the young men to their revels. Falling insensible from drink and sleeping on the hall's hard floor held little appeal. He much preferred the comfort of his bed. He was already stiff enough in the mornings. He grimaced. Soon he would be an elder, nodding by the fire.

He also did not relish the sore head he would have come morning, but at least he would not be alone in his suffering. Most of Bebbanburg would move slowly tomorrow.

Rain pattered around him as he made his way to his house, and a stiff breeze caused him to draw his cloak tighter around him. But at least it blew some of the ale fumes from his head.

When he reached his house, he slowed. The windows glowed brighter than they should. He had left the hearth fire banked. But nothing else seemed out of order, and after a moment's hesitation, he opened the door.

"Mam o dduw! Rydych chi'n ôl!" The words erupted from him in a spasm of startled joy at the sight of Thomas sitting by the fire. "You're back!" he repeated, pulling the door shut behind him. He strode over to the boy as Thomas rose to greet him, grabbing him by the shoulders and pulling him into an embrace. "Praise the good Christ, you are back."

"Celyn," Thomas choked out, returning his embrace.

Noting the despair in his friend's voice, Celyn pulled back, keeping his hands firmly on Thomas' shoulders as he peered into the young man's eyes. He frowned as he saw what he first missed.

Thomas' face was drawn, and he looked hungry. And exhausted. But worse was the defeat that lurked in Thomas' eyes. "What has happened? Did you find the man you sought?"

Thomas' lips thinned, and a shadow crossed over his face. "Yes." He opened his mouth to say more, but then shut it again.

Celyn gestured at the low benches before the fire. "Sit down. Did you just get back?"

Thomas shook his head. "No. We've been here a couple of hours." He nodded his head at the sleeping pallet in the shadows against the wall, where a boy of about ten years lay under the furs. "This is Odda. He was Wulfram's slave. I brought him with me." His gaze slid away from Celyn's and his cheeks flushed.

And there's a story there. "You bought him from this Wulfram?"

Thomas' jaw bunched. "No. I rescued him." He stopped and exhaled. "Look. We need to talk. But I can't start there." He sat down by the fire again.

Unease crept up Celyn's spine at the silver edge that had gleamed in Thomas' eyes. He felt light-headed for a moment. The effects of the ale, perhaps.

But perhaps not. There was something off about Thomas. Had the other *tylwyth teg* put a spell on him and sent him back to Bebbanburg to fulfill his plan?

He reined in his speculations and sat down beside Thomas, who was leaning on his elbows and looking into the fire, brooding. "You say you found the one you sought. What happened? And where is the harper?"

Thomas glanced over at him, his jaw tightening. "Godric is gone. But he'll be back, I'm sure." He raked his hand through his hair and grimaced, looking back at the dancing flames.

Celyn frowned, but before he could answer, the door opened.

Nona stepped in, her head down against the gust of wind that caused the flames to flare brighter. She held a jug in her hand. "Celyn I—" She lifted her head and froze. "Thomas!" A smile wreathed her face. "Praise God and all His saints!" Her smile faded, replaced by a slight frown. "What is wrong? What has happened?"

The boy on the sleeping pallet stirred, and her gaze flew to him and back to Thomas, fear flashing across her face. "What is this? What have you done?"

Thomas flushed and looked back at the flames.

Another spike of fear pierced Celyn at his cousin's tone. What had she discerned?

But Thomas remained silent, so Celyn stood and took the jug from Nona's hand. "What brings you here?" He caught a whiff of the contents in the jug and grimaced. Her remedy for a sore head. "Ah."

"I meant to bring this before you got back, so you might have it for the morn. But I left the hall later than I had planned."

Celyn put it on the table. Her remedy for the excesses of ale was effective, as he well knew, but the taste of it was nothing short of foul.

Nona divested herself of her cloak and sat down beside Thomas. "When did you get back?"

Celyn had left some cider warming by the hearth fire for when he returned. He poured out a mug for Thomas, sitting down with an inward sigh. The boy would get no peace, now.

"I've been here a couple of hours," Thomas replied, taking the mug from Celyn.

"Why didn't you join us in the hall? You look as if you could use some food."

Thomas grimaced. "Too many people. I just…" His voice trailed off. "I wanted to be alone."

Nona glanced at the sleeping boy and then looked back at Thomas. "This boy," she said, her voice crisp.

Thomas flushed again, his fingers tightening on the mug.

"Leave him be, cousin," Celyn said. "He will tell it in his own time. He was going to start when you arrived. Hold your tongue and we will hear all." He turned to Thomas. "It seems you have not dissuaded this Wulfram from his plan, or you would not be so troubled. Tell us what happened."

Thomas glanced at him, his eyes shadowed, but remained silent.

"But perhaps your tale is not one for my ears. I will leave if you wish to speak to my cousin alone." His pride stung, but he could not deny the relief that pricked him. The tales of the *tylwyth teg* were ones he had no wish to know.

He rose, but Thomas caught at his arm.

"No." His voice was quiet. "It's not that. I will speak to you both, but only if you want to hear it. I've already told you too much. The more I tell, the greater the danger."

Celyn snorted to hide the unease Thomas' words brought. "As to that, I cannot help you fight against what I don't know." He looked at Nona. "I will hear it all."

Nona shifted on the stool, resignation filling her face as she nodded.

Celyn sat again, bracing himself. God had given him this task. He had to see it through. "Tell us what troubles you, ere I lose the courage to hear it."

Thomas grimaced again and took another drink of cider. The flames cast wavering shadows on his face, highlighting the sharp angles of his cheekbones. He took a deep breath and began, the gusting wind that rattled the shutters a wild counterpoint to his words.

Celyn forced himself not to interrupt. But as Thomas described what happened after he defied Wulfram, he leapt up with a cry, his hand out to stop Thomas' words. "A *demon*? Good Christ and all the angels preserve us!" He crossed himself. "How did you escape?"

Thomas flushed. "I didn't."

Nona crossed herself also, her face white. "God, have mercy," she said under her breath.

Celyn sat down, drawing a hand over his face. "Mother of God, pray for us," he muttered. He longed for an enemy he could fight with cold steel. This was beyond him, he feared. "Go on, and may God give us strength."

His dismay increased as Thomas recounted how Wulfram took him to a group of *tylwyth teg* whom he called *Unseelie*, and of Wulfram's plan to make Thomas an unwilling participant in their dark scheme of destruction and betrayal.

But then he stopped and fixed Celyn with a silver-edged gaze. "I escaped. I can't tell you more."

Nona's eyes narrowed. "And what of Wulfram? And Godric?"

"The Unseelie King turned against Wulfram and cast him out. But it's clear Wulfram has convinced some of the Fey. His plan hasn't changed. He seeks to overthrow Oswy and to destroy the monastery."

Celyn let out a breath, seeking calm. "And the harper. You say the Devil possesses him."

A shadow passed over Thomas' face, and his jaw tightened. "Wulfram uses a demon to control him somehow. But I don't think that Godric is completely under its control."

A shiver went up Celyn's back and unreality stole over him again. *Christ, be my shield.*

"You should know one more thing." Thomas took another drink of the cider. "When Wulfram took me to meet the Unseelie King, we met Oswine of Deira on the road."

Celyn drew back, startled out of his contemplation of the evils that Thomas had described and the questions they posed. "The king?"

"Yes. Wulfram told him stories about me, that I am a sorcerer at Oswy's Court. He implied Oswy is directing me to use my black arts to sway men's hearts towards him."

Celyn managed not to show the alarm he felt at Thomas' words. "We heard these tales as well. Whispers and questions." He kept his tone dismissive.

"Worse than whispers," Nona said, her face grim. "The talk increased while you were gone, cousin. I heard it on my visits to the sick and injured. Many asked me about Thomas and his father, always quoting someone passing through. Wulfram's Unseelies, likely, spreading lies and fear."

Thomas nodded. "People told me the same stories on my way back. Some even used my name."

Once again, Celyn wondered how many of the *tylwyth teg* roamed the land, causing mischief. He shifted on the bench, another icy chill running down his spine.

"But that's not all," Thomas said, interrupting Celyn's forebodings. He held Celyn's gaze. "Oswine wasn't alone. He had warriors with him, men of Gwynedd. One of them was your brother, Griffith."

CHAPTER 3

CHOICE

Celyn froze. "Griffith? How do you know?"

Nona's eyes widened in shock at Thomas' words.

A wry smile touched Thomas' lips, lightening the shadows in his eyes, and he shrugged. "He is much like you. And besides, he spoke to me of you."

"He spoke—" Celyn cut off, trying to get his thoughts in order. "What did he say?"

"He asked if you were a monk. When I told him no, he said he was glad that killing a monk would not be on his conscience."

Celyn snorted. "Conscience. I fear he has long stopped listening to it." *Betrayer. Coward.* Griffith's voice whispered through his mind, but he ignored it. Harder to ignore what Thomas had said, though. Griffith was closer to the truth than Thomas suspected.

Ever since he had avenged his family's murder by the wild Saxon's capture and death, a longing for the ordered peace of the monastery had grown within him. A chance to set aside his sword forever. But every time his thoughts strayed that way, he dismissed the idea. He could not enter that life until he helped Thomas confront the danger that Wulfram posed. That unshakable conviction always prevailed.

"Griffith would only be there with Cadafael's blessing," Nona said, her face bleak. "And we know the ties between Cadafael and Mercia. You must tell Oswy of this, Thomas."

Thomas shifted on the bench, raking his hand through his hair as he often did when agitated. He looked at Celyn. "And if I do? Will that cause you problems?"

"Problems?" He shook his head. as he discerned Thomas' meaning. "Ah. No. As to that, I have pledged my sword to Oswy. Our king knows I have done so against my brother's wishes. He knows where my brother's loyalties lie and that they have no bearing on mine."

A shadow passed over Thomas' face. "You lost your home, your family, in pledging to Oswy. Don't you regret it sometimes?"

Celyn's lips closed on the ready denial that sprang to his tongue. Thomas, too, knew the pain of exile. Trite answers would not convince him.

Celyn thought of the rocky mountains of his homeland and the holding where he and Murieann had lived in such happiness. He closed his eyes as sudden grief seized him for all that he had lost. But grief without the burning gall of guilt. He had brought his family justice, and now their memories rested easier in his heart. As did the memories of his homeland. "Aye," he managed, his voice rough. He opened his eyes and swiped at a tear that wet his cheek. "But I had seen enough of blood and revenge at my brother's side. I could not stay without losing my soul. And at Hii, I met Oswald, and glad I was to serve him and rid this land of Cadwallon's scourge." He shook his head. "I am bound here by duty and honour. I pledged my sword to Oswy's service. Here I will stay until he releases me, or I die serving him. There is no other choice." His eyes met Nona's over Thomas' head. "And perhaps I have not lost all my family, even so."

Her eyes filled with tears. "Celyn, *cefnder*...you have not. I swear it. *Rydych chi bob amser yn un ohonom ni.*"

You are always one of us. Her words were a balm upon his heart, and his eyes filled with tears again.

"Choice," Thomas muttered. He shook his head. "There's always a choice, though, isn't there? You could break your pledge, take another path. Just like you did when you pledged to Oswy in the first place and broke your oath to your brother and your king."

"Thomas!"

Nona's shocked exclamation accompanied Celyn's jump to his feet, goaded by Thomas' words. He fought to restrain his temper. "I broke my oath to Griffith because what he asked of me was wrong in the eyes of God and man alike. You know this."

Thomas stood too, his hands tightening into fists. "But that's it, isn't it? Sometimes doing what's right fixes one problem but causes another. You left your family to serve your king, and an evil man murdered them. Your quest for vengeance led you to do evil yourself. Breaking your vow to your brother and your king has caused him to seek *your* death." Anguish filled his face, and he crossed his arms over his chest.

Nona rose and put a hand on his arm. "Thomas," she repeated, her voice steady. "God knows our hearts. We can never see all of what might come from our actions."

Thomas flinched at her touch, closing his eyes. Anguish flashed across his face, but then he heaved a deep breath. When he opened his eyes again, bitterness filled them. "No. We're just left to pick up the pieces."

Nona's eyes met Celyn's, and her jaw tightened. She dropped her hand. "You look tired. And you must be hungry. These questions need a clearer mind to think through them. I will get some food from the hall. You must eat and rest. We can speak more of this in the morning." She gathered her cloak and threw a warning look at Celyn. "I will be back soon."

Celyn wasn't sure what the look meant. Ask no more questions? Or find out more in her absence?

Before he could decide what Nona wanted of him, Thomas glanced at him, his face grim. "She won't want me to tell you this, but I want you to know." He gestured at the bench. "Sit down."

Celyn sat down on the bench again, wary. "Think you, are you sure? You have said of the dangers of knowing too much of the ways of the *tywlyth teg.*"

Thomas sat beside him. "Too late for that. Which is also my fault." His lips twisted.

Celyn forced aside his fears. "Never mind. Speak of what troubles you."

"You know of the Charms. That the Fey can bend another to their will."

He had tried hard to forget the odd sensation that had enveloped him when he met Thomas' father for the first time, but sometimes a ghost of it tickled against his mind. As it did now. *O Mighty Three, envelop me.* He forced himself to concentrate on Thomas' words, and the feeling faded.

"There's another way to influence a human. Something deeper than a Charm. A Binding of their will. Wulfram did that to Odda." Thomas' jaw hardened. "He showed it by telling Odda to cut off one of his own fingers. Odda did it without even thinking about it."

"God, have mercy!" Celyn's gaze darted to the slave boy, the odd tickle of sensation returning. The sense that, for a moment, he had been a mere puppet in Matthew's hands.

He gathered his thoughts together and forced himself back to the matter at hand. "So, you saved the boy from this Wulfram. A good, as you say. What evil has come of it, then?"

Thomas looked away again, back into the flames. "That was just the beginning. Wulfram had Odda hold a knife to his own throat and told me he would command him to cut it. It was up to me to stop him. Godric restrained me, so I had to use my power to do it. And it worked."

Celyn forced himself to speak. "What pains you now, then?"

Thomas looked at him, his eyes bleak. "I freed Odda from Wulfram, but somehow I Bound Odda to me, instead."

"Bound..." Celyn's voice trailed off as he struggled to understand Thomas' meaning. "He is your slave, you said as much. He must do your bidding, as all slaves must obey their masters. Free him, then. What is the difficulty? Aidan will pay for his freedom and welcome him in, as you have seen him do with others."

"No, you don't understand. He's not that he has to do what I say. It's like I said before. He's Bound to my will. I can feel him in *here*." He tapped his temple. "He has no choice in his obedience. Fetch water, cook supper, weed the garden. But not just that. If I told him to take a torch and light this place on fire while you slept in your bed, he would. Or to drive a *seax* through Oswy's heart, or Nona's. And he would do it with a smile on his face, happy to serve his *Master*." Thomas' mouth twisted on the last word, and he dropped his head into his hands. "God, forgive me."

Horrified understanding swept over Celyn. He darted a gaze at the boy and back at Thomas, gathering his thoughts. "What is done can be undone. Free him and escape this evil!"

Thomas looked up at him, his eyes shining silver in the firelight. "That's the problem. I can't. I don't know how. It was a mistake, an accident. I don't know how to undo it."

Celyn got up and paced, trying to find the right question. "How is it you have a power you cannot control?"

Bitterness flashed over Thomas' face. "Fey parents teach their children how to use their power. But my father left me when I was too young to know what I was. I had no one to teach me."

"And is there no one else, no one of the *tylwyth teg*, who can help you?" His stomach twisted as a thought struck him. "Perhaps Nona—"

"No." Thomas interrupted. "She won't know. It's an evil in their eyes. At least to the Seelie Court."

Celyn sat down. "Thank the good Christ for that," he muttered. He drew a hand over his face, weariness settling over him. He eyed Thomas, whose hunched shoulders and bleak expression spoke to his despondency. "Nona had the right of it. We cannot solve this tonight. When she returns, eat and then get some sleep. We will not speak of this. The morning will be soon enough to tell her what has happened. Perhaps she may have some ideas after all." He blew out a breath. "But we must pray. God may yet reveal a way out."

Thomas met his eyes. "Perhaps." He made an impatient gesture. "I'm sorry, Celyn. This is all—"

Celyn waved a hand, cutting him off. "God will show us the way. Do not fear."

The gusting wind rattled the shutters, the sound filling the silence left behind. Celyn's thoughts were as chaotic as the wind gusting against the house. His confident words sounded hollow, even to him.

They had to undo this evil, but how?

CHAPTER 4

ROUSED

Thomas stood by his father's grave, the morning mist curling around his ankles as the sun rose over the horizon. He had left Odda with Celyn so that he could avoid Nona. He wasn't up to confessing what had happened, even with a night's sleep behind him.

A simple marker in the small cemetery next to the village church was the only sign of Matthew's grave, much different from the other one at home. He had grieved at the grave of a stranger all those years when he thought Matthew had died, but in fact was here, alive.

Not anymore. The thought pierced him like a knife. Once again, his father had left him alone. And although he knew it was irrational, he couldn't help the anger that boiled up at the thought. What had Matthew been doing that night?

I killed your father. Godric's confession whispered through his mind. It rang true. But the harper's tale of seeing Frithlac push Matthew off the embarkment also held the ring of truth. The complete story had yet to be told. Perhaps he would never know.

But no matter who was there that night, he was convinced Wulfram was behind it. Wulfram had implied as much. He wished he had pressed the other Traveller on the details. Perhaps the subtle influence of the demon had directed his attention away from that topic.

He exhaled sharply. His father was truly dead this time, killed through Wulfram's doing, no matter how it had happened. Because Matthew had determined to stop the other Traveller. And even though the thought filled him with dread, he knew the task was now his.

"But how?" Whether his murmured question was for his father or God, he wasn't sure. Either way, no answer presented itself.

"Thomas."

He whirled around as the tingling sense of another Fey alerted him at the same time as the whispered word. Nona stood behind him, wreathed in mist. So much for trying to avoid her.

"I'm sorry to disturb you, but I thought it best we spoke alone." She joined him at the grave and looked down at it for a moment, her lips moving in a silent prayer before she crossed herself and looked back at him. "How are you?"

Thomas shrugged. "Alive."

A faint smile touched her mouth. "Thank God," she murmured. The smile faded. "Tell me now what you left out last night. I sent word to Brorda and Nectan before you went to Eoforwic, as you asked. Did they find you? Is that how you escaped from Raegenold's Court? And the slave boy. There is more to be told of him."

The slave boy. Thomas' gut tightened. Best to tackle the first question first. "Yes, Brorda met us on the road. Godric wasn't happy about it, but I told him I wouldn't go to Eoforwic without him. But we were ambushed along the way. Wulfram used Brorda against me, to ensure my good behaviour. Nectan caught up with us at the Unseelie Gathering. If he hadn't shown up when he did, Wulfram and Raegenold would have made me their puppet."

"Thank God for His mercy," Nona exhaled. "But how did our king persuade Raegenold to release you?"

"Wulfram neglected to tell Raegenold that I'd pledged to Nectan. He wasn't too pleased to find that out. And I guess he had second thoughts about Wulfram once he heard about the Undying. He seemed happy to have a reason to release me." He let out a breath. "He kicked Wulfram out of his Court. But there are Unseelie who support him, even so."

"Wulfram's anger will be roused against you. Yet it seems he needs you for his plan. Otherwise, he would have killed you once you defied him, rather than taking you to Raegenold." Her face clouded. "But what drives him to such evil?"

Thomas shook his head, remembering the desire that had flared in Wulfram's eyes when he had seen the demon in Godric. "He didn't give me details. I'm not sure he has any. He's just obsessed with the monastery, with the Church. He thinks if he can get rid of Oswy and put Penda on the throne, Lindisfarne will disappear." He hesitated. He had to tell Nona more, but even with the Fey he had to be careful of how much of the future he revealed. "In his time, he sees his twin brother die at the hands of men who are motivated by hatred. Part of that hatred stems from the actions of the Church. And so Wulfram thinks that if he destroys the Church now, in the future his twin won't die."

Nona frowned. "But that is madness." She eyed him, wary. "You have never told me how far in time you have Travelled. And I don't want to know," she added, hastily. "But I know you come from a time far from us. Surely it cannot be as easy as all that, to change something now that will have that great an effect then? Is Lindisfarne so important?"

"I don't know. But the important thing is that he believes it is. I told you, he's obsessed with it." He spread his hands. "Once he tries something here and goes back to his own time, if he doesn't find the result he wants, he'll come back and try something else. On and on until he gets what he wants—the Fey triumphant. And most importantly to him, his brother alive."

Nona's face paled as the implications struck home. "God have mercy," she breathed. She gathered herself, her gaze sharpening on him. "If he needs you for this plan, the best thing is for you to go back to your time. Now. Before he gets his hands on you again. If you're not here, perhaps his plan will fall to pieces."

"No!" He modulated his sharp tone. "Don't you see? If it wasn't me, he'd latch onto someone else. Maybe you. Or Celyn. How hard would it be to direct him to slit Oswy's throat one night while he slept? Just like he compelled Frithlac to kill my father." He shook his head. "Better that he keeps his eyes on me." His fists curled. "I have to stop him. Finish what my father started by being here, waiting for me. Because of that, he drew Wulfram and Godric here as well as me. I can't leave. Running away isn't the answer. My father taught me that." Grief choked off his voice, and he heaved a breath, fighting the despair that seized him.

"Thomas," Nona said, her emerald eyes filling with compassion. Mist wreathed her form, cutting them off from the world.

It was too much. His fragile self-control broke. He reached out and cupped her face, her cheek satin against his palm. With a groan, he bent towards her, slanting his lips over hers. The buzzing Fey-sense, the sweetness of her lips, the press of her body against him obliterated everything else.

They clung to each other for a long moment before Nona wrenched away with a gasp, her hand pressing against her mouth. "We should not—" she choked out, her other hand out, warding him away.

Misery filled her face, and then she turned on her heel, her slender form dissolving into the mist as she rushed away.

Thomas took a step after her and then reason returned and he froze, wrapping his arms around himself. *Christ, have mercy.* What had he done?

Nothing had changed. He was a Traveller. She belonged here. She was going to be married to another. He could not interfere.

He told himself all these things and more. But all of them seemed hollow in the light of the sweet thrill of her lips on his.

You've just made things ten times worse, idiot, he told himself.

But he'd do it again in a heartbeat.

He heaved a breath. He had forgotten to speak to her of Odda. After he and Celyn spoke to Oswy, he would seek her out and tell her what happened. He'd have to apologize, too, although he was finding it hard to feel sorry about their kiss. The silky feel of her lips against his remained, kindling a glow in his heart that brought welcome warmth.

Not yours, Tommo. He clenched his jaw as his father's voice whispered through his mind.

Right, he thought back at it, defiant. *And what are you going to do about it?*

But there was no answer.

Celyn insisted on waiting to seek out Oswy, and after seeing his bloodshot eyes and careful movements, Thomas curbed his impatience. He'd seen the signs of a hangover in his mother too often to press the point. According to Celyn, Oswy likely felt the same.

After breakfast, he left Celyn nursing his headache and sipping on Nona's draught. He bolstered his courage and went to find the Healer. Bronwyn told him she had gone to dress a burn caused by someone tripping and falling into the hearth fire the night before, likely the result of too much ale. She made it clear that several others would need Nona's services after that, so Thomas left her to her task of gathering the supplies Nona had requested. He couldn't help but feel relief that his conversation with Celyn's cousin would have to wait.

He turned back to go to Celyn's house, but a shout stopped him.

"Master Thomas! God be praised, ye be back!" Oswy's priest and scribe, Father Colm, hurried towards him, a friendly smile wreathing his face.

Thomas smiled back, relieved to be rescued from his gloomy thoughts. "I just arrived last night."

Colm's gaze skimmed over him. "Ah, ye look fair worn out, so ye do. A hard journey, then? Your father's wife, is she well?"

"She grieves. But her family will help her. She is going back to her uncle's holding in Dál Riata."

"Ah," the priest said, sympathy in his face. "May the God of all comfort bring her peace. I will pray for her, so I will, and for ye as well. Grief can be a hard journey."

"Yes." His heart eased at Father Colm's words. "Thank you."

A family walked by, and the father's eyes narrowed as he saw Thomas. He lifted a hand in greeting to the priest, but hurried his family along without stopping. The oldest child, a young boy around Odda's age of ten years, looked back over his shoulder at him, his eyes wide.

Father Colm glanced at him. "Be careful, me son. Tales have sprung up in your absence, I fear. Raedmund still seeks an answer for his brother's disappearance. His mistrust of ye only grows, and he is not careful to hide it."

Thomas nodded, keeping his face neutral. "Thank you, Father. I'll watch my step."

His unease deepened as he watched the priest hurry off towards the church. Deorwald's disappearance on the night of the Wild Hunt was the price paid for the Alder KIng letting his father go. The long fingers of fear from that night lingered still. Fuelled by Wulfram's Unseelies. The rumours of the black sorcerer in Oswy's Court would only increase now that he was back. Lindisfarne would be a better shelter for him. But he had to free Odda before he went there.

But how? Anxiety speared through him, but he forced it down and closed his eyes. *God, show me the way.*

He waited a moment, but with no answer forthcoming, he sighed and opened his eyes. *The way of the Fey comes by doing.* He sighed. *Right. Doing what?* The road ahead seemed shrouded, a looping circle that led to nowhere.

CHAPTER 5

THE WAY OF KINGS AND WARRIORS

It was mid-afternoon before Celyn felt human enough to accompany Thomas to meet the king. They found him at the church, consulting with Father Paulus and Father Colm regarding his brother's remains.

They waited outside in the spring sun, neither of them wishing to intrude. Celyn winced at the brightness of the light, a sour look on his face.

"Nona's draught not working?" Thomas asked, unable to resist teasing Celyn.

The other man scowled. "As to that, I've had enough of drinking piss water. Why she can't make her potions more palatable only the good Christ knows."

Thomas could only briefly wonder what Celyn would have thought of the bitter black coffee his mother preferred as a hangover remedy before the church door opened and Oswy came out.

He stopped short. "Master Thomas!"

Thomas only saw the slight tightening around Oswy's eyes because he was looking for it. That, and the lack of welcome in his tone, told him everything he needed to know about the king's enthusiasm at seeing him again. He bowed his head. "My lord king."

"Master Thomas has news for you," Celyn said. "We thought it best he bring it to you without delay."

Oswy nodded and gestured at the path through the village. "My wife has need of me, so Father Paulus tells me. Walk with me. We will speak of your news where there are not so many ears to hear."

They fell into pace beside him as he headed towards the craggy upthrust of rock that loomed over the village. His hall and other buildings perched at the top, looking out over the sea on one side and his domain on the other.

Thomas couldn't help noticing the suspicious looks directed his way from some of those out and about. He guessed that the stiffness in Oswy's manner was not just from his excess of ale the night before. Wulfram's tales had taken hold, it seemed.

Celyn broke the silence. "All is well with Lady Eanflaed, I trust?"

Oswy glanced at him. "She is with child. She frets more than usual, that is all. Time hung heavy on her while I was gone."

Celyn grunted. "As to that, my Murieann was the same. She was none too pleased with my absences when she was carrying our child."

It was the first time Thomas had heard Celyn speak of his wife since the awful day they found the remains of Uirolec's family. But he saw only a fond remembrance on Celyn's face, not the bitterness that had marked him before.

"Aye, that is the right of it. The babe is not due until after Solstice. It may be a long summer for her, for I will be away much."

Solstice. An odd quiver thrummed through him and he frowned, trying to seek the source, but it faded as quickly as it came, and as Celyn spoke again, he dismissed it.

"'Tis the way of kings and warriors, my lord king. She knows that. But I learned to my cost not to ignore my wife's fears. Murieann—" His voice choked off as his hand fisted on his sword hilt, bright tears springing to his eyes.

"News about the return of your brother's remains brought much joy to those I met on my way back here, my lord king," Thomas said, changing the subject. Celyn's heart might rest easier, but he knew too well how grief could catch a person unawares. "The *scops* sing your praises in Bernicia's halls."

A grim smile played around Oswy's lips. "Ah, yes." He glanced at Celyn, the smile widening. "A story fit for the mead hall, indeed. You should ask Lord Celyn for his part in it."

Celyn wiped his eyes and waved a hand. "All did their part, my lord king."

Oswy slapped him on the back. "Aye, but I know your worth."

When they reached the base of the rocky hill upon which the fortress stood, Oswy drew them off the path. "We may speak freely here without other ears to hear. Tell me of your news, then. Did you find the man you sought in Eoforwic?"

Thomas ignored the flutter of nerves that tumbled in his gut and prayed his face wouldn't reveal his lies. Oswy was no fool. "Yes, he was there. I followed him and watched who he spoke to. Listened in where I could, and to what others said about him. There are many who come and go from his house. Mercians and Deirians alike." He hesitated, but before he could say more, Celyn spoke up.

"Thomas tells me that Oswine spent time at Wulfram's table. And with him was Griffith of Gwynedd, my brother."

Oswy frowned, giving Celyn a sharp look. "Your brother. With Cadafael's blessing, do you think?"

Celyn's face darkened. "Aye. He would not go where his king had not bid him."

"So Cadfael seeks to welcome Deira into his hall, along with Mercia," Oswy mused. His face hardened. "They've likely promised him Bernicia. My cousin Oswine is too trusting. He will not see the blade that slits his throat when it's held in the hand of a friend. Penda would use him as a stepping stone to gain supremacy over all of Bernicia and Deira as well." He squeezed his hand into a fist and lapsed into silence, deep in thought. "Yet these whispers are without substance, so they are. And there could be other explanations as to Oswine's presence at Wulfram's table."

Thomas shook his head. "No. There's no doubt." He hesitated. "Wulfram had a slave boy, a Saxon. I stole him away. He heard and saw much while serving him. Wulfram seeks to force you off the throne, that much is certain. And not only that. He sets himself against Lindisfarne, too. He wants to destroy it."

Oswy's eyebrows raised, and a sudden bark of laughter escaped his lips. "Stole his slave—" He clapped Thomas on the back. "Ah, another tale for the mead hall!" His amusement faded. "But why the monastery? This seems an evil plot."

"Wulfram does not believe in the Christian God. His ways are the ways of Woden. He wants Aidan and the monks gone, so he's coming after you, too. That will be easier with Penda on your throne."

Oswy frowned. "He will not find us an easy target all the same. God will fight for us against this evil."

Although it was tempting to agree, Thomas knew the Viking raids within the century to come were proof that this kingdom and the monks were vulnerable against those who might want to do them harm. And where was God when that happened?

Celyn spoke up, covering Thomas' hesitation once again. "But God would not want us to be foolish, my lord king. He has brought us news of this threat so that we might prepare to meet it. We must be wary."

Oswy's eyes hardened. "My blade will be ready. Do not fear, Lord Celyn. I only meant that we must not trust only to our own strength." He looked at Thomas. "And what of your father's death?"

I only wish I had been there to see him die. Wulfram's voice ghosted through Thomas' mind, but he ignored it. "Odda didn't know. But he said a monk came to visit Wulfram at least once. He described Frithlac perfectly." That much was true, although he hadn't gleaned it from something Odda said. He had seen a picture in Odda's mind of Frithlac arriving at Wulfram's door, stepping inside with his peculiar stumping gait. His jaw tightened. "I am certain that Wulfram used him to kill my father. But I can't prove it. I didn't think it wise to confront him by myself."

"Aye. You will find those to help you make him pay for your father's death when the time comes."

Thomas nodded, his jaw tightening. "I am not done with him yet."

Celyn's voice was grim. "As to that, you will have my sword to aid you when the time comes." He turned to Oswy. "Bishop Aidan is close to Oswine. Perhaps he could dissuade him of this path."

Oswy's lips tightened. "Aye. Perhaps." His fingers tapped against his thighs, and then he let out a breath. "We must tell the bishop of the plot against Lindisfarne so that he can set his prayers against these schemes that seek to destroy God's work." He paused, looking at Thomas. "This slave boy, do you still have him?

"Yes."

Odda was chopping wood at Celyn's house, and for a moment Thomas felt the axe in his hands, the warmth of the sun on his back, the griping of hunger pains in his stomach. *Master?* Thomas turned his mind away from Odda, and the boy's presence faded.

"Take him to Aidan and tell the bishop of these evils. He will welcome the boy." His eyes hardened. "Tell him I will come speak to him soon. I would value a time of prayer with him. These dark tales nip at my heels like an untrained hound, and I would settle my soul."

Thomas fought down the flaring panic that speared him at Oswy's suggestion. Even though it had been his plan, hearing someone else say it brought excuses clamouring to his tongue for why he could not do it.

He forced himself to nod. "Of course, my lord king," he managed.

He couldn't leave Odda there. He first had to undo the Bond. Panic flared again. By the good Christ, how was he supposed to do that?

The blue sky dazzled above them, sea birds wheeling against its vast expanse. Their faint screeches came to them on the salty breeze, over the sound of the pounding waves. It felt as if they were laughing at him.

"These dark shadows do not chase me alone," Oswy said. "They surround you as well, Master Thomas. We spoke of this before you left. Whispers. Murmurings of magic, of the work of the Devil."

"Yes, my lord king." Thomas' face flushed. A spiralling sense of impending doom seized him as Oswy continued.

"I cannot ignore these tales any longer, not now, when by your own admission there are those plotting to take my crown. These whispers add fuel to that fire. I had hoped they would die down, but Eanflaed tells me they have only continued to grow. She half believes them herself. She fears for our babe." He shook his head.

"You have done well to bring the news from Eoforwic, but you cannot stay here. You must leave Bebbanburg without delay, ere the tales entangle us all."

The screeching laughter of the seabirds filled the silence as Oswy's words sank in.

CHAPTER 6

DARK SHADOWS

Dismay flashed across Celyn's face. "My lord king, this is unnecessary. Thomas will go to Lindisfarne, as before. Aidan will speak for him to any who ask. These tales will die out."

Before Oswy could answer, Thomas beat him to it. "No. He's right, Celyn. I shouldn't stay." Despite his fear at the thought, he knew Oswy was right. He'd known it the night before, after hearing the guard's words at the holding he'd stayed at, but he hadn't wanted to face it. His presence at Bebbanburg only played into Wulfram's hands. He would only harm Oswy by staying, and Aidan, too. "Brother Frithlac has already cast doubts about Aidan's judgement in allowing me at the monastery. Wulfram is spreading these rumours, I am sure. The only way they can die down is for me to leave."

Celyn's face flushed, but he remained silent. He saw it, too.

You are alone. He ignored the dark whisper that coiled through his mind and bowed his head to Oswy. "I will go to Lindisfarne first and speak with Aidan. Then I will leave. If I hear any more about what Wulfram plans, I will get word to you."

Oswy nodded. "Go with God, Master Thomas." He spread his hands wide. He looked up the hill at the fortress. "My wife awaits. I will give my leave." He nodded at Celyn and then walked up the path.

Thomas and Celyn watched him go, and when he was out of earshot, Celyn turned to him. "We can find a place for you to stay nearby. Somewhere out of sight."

Thomas shook his head. "No. It's too risky. It would just take one sighting of me for the tales to start again. I have to go." His hands clenched. "But not forever. I have to be here when Wulfram makes his move."

"As to that, how when you know when that will be? Or what he will do?"

Frustration filled Thomas. "I don't know. I told you that."

Celyn stepped nearer to him and put his hands on Thomas' shoulders, his face intent. "Think. There must be some clue in what he said. Will he strike soon, do you think? Even knowing that would be helpful."

Thomas forced himself to think through all that had happened. Raegenold had thrown Wulfram out of his Court. Some Unseelies would follow, he knew that, but Wulfram would need more than a few to do what he planned. Taking down a king would not be easy.

"No. He'll need more help," he said, thinking it through. "Whatever he plans, he can't do it alone."

Celyn grunted, dropping his hands. "Neither Penda nor Oswine will hasten to strike against Oswy. As to Cadafael, I know him well enough to know he will only go where he is assured of victory."

"All I know is that it will be sometime this summer." Wulfram could not stay overlong in this time or he risked being unable to Cross back. Thomas wasn't sure when Wulfram had Crossed, but he guessed it had been during the summer before Thomas arrived. Which meant he had been in this time almost a year. He wouldn't wait too much longer.

"So. We must watch and wait."

Thomas nodded, a niggling thought chasing through his mind, but he couldn't quite pin it down, and he gave up in frustration. Maybe it would come to him later. "Yes. That's all we can do for now."

"A few months to prepare. And maybe less than that."

So little time. How could he possibly be ready?

Celyn eyed him. "And the slave boy? You will free him?"

"I don't know how. I told you that." His voice came out sharper than he meant. He took a breath and continued in a milder tone. "I suppose I don't have to, not yet. I could take him with me. Maybe I'll find someone who can tell me how to undo the Bond." Relief flooded through him at the thought. Too much relief, perhaps. But wasn't that a better idea than harming Odda by flailing around in the dark?

Celyn shifted, discomfort flashing over his face as it did whenever they discussed the Fey. "My cousin had no ideas for you when she spoke to you this morning?"

"No. We got interrupted. I didn't get to that." For a moment, the sweet feel of her in his arms flooded through him and he had to duck his head to hide the blush that had suddenly stained his cheeks. He raked his fingers through his hair and looked up at Celyn, his face composed. "I'll try to track her down again before I go. But I can't take too long."

"Aye. Our king will not be pleased if you linger." They started up the hill to the fortress. "But where will you go?"

Good question. Thomas shook his head. "I don't know." He heaved a sigh, trying to think it through. "First I have to go see Aidan." He listened for a minute to the booming sound of the surf to determine whether it was close to the fortress. "I think the tide is in, don't you?"

Celyn listened. "Aye, I would say so."

"I'll check with Father Colm at the church and see if he can tell me when it will change. But I shouldn't wait here in Bebbanburg." He thought for a moment. "Maybe I'll go to Torht's. It's on the way. And I can ask if he knows anything about what to do with Odda."

Celyn grunted in response. "He will be happy to see you, I am sure."

His lips twisted. He wasn't sure of that, considering all that he had cost him. "You'll have to keep a careful eye on Oswy."

"As to that, you need not fear. Anyone seeking to harm him will meet my blade first."

Thomas didn't bother to remind him that his sword might be useless against whatever scheme Wulfram was plotting. Celyn knew it well enough.

The Welshman heaved a sigh. "Send word to me of where you will go once you know." He shook his head, his face troubled. "I mistrust this plan. Oswy had the right of it. Dark shadows are forming. I sense it too. But sending you away will not disperse them, I fear."

"No." He ignored the unease that clutched at him with icy hands. "I won't stay away for too long. When I come back, I'll go to Torht's, or to Lindisfarne, and send word."

Celyn nodded. As they reached the top of the hill, the sea breeze caught at their cloaks, causing them to flap around their legs. "I'll do what I can to stamp out these rumours." He put a hand on Thomas' shoulder. "I will pray for you, *periglour*, and I ask for your prayers as well."

Thomas smiled, heartened as always by Celyn's steady friendship. "Of course."

He kept his fear to himself that all of their prayers might not be enough to dispel the cloud that Wulfram and the Undying had cast over this kingdom.

Christ, have mercy. As good a prayer as any, and better than most.

Chapter 7

Unseelie Work

Thomas was cinching up Missy's saddle when a shadow darkened the stable door. He turned, sensing another Fey, and saw Nona. Apprehension and relief touched him in equal measure. He hadn't wanted to leave before he could resolve some of what hung between them. But he also knew he would have to speak of Odda.

She came into the stable, a bag in her hands. "Celyn told me you are going to Lindisfarne. I've brought some herbs for Brother Eadric."

Badulf, who had been fussing with Oswy's favourite mount, peered around the horse's rump at her. "Good day, my lady. Did ye bring me the herbs I asked ye for? They did the trick for the gelding here, so they did."

She frowned. "Oh yes, of course. I've left them in the cookhouse, in a bag. When I gathered these things, I put them down. I'll go get them once I've said goodbye to Master Thomas."

"Ah nay, Lady, I will get them; 'tis no trouble," Badulf said, knuckling his forehead as he came around the horse. "In the cookhouse, ye say?"

She nodded. "Yes, you will find Mistress Bronwyn still there, mixing some potions. She will know where it is."

He nodded his thanks as he left.

Thomas snorted. "Nicely done." He waved at Missy. "Celyn must have told you what Oswy said. I'm getting ready to go."

She grimaced. "Aye. I am sorry, Thomas." She entered the barn, halting in front of him.

A faint scent of cinnamon and cloves met Thomas' nose, and he stopped himself from reaching for her with an effort. "I had already decided to leave. Staying here plays into Wulfram's hands."

"As does leaving, perhaps. You will be on your own."

He shrugged. There was nothing he could do about that.

She glanced out the stable door behind her, making sure no one was around, and turned back, her gaze meeting his. "I wanted to speak with you alone before you left."

Thomas swallowed back the knot in his throat. "Me too," he managed, and almost without volition, his hand raised to touch a soft waving lock of black hair that had escaped her head covering.

Her eyes shut as a pained expression flashed over her face and Thomas dropped his hand as if burned. "I'm sorry. For before, I mean. I shouldn't have—"

Nona's eyes flew open. "Don't be sorry," she said with some asperity. "I'm not." His heart leapt at the longing in her eyes. But she shook her head. "We cannot speak of that now. There's not much time before Badulf comes back. We must speak of the boy."

Thomas looked at Odda, who was watching them from where he sat on a hay bale in the corner. "Odda, we must fill our water bags before we leave. Can you do that while the Lady Nona and I speak?"

Odda nodded and scrambled off the hay bale, grabbing the leather bags on his way out.

Nona watched him leave and then faced Thomas. "Tell me what you left out last night. About this slave boy. How is it that you Bound him?" Her face was impassive, but judgement coloured her words all the same.

His heart sank. Nectan and the other Fey had discerned the Bond through their Fey power, but he had harboured a small hope Nona wouldn't notice.

"By mistake." His voice was sharper than it should be, but he was sick of being judged for doing things no one had warned him against.

One elegant black eyebrow rose in a Celyn-like expression. "Mistake?"

Missy stamped her foot and tossed her head, and Thomas let out a breath, struggling to control his temper. He stroked the horse's smooth neck. "Easy, girl." He looked back at Nona. "Look. We won't have long before Badulf comes back. Do you want to hear what happened or not?"

"Go on."

"Odda was there when I came to Wulfram's house. I sensed there was something off about him. I didn't know about the Bond. That isn't something you Fey had bothered to tell me about yet." He regretted the words as soon as they left his lips, and he waved a hand, heaving a sigh. "Never mind. Wulfram used Odda as a demonstration, I guess. A way to show me my power." His hand tightened on Missy's mane, anchoring himself to the present as the memory of that night swept through him.

He summarized the rest. "I didn't know what I was doing," he concluded. "I saw the Bond in his mind, joining him to Wulfram. I broke it. But somehow, in doing that, I Bound him. I didn't realize it right away. Wulfram turned the demon on me and then…" He shook his head, uncomfortable at the memory. "I resisted it and it went away. But I couldn't fight off both Wulfram and Godric. Physically, I mean. They didn't use Fey power on me." He paused. For the first time, he wondered why they hadn't, and then shook his head, continuing the story. "They tied me up. Odda was asleep, or something. He didn't wake up. Wulfram just left him there in his house when we left. But Nectan found him on the road when he and Brorda came looking for me. Odda led him to me. When I saw him there, I realized what had happened."

Nona let out a shallow breath, her eyes wide. "Christ, have mercy," she said. She drew herself up, setting aside the dark mood that had gripped them at Thomas' story. "So. What does Nectan say of this?"

Thomas' lips twisted. "He says I have to break the Bond. But he can't tell me how. Can you?"

Nona shook her head. "Nay. 'Tis Unseelie work." She made an impatient gesture at his expression. "I did not mean it that way. The fault for this lies with Wulfram, not you. You tried to help Odda. But now you must free him. Do you not have any idea?"

"I can see the Bond. I think I could break it." He swallowed. "I know I could. But I—" He broke off, fumbling for the words to explain what he felt. "I think that will harm Odda. It feels wrong to me. But I'm not sure. Maybe that's what the Unseelies do."

Nona frowned. "Aye, 'tis possible. The Unseelies are unlikely to care overmuch. They Bond humans for a willing slave, or so the stories tell. They sometimes use Bonded humans for evil deeds that they are unwilling to do themselves."

Thomas clenched a fist. "Yes. He would do anything. I know it." Self-disgust filled him. "He does anything I ask, anticipates my needs. I'm afraid I'm starting to like it. I'm my father's son, in more ways than one."

Nona's eyes flashed. "Don't be foolish. You have pledged to the Seelie Court. I see none of the Unseelie in you."

Thomas snorted. "No? What about Odda, then? How do you explain how I Bound him?"

A flush stained her cheeks, and she opened her mouth to reply.

Thomas pressed on before she could speak. "And, as you all constantly remind me, I am a wilding. Worse than being Unseelie, it seems."

Nona made an impatient gesture. "You can't give in to despair. God will lead you out of this trouble. You must trust Him."

"Right. But what if I can't trust myself?"

She drew back, frowning, but just then Badulf returned.

"I've got it, my lady, and many thanks. Tell me now, what think ye of this one here?" He gestured at another horse whose long nose poked over a stall. "'E has a limp that comes and goes, and I canna find the cause..."

Nona threw Thomas a frustrated look behind Badulf's back as he rounded the horse again. "I will have a look," she said to Badulf. Her gaze held his. "Safe journey, Master Thomas."

There was much more he wanted to say to her, but, as always, he could not. Should not. He had to leave her be.

He managed a nod and then turned back to his task, trying to block out the sound of her voice as she conversed with Badulf, trying to ignore the ache in his heart.

CHAPTER 8

FREEDOM TO OBEY

Relief filled Thomas as he and Odda headed down the path to Torht's workshop. Leaving Bebbanburg not only left behind his tangled relationship with Nona but also the dark whispers that murmured behind his back at Oswy's fortress. The bright sunshine and clear blue sky helped to lift his spirits further.

Missy's ears perked forward as she stepped along the path. Thomas suspected she recognized the path and was eager to get to the house of the Horseclan Fey.

But he could not leave all his troubles behind. His most immediate problem could not be so easily escaped. It was as close as Odda's arms encircling his middle, and more to the point, to the feeling of the boy in his mind, nestled up against him like a devoted puppy. That feeling had gone from being an alien sensation to a familiar comfort. The panic that seized him whenever he thought about breaking the Bond was a warning he could not ignore. A warning that if he waited too long, he would not be able to do it.

He couldn't imagine how Wulfram had left Odda behind in Eoforwic after being Bound to him for so long. Nor how he could have invited Thomas to break the Bond. The only thing he could come up with as an explanation was the influence of the Undying, and Thomas didn't like to think about how tightly Wulfram must have tied himself to the creature in order to be shielded from the loss of Odda.

With an effort, he set his mind away from the thoughts of severing the Bond. Father Colm had told him that the next time he could cross to Lindisfarne was the next morning. In the meantime, Torht might know of something. And if not, well, Odda could come with him. It might be some time before he would have to face that task.

But he was not to enjoy the bright spring morning for long, it seemed. A big raven lifted off a tree alongside the path, croaking its deep throaty call as it flapped away at their approach. Thomas hauled Missy to a halt, bitterness filling him. Was there nowhere that Wulfram did not stalk him?

Odda twisted in the saddle to look back at him. "No, Master Thomas. Not his."

Startled, Thomas looked down at him. "Not—? Wait. You can tell which one of the birds are *his?*"

The boy nodded.

A flash of a memory came through the Bond, and then more. Thomas had to shut his eyes to concentrate as they swirled through Odda's mind like a bright blur of disjointed images, too fast for him to comprehend.

The flashing kaleidoscope stopped, narrowing in on one memory. Wulfram stood in a field with his arms outstretched and eyes closed, covered with a flock of about fifteen black, noisy birds. Ravens and rooks rose and descended upon the Unseelie with short flaps of their wings, smaller jackdaws and crows lined up on his arms, fighting and squabbling among themselves to stay perched in their positions. A sudden glow of Fey power enveloped them all, obscuring Wulfram and the birds from view.

Thomas opened his eyes as the image blinked out.

Odda's eyes opened, too, and his gaze met Thomas'. "Not his," he said again, insistent.

"Only *those* birds? And you know which ones they are?"

Discomfort flashed over Odda's face, and Thomas knew the answer even before the boy nodded. Odda had been Bonded to Wulfram when Wulfram had commissioned the birds to be his eyes. Somehow Odda could still sense Wulfram's touch on certain birds, even though his Bond with Wulfram had been severed.

Thomas suspected that perhaps he, too, could sense which specific birds belonged to Wulfram if he used his Gift and probed deeply enough into the connection he had with Odda. But the thought of doing so churned his gut, and he dropped it. For now, it was enough to know that Odda knew, and could tell him.

Another thought struck him. *Of course. Why hadn't I thought of this before?* "You know Wulfram plans to do something bad."

Odda looked away, uncomfortable. "Yes, Master Thomas."

"Something against our Lord King Oswy and the monks."

A tremor rippled through Odda. A rising discomfort leached through the Bond into Thomas.

Thomas pushed past it. "Do you know what he plans?"

Sharp panic flooded Odda's face, and his body went rigid as his eyes fluttered shut. "Can't tell, can't tell, don't know." He chanted the words in a thin voice through gritted teeth. "Can't tell, can't tell, don't know. Can't tell—"

A deep *twisting* rippled within the boy. Wulfram had compelled Odda not to speak of what his Master planned, had ordered it in no uncertain terms. Threatened the boy with dire consequences. It was an extra compulsion on top of the Bond, using Fey power along with the Undying's will. All of that Thomas saw in an instant, and saw, too, how Odda's new Bond fought against the compulsion. But it would be a losing fight and could harm Odda if it continued.

He clutched the boy to his chest. "Never mind. It's okay. You don't have to say."

Odda fell silent, gasping for breath as the competing commands faded. He looked up at Thomas. "I can't tell, Master. I can't tell."

Thomas' mouth twisted as he released his grip. "It's all right. I should have been more careful." He heaved a breath, trying to steady both himself and Odda, and lifted the reins again. "Come on, let's get going." Odda settled back against him, his earlier panic forgotten, it seemed.

But Thomas didn't have as easy a time of letting it go. He was sure that Odda likely knew the plan, or at least more of it than Thomas knew. But it was as inaccessible to him as the moon.

He cast away his frustration and set his mind to the problem once again. Wulfram wanted the monks gone. There were hints he was plotting to take down Oswy, install Penda as king, and twist that pagan ruler to expel the monks. Did he plan to nudge Oswy into a full-blown confrontation with Penda? Or maybe just urge Oswy's *ealdormen* and *thegns* to cast him aside and place Oswine on the throne, as Oswy seemed to think might happen. Then urge Penda to strike against Oswine. That seemed too convoluted a plan. Thomas thought Wulfram would want to do something more direct, something that might push more conclusively towards the outcome he sought. Burn down the monastery? Kill Oswy?

As always, the unknowns haunted him. He couldn't stop what he couldn't see. Frustration filled him, and he urged Missy to go faster, as if he could outrun the dark thoughts that followed him.

As Thomas rode up to Torht's holding, the Horseclan Fey came out of the barn. Thomas slid off of Missy's back and then helped Odda dismount. As he straightened, Torht stopped in front of Missy, stroking her nose as she huffed at him, her large nostrils quivering.

"Aye, lass, aye," Torht murmured and then glanced at Thomas. "Wilding," he said, with a slight nod of his head. "We are long parted."

"But never far apart," Thomas replied. "It's good to see you. Are you well?"

Torht nodded. "Oh aye, well enough," he replied. He rubbed Missy's ears and the horse snorted, leaning closer to him, and he smiled, ruffling her mane. He glanced back at him, the smile fading from his face. "Trouble, is it?"

Thomas let out a breath. "Yes."

Torht nodded, his hands running over the mare, crooning to her under his breath. "Let's get her settled first." His hands froze on the horse, and his face went vacant for a second; then he glanced at Thomas. "She is tired, young Master."

Thomas flushed under the disapproval he saw in the Horseclan's eyes. "Yes, well, we've done a lot of travelling lately. We didn't get to rest in Bebbanburg as long as I had hoped."

Torht grunted and walked back to the barn. Thomas followed, the reins in his hands, but he didn't need them to lead the mare. He was very much second to Torht in Missy's affections. She would follow the bone carver anywhere with no encouragement from him.

They stripped the tack off of Missy and turned her out in the pasture with the others, who greeted her with loud whinnies. Thomas stood beside Torht at the fence, the bone carver's steady calm a peaceful bulwark that soothed him as much as it did the horses.

After a moment Torht walked over to the porch attached to his house and sat down on a chair. Thomas followed and sat down beside him. The door opened and Torht's wife, Hilda, stuck her head around the door. Seeing Thomas, a frown flashed across her face before she nodded at him. "Master Thomas."

Her gaze took in Odda, who sat on the edge of the porch, leaning up against Thomas' legs. She looked from him to Thomas, her eyes narrowing as sudden comprehension filled her face, and her mouth twisted in disgust. She hissed and pulled her head in, shutting the door.

Torht shook his head at her discourtesy. "She blames ye for this," he said, lifting his hands, fading scars still evident on his palms.

Guilt assailed him. He didn't blame Hilda. He felt the same way. If he hadn't been there, Torht would not have suffered the Ordeal. "Yes, well, I understand."

"It is as God wills." Torht lapsed into silence again.

"Yes," Thomas replied. He shifted on the chair. He wished God's will wasn't quite so mysterious.

The trilling song of a wren erupted from the hedge nearby, and a bee buzzed over the mustard and mint planted in Hilda's small garden. The spring sun held some warmth, and for a moment his gloomy thoughts fled from its golden touch.

Torht nodded at the boy. "Now then, lad, my barn needs mucking out. The Mistress Hilda will be glad to share the honey cakes she made with one who could help me with the task. You'll find the rake inside."

Odda looked to Thomas.

"Go on," Thomas said, waving at the barn. "I want to speak with Master Torht for a moment."

After Odda was out of sight, Thomas turned to Torht. "Our Lord King Oswy does not want me at Bebbanburg. Too many rumours about me. People are wondering why he harbours a sorcerer."

"Aye, I have heard the talk." A small smile flashed across Torht's face. "They still say the same of me. Hilda and I will not linger long here. 'Tis time for us to go."

"I'm sorry, Torht. This is all my fault."

"Nay, wilding, do not fret. If not you, there would have been some other cause to drive the humans' thoughts to suspicion." He shrugged. "'Tis the way of the Fey."

Thomas' mouth thinned. "Yes, I suppose." He was beginning to understand how difficult it was for the Fey to live as they did, hidden in plain sight. He heaved a breath. "The boy. Odda." He waved towards the barn, where they could just see Odda's form in the gloom, bent over a rake.

"Ye have Bound him."

Thomas nodded, his face flushing. There was no condemnation in Torht's manner, but he felt ashamed even so. "I didn't mean for it to happen. He was Bound to Wulfram, and I tried to free him. But he ended up Bound him to me instead." *The golden rope, whipping back and forth, Odda reaching for him....* Thomas set aside the memory with an effort. "Do you know how to undo it?"

Torht grunted. "'Tis Unseelie work. The Seelies know not the way of it."

"So I've heard." He sighed. "I can't seem to find anyone who can tell me how to undo it without harming Odda."

They sat in silence for a moment, watching the bees, and then the bone carver spoke again. "Sometimes a young colt will not do as I wish. Take the bit, or the saddle. They have their own minds, these young ones. They can resist even the Horseclan." A small smile touched his mouth, and he shook his head. The smile faded as his gaze met Thomas' eyes. "I give them the freedom to obey. That works." He stood and nodded at him, and then made his way to the barn.

Thomas knew Torht was trying to give him a solution, but he couldn't see how it applied. Odda had no choice to obey. That was the whole point. Was he just supposed to command him to—

Shock washed over him as an idea presented itself. Had Torht just provided the solution after all?

CHAPTER 9

THE FEY AND OUR WAYS

The idea that bloomed full force after Torht's comment chased Thomas through the rest of the afternoon. Even though it held danger for him, he couldn't let it go. But as his conviction grew that he should try it, the reasons for not doing it multiplied as well.

Odda couldn't read his mind through the Bond, but he could sense his emotions. The boy became more of a constant shadow than usual, the turmoil that churned through Thomas causing him to seek reassurance from his Master.

Thomas tripped on him twice while they helped Torht in the workshop. The second time, he barked at Odda to get out of the way. The boy cringed away, and remorse flooded through him. "Sorry," he muttered, exasperated with himself and Odda in equal measure.

Torht put down the antler he was carving. "Master Thomas, there are bones in the ant nest ready to come out. Perhaps you could get them for me." He put his hand on Odda's shoulder, looking down at the boy. "You stay with me, lad. Master Thomas will be back soon."

Thomas nodded, grateful for the bone carver's intervention. He needed a moment to himself.

He took a deep breath of the spring-scented air as he closed the door behind him. Torht's reassurances to Odda faded as he got further away from the workshop. But Odda's anxiety at his departure wasn't so easily left behind.

He turned back without thinking and then stopped, fear seizing him. *The longer I wait, the harder it will be.* New resolution filled him, and he shook off his doubts and strode into the forest along the well-worn path. He should enlist Nona's help to use her herbs to put Odda to sleep before he attempted to break the Bond. Perhaps Torht would take a message to Bebbanburg for him.

He found the nest of wood ants without trouble. He and Matthew had done this task together while his father healed from his injury. A pang pierced him at the memory, and loss filled him once again. *Alone.*

He silenced that gloomy voice and looked for the long stick that Torht used as a tool to push the cleaned items off the anthill. The ants were vicious creatures that gave a nasty bite when disturbed. He spotted the stick leaning up against a nearby tree and turned to grab it.

A slight pressure against him was the only warning before the forest flared white around him and he staggered, losing his balance.

The white faded, leaving behind the shimmering outline of a Fey in the shadows of the trees a few paces away. The pointed cap on his head confirmed what Thomas had guessed: Jack Redcap had returned.

Sudden silence filled the woods, the spring birdsong quieted by the other Fey's arrival. Thomas gripped the stick, raising it. "What do you want?"

The other Fey cocked his head. "Long parted we are, yet he greets with a stick. No manners in his manner."

The odd shift in his mind when people spoke different languages had become familiar. But it was still a shock to realize that Redcap spoke in modern English. Curiosity flared again about this enigmatic wilding. "What do you want?" The English words were both odd and comforting on his tongue.

A small smile flitted across Redcap's face. "Want? Need? A coin with two sides, a jar with no lid." The smile faded. "If I had meant to spill your blood, I would have done it by now, youngling. Put the stick down. It's of no use to you."

Thomas lowered the stick but didn't release it. "Fine." His heartbeat slowed. Redcap was right. The other Fey hadn't meant to harm him. Yet.

Redcap's gaze travelled over him, and he inclined his head. "Power and more power and yet you have learned." His eyes narrowed. "But what is this? Someone beside, someone inside, a Binding do I see?" He clapped his hands together, delight blooming across his face as he grinned. "What a surprise. Did it open their eyes?"

Thomas gritted his teeth together. "It was a mistake. I'm going to undo it."

"Going to, will do, trying to." Redcap chortled. "A path to take, a path to make. You will see, you will see!" He erupted in laughter.

He's lost it. Pity seized him and then disgust, as a faint scent of corruption wafted over to him on the breeze. "So tell me how to undo it. I assume you know."

Redcap's laughter faded, but amusement still filled his face as he wiped his eyes. "Ah, youngling shepherd, ant master, stick lord. You know as well as I. Try by doing, the way of the Fey. The Fey and our ways. My ways are games."

A chill touched him. *The best games.* At Bebbanburg those games had involved the slaughtering of the animals in strange and mysterious ways. Which had led to Torht's Ordeal. "Look. If you can't be helpful, just leave me alone. And leave these people alone. No more of your games around here. You've brought enough harm."

Redcap laughed again. "He speaks, he tells." The laughter stopped, and a light in his eyes flared. "But does he command?"

Thomas' senses screamed danger as a slight push of power signalled the other Fey brushing up against his mind. His own power leapt in response, and the feeling snuffed out.

Redcap smirked. "No. Not yet." He crossed his arms. The light disappeared in his eyes, along with the menacing threat. "I watch. A wilding Fey can use some help."

Did Redcap seek his help or offer his own? The other's words were, as usual, ambiguous. Sensing no further threat, Thomas let go of his power with an effort. "If you want to help, tell me what you know of Wulfram."

Redcap giggled. "Ah. You'll not want the Knowing of him." The giggles stopped. "Nor do I."

Thomas' stomach curdled as he forced away the memory of Nectan and how the king had seen to the depths of him at his first Gathering, after Thomas had pledged to him. He had narrowly avoided enduring the same at Wulfram's hands. "You know what I mean. What does he plan? If you know something, tell me."

Redcap cocked his head. "You know as well as I what he plans."

"Only the big picture. Not specifics. Not timing."

"Time serves the Traveller, Master of Ants. Timing and time and time again. You will see it, you will know it."

"What do you mean?" Thomas' frustration made his words sharp. "If you have something to say, say it!"

"The Speaking is yours, youngling Traveller. We will play games, you and I, when you Call." He grinned again, doffed his cap, nodded his head, and then turned and scampered into the woods.

The white flared again, causing Thomas to stagger as a small echo of Redcap's voice whispered through him.

The Speaking is yours.

Thomas spun around, looking in the shadows for the other Fey, but he had disappeared. He swallowed and shut his eyes, seeking calm. What did Redcap want from him? *We will play games when you Call.* Just what was that supposed to mean?

He shook his head. Easier to untangle a ball of yarn than to figure out what the Redcap meant.

A sudden longing for the peace of the monastery seized him. Tomorrow, he would speak with Aidan. Perhaps the bishop would have some answers for him. Answers to calm the storm of doubt and fear in his heart.

The birds started up again, their cheerful song a balm to his ragged emotions. He gripped the stick and focussed his attention on the large ant pile and the bones that lay upon it, setting his scrambled thoughts aside.

CHAPTER 10

THE HAND OF WULFRAM

Hilda tolerated Thomas' presence, but Thomas didn't want to press his luck. The next morning, after suffering her black looks during breakfast, he took the hint and decided he would leave by noon. In the meantime, Torht asked that he and Odda go to the woods to search for discarded antlers while the bone carver worked on a knife handle for Eanflaed, a commission from Oswy.

Thomas was apprehensive that they might encounter Redcap once again, but there was no sense of the other Fey disturbing the peace of the morning. They looked where Torht had told him he had found antlers before—on game trails through the underbrush where overhanging branches would snag the antlers and in places along the trail where the deer would have to jump over an obstacle or ditch. Torht had warned them not to get their hopes up, but it turned out they found a large one after only about an hour of searching. Flushed with their success, they came back to the holding with their prize clutched in Odda's hand.

But when they reached the workshop, they found Torht standing outside, looking up at the sky, shading his eyes as he squinted against the sun. "Our king comes."

Thomas followed his gaze. High above, a falcon hovered in place, facing into the wind, almost stationary. The black band of feathers that edged its tail was plain against the blue sky. It screeched and darted off to the west.

Nectan. Unease touched him. "What does he want? Do you know?"

Torht shook his head, solemn. "Nay. But he will be here soon. I will tell Hilda."

Odda stepped close to his side and pressed against him as they watched Torht enter his house. Thomas looked down at him. "Don't worry. The king won't hurt you."

He was less confident of saying the same about himself, but he kept that thought away from Odda.

Thomas had braced himself to see Nectan, but when the king came into view, he saw both Domech, Nectan's nephew, and Nona accompanying the king.

A slight flush touched her cheeks as her gaze met his briefly, but otherwise her face was cool and composed. What could her presence mean? Thomas forced himself to rein in the speculations flitting through his mind as the visitors dismounted.

Torht inclined his head. "We are long parted, my lord king. Your visit honours us."

"But never far apart," Nectan replied. "Forgive us our intrusion, Master Torht, but we must speak with the wildin'."

Thomas' gut constricted. He glanced at Nona, but she ignored him, busying herself by tying up her horse to the wooden rail.

Dread haunted Thomas as he followed them in, enduring the pleasantries as Hilda brought them some ale, along with the honey cakes she had baked that morning.

Once they had been served, Nectan turned to Hilda. "Mistress, I ask that ye take the lad out. What we speak of is no for his ears."

Hilda pressed her lips together, but nodded. "Yes, my lord king." She stood, giving Odda a stern look. "Now then, lad, come with me. There's work to do in the garden."

Odda darted a glance at Thomas.

"Go on. It's all right."

The boy slid off the bench at the table and followed Hilda out, reluctance in his manner. Thomas bit back his own unease at seeing him leave, unable to stop the quick search in his mind for the boy's presence as the door shut behind him. The flood of relief as he found it was both comforting and disconcerting.

Torht stood to follow his wife, but Nectan held up a hand. "Nay, Master Torht. Stay." As the bone carver sat, Nectan spoke again. "Tell me: has the Lord Strang been here to visit ye?"

Strang? It wasn't the question Thomas had expected.

Torht answered in his usual quiet manner. "Nay, my lord king. The night Thomas' father came to us was the last time I saw him."

The liquid, dark forms of the Hounds boiled out of the woods, pursuing the rider who shone like a star in the night—

The crystal-clear memory flashed through Thomas' mind. He wrenched his thoughts away from it as Torht continued to speak.

"But two days past, Puttoc of the Horseclan Fey came to me." Torht's left thumb massaged the scars from the Ordeal on the palm of his right hand as he spoke. "He spoke of the Lord Strang. I sent you a message, but it must have reached your holding after you left."

Nectan and Domech exchanged glances, their faces grim. "'Tis no secret the wee upstart wants the Seelie Throne restored to his kin. To him. But lately his talk ha' turned to action. He gathers the Seelie against me. 'Tis sure that he will seek to bring a Charge at the Solstice Gathering."

Torht's face tightened, and he nodded. "Puttoc hinted at it. My message warned you to be wary of him."

"A Charge?" Thomas asked. Again, something niggled at him at the thought of Solstice, but he couldn't pin it down.

Domech's face darkened. "He will seek to prove to the Gathered Seelies that my uncle is unfit to be king and ask them for their support for him instead." He scowled, anger flashing in his eyes. "And all because of ye, wildin'." He practically spat the last word.

Nectan's eyes flashed. "Nay, Domech, hold your tongue." He looked back at Thomas. "Ye be the excuse, not the cause. Last summer after the Solstice Gathering when I became king, we knew Strang would not rest easy. He said himself that he would bring a Charge against me to the Court." His amber eyes hardened. "But 'tis sooner than I expected. I see the hand of Wulfram and his Unseelies in this."

Thomas' heart skipped a beat. "What do you mean?"

Nectan's lips thinned. "Too many whispers. Too many rumours. The wind blows ill against us." His jaw tightened. "I must make my case with the Seelies, visit them in their holdings. Counter the rumours. I ha' already planned to do this. But ye must come wi' me, to show them ye are no to be feared."

"Me? How can I help? If the Seelies are upset because of me, having me with you will make it worse."

"Nay. Strang whispers that ye ha' twined me around your fingers, that I follow your orders." His lip curled. "That I fear your wildin' power, that ye Bound me to ye in the Knowing. All the talk distracts from Wulfram and his purposes here. If ye are wi' me, the Seelies will see the truth of it. And they will hear from your lips what Wulfram proposes." He fixed Thomas with a hard glare. "Ye must come with me. But ye must come alone."

The blood drained from Thomas' face as Nectan's meaning struck home.

But before he could speak, Nectan continued, relentless. "The Binding is Unseelie work. I canna bring ye to the Seelie Fey to show ye are harmless with a Bound human in tow. Ye will Unbind him. Today."

Alarm propelled Thomas to his feet. "But... I don't know how. Do you? Have you learned something?"

From outside, Odda's voice cried, "Master!"

Hilda's voice followed, raised in inarticulate scolding.

Nectan scowled, and he stood and crossed his arms, muscles bulging. The Pictish tattoo on his face cast one side into darkness, but his eyes blazed with Fey power. "Nay. 'Tis Unseelie work, as I ha' said. But ye ha' done it, and ye will undo it. The Healer will aid us. The way of the Fey comes by doing. Ye'll find the way once ye try."

The door flew open and Odda charged in, grabbing onto Thomas, the boy's fear adding to Thomas' own. With an effort, Thomas tamped down their shared alarm, putting an arm around the boy protectively. "Never mind, Odda; I'm all right," Thomas managed. He looked back at Nectan. "I can't.... Just give me a minute. I need to think about this."

"Now, wildin'." Nectan's voice was a low growl. Domech stood as well, his hand resting lightly on the knife at his belt, his eyes hard as flint.

Torht's eyes held some sympathy, but the bone carver remained silent.

Nona stood quickly, glancing from one to the other. "My lord king, perhaps we should give Thomas a moment to think through your request. Let us give Odda some cider and a honey cake, and Thomas can take a short walk. He will see the sense of what you say." She darted Thomas a narrow-eyed look.

He couldn't help feeling betrayed, even though he knew it was unreasonable. Nona had hardly more option to disobey the king than he did.

Nectan's lips thinned, but he nodded. "Verra well. We will await ye here, Master Thomas. But we will no wait long."

Thomas forced himself to walk out the door with some dignity, but after closing it he collapsed back on it, heaving a breath. *Christ Almighty, give me strength.* He shoved away from the house and headed blindly past the workshop into the woods.

Alone. The word beat through his mind as he stumbled down the same path he had taken to the anthill. Once Torht's holding was out of sight, he stopped under a towering ash tree. With a groan of despair, he leaned up against its smooth grey trunk, trying to stifle the spikes of panic that speared through him.

Objectively, Nectan was right. Puzzling out how to Unbind Odda would not work. The only option was to try. Further delay would get him no closer to the goal. So why did the idea of it make him want to puke?

Alone. The word drifted through his mind again, and his jaw tightened. Perhaps that was it. The same haunting emptiness that had chased him all his life since his father died when he was nine was a black cloud that waited to suffocate him once again. It had dispelled somewhat when he had accepted Christ. But since his mother had died, its familiar presence clutched at him.

He was used to being alone. But this panic was different. The thought of severing the Bond was like the thought of cutting off his own leg. Which was precisely why he had to do it. But he couldn't talk himself out of the feeling, no matter how hard he tried.

He shut his eyes, seeking calm, and, as it often did, the words of the Breastplate prayer came to his mind. He grasped at them like a drowning man grasps a rope. *I bind to myself today the power of God to guide me, the might of God to uphold me, the wisdom of God to teach me, the eye of God to watch over me.*

He heaved in a breath, remembering Celyn in the haunted *coed*, the words of his muttered invocations bringing peace in their wake.

He spoke the prayer out loud again. He took a deep breath and opened his eyes. *Now or never.* He pushed himself away from the tree and forced his feet down the path towards the holding.

He could do this. He had to.

CHAPTER 11

NETHERWORLD

"He's asleep now." Nona straightened up from where she had been bending over Odda, apprehension on her face as she looked at the boy. She put down the flask that held the draught she had made.

Thomas felt the same. Resolution had taken him this far, but his courage was quickly draining away as the time drew near.

"It's time," Nectan said. "Do what ye must."

Icy panic gripped him. But faced with the hard glint in Nectan's eyes, Thomas' protest died on his lips. He took a deep breath to steady his nerves, his heart pounding. His eyes sought Nona's, and she nodded. Beside her, Domech glowered at him.

The Speaker's surly expectation of his failure strengthened Thomas' resolve. He clenched his jaw and knelt beside Odda, determined to prove the Speaker wrong. He reached out a hand and touched Odda's forehead, battling the reluctance that fought against his resolve. *Oh God, make haste to help me.* He inhaled, seeking calm. *I arise today, through the strength of Heaven: light of Sun, brilliance of Moon, splendour of Fire, speed of Lightning, swiftness of Wind, depth of Sea, stability of Earth, firmness of Rock.* He heaved another breath and opened the door to his power. It flooded through him, scouring away doubt and fear under its bright onslaught.

He opened his eyes. A dark place of mist and shadows surrounded him. In the distance, the billowing mist revealed and hid low hills on the horizon.

Disoriented, he turned around, fear flooding back as the rush of power faded. *The mist.* The dream that had haunted him from his first days after his arrival in this time was eerily similar to this, including the strange feeling of dread.

What...? His thoughts scattered, unclear as the misty shadows. He sucked in a breath. The air felt thinner, harder to breathe. The fear that tightened his chest didn't help. *Get a grip, Tommo.* He focussed on breathing, shaking his head to clear it. *Odda. The Binding.*

He must free the boy. But where was Odda? Shouldn't he be here, wherever *here* was? He shut his eyes, fighting down rising panic, forcing himself to think through that chaotic moment when he had freed Odda from Wulfram's Binding. Memory flashed: a golden rope, whipping back and forth like a snake after he broke it. The rope that tied Wulfram to Odda.

He opened his eyes. Where was it? Odda must be in this strange landscape somewhere, and that rope would lead Thomas to him.

The wisdom of the Fey comes by doing.

He spun around again, the echo of a voice fading in his ears, shock making his heart pound. His father's voice, as close as a breath. He squinted through the mist. Was that a shadow there…? He had the eerie sense of someone watching. Not just *someone.* His father.

"Dad?" His voice croaked out of him, and he took a step towards the shape. Another memory flashed through him: his father, turning towards him with a smile lighting his face. *Tommo.*

The memory disappeared, along with the sense of his father. Shaken, he turned again, seeing nothing but the billowing, dark mist. Frustrated, he raised his hand to push the hair off his face and froze.

His hand grasped a golden rope that stretched away from him into the dark. Surprise loosened his grip, and he dropped it, but then grabbed at it before it hit the ground. He looked at the rope to see if it went somewhere behind him, but when he twisted around, it was not there. Peering at it, he saw it dissolved into a misty golden shadow of a rope that looped around him, moving with him as he experimented, twisting this way and that. He let go again, and it stayed in place, stretching away from him.

He looked around again. Had he truly seen his father? He couldn't be sure. But whether it had been a figment of his imagination or not, the encounter had bolstered his courage. Time to get going. The wisdom of the Fey comes by doing.

He clenched his jaw and started following the shimmering rope that extended away from him into the dark, piercing through the mist.

The landscape, such as it was, did not waver. The billowing grey mist, the darkness that encompassed him, the small glimpses of a far horizon ringed by hills—all stayed the same as he walked.

After a few steps, the sense of purpose and the lingering comfort of the encounter with his father faded, and the menacing foreboding grew. The disorienting place in which he found himself was more like a dreamland than reality. Just as in dreams, things shifted around him, changing in a flash and then back again. A slight weight dragged at his limbs as he walked, as if he were trying to push through air that was thicker than normal. His heart thudded loudly in his ears.

He was not always alone. He had flashing impressions more than once of someone with him. Not his father, not always, but once or twice he thought he had the same sense of Matthew's presence as he had before. Never as strong, but fleeting, insubstantial as the mist. But it heartened him all the same.

Others were darker companions. A throaty chuckle, or a strange, hunching shape. Once, a far-off moaning howl that stopped him in his tracks. But it faded, and he hurried on.

Was he going mad? Had the use of his power tripped him into the netherworld, never to return? He thrust such thoughts aside and kept his eyes on the golden rope. It helped if he focussed his mind on something other than the distracting flashes of other realities, and he muttered the *lorica* under his breath. *Christ above me, Christ beneath me.*

As was usual in the grip of Fey power, time became meaningless. The act of walking became all, one plodding foot in front of another, pushing onward towards a half-remembered goal. *Odda,* he reminded himself when he found his attention wandering and his feet faltering. *Odda.*

The golden rope cast a slight glow, its shimmery substance a comfort in the grey billowing mist. Muted sounds came to him as if from far away. Suddenly, he stopped short at the harsh caw of a crow splitting the silence. He squinted ahead. *A light?* He forced himself to move more quickly, pushing through the odd resistance. As he approached, details emerged from the surrounding fog.

Odda sat huddled in the dark, his knees drawn up and his head resting on his knees. The rope looped around him, casting a golden light that held him in a warm embrace.

The boy didn't seem to notice him as he approached. His eyes were closed, his breathing even. Asleep under the effects of Nona's herbs, Thomas presumed.

Just forget it. It won't work. Try another time. The thought whispered through his mind. Thomas gritted his teeth, ignoring both the temptation and the burgeoning need for escape that arose on its heels. He stretched out a hand and touched Odda's shoulder, avoiding the bright rope. "Odda."

The boy stirred and looked up. His eyes focussed on him. "Master?"

Thomas sat down beside him, careful not to touch him. "I need to talk to you."

"Yes, Master Thomas."

A perverse twist of pleasure flooded through him at Odda's words. "No!" He spoke more harshly than he meant.

Odda recoiled, panic in his eyes.

"Don't be afraid," he said, seeking control. He heaved a breath. "Look. I need to fix this. But I'll need your help."

Odda nodded, his eyes brightening. "Yes, I'll help you."

Thomas curled his hands into fists. "Just listen. This is important." For a moment, indecision seized him and he couldn't continue. *Strength of Heaven.* He forced himself to speak. "This has to stop. I have to free you." He tried to keep his voice calm, despite the panicky voice that yammered away in the background. *Don't do it, don't do it, this is nuts, it won't work, don't do it—*

"I want to serve you. You are my Master." The words echoed through the mist, reverberating unpleasantly. In the distance, a faint screech sounded.

"Stop it." Thomas gritted his teeth, trying to ignore the distractions. He had to break through to the boy's real self, hidden under the slave. "Listen. It doesn't have to be this way. I can break the Bond. You can be free, like before. Before Wulfram."

Odda shuddered and drew his knees tighter against him and rocked back and forth.

Thomas wasn't sure if the panic that rippled through him came from Odda or from himself. He fought against the urge to get up and run away. "He hurt you. I hurt you. But you can be free." He floundered, his words hollow in his ears, as he forced himself to lift his hand, bracing himself to touch the shining rope and make it snap.

But not yet. *Freedom to obey.* Torht's voice came back. That was the key. It had to be Odda's choice.

Thomas could touch the rope and destroy the Bond. But that was just another way to override Odda's will. What if Odda had been so damaged that he didn't want freedom? If Thomas broke the Bond, the boy would forever seek a Master. Easy pickings for those who might want to use him again. Wulfram again, or worse.

But giving Odda the choice meant the boy could refuse. Which would bring other dangers. He knew the creeping danger that the Bond posed to him. Its corrupting power already corroded his will. Worse, he would be stuck in this time, for Crossing back home would sever the Bond, leaving Odda lost.

A burgeoning sense of panic swept through him. He looked around, peering through the fog that had closed around them. He saw nothing, but he knew without a doubt that something was coming for them out of the mist.

His muscles tensed and he half-stood, searching for danger. A loud sound erupted above him—the harsh, strangled cry of a crow, abruptly cut off, followed on its heels by two more. Three crows thudded to the ground, their necks twisted, glittering eyes dulling in death.

Thomas gaped at them, but a movement out of the corner of his eye caused him to whirl around in a panic. But it was merely Odda, lifting his head.

Their eyes met, and everything fell away.

CHAPTER 12

THE THING IS DONE

"Thomas! Thomas!"

Thomas heard Nona from a distance, but he tumbled and twisted in the darkness, unable to respond, speeding towards an unknown destination.

Suddenly sensations returned. He gasped a great shuddering breath as his eyes flew open. A wrenching sense of loss washed over him, tearing a groan from his lips.

He lay on the floor. Nona knelt beside him, concern in her eyes. He tried to sit up, but everything swayed around him and he slumped back down.

His thoughts swooped and whirled in his mind, moving so fast he couldn't catch them. Something was wrong. He closed his eyes again, fighting the nausea that gripped him.

"Help me, my lord," Nona said with urgency.

Strong arms grasped Thomas under the arms, pulling him to a sitting position. "Are ye well? Did it work?"

Nectan. He opened his eyes again. The Seelie King peered at him; his amber eyes concerned. He was sure he should be able to understand what the king meant, but he couldn't concentrate, not with his mind whirling around and around like water draining out of a sink, tumbling into the black hole at the bottom...

Suddenly, memory returned in a crash. *Odda.* "He's gone. G—" He choked on the word. The vacancy in his mind Odda's presence left behind exerted a pressure that compelled him to seek it out, like the urge to probe an empty spot left by a pulled tooth. Panic flooded through him. "Where is he?" He tried to rise, but Nectan held him down.

"The lad is fine. He sleeps. Ye ha' broken the Bond."

"Let me go," he insisted. He had to see the boy for himself. Maybe then the aching emptiness that threatened to overwhelm him would ease. He strained at his memory. The Bond had been severed, that much was certain. But how? What had he done? *The mist, the rope. Odda.* What happened next was a blank. Had the boy chosen freedom? Or had he chosen to stay Bound? Thomas' blood ran cold at the thought. If that was the case, he had forced his will on the boy and broken the Bond without his consent.

The details wouldn't come. The Bond was gone. That much was clear. Why couldn't he remember what he had done? He tried to push himself up, but his strength failed him. "I must see him."

Nectan glanced at Domech, and the two of them helped Thomas to rise. Odda lay on the bed, sleeping. A violent urge seized him. *Take him, take him, he's yours.* He recoiled from the insistent mantra and turned blindly, shaking off the hands that restrained him. He staggered to the door, wrenching it open.

Nectan caught up with him, Domech on his heels. The king grabbed his shoulder, pulling him back.

Thomas shook off his hand, spinning back to face the king. "Don't!" he snarled, his power surging. If he stayed there one more second, the consuming desire to Bind the boy again would overpower him.

Domech pushed past the king, his dagger in his hand, murderous intent in his eye, but Nectan grabbed him, shoving him away. "Nay, Domech, hold!"

Thomas flung himself outside as Domech protested, his head spinning. He leaned against the wall. Nausea seized him, and he bent over and retched.

Angry voices raised from inside, Nectan and Domech clashing, but Thomas paid no notice, consumed by trying to stitch himself together without the solid feel of Odda to anchor him. *Christ.* He leaned over and heaved again.

Nectan stepped out, shutting the door behind him.

The shut door helped, a barrier between him and Odda. Thomas caught his breath and beat down the surging desire to leap past the king and throw himself inside.

Nectan crossed his arms, regarding him through narrowed eyes. "Pull yourself together. Let the power go. Ye'll burn yourself to a husk."

Thomas blinked at him. *Power?* Sudden understanding swept through him. His power still surged through him, bright as the sun and sharp as a knife. He shook his head, words tumbling out. "I need it. I want Odda back. I need him back. The power fills the spot where Odda was. If I don't have it, I—" His words choked off again as the need for the boy flooded through him, pushing him off the wall. *Odda.*

Freedom to obey. Torht's solution had worked. He had given Odda the choice, and now Odda was free. He strained again at that last moment, but everything after Odda looked up at him was frustratingly opaque.

Something flickered in his memory. A feeling. *Doom. Loss. Grief.* "I've gotta stop it," he muttered, hardly knowing what he was saying, but certainty fell on him all the same. Something he had to do. Or not do. Something about Odda. "I have to!" He pushed against Nectan as panic surged through him. "Odda!"

A flash of alarm crossed the king's face. He grabbed Thomas' shoulders, pressing him back against the wall. "That's enough," he snarled, a wisp of power threading through his words. "It's done. Release your power. Ye canna sustain it. I wilna let ye harm yourself."

Through the confusion that roiled through his mind, Nectan's words struck like a hammer. Holding his power now would drain him completely. The shuddering quivers that wracked him were the last warnings before... what? Thomas didn't know exactly what might happen, and he didn't care. The thought of facing the yawning emptiness where Odda had been without the power to shield him was too much. "Let me burn, then." His voice rasped in his throat. "Or I just might march back in there and get him back."

A flicker passed through Nectan's eyes as the king raised his own power. "I wouldn't let ye, wildin'. It wilna happen."

Instinctive anger flared at the snap of Nectan's power against him. He snarled, pushing against the king, but Nectan held him pinned to the wall.

Thank God. Sudden relief flooded through him. Odda was safe from him for now. With a gasp, he let his power go; the strength draining from his limbs at the same time. He would have collapsed in a boneless heap had Nectan not been holding him up.

"Come wi' me." Nectan slung his arm around Thomas' shoulder and began to half drag, half support Thomas as they walked towards Torht's house.

The bone carver must have been watching from the window. He opened the door as Thomas stumbled up the steps to the porch and reached out to help Nectan. Together the two Fey got Thomas into a chair, and Nectan shoved a mug of a hot cider into his hand—the same concoction Nona had brewed earlier for Odda.

"Drink," the king ordered. He kept one hand on Thomas' shoulder, preventing him from getting up. Thankfully. The raging need to see Odda flooded through him again. Without Nectan's restraint, he would have made a run for the door.

But he wouldn't have gone very far. He was as weak as a kitten, his arms made of lead. Even lifting the mug was beyond him. He sucked in a breath, his eyes fluttering shut as a bone-deep weariness pulled at him, his mind filling with cotton wool.

"Wilding."

Thomas felt Torht's hand on his arm, heard the bone carver's grave voice from a distance, calling him back from the spinning void that beckoned him, the one that whirled around and around a black hole, dragging him closer and closer…

Thomas blinked his eyes open with an effort. "Odda," he mumbled.

Nectan grabbed his chin, forcing his head up to meet his eyes. "The Binding is gone. Ye ha' freed him."

Thomas blinked. Nectan's words merely skipped along the surface of his roiled brain. Below, a vast aching emptiness echoed with loss. *Gone.*

Nectan's eyes narrowed, and he muttered a Pictish curse. He grabbed Thomas' arm. "Speak. Tell us what ye ha' done. The tellin' will help ye."

The king's sharp voice pierced through the confusion in his head. He frowned. "There was a mist," he began, fumbling to explain something that he didn't understand. "A strange place. Dark. Misty clouds."

Nectan and Torht exchanged a glance.

"The Otherworld." Nectan spoke in a low voice. "The world between the worlds. A place of dreams and shadows." His jaw tensed. "A dangerous place."

"The boy was there?" Torht asked.

"Yes. There was a rope that led me to him…" His voice trailed off as he tried to remember. The circle of golden light. Thomas gritted his teeth against the sudden need for Odda that seized him, and he crossed his arms over his stomach, trying to hold himself together. *Focus.* "I found him. And I realized I could break the rope that tied me to him. Just by touching it and willing it to be gone." He raised his eyes to Torht. "But it was more complicated than just breaking the Bond. You gave me the key. Odda had to choose." Sudden grief choked his throat shut.

"Freedom to obey," Torht said. "Aye, indeed."

The calm quiet of the bone carver's voice was a balm on Thomas' roiled emotions. He took a deep breath. "Yes. Breaking the Bond without allowing him the option of staying where he was would have been the same as when I took his freedom away the first time. My will, not his."

Nectan nodded slowly. "Aye, I see it. 'Tis wisdom there." He thought for a moment and then stirred and fixed his gaze on Thomas once again. "And so he chose to be free."

A tendril of fear touched Thomas, an echo of the mist. "I don't remember."

Nectan raised an eyebrow. "Ye dinna—" He gathered himself and tried again. "He is no longer Bound to ye. What did ye do?"

"I can't remember what happened. I gave him the choice. But then—" He closed his eyes, concentrating, but everything after that moment remained blank. He shook his head. "I don't know what happened."

What had Odda decided? Obviously the boy was free. But had that been his choice? The thought that Odda chose to stay Bound and that he overrode that choice haunted him. Was he compelled to Bind the boy again because his subconscious was telling him to heal a wound Thomas had caused in Odda by freeing him?

Something surfaced at the edges of his mind. For a split second, a tumble of images spun through his mind like a kaleidoscope.

Nectan, facing him with his arms crossed over his chest, wreathed in firelight.

Godric, singing in a crowded hall, his fingers on the lyre burning with fire.

Stumbling in the mist, a raven's call harsh in his ears.

A bright flash of a blade descending.

A horrified cry wrenched out of him as he leapt to his feet. But just as suddenly as they had come, the images disappeared. He heaved a breath, seeking to calm his pounding heart, and sat down again.

Nectan and Torht had leapt to their feet in response to Thomas' cry. "What is it" Nectan scanned the room, his hand on the knife at his belt.

"Nothing," Thomas managed. "There was something I remembered, but..." His voice trailed off again. Whatever it was had disappeared into the black hole in his mind again. He took another deep breath as they sat down once more. "I don't know what happened," he managed. "Maybe he wanted to stay Bound, but I broke the Bond, anyway."

Nectan's eyes narrowed as he gazed at Thomas. "We wilna know until the boy wakes up. The Healer will watch him. 'Tis all we can do."

Self-disgust flooded through Thomas. "And if I have harmed him by taking that choice from him? What will you do?"

"You did not." Torht spoke before Nectan answered. "You are no Unseelie, to treat him so."

Bitterness twisted through Thomas. He leaned forward, holding his head in his hands. "No? I'm not so sure."

Nectan made a noise of disgust in his throat. "Ach, dinna be a fool. Torht is right, and ye know it. Ye couldna have released the boy if ye had waited much longer. That much is clear. But ye did it. Odda is free. Ye are young, untrained, and a wee fool, besides. Full of more power than is good for any of us. Ye used it unwisely, 'tis true, but out of ignorance, and to save another's life. Not Unseelie work, any of it. I've had the Knowin' of ye, dinna forget."

Thomas sat back, weary. "But my father—" His words cut off. The strange misty darkness, the sudden voice in the dark. Had Matthew truly been there?

Nectan's reply cut into his thoughts. "Your father's destiny is not yours." He stood up. "No Unseelie could ha' torn himself away from his desire as ye did. Dinna forget that."

Thomas wanted to protest, but he was too tired.

Nectan rose to his feet. "Rest now. I will see to the boy. We will speak more of this later."

Silence fell after the king left. Torht nodded his head at the mug on the table. "Drink the draught the Healer made and then lay yourself down. Hilda won't be back from town for some time."

Thomas sighed and drank the bitter liquid in one swallow. He stood up with an effort, swaying. Torht supported him as he led him to the room in the back where their sleeping pallet lay.

Nectan's words tumbled through his mind as he lay down. *No Unseelie could ha' torn himself away from his desire as ye did.*

But no Seelie would have done it in the first place, he countered, despair rising again.

The haunting thought chased him into sleep.

CHAPTER 13

DESOLATION

Thomas blinked his eyes open. *Odda.* He winced. The wound of the boy's absence still throbbed, but the relentless, overpowering sense of loss had eased. The sleep had helped.

He pushed himself up, taking stock. A rooster crowed, the cry loud, and in the distance a horse squealed, answered by another.

He must have slept through the night. He got up, fighting dizziness, and pushed past the curtain that divided the sleeping area from the rest of Torht's house.

Nectan, Domech, and Nona sat at the table, eating hot porridge. Hilda had her hand on the latch of the door, the other arm cradling a large bowl of porridge. She turned back at the sound of his entrance. Seeing him, she grimaced and slipped outside, shutting the door behind her.

"Thomas!" Nona rose and hurried over to him. "Are you well? You have slept long. You must be hungry. Come, sit and eat."

He sat down at the table, nodding at Nectan, who regarded him through narrowed eyes. "My lord king," he managed.

Nectan nodded back, but Domech, as usual, scowled at him.

Nona put a bowl of porridge laced with honey and cream in front of him, but he ignored it for a moment, even though his stomach contracted in hunger as the aroma wafted to his nose. "Odda?" He couldn't help the waver in his voice, and he cleared his throat. "How is he?"

Nona sat beside him. "As to that, he is well. I spent the night in the workshop with him. He did not stir, and woke up hungry. Hilda is taking him some porridge, and she and Torht will eat there with him. Never fear. He is young. He will recover. Do not worry on his account." Nona's gaze roved over him. "You look worse than he does."

He waved a hand. "I am fine." Which was partially true. A headache pounded in his head, and he still felt raw and torn inside. Empty. But not as if his mind were teetering on the edge of a black hole of nothing.

Nona frowned. "You do not lie well, Thomas." She nodded at the bowl in front of him. "Eat."

Thomas gave into hunger and attacked the hot porridge, his strength returning with every bite. But his thoughts whirled around Odda. "Has he spoken of me?"

"He asked where you were when he woke up. I told him you were sleeping. Do not worry." Nona hesitated. "You can see him if you like—"

"Nay, Healer." Nectan's voice was flat. "That wouldna be wise. The wildin' will eat and then we will be leaving."

Cold horror gripped him, but Thomas tamped down the denial that sprang to his lips. He put down the spoon. "I should make sure he is fine before I leave. The unBinding might have damaged him."

But Nectan's face hardened. "Lady Nona will see to the boy. We will leave once ye have eaten."

Nona laid a hand on his arm. "I will make sure no harm comes to him."

Thomas swallowed back a complaint. He wanted to rail against the king. But he knew Nectan was right. His control was too fragile. The only thing that would stop him from Binding Odda again and filling the hole he'd left behind was leaving. The sooner the better. "All right," he managed. "I'll go with you. But I must see Aidan first."

Nectan's eyes narrowed. "The bishop has no place in this."

Thomas held the king's amber gaze. "Oswy wanted me to tell him of Wulfram's plans against the monastery." He waved his hand at Nectan's hardened expression. "He needs to know. I won't tell him of the Fey." He swallowed. "Besides, I need—" His voice choked off. He heaved a breath and gathered himself together. "I need his wisdom. And his blessing. I checked the tide charts with Father Colm before I left Bebbanburg. The tide is out this morning. I can be back before it turns."

Nectan regarded him with a long, measured look. "Verra well. See to it ye dinna linger long." He rose. "The Lady Nona has words for ye. Come, Horsemaster. Domech. We will leave them be."

Words for him? That sounded ominous. He looked at Nona as Nectan and Domech left, but she avoided his gaze, busying herself by pouring out warm water from the pot over the hearth fire into a bucket and putting the dirty bowls in to scrub clean.

Suddenly, he knew. He clenched his jaw, fighting back the emptiness that threatened to overwhelm him. *First Odda, now this?* "Nona," he managed. "Sit down." If the table were between them, it would make it harder for him to give into the urge to take her in his arms.

She froze, her back to him, her hands going still in the bucket, and then she turned, but remained standing.

His heart plunged at the sorrow and reluctance in her eyes. He stood. *Get it over with.* "Look, I—"

She stopped him with an impatient gesture. "Nay, let me speak." Her hands twisted together as she took a few steps towards him. "When I came to Bebbanburg, it was with no thought but to visit with Celyn and wait here for my betrothed to arrive in the spring, and after that, the marriage. But God brought you here on the wind, too." She faltered for a moment and then gathered herself. "All my life I have been warned of the wilding Fey. They bring danger, disaster, destruction. I was frightened of you at first, 'tis true. But then..." She waved a hand, a flush staining her cheeks, her eyes darting away. "I did not expect to feel as I do for you. I should not have allowed it. My duty calls me elsewhere." She met his gaze, her chin lifting. "I have had word. My betrothed is coming. He will arrive in Bebbanburg within the week."

Even though he had expected it, the words hit him like a hammer. *Not for you.* He knew that from the beginning. Why had he allowed himself to forget it? It would have spared him the pain that assailed him now.

"I understand." His throat closed, but he forced the words out. "I'm sorry. I should not have—"

She stepped around the table and placed her hand over his lips, stopping his words. Her eyes shone with tears as they met his. "I am not sorry."

He couldn't help himself. He took her hand and turned it to his mouth, kissing her palm.

She closed her eyes, stricken, and wrapped her fingers around his, bending her head to his chest, and he enfolded her in his arms.

They stood for a moment, silent. Thomas breathed in her scent, imprinting the sensation of her pressed close to him. Then he stiffened and stepped away, allowing his arms to fall. "You had better go."

She looked at him, her eyes shining with tears, and nodded, turning away from him.

"Wait." The words burst out of him as she reached the door. She froze with her hand on the latch. "Tell Celyn what's happened, where I've gone." He heaved a breath. That wasn't what he needed to say, but anything else was irrelevant.

She looked back over her shoulder at him, tears streaming down her face, and nodded once. "Go with God," she choked out. "I will pray for your success. I will help if I can." She opened the door and left, shutting it behind her.

Thomas stood still for a moment, desolation freezing him in place. It was too much. He had suffered so many losses that it was suffocating. *His mother. His father. Odda. Nona.*

He sighed deeply, pushing aside the weight of sorrow that threatened to crush him. He couldn't dwell on it now. It would only distract him from his purpose.

But he stood still for a moment, his heart aching. *God, give me strength.*

It was as true a prayer as he had ever prayed.

CHAPTER 14

THE WILLING

Thomas got Missy ready to go as quickly as he could, the task a good distraction from his thoughts. According to Father Colm's charts, it was safe to cross until about an hour after noon, so he needed to get to Lindisfarne without delay if he was to return this day.

Yesterday's sun had disappeared behind a low bank of clouds. A few raindrops spat down as he rode towards the tidal island. Its rocky outcrop, twin to the one at Bebbanburg, soon loomed ahead, a black silhouette against the grey clouds.

He did his best to keep his mind on the task at hand, avoiding the yawning black hole inside him that sought to draw him in and rip him apart. Blackness that whispered to him of his failures, his inadequacies. Of Odda and Nona, his father and his mother. Those whom he had lost.

He recited the Breastplate as he urged Missy into the teeth of the wind and rain that strengthened as he rode, the words a bulwark against the despair that threatened to overwhelm him.

The wet sands were dull under the slanting rain. Gulls wheeled above, their piercing cries a perfect lament of loss that matched his feelings. He urged Missy to go faster until the mud flew off her hooves as she galloped across the sands.

The prior, Father Gaeth, told Thomas that Aidan was in his cell. Thomas left Missy eating hay in the horse shelter, but he left her saddled as he would need to get away before the tide turned again. He hurried towards Aidan's cell. The midday prayers were nearly upon them. He had to speak to Aidan before they began.

Aidan and a novice stood speaking outside of the bishop's cell. As Thomas approached, Aidan looked over. His eyes widened, and a smile split his long face. "Master Thomas! God be praised, ye be back!"

Thomas' heart lightened at the bishop's warm welcome, and as Aidan wrapped him in a hearty hug of welcome, some of the tension that had gripped him melted away.

Aidan pulled back, examining his face. "Ye have a tale for me, so ye do." He looked down at the novice. "Away wi' ye then. Tell Brother Eadger that I will speak to him after Sext."

The novice nodded. "Yes, my lord bishop." He darted a curious glance at Thomas before hurrying off.

"Come now, I would hear of your journey." Aidan opened the door to the cell and gestured Thomas inside.

They sat down across the table from each other, and Aidan fixed him with a searching gaze. "Tell me then, Master Thomas. Did ye find the man ye sought?"

Thomas recounted the same tale he had told Oswy. "His target is the monastery," he concluded. "He thinks that by getting rid of Oswy, Lindisfarne will soon follow." He leaned forward. "Is that true, do you think? Are you that vulnerable here?"

Aidan looked troubled, but his voice held confidence as he answered. "We have the protection of God and all his angels, so we do. Prayer shields this work. It will not be easy to root out." He shook his head. "But 'tis true we exist under the king's favour."

"What if Penda killed Oswy in battle and took Bernicia's throne?".

Aidan drew back, startled. "This is Wulfram's plan? To make Mercia supreme?"

"He implied as much."

Aidan shook his head, but Thomas saw unease in his eyes. "Mercia is strong. But to face Oswy and win, he would need more allies than he has. He has Powys and Gwynedd, but Wessex would never—"

"Deira," Thomas interrupted.

Aidan's eyes narrowed. "Oswine is a Christian king, and cousin to Oswy. He would not betray Oswy to Penda. He would never allow us to be removed." His gaze sharpened. "But I see ye are not convinced. Tell me what ye know, me son."

Thomas' cheeks flamed, but he forced himself to speak. "The tales that Brother Frithlac began have spread, as you must know. Tales of the sorcerer in Oswy's Court, who uses black arts to sway Oswy's *thegns* and *ealdormen* on Oswy's orders." Thomas let out a breath. Aidan was going to hear all this anyway, from

Celyn or Oswy himself. He may as well tell him. "Lord Griffith of Gwynedd was seen with Wulfram."

"Griffith!" The word burst out of Aidan, and then he collected himself. "Celyn's brother, who pledged to Penda."

Thomas nodded.

Aidan got up and paced, disquiet in his face. "God, have mercy," he muttered, and then swung to Thomas. "Ye ha' told Oswy of this?"

"Yes, of course, my lord bishop. He asked me to tell you of what I learned."

Aidan shook his head and sat down, his gaze sharpening on Thomas once again. "The Brothers bring me word of what they hear in their travels. They've told me the tales of sorcery and evil at Bebbanburg ha' no died out." He sighed. "I do what I can to ease their fears, but these stories spring up faster than I can stamp them out, as if they be borne on a wicked wind."

Thomas nodded. "I saw the harper Godric again, in Eoforwic. With Wulfram. He is likely spreading these tales as he travels around. And Wulfram has others to help him, too."

"Aye. I've heard talk of strangers roaming throughout Bernicia, who come and go like the wind." The bishop paused and then continued, his voice lowering. "Dark clouds hem us in. Evil sets its face against us, to be sure. I ask ye, do ye think Wulfram is in league wi' the *sidhe*? Could he be one of them himself? I ha' heard tales of him, too. Strange tales, so they are."

Thomas wished he could confess all, but he dared not. "It's possible."

Aidan eyed him and then let out a breath. "Ye were wise not to confront him. The *sidhe* do not willingly give up the mortals they claim as their own. If he hails from the Otherworld, he will seek to use ye for his purposes, so he will."

"Yes." He switched topics; the less he spoke about the Fey to Aidan, the better for both their sakes. "I just wish I knew what Wulfram was going to do. It would be a lot easier to stop it if we knew that."

"A king can lose a throne through death from battle or illness, or by treachery within his kingdom. 'Tis no other way," Aidan mused. "We will no stop Oswy from war, 'tis the nature of kings. There will be skirmishes, raids, and battles over the summer. No king will keep his sword idle when there is an opportunity to gain land and wealth. Oswy will need to prove his worth to his warband, reward them with the spoils of war. Whether he dies or lives is up to God. As is illness. But treachery..." His voice trailed off. He blew out a breath before continuing, the rain pattering down in counterpoint to his words. "Oswy will hold the *witenagemot* at Yeavering on Midsummer's Eve. I tell ye this now, I have had some come to me questioning Oswy's worth. More than one. All these rumours are a noose around his neck. If the murmurs against Oswy are strong enough to sway the *witan*, he could face a challenge to his throne."

"The wit-a-..." Normally Thomas didn't think about what language he spoke, for his Traveller's Gift gave him the ability to understand and speak the languages he heard. But occasionally it had a hiccup and wouldn't work. This unfamiliar Saxon word spoken amid the Latin derailed him, and he had to scramble to keep up as Aidan continued.

"Aye. The gathering of the king's council." Seeing his puzzled expression, Aidan clarified. "They meet every year to discuss the affairs of the kingdom, so they do. And if they are no happy wi' the king, they can take the throne away."

"Take it away? You mean replace him?"

"Aye. It does not happen often, but it is possible."

Dread coiled in Thomas' gut. "They would give it to Oswine. And soon after, he would be disposed, and Penda would march in." He thought for a moment. "Midsummer's Eve. When is that?"

"St. John's Feast, when the herald of our Lord was born, bringing the light of life to all men. It comes a few days after the pagans celebrate the summer Solstice."

Solstice. The word tumbled around his mind, a key fitting a lock. A time of turning, just like Samhain, when he had Crossed to this time. A time when Wulfram's Fey Power would be strongest. That's why the word had been chiming a warning at him. "That's it." He jumped up, his agitated thoughts causing him to pace. "Solstice. That has to be when Wulfram is going to act."

With a lurch, Thomas realized something else. Nectan would be facing Strang's Charge at the Solstice Gathering. Oswy's meeting with his council would be a few days later. The Unseelie Traveller had to be planning something for Oswy's meeting, too—something that tied in to whatever he would do at Solstice. Something that would undermine Oswy's kingship, or strip it from him entirely. Or worse. Both Nectan and Oswy would face opposition because of Wulfram's interference.

"Aye, I see it." Aidan's words interrupted Thomas' thoughts. The bishop frowned. "The walls between the worlds are thin at Solstice. He can bring all the powers of darkness against us." He crossed himself. "We will set our prayers against it, so we will."

"It won't be just Solstice that we have to worry about. Whatever Wulfram does that night will cause Oswy to lose his throne at his meeting. I'm sure of it. The two events are tied. Can you ask the king not to hold it on that date?"

Aidan shook his head. "Oswald started the tradition of holding the *witenagemot* at Midsummer's Eve. Word has already been sent throughout the kingdom that Oswy will do the same. Changing it now will bring questions that he wilna want to answer."

Frustration caused Thomas' fists to clench. "Right." He always seemed two steps behind. "These people who come to you with questions of Oswy's leadership are asking for your support for Oswine, aren't they?"

Aidan's face was mild. "As a bishop, I will no pick sides."

"Of course not. But that doesn't stop people from asking your opinion." He forced himself to stop and think. He had to be very careful. Wulfram was interfering in history, but so might he be, if he swayed the bishop's thinking. He might already have said too much. "It's not my place to tell you what to do. You know my fears. I just ask that you be careful in what you say."

"Aye. I will ask God for wisdom, so I will."

A bell rang, calling the brothers to prayer. Aidan rose at the sound of it. "Come then, it is time for prayer. Will ye no join us?"

Thomas shook his head. "I'm sorry, my lord bishop. The tide will come in soon." He paused, then continued with the rest of his news. "Oswy has asked me to leave, because of the rumours. I don't blame him. I had already decided the same thing. I have to go. The less I am seen around here, the better."

Aidan's face was full of sympathy. "Aye, the king discussed this with me. I am sorry, me son. But where will ye go?"

Thomas shrugged. "I am not sure. I'll try to find out more of Wulfram's plans. But I'll come back before Solstice."

Aidan put a hand on his shoulder. "Dinna be troubled, me son. God ha' brought ye here to reveal these schemes, and to undo them."

He grimaced, despair filling him. "Feels more to me like I'm in the cause of them. And as for undoing them... I don't know. I'm not sure what I can do."

Aidan fixed him with a penetrating gaze. "Ah, Master Thomas. Ye must not fear. God uses the willing, not the perfect. He will stand wi' ye, of that I am certain. He will show ye the way. St. Augustine said, 'God provides the wind; man must raise the sail.' Raise your sail, Thomas. Go where God leads ye, trusting that He will provide the answers ye seek."

Thomas' protests died at the conviction in Aidan's voice, and he could only nod in response. "There's one more thing. Wulfram had a slave boy I took with me when I left. He's at Master Torht's holding. But he can't stay there. Could you take him in, if he is willing?"

Aidan smiled. "Of course, me son. Ha' no fear." His face grew solemn. "Kneel, and I will give ye me blessing, so I will, afore ye go."

Thomas knelt before the bishop, closing his eyes as the words of the blessing prayer washed over him. When he arose, a fragile peace surrounded him.

"Do not forget your prayers, me son. Evil bends its will against ye. Be alert." Aidan squeezed his shoulder and left without a further word.

Thomas stayed for a moment longer, not wanting to be seen leaving with him, and then headed back to the barn. The chanting prayers of the monks faded behind him as he retrieved Missy and headed back towards the mainland.

After he had crossed the wet sands, he turned back to look at the blurry outline of the island against the rain-lashed sky. Even as he watched, the waves swallowed the last of the path and Lindisfarne was once again an island. For a moment, longing seized him to be there, cut off from all the troubles that plagued him.

He couldn't hear them anymore, but he knew the monks continued their prayers, their voices rising to God as they did throughout each day, their schedule as regular and timeless as the tide. Sudden conviction seized him once again of the need to protect the monastery. Aidan's voice floated through his mind. *God uses the willing, not the perfect.* Perfect, he was not. But willing...

Resolution filled him as he turned back and urged Missy towards Torht's holding, the gulls circling in their endless dance above him.

CHAPTER 15

BE A FEY

Thomas drew Missy to a halt at Torht's holding, noting with a pang that Nona's horse was missing from the group tied out in front of Torht's house. As he slid off the mare, Nectan and Domech exited the house, followed by Torht.

"We will leave right away. Our horses are ready," Nectan stated, gesturing at the saddled mounts.

Torht thrust a small package at Thomas. "Some bread and cheese for you for your journey, young master."

"Thank you," he said, accepting the package. He opened his mouth to ask if he could check in on Odda, but the gimlet gleam in Nectan's eye told him the king would deny the request, and he bit back the words.

But Torht must have discerned his question. "The boy still sleeps," the Horsemaster said. "Lady Nona has left some herbs for Hilda to brew if he becomes distressed." He gripped Thomas' shoulder, empathy in his eyes. "Never fear. We will care for him."

Thomas nodded in reply, grateful again for Torht's kindness. He turned to Nectan, impatient to share what he and Aidan had discussed. "Solstice. Wulfram will try something that night, when his powers are strongest. I realized it when Aidan told me that Oswy will hold the meeting of his council on Midsummer's Eve a few days later. Whatever Wulfram does at Solstice will take Oswy from Bernicia's throne at that meeting."

Nectan's eyes widened slightly, then narrowed as he thought it through. "Aye," he said, frowning. "Ye could be right."

"I am right," Thomas said, insistent. "I feel it."

The king frowned. "We will go to my holding, near Dún Duirn. The journey will be a week, at least. I ha' already sent messages ahead to prepare for a Gatherin' to be held after we arrive." He glanced at Domech. "What do ye think, nephew? Seems best to me that instead of staying at the *crannog* after the Gatherin' we should journey southward instead, to meet with the Seelies of Dál Riata and

Deira, and be back here in time for Solstice." He glanced at Thomas. "'Twill allow us to show them that ye are free of the boy, and ye can tell them of Wulfram and the Undyin'."

Domech's eyes flashed. "Having the Solstice Gatherin' here will only help Strang, and ye know it. More of his kin live near here than in our land."

Nectan's mouth twisted. "Oh, aye. And how better to show the wee shite that I dinna fear his Charge?"

Domech glowered at him, but kept silent.

Nectan turned to Torht. "Horsemaster, send word to the Seelies that I will hold the Solstice Gathering near Bebbanburg. More will come if I give them enough notice so they have time to travel. We will need as many as possible to deal with Wulfram and his Unseelies. And to stop Strang's ambitions."

Torht inclined his head in a bow. "Yes, my lord king. It will be done."

Thomas wasn't looking forward to being displayed as "Exhibit A" at the meetings and Gatherings Nectan had planned, but he could hardly refuse. Nectan was right. The more Seelies they had behind them, the better.

Nectan and Domech mounted their horses, and without further words, they set off.

Distracted by musing over the journey that Nectan had described, as well as the political implications in the Seelie Court of having the Solstice Gathering near Bebbanburg, the sudden wrench in Thomas' heart at leaving Odda behind took him by surprise. He clenched his hands on the reins, concentrating on not giving in to the impulse to turn Missy's head and go back. *Christ, have mercy.* If he turned back, he suspected he would give in to the next impulse that he was sure would follow: to Bind Odda again to relieve the aching emptiness the boy had left behind. A cold sweat broke out on his brow. Nectan was right to insist on them leaving right away. The thought was a bitter bone to chew on.

A cold rain drizzled down, mirroring his gloomy mood. He hunched down in the saddle, miserable, feeling as lost and alone as he did when he had first Crossed to this time.

We wilna waste our journey.

Nectan's voice in his mind almost caused him to drop the reins. He looked over at the king, anger replacing the shock. "Stop that," he growled. "I'm not in the mood."

Nectan's eyes narrowed, but his tone was mild when he answered. "I suppose ye'll say the same to Wulfram when he tries to Bind ye? Ye dinna think he will wait until ye are in the mood to handle him, do ye?"

Thomas clamped his jaw shut. He shifted his shoulders under his cloak, uncomfortable.

"So then," Nectan continued. "As I said, we wilna waste this journey. I ha' neglected your training, and ye ha' suffered for it. We canna risk your ignorance any longer. Ye must learn the ways of the Speakers: to sense them afore they Speak, to keep them out if ye dinna wish to hear them. 'Twill only come by practice. Domech and I, we will Speak to ye as we ride. Ye will learn to keep us out."

"Right," he muttered. "How?"

Be a Fey, wildin'. If ye can. Domech's voice in his head held the same smug superiority as his smile, and Thomas forced back his angry response. He wouldn't give the other Fey that satisfaction.

His already foul mood deepened at the thought of having the king and Domech stomp around in his mind whenever they wanted. His teeth ground together. *Not if I can help it.*

But despite his resolve, the first few times they tried it, he failed utterly to stop them, their sudden voices in his mind proof of his inadequacy. It was the sharp glance Nectan gave him after his second successful attempt that snapped Thomas out of his despair.

It reminded him of the way Matthew had looked when his father had encouraged him to embrace his Fey nature. *Tell me what you see,* he had said, sweeping his hand across the vista that fell away from where they stood at the top of a high hill. And with the memory came the solution to his present dilemma. In order to stop the other two from Speaking into his mind at will, Thomas had to sense their small gathering of power needed to do it. And in order to do that, he had to tune into his Fey nature—something he had been trying very hard not to do since he had Bound Odda, out of fear of what he might inadvertently do with that power. But Nectan was right. As was Domech. He had to learn this or risk being overwhelmed by Wulfram.

With a silent prayer, he let out a breath and opened the door to his Fey power, allowing a trickle to escape. Allowing himself to be Fey. His fingers loosened on the reins at the same time as muscles that he had unconsciously been clenching relaxed. As before, the rush of awareness that flooded over him was intoxicating, and he straightened up in the saddle, taking a deep breath of the salt-scented air.

As he did so, a small sensation like a feather brushing against his mind touched him a split second before he heard Nectan's voice. *Now ye can truly begin.*

He looked over at Nectan. The surging confidence that followed his discovery caused him to Speak back to the king. *Give it your best shot, my lord.* Now that he knew what to look for, he was sure he could stop them.

He shouldn't have been so confident. He barely sensed the subtle touch of Nectan's mind before the king replied. *Oh aye, wildin'. We will.*

Thomas gritted his teeth together, his face flushing. The screech of Nectan's falcon overhead gave expression to the king's triumph. The sound filled him with resolve, pushing aside his anger. *The way of the Fey comes by doing.*

CHAPTER 16

A Wilding, UnTamed

The Fey proverb was cold comfort as the miles passed and Nectan and Domech continued their training. The odd sensation of their minds brushing against his in the split second before they Spoke became easier to discern. But blocking them was another matter entirely. That was harder, especially since Domech always left behind a mocking sense of superiority when Thomas failed, and the words he Spoke were always insults.

The constant vigilance wore on him. Already on edge after losing Odda, his nerves stretched to the breaking point. Missy grew tense, sensitive to his mood. She shied and fidgeted, causing him to either haul on the reins or soothe her as they rode.

In contrast to his worsening mood, the rain clouds fled before a quickening wind, revealing the sun in their wake. True spring had come at last, and everywhere the land showed fresh growth. The path they rode entered a shadowy forest, and Thomas had a moment's qualm as memories of the haunted *wold* crowded in. But his fears soon dissipated under the spring spell of trilling bird song that filled the woods and the carpets of bluebells that bloomed in the shady forest glades.

It was glorious, truth be told. He took a deep breath, the tension that had gripped him easing under the beauty that surrounded him. As the path narrowed through a stand of oak, Nectan took the lead, followed by Thomas and then Domech. Suddenly, Nectan's horse shied, bumping into Missy, who squealed and reared. Thomas glimpsed a snake flashing into the undergrowth as he grabbed at the reins. Domech's horse, too, started.

Missy's hooves hit the ground and, quick as lightning, she bucked. Thomas went flying and hit the ground with a jolt, the breath knocked out of him. He lay stunned, trying to get his lungs working again, aware of Nectan's muffled curse.

The subtle shift of power touched him, but he couldn't mount any defence as Domech's mocking voice slid into his head. *Nice landing, wildin'.*

Frustration boiled over, flashing into anger as his breath returned in a rush. He leapt to his feet, a flood of power rushing to life within him in a full-blown tsunami.

Get out! The command, and his power, roared through him as he shoved at Domech's presence in his mind. But as before, when he had cut Wulfram's Bond with Odda, his mental shove had physical results as well. Domech flew off his horse, landing hard against a tree and crumpling at its base.

Satisfaction at the sight swept through him for a split second until Nectan crashed into him, knocking him to the ground again.

"ENOUGH!" The king hauled Thomas to his knees, grabbing his hair and wrenching his head back. His eyes glowed amber, lit with the Fey power that coursed through him. "Are ye mad?"

Domech stirred, groaning as he picked himself up from the ground.

Nectan glanced over his shoulder. "Nephew, are ye well?"

Domech mumbled something that Thomas didn't catch, but it seemed to satisfy Nectan. When the king turned back to Thomas, the fire in his eyes was banked. Good thing, too, for surely his death would have followed on the heels of Domech's if Thomas had mortally injured the other Fey.

"Wee fools, the both of ye," Nectan snarled. "Domech shoudna have goaded ye, but ye ha'—" He sputtered to a stop and heaved a breath. He let go of Thomas' hair and stood over him. "I mean to Teach ye, so I ask ye: what ha' ye learned?"

That Domech's an ass, Thomas wanted to respond, but he doubted Nectan would appreciate that reply.

Domech joined his uncle, his arm holding his middle and his face white, anger burning in his eyes.

The same satisfaction flashed through him that had filled him at the sight of the other Fey's crumpled form. His cheeks flushed as shame came on its heels.

"Speak. What ha' ye learned?" Nectan crossed his arms, glowering down at him.

Cornered, Thomas had no choice but to speak the truth. "I can't trust myself," he snapped. "Is that what you want to hear? My power is too strong for me. I can't control it." Despair flooded over him, washing away the anger.

What was the point of all this? He could never best Wulfram.

"He should die," Domech snarled as he rounded on Nectan. Fey power rippled around the two of them, causing a painful sensation on Thomas' nerves. "Ye heard it from his lips. A wildin', unTamed. Ye know the Rule, O king. He is an anvil around your neck. I canna understand—"

"Hold!" Nectan snapped, his eyes flashing. "Thomas pledged to me, as ye did. I ha' Known him twice now, and I tell ye, there is nothing to fear." He held

Domech's gaze for a moment, and then his eyes softened. "Trust me, lad. I ha' told ye, this one is no what he seems. His fate is bound to that of the other Unseelie Traveller. They dance together in our time, forging the destiny of our time and theirs. I ha' seen it in the wind, I tell ye! The wildin' must be there to stand against the other when he comes against Oswy and the monks. If not, destruction will follow for the Fey and humans alike. We must lend our aid. I ha' told ye this before. Nothing ha' changed."

Domech flushed, and his jaw tightened, but after a moment he bowed his head. "I stand wi' ye, ye know I do. And I will protect ye from him, when the time comes, for I am certain it will." He shot a vicious look at Thomas.

Nectan smiled and squeezed his shoulder. "Are ye able to ride, then?"

"A rib is broken, my king. But if I bind it, I will be fine."

Nectan turned to Thomas. "Get up."

Thomas rose, ignoring Domech's glower.

"Every Fey feels as ye do, at the Quickening when we first come into our power. None master the use of it without some mistakes along the way. 'Tis normal. Ye will learn, wildin', but ye will only learn by doing. Ye canna shut yourself off from it. Ye are Fey. Ye must learn to master it, or it will be your master. Now, do as I say. Use your Gift and Speak to Domech."

Domech drew back. "My lord king—!"

Thomas spoke at the same time. "I can't! Don't—" He didn't get any further. Nectan reached out as quickly as the snake that had flashed past earlier and grabbed Thomas' throat. Thomas scrabbled at the king's arm, but Nectan's muscles were like iron.

"Do as I say! I command ye, as your king!" He let go, shoving Thomas away.

"My lord king," he rasped. "I'm not ready. I just about—" He snapped his mouth shut on what he was going to say. But the word hung between them. *Killed.*

Nectan's eyes shone like burnished copper. "Name your fear, wildin'."

"It's too dangerous," he ground out between his teeth. "The last time I tried to use it like that, I Bound Odda to me." He raked his hair back from his face, his hand shaking. "And just now, you saw what happened. I could have killed him. I can't risk it."

Nectan snorted, amusement filling his face. "Ach! Ye can barely stand." He put his hands on his hips. "Overusin' the power has weakened ye. Ye dinna have enough left to kill a fly, never mind enthrall my Speaker." The smiled faded. "I will no allow ye to harm him, never fear. Speak to him, now. There is no better time."

Thomas glanced at Domech, who regarded him with mingled scorn and fear.

"Now, Traveller." Nectan's words held no more patience.

Thomas heaved a breath. "Fine," he muttered and closed his eyes, trying to ignore the fear that fluttered in his gut. He had lost hold of his power when Nectan tackled him, and he had to find it again. He pictured his hand reaching for the doorknob and opened the door, bracing for the bright torrent to fill him.

But it wasn't a flood of power, just a warm glow that prickled over his skin like a shower. Nectan was right. He wasn't likely to hurt anyone with it.

He hesitated. Before when he had Spoken to another, he was in the grip of a powerful emotion and it came without thought. He didn't know how to do it on purpose.

He concentrated. Nectan and Domech's power danced along his nerves. After a moment, he distinguished between the two.

There. A connection bloomed between him and Domech. The sensation was odd, almost like having Odda in his mind. An echo of the pain from Domech's cracked ribs, and the Speaker's simmering anger, brushed through him. *I'm sorry.* As soon as he Spoke the words, he broke the connection and opened his eyes.

Domech's gaze met his. Anger still sparked in his eyes, but he nodded, once.

"Now ye see, wildin'," Nectan said. "Ye are Fey. Ye canna hide amongst the monks. Our blood runs in ye. Ye must accept who ye are, Fey and human alike."

The high-pitched trilling of a goldcrest broke the silence that fell, and Thomas spotted a flash of yellow as it flitted about a spruce that stood opposite the oaks. Thomas envied its unconscious acceptance of who it was.

It wasn't quite so easy for him. But Nectan waited for a reply, so he nodded.

The king regarded him for a moment longer and then spoke. "It is through your doing that Domech was hurt. Ye will help him bind up his ribs, and then we must be away. We are expected in Hawkham tonight."

He supposed it was the least he could do. He tore his extra tunic to use as the binding and wrapped it around Domech's middle. The Speaker bore his ministrations with ill-natured patience. Once Thomas finished, Domech stood up and pulled his own tunic back over his head, wincing at the movement. He glanced over at Nectan, who mounted his horse some paces away, and then back at Thomas.

Thomas felt the faint pressure in his mind but steeled himself and allowed Domech's words to touch him.

Ye live only at our king's forbearance.

Domech held his gaze for a moment and then turned to join Nectan.

Thomas' lips twisted as he swallowed back the despair that threatened to overwhelm him. He mounted Missy and fell into line behind Nectan on the narrow path through the trees, feeling Domech's hostile glare at his back all the way.

CHAPTER 17

A GATHERING IS FOR THE FEY

It took a couple of days to reach the small settlement at Hawkham, where a few families lived by a stream that tumbled along the valley, winding its way through high rounded hills. They arrived before sundown, in time for the evening meal.

The Fey who took them in was a distant relation of Nectan's, a Pict living among the Alt Clut British. Thomas was tired, and anxious about the coming Gathering, so when the meal was over he went to the stables where they would shelter for the night.

He woke with the Call to the Gathering ringing in his mind. Nectan and Domech were gone. The holding was quiet and dark under the stars.

Another test, he supposed, to find his way to the Gathering by himself. But he wasn't worried. The Call would lead him. Going alone would give him the time he needed to prepare.

He fingered the bone whistle Torht had given him. Nectan had told him that Thomas must play for the Gathered Fey. Fey music revealed much about those who played it. He was both frightened of the opportunity and eager for it. The music would speak far better than he could, but what it might expose to the Fey could prove dangerous for him and Nectan alike.

He slipped into the shadows along the buildings and headed into the woods, following the stream that sparkled silver under the moonlight. The sounds of the night accompanied his journey; the hoot of an owl, the rustle of the branches, the small skittering of an animal in the undergrowth, the music of the water over the rocky stream bed.

A fog had risen. The night was full of misty wisps, shining grey in the light of the full moon. This mist prompted no fear, not like the dark vapours he encountered in the Otherworld. His Fey nature responded to its ethereal beauty, filling him with excitement.

But he took a deep breath, forcing it away for a moment, and contemplated the *lorica*. *God's might to uphold me, God's wisdom to guide me.* His task would require all of him, both his feeble human faith and his uncertain Fey Gifts.

He prayed they would be enough as he hurried towards the Gathered Fey, moving as silently through the night as the mist.

He lost track of time in his journey through the moon-bright woods, but after a time faint music floated through the trees, and he knew he was getting close to the grove where the Fey Gathered. Soon the aromas of wood smoke and roasting meat drew him towards a dark clump of trees. As he approached, Domech stepped out from among them, his form glowing in the night.

Thomas stopped, eyeing the Speaker.

"I am watchin' ye, wildin'." Domech's voice was a low growl.

Thomas bit back the retort that sprang to his lips and just nodded his response. He couldn't blame the Speaker for his hostility.

Domech held his gaze for a moment, then stepped aside, letting him pass.

An enormous bonfire threw off sparks that rose like fireflies into the night sky. Perhaps a dozen Fey milled around the grove. A small Gathering, as Nectan had predicted. Thomas spotted Brorda, speaking to Nectan. His spirits lifted, dispelling the threat of Domech's warning. He would have at least one friend to speak for him.

Brorda's wife, the Healer Emma, stood nearby, her hand resting on Brorda's forearm. With a jolt, Thomas realized she was pregnant. Her rounded belly was evident under her colourful embroidered dress.

Glad surprise filled him. A baby born to Fey parents was a rare occasion.

A knot of Fey danced to the music, small children leaping and running back and forth among them. The adults swirled in an intricate pattern, and one of them, a slender woman with fiery red hair, glanced over at him. Thomas saw a flash of blue eyes and a mischievous grin before the other dancing Fey blocked his view.

Heat rose to his cheeks at the invitation in those eyes, and he looked away. Off to the side of the dancing Fey, more gathered around someone whose hands gesticulated as he spoke. Thomas stiffened in surprise. It was Strang, the sour-faced Fey who had challenged Nectan for his throne.

He looked back at Nectan and saw the tension in the king by the set of his shoulders, his clenched fist at his thigh. Strang's presence must be unexpected. It could only mean trouble.

Nectan and Brorda spoke to a Fey whom Thomas didn't recognize—a man with a full reddish beard and dark hair that sparked ruddy highlights in the firelight. It was hard to see more details as they were back-lit by the flames. But there was no time to register more than a fleeting impression before Nectan looked over and met his eyes.

Wildin'.

He forced himself to Speak back to the king as he nodded at him through the crowd of celebrating Fey. *My lord king.*

A few heads turned, Fey-sense alerting the Gathered Fey to his presence. The music stopped. Whispers and murmurs flitted through the crowd as he stood at the edge of the grove under the intense regard of the Gathered Fey.

Wariness filled most faces, but outright hostility radiated from the group around Strang. The news of his latest adventures had travelled far. The only ones who looked even half-friendly were Brorda, who smiled at him and raised a hand in greeting, and the red-headed woman, whose slow smile held anticipation.

Nervousness fluttered in his gut. Strang's presence meant that he would have to be extra careful. He would not help Nectan if he made a foolish mistake.

Nectan's voice rang out in the sudden quiet. "Thomas mac Cadán, wildin, Traveller, and Speaker! You are welcome here, to this Gatherin' of the Seelie Fey." He beckoned towards Thomas to join him.

Thomas forced his feet to move and made his way through the others to where Nectan and Brorda stood. A young boy hurried over and thrust a silver mug containing liquid into his hand and scampered off again.

Thomas raised it to his lips and took a sip. It was mead, sweet, thick and potent. He would have to drink sparingly.

Nectan faced the Seelies again. "Our Gatherin' is complete. Dance and be merry!" He glanced at the Fey holding the instruments, and they began a lively tune.

Brorda turned to him. "We are long parted indeed. 'Tis good to see you, Thomas!" He clapped him on the back, grinning.

"But never far apart," Thomas replied, grinning back. "I'm glad to see you here, too." He wanted to ask Brorda about Strang, but the other Fey who stood with Nectan was listening, so he turned to Emma. "Congratulations. When will the baby be born?"

Emma's smile was strained, but before she could speak Brorda answered, bashful joy lighting his face. "Come harvest time, or so she says. But until Frigga carries my wife through childbirth and brings the babe to us, I will not celebrate." He let out a breath. "But I am not too worried. The humans have more children, but they often lose the babe or the mother to death during the birth. We Fey have fewer children, but 'tis rare for our women or babes to have difficulty." He smiled. "Even so, I would value your prayers to the White Christ on their behalf."

"Of course."

Emma's nostrils flared, and she spoke to her husband. "I will go sit down, husband. I grow weary of standing."

"Of course. I will come with you." Brorda threw an apologetic look at Thomas and escorted her around the edge of the dancing Fey.

Thomas watched them go, wondering at the anger that flashed in Emma's eyes when she had looked at him.

Nectan gestured at the other Fey. "This be Conaire mac Alpin, of Dál Riata, Wolfclan and Ward. The betrothed of the Lady Nona. 'Twas fortunate indeed that his journey to Bebbanburg enabled him to attend our Gathering. He will take your news to the Fey of Dál Riata."

Shock pierced him, robbing him of words. *Betrothed.*

The man's gaze travelled over him, his eyes narrowing as their gazes met again. "We are long parted." An Irish accent coloured his words.

Thomas scrambled to collect himself. "But never far apart," he managed, taking in other details as the shock faded.

Nona's future husband looked to be a couple of years older than him. His grey eyes regarded Thomas with polite but cool reserve. "Our king tells me ye ha' been with my betrothed at Bebbanburg over these past months, so ye have. How does she fare?"

The memory of the kiss he had shared with Nona flashed through his mind. "She is well," he managed, helpless to stop the blush he felt staining his cheeks. He hoped it was dark enough to hide it. He took a sip of the mead to cover his discomfort.

Nectan spoke before Conaire could continue. "Ye must forgive us, my lord. I must speak to Thomas alone for a moment. I'm sure he will be happy to tell ye of the Lady Nona later."

Conaire inclined his head to the king. "Of course, my lord king," he said. He glanced at Thomas again. "I will welcome it, so I will."

The words were polite, but they felt like a threat. Unease filled him as the other Fey walked away, joining a group of the Fey who were watching the others dance.

"Lady Nona will marry him," Nectan said. "'Tis an excellent match, both for the Fey and the humans."

Thomas didn't need to look into the king's thoughts to know the rest: *And ye are not.*

It stung his pride, but it was only what he had been telling himself ever since he had met Nona. It was impossible to be with her. But he didn't have to like it. "I know that."

Nectan inclined his head in acknowledgement. His gaze roved over the Gathered Fey for a moment and then he looked back at Thomas. "Ye will play for them soon."

Fear and anticipation warred within him at the thought of abandoning himself to the music under the regard of the Gathered Fey. "And Strang? Why is he here?"

Nectan's mouth set in a line. "To cause trouble, no doubt. Pay him no mind. Let the music take ye, that is all."

He forced his tangled emotions aside as Nectan fixed him with a hard look and left him to join the dancing Fey.

But he was not alone for long. The red-haired woman danced over to him, her eyes shining in the moonlight, tossing her copper hair over her shoulders. She stopped in front of him and smiled, showing even white teeth, her slanted cat's eyes a dark blue in the night. "I have heard much about ye, Thomas the wildin' Traveller." She cocked her head, examining him. "Ye not be as fearsome as they say."

She was beautiful, the welcome in her manner an antidote to the hostility he sensed from most of the Fey. And a welcome distraction from his task. He dipped his head. "My lady," he said.

She laughed, a throaty sound. "Nay, not tonight. A Gatherin' is for the Fey, without the boundaries that the humans place between us. I am Languoreth, Catclan, and you, Thomas the Traveller. 'Tis more than enough, tonight."

A knot within him eased at her words, and he couldn't help his answering smile. There was a freedom being among the Fey, no matter their suspicion of him. They were used to living in a world where they had to hide. At the Gathering, they could be themselves. So could he.

The music changed, mirroring his mood. The beat sped up and became more complicated. Thomas's fingers beat against his thigh in counterpoint as a sudden urge to dance seized him.

Languoreth laughed. "Aye, 'tis wonderful, no? They know the way of the music well!" She turned to listen, her face bright with laughter, her feet moving as she swayed to the beat.

The musicians played with blistering speed, egging each other on to follow the rhythm. A woman played the lyre, accompanied by a man on a flute. By the looks they gave each other, it was obvious they shared a bond deeper than just the music.

The woman played with great skill and speed, but with a certain careful reserve. But the man played with recklessness, the notes a fiery accompaniment to his wife's melody.

The song invited dance and celebration, and something more. Grief hid behind the riotous notes, a shadow that coloured the song, no matter the upbeat melody.

"They lost their babe after the last Gathering," Languoreth said, seeing his frown. "A fever took him, no matter that she is a Healer. She about died herself, trying to save him."

The eager fire in his blood that the music sparked cooled at Languoreth's words. The dancing Fey seemed grotesque now. But the music changed again. A new melody bloomed, one without the underlying sadness. An older man joined the couple and picked up a drum, tapping out the riotous beat in complicated rhythms.

Languoreth laughed and grabbed his arm. "Come, let us dance! This is how we honour them and their babe!"

A sudden need to honour his own losses swept through him, and he abandoned himself to the music, following Languoreth and joining with her in the dance under the light of the brilliant moon.

CHAPTER 18

I Am Fey

"Thomas," Languoreth said, her voice a breathy whisper in his ear. "Come away with me. Now..."

The words served as a dash of cold water, jolting Thomas back to himself. His arms were around the Fey woman, both of them swaying to a slow, sensual song. His heart skipped a beat, tripping out of the heavy, languid beats that pounded in time to the music.

It was hard to tell how much time had passed. He shook his head to clear it and glanced up at the moon. It looked like it had been at least an hour since he stepped into the clearing.

"Ah," Languoreth said, disappointment in her voice. "I shouldna have spoken, I see."

Thomas released her with reluctance. His whole body ached for her, but now that reason had returned, he could not allow himself to touch her. "I'm sorry," he managed, his face flushing. He felt like a fool. "I can't."

"Can't?" One eyebrow arched. "Or won't?" She leaned against him again, smiling up at him. "We are Fey. We take our pleasures seriously, especially at a Gatherin'." She twined her arms around his neck and pulled his head down.

Fire shot through him as their lips met, burning his resolve to ashes. A groan escaped him as he cupped her head, his fingers slipping through her hair.

For a moment he was back in Nona's arms, and it was her lips he kissed. Then he came back to himself and tore himself away before he lost control. *Idiot.* He clasped Languoreth's arms and moved her away from him. "Stop. I can't. I told you."

Anger sparked in her eyes. "I desire ye, and ye desire me. 'Tis enough. There is none to stop us. Your monkish beliefs hold no weight here."

He let his hands drop. "Maybe not for you. But they do for me." He let out a breath, raking his hand through his hair to push it back off his face. "Look. I'm a

Traveller. I'll be gone soon. There is no future for me here. For us. You may not care that you might have a baby, but I do. I won't leave a child without a father."

She tossed her head, the anger in her face deepening. But before she could speak, Brorda joined them.

He glanced at Languoreth, a warning look, and turned to Thomas. "I would have words with you."

Languoreth's lips curled in scorn. "His words are nae worth much, Ward." She swept a scorching gaze over Thomas, then turned on her heel and walked away.

Brorda looked over at Thomas. "She will only bring you trouble. Best to stay away."

"No kidding," he muttered. With an effort, he set aside the lingering sensation of Languoreth in his arms, which reminded him painfully of Nona. Regret and desire throbbed through him with every beat of the music. He took a deep breath, willing his addled brain to focus. "Did you want something, or were you just playing the hero to rescue me?"

Brorda smiled. "Both. Our king sent me to tell you it is time."

As he spoke, the song ended and the couple who had been playing set down their instruments, joining the others.

Nectan took his place in the space the musicians had abandoned. "Thomas the Traveller has words for us. But first he will give us his song." He looked at Thomas and stepped aside, inviting him to come forward.

Thomas forced aside the lingering effects of his encounter with Languoreth and made his way to the front. Anxiety filled him now that the time had come. If he failed to convince the Gathered Fey, he had no hope of stopping Wulfram. It was as simple as that.

He had been intending to play the whistle, but when he saw the lyre abandoned against the log, an impulse seized him. He picked it up and cradled it against his chest as he plucked a few of the strings.

Grief seized him as he remembered Matthew doing the same at Achan's holding, and for a moment his hands stilled on the strings. *They must know who you are.*

But who was he? The son of an Unseelie, a Traveller from a distant time they could not fathom. A wilding, who knew little of their ways. All the reasons they might reject him tumbled through his mind.

Get a grip, Tommo. His father's voice intruded into his fearful imaginings, and he swallowed. He closed his eyes, composing himself. *God, help me*, he thought, and then he bent his head to the strings.

At first he tried out melody lines and rhythms, getting the feel of the instrument. Matthew had shown him the basics and his innate Gift helped with the rest. Soon his fingers were moving without thought as memories and feelings swept through him, tumbling together and flowing out through his fingers into the notes that shimmered through the glade and wove around the Gathered Fey.

They danced, their movements becoming part of the song, mirroring the terror of his arrival, the discovery of his Fey nature, finding his father and then losing him again.

He couldn't hide his love for Nona, and the bitter grief of his separation from her, nor the emptiness left behind by the severing of the Bond with Odda.

But bright notes thrummed through the song, too. Celyn's steady friendship. The monks' devotion and sacrifice; the early morning prayers as dawn touched the horizon, the discipline of work and worship that bound their days. Boundaries that hemmed in a path leading him back to God, despite his doubts.

A subtle discordance underneath the melody pointed to Wulfram, a minor tone that grew as the song progressed. It spoke of the devastation to come if Wulfram succeeded, of the dark shadow that inhabited Godric and that he feared would embrace them all.

The Fey spun through the grove on the wings of his song. And through their dance he sensed their fear of him, of his power and Gifts. Their uncertainty of him, a wilding and a Traveller both.

The song swept through him, his fingers burning on the strings, leaving nothing behind. *I am Fey,* it said. An acknowledgement came through the dance. *You are Fey.*

And then it was over. As the last note faded, he came back to himself, his fingers falling from the strings. He lifted his head, disoriented. The Gathered Fey slowed and stopped their dance, regarding him with solemn faces.

His earlier nervousness vanished. The wild release of music had left a settled determination in its wake. *Now or never.* He took a deep breath, his fingers grabbing for the cross at his chest. With a pang, he remembered its absence. He swallowed and closed his eyes, saying a quick prayer that what he said would be enough.

Chapter 19

Stand in the Shadows

A slight breeze caused sparks to fly up from the bonfire, flitting upward in a riotous whirling motion that echoed the dance of the Fey.

Thomas set down the lyre. *Here goes nothing.* "Wulfram, the Unseelie Traveller from my time who lives in Eoforwic, wishes to destroy the monastery at Lindisfarne. He seeks to do this by pushing Oswy off his throne. He believes that will change the fortunes of the Fey so that in my time, we will be triumphant over the humans."

His gaze roved over the Fey. The song had won him a chance to speak. He couldn't waste it, nor could he lie. They would see it in him. He heaved another breath. "He might be right. I don't know. But the Rule of the Fey forbids the Travellers to change the future. Those who crafted the Rule knew the danger of what Wulfram seeks to do." He shook his head. "It is true that wrong will happen in the name of the God that the monks serve. The death of many Fey might be laid at the doors of the Church that grows out of these monasteries. But there is much good that comes from them as well, more than I can tell. Lives saved, Fey and human alike. All of that could be swept away if Wulfram is successful."

He scanned the crowd. Most of the Fey regarded him with dispassionate interest. He had not yet won them over. His hands curled into fists. He had to make them see. "Think of your own past—the history of your clans, of the Fey. The tales you tell around the fire. In the past, things may have gone differently if other choices were made. Things can change for better or worse depending on a decision made, a battle won or lost. But if you could go back and force those events in a different direction, would you? Knowing that what actions you took then, however small, could make untold changes now?" Now he had their attention. He pressed home his point. "None of you are Travellers. You think you will never have to make that decision. But you're wrong. It's in front of you right now. If you do nothing to stop Wulfram, if you won't help me, you are making a choice.

He says his plan will bring the Fey to triumph. I say it will bring disaster. Are you willing to risk it?"

He fell silent, not knowing what else to say.

There was a moment's pause, and then an older Fey stepped forward. Thomas recognized him as the bowman who had stood guard at the first Gathering he had attended with Nona.

"What do you ask of us, then? The Traveller Wulfram has pledged to Raegenold. Many of them follow him. Is it war against the Unseelies that you require?" He spread his hands and looked around at the other Fey with his eyebrows raised to emphasize the ridiculousness of that request.

He forced himself to speak calmly. "No, of course not. I don't—"

"It may come to that, my people," Nectan interrupted, stepping forward to stand beside him.

A chill snaked up his spine at Nectan's words. Would war be the result from all this?

Nectan put up his hands to silence the murmuring that arose at his statement. "It may come to that," he repeated, "but I dinna think so. Raegenold has cast Wulfram out of his Court. I dinna think they will welcome him back. Even the Unseelies are not that foolish." He paused, his jaw hardening. "I tell ye something now that Thomas and the Ward Brorda both ha' seen. Wulfram ha' Bound the harper, Godric, using one o' the Undying."

A dog whined, accompanied by the sharp whinny of a horse and the sudden screech of a bird. The beasts of the Animal Clans were expressing the anger and fear of their Bonded Fey. Nectan spoke over the noise. "Many of ye have reported to me of Unseelie mischief in your towns and holdings. Cast out or no, Wulfram has gathered some of that Court around him, wooing them with tales of glory. Tales hard for Unseelies to resist. He has some of them with him, to be sure. But 'tis no just the usual Unseelie mischief that plagues us." He nodded at Brorda.

The Ward joined Thomas and Nectan. "I have heard talk in the inns and halls of Bernicia these last weeks. Whispers of Oswy, saying that he has used a sorcerer to gain the throne, and that he will use black magic to keep it." He paused. "There is also talk of Oswine, the follower of the White Christ whose life in is danger from the witchcraft of Oswy's sorcerer. Some say he seeks Penda, King of Mercia, to gain his aid in taking the throne from Oswy. You may think these are mere chatter over ale. But I heard Wulfram speak these very things to Oswine himself, when Thomas and I were taken in bonds to Raegenold's Gathering."

Silence fell at this announcement. Thomas saw shock on some faces, but not all. Some of these tales had reached them, too.

Strang's reedy voice broke the silence. "True. The humans are nervous. I have seen it myself. I have heard the stories." He made his way to the front and stood beside Brorda, spreading his arms wide as he looked out over the Fey. "But it is the wilding who has brought this amongst us. It seems to me we are more in danger from him than from Wulfram. If this wilding were removed, these tales would cease!"

Cold tension gripped Thomas at Strang's words. It was the same argument Oswy had used, more or less. An argument hard to refute.

Another voice spoke up from the crowd. A tall, dark-haired Fey, whose face held some similarities to Strang's. "My brother is right, my lord king. The Unseelies always dabble in foolishness. It is no surprise a Traveller could prod them into an ill-advised plot. But the unrest centres on this wilding—this wilding of Unseelie blood," he added. "Without him, this plot would collapse into dust. We should rid ourselves of him and dull this Wulfram's blade! Lord king, I do not understand your protection of this Traveller. A Traveller's business is their own, so the saying goes. Why are we now interfering in Traveller business? That is the way of danger."

A sudden loud snap of the fire put an emphasis on the Fey's words. Thomas searched the crowd to determine how many agreed with Strang and his brother.

Four Fey gathered around Strang's brother, all with hostile expressions on their faces. One of them was Languoreth. The musicians stood with Emma, Brorda's wife. The rest seemed not to have decided, their faces neutral as they looked to Nectan for a response. They would throw their support behind whomever was the victor.

Nectan looked at Strang. "I protect this Traveller just as I protect all who ha' pledged to me and to this Court." He spoke calmly. But tension was clear in the set of his shoulders, in his careful stance.

Strang dismissed Nectan's words with a sharp wave of his hand. "But this one is a wilding. Dangerous. Look at the trouble he has caused so far! You make much of his pledge to you. I say it is his actions that count—actions that mark him as Unseelie! He Bound a human—"

"Enough!" Nectan's voice was edged with steel and laced with power. He stepped closer to Strang, their gazes clashing. "My patience for this is at an end. Wulfram dragged this Fey in chains to Raegenold's Court. Does that sound like someone who wished to forsake his pledge to us? Dinna be foolish, Lord Strang!"

But Strang did not flinch. "It is you who are foolish! You cannot predict what he will do! It is too dangerous to trust him. You must see that!"

"Trust?" The word burst out of Thomas before he could stop it. Anger spurred him on, despite knowing he should keep silent. "Right. You all sit back and wait for me to make a mistake, and then you condemn me for it." His gaze raked over the Gathered Fey. "You think I'm the problem? You're playing right into Wulfram's hands. Getting rid of me is what he wants you to do. He plans to get rid of Oswy, destroy the monastery. I will do what I can to stop him, but this is bigger than just him and me. His plot affects all of you here and now, never mind the future."

"Our king is right." To his surprise, Conaire, Nona's betrothed, stepped forward. "We canna get distracted. Our problem is nae the wildin'; rather 'tis the Unseelie Traveller—this Wulfram—and his plot. If he didn't have the wildin', he'd use something else. Bernicia is vulnerable, so it is. Oswald's death has left a hole big enough for Penda of Mercia to march right through if Oswy and Oswine lose sight of him in their ambition to snatch the crown of High King." He scanned the crowd. "This will be good news to some of ye, who ha' no love for Bernicia. Perhaps ye would want this plot of the Unseelie Traveller to succeed. But we all know the Rule. We live hidden but not separate from the humans. We seek the good of the Fey over all. Sometimes our duty to the Fey interferes with our duty to our clans and kings. Ye ha' heard our king. This Wulfram calls the Undying to him. He ha' been thrown out of Raegenold's Court. He is a danger to us all, no matter what he plans. We must drive out the Unseelies who are sneaking around our holdings and villages like mangy curs sniffing out trouble. Stay alert, and to be ready for our king's Call, when he ha' need of us. This Wulfram must be stopped. He ha' brought the Undying amongst us. We cannot allow him to succeed."

He turned to Strang. "And in the summer, Lord Strang, at the High Gathering, if ye wish to pursue Nectan's throne, I will watch your bid with interest, so I will. Until then, our duty is to obey our king whom we have pledged to serve."

Strang's nostrils flared, a hound catching scent, but he nodded, and then bowed to Nectan. "I ask questions that others have not the courage to ask." It was an apology of sorts, however ill-mannered.

Nectan's eyes narrowed, but he nodded at Strang and turned back to the Fey as Strang re-joined his brother. "We Fey stand in the shadows for our own good. But we must be wary. This plague o' Travellers amongst us requires more than our usual vigilance. Stand firm in the Rule. Protect our people and the humans from the folly of Wulfram. Send word to me of anything you see that might be his doing. Keep watch for the harper, Godric. We dinna know how Wulfram will strike. But he will, and soon. Take these words to your clans and your holdings." He paused. "'Tis possible Wulfram will strike at Solstice, but how? We dinna see as yet. Keep watch. Report to me of what you hear." He raised a hand. "Go now in peace, with the brotherhood of the Fey as your bond."

Thomas let out a breath. Without the unexpected intervention of Nona's betrothed, things could have gone worse. He eyed the Lord Conaire, who spoke to Brorda and Emma. Why had the other Fey supported him? He pondered the question for a moment and then dismissed it. Whatever the reason, it had provided opposition to Strang's ambitions, and that was a good thing.

CHAPTER 20

I WOULD HAVE WORDS WITH YE

Murmured conversations broke out among some of the Fey as the Gathering dispersed. A few put out the fire and others readied their horses for leaving. Some melted away into the trees. Strang looked at Thomas with distaste as he departed with his brother, followed by others. Nona's betrothed left on foot, his wolfhound at his side.

Brorda drew Thomas away from the Fey who had collected around Nectan. "The Seelie Fey will stand with you," he said in a low voice, so no others could hear. "Do not take Strang's words to heart. They can see Wulfram goes too far."

"Can they? It seemed like a lot were listening to Strang."

"Listening, yes. But not action."

Thomas wanted to argue the point but kept silent. Brorda was only trying to make him feel better.

Emma joined them. "We must depart, my husband, to get home before daybreak."

Brorda nodded at her and then looked back at Thomas. "Send for me if you need me. I will come."

Emma's eyes flashed as she looked up at Brorda. "Your last offer of aid to this wilding nearly cost you your life. I would not be so eager to offer again. I wish this child to know his father."

Brorda's jaw hardened. "'Tis for the sake of our child that I must aid Thomas. Our king has spoken. Wulfram's plans will only bring destruction."

Emma pressed her lips together, but she nodded. She shot Thomas a hard look and left to speak with Nectan's wife as she waited for her husband.

Brorda turned back to Thomas. "I am sorry. Emma is like a boat in a storm these days. She does understand the danger, I promise you."

"Never mind. She's bound to be more anxious now. And she's right. Last time, you could have died because of me."

"And yet, here I am." Brorda squeezed his shoulder, his eyes growing sombre. "Be careful, Thomas."

Thomas watched as Brorda gathered Emma and they went to their horses tied at the edge of the grove. It had not escaped him that none of the other Fey had bothered to speak to him. He wasn't sure if that was good or bad.

He let out a breath, deciding to consider the night a success, despite its ups and down. *One day at a time, and to God be the glory.* Brother Shamus, the shepherd, often said that. He had done all he could do. Now all that remained was to pray for divine help to make his efforts successful.

Thomas slipped into the trees and began to make his way back to Nectan's *crannog* without waiting for the king. Nectan had lingered at the Gathering, speaking with his supporters, and it seemed best to not intrude.

The night was peaceful. The wind sighed in the trees, their branches dancing shadows against the stars that blazed in the sky. A memory seized him, of travelling through a night similar to this with his father, searching for the Hound.

He stopped. The peace of the night evaporated, bringing loneliness and despair in its place as grief grabbed him by the throat, choking him. *Alone. Again.* Longing for his father filled him. Matthew would have handled this differently. Better. He took a deep breath, fighting the bleak thoughts that battered him. *Christ within me, Christ beside me—*

He froze at the sudden sense of another Fey. For a wild moment he thought it was his father, impossibly returned once again, until the tall form of Nona's betrothed stepped out of the trees with his rangy wolfhound at his heels.

"I would have words with ye." The other's voice held a frosty edge. But in the dark it was hard to see his face, despite the glimmer of Fey power that wreathed him.

Thomas willed his tripping heart to calm. If the Wolfclan Fey had wanted to harm him, it would have been easy enough to send his dog to rip out his throat. But even so, he guessed the other Fey did not have his best interests in mind. "So talk, then."

"Ye left before we could speak of the Lady Nona."

Thomas gritted his teeth. He did not want to have this conversation. "I told you. She is well."

The other man moved, stepping out from the trees. He came to a halt a few paces away, his arms crossed over his chest. "Ye pine for a lost love. I heard it in your song. Tell me, wildin', is she the one that holds your heart?" He spoke in a low voice, his eyes a hard silver.

Thomas lifted his chin, forcing back the fear that seized him. There was no point in lying. Conaire would see it in his face. But he didn't know what to say, so he kept silent.

The dog growled once, low in its throat. Conaire's gaze narrowed. "I knew your father in Dál Riata. Fidelma, his wife, is one of my kin. Matthew had a way with the women, so he did. When I heard his son was in Bebbanburg, and a wildin' at that, I feared ye might hold the same charm." His mouth twisted as anger flashed in his eyes. "I see I had reason to fear."

"So why did you speak up for me?"

Conaire made an impatient gesture. "Nectan told me what happened in Eoforwic. 'Tis obvious the Unseelie Traveller must be stopped. I supported Nectan's bid for the throne and I support him still. The Seelies would suffer under Strang, so they would. I spoke tonight for Nectan's sake. Not for yours." His jaw hardened as his gaze narrowed. "I go to Bebbanburg to collect me betrothed, and I will find out what I can about this Wulfram in Dál Riata. But on Nectan's request. Whatever aid I give will be for him. Ye will keep away from me and mine."

His gaze swept over Thomas once more, and then he turned on his heel and stalked away, his dog following on his heels. They vanished back into the trees without a sound.

Thomas let out the breath he had been holding, uneasy speculations jostling through his mind. First of which was that he had made things worse for Nona. Yet again.

He stood for a moment, allowing the faint sense of the other Fey's presence to fade. After he knew he was alone, he followed, slipping through the dark woods, as silent as a shadow.

He berated himself as he walked, thinking of other things he could have said. He exhaled in a deep sigh. *Focus. Stop Wulfram. That's what I have to do.*

Everything else was a distraction.

CHAPTER 21

COLD AS A WINTER'S DAY

May 4, AD 643

Nona waited outside Bebbanburg's hall, squinting in the bright spring sunshine. She stood beside Oswy's queen, Eanflaed. Oswy was beside his wife, along with three of his trusted Dál Riatan warriors who had come out of exile with him when he came to take the Bernician throne. Celyn waited next to Nona, and behind her, Bronwyn's steady presence was a comfort.

Conaire mac Alpin would arrive within minutes. Her future husband was a high lord of the Dál Riatans and would be welcomed to Bebbanburg with honour. The king and his warriors, who all knew Conaire from Oswy's time of exile in Dál Riata, were eager to make his acquaintance once again.

And of course, as his betrothed, Nona must welcome him as well. But oh, how she wished she could have stayed in her bedchamber, nursing the headache that had settled behind her eyes ever since she woke. A headache that wouldn't subside no matter how much of the willow bark draught she drank. It mirrored her heartache, which was a wound for which she had no cure.

"He comes! Look!" Eanflaed pointed down the slope where sunlight flashed on a group of riders. They had come into view as they exited the village huddled at the base of the rocky outcrop upon which Oswy's fortress perched.

The queen looked at her, excitement in her eyes. "Finally, you will meet your betrothed! Thanks be to God that the day is here at last!"

Nona forced herself to smile, but her throat knotted, robbing her of speech. *Mary, Mother of God, give me your aid.* She willed her unruly stomach to settle and took a deep breath as the riders approached. When she had first arrived here in Bebbanburg last fall, she could hardly wait for this day to come. Now she dreaded it.

As the riders drew closer, it was clear which of the men was her betrothed. He wore finer clothing than his warriors, with golden thread edging his cloak, impressive leather boots, and a gold torc and armband. His hair shone with ruddy highlights, and his beard was a lighter red. His horse, a powerful black stallion with a coat that gleamed in the sun, sported a finely tooled leather saddle. It was his mount's silver fittings that flashed in the morning sun.

A wolfhound loped easily beside the beautifully fitted horse. Her betrothed was Wolfclan, so it was no surprise to see a hound accompanying him, even all the way from Dál Riata.

As the group halted before them, her gaze flew to the man who sat with easy self-assurance on the back of the stallion: Conaire mac Alpin of Dál Riata, her future husband. He had a strong face, with a firm chin and a confident manner. Handsome enough, she supposed, not allowing herself to compare him with Thomas.

His Fey power tingled against her in a powerful buzz, eclipsing all other details, and an errant thought broke through her determination. *But not as powerful as Thomas.* She banished the thought with an effort. Few Fey were as powerful as the wilding.

Then all thought fled as their eyes locked. She wasn't sure what she had been expecting, but the flash of anger she saw in his gaze startled her.

Oswy stepped forward and spoke. "Greetings, Conaire mac Alpin of Dál Riata, and be welcome."

Conaire's attention turned to the king. Nona sucked in a breath, disconcerted. Her thoughts raced. What caused that anger? Or had she imagined it?

The men dismounted, and Conaire and Oswy embraced in a back-slapping hug. The Dál Riatan stepped back, his face solemn. "We grieved at the news of your brother's death, so we did. His loss was a great blow."

Oswy's gaze sharpened on Conaire. "Aye, indeed. As was the death of Domnall Brecc. Tell me, my lord: how fares your king, Ferchar?"

Conaire's eyes tightened, but he smiled. "He fares well and brings his greetings, so he does." He gestured to one of his men, who dismounted and handed the king a sealed scroll.

They spoke the language of the *Scotti* between them. That the words fell easily from Oswy's lips was a reminder of his long exile in that kingdom after his father's death and of the ties between him and the warriors who had accompanied his brother from Dál Riata ten years ago. Oswald had come to Bernicia to wrest his ancestral throne back from the usurper, Nona's own erstwhile king, Cadwallon of Gwynedd.

Battles won and lost, alliances forged and broken. Thus went the ways of men and Fey alike, Nona mused. She prayed that the alliance forged with her marriage would prove to be a good one for all. That outcome would help to ease the death of her own dreams, taken from her when Thomas left Bebbanburg with Nectan.

Perhaps she could also help to ease the strain that had developed between Bernicia and Dál Riata at Domnall Brecc's death. Rumours flew that Ferchar was not supportive of Oswy's overlordship of Dál Riata, as Domnall Brecc had been.

"We will speak later, during the feast," Oswy continued. "But now I am sure you are eager to meet your betrothed." He swept his arm towards Nona, whose heart took a lurch as Conaire's gaze met hers again, and he came to stand in front of her.

His eyes were the same clear grey as those of Thomas. But these eyes were cold as a winter's day. With a sinking heart, she realized she had not imagined his earlier anger. It was still there, lurking in the depth of his gaze. "My lady," he said in a clipped voice, dipping his head.

She gathered herself and nodded back. "My lord."

His lips tightened as if he were holding back further words, and then he moved on to Celyn, whose impassive greeting was more than a match for the Dál Riatan's own.

She had warned Celyn that her betrothed was Fey, which might account for the tightening around Celyn's eyes as he spoke. But she suspected her cousin was as put off by Conaire's manner as she was.

She had not expected that Conaire would greet her like a long-lost friend. But she had hoped for more than the little regard he had shown her, as if she were a mere servant of Oswy's hall. The stiff formality and his anger confused her. Her heartbeat pounded in her ears, making her headache worse. How had she displeased him already?

Oswy interrupted her thoughts. "Come now, my lord, take your ease in my hall where we can speak in comfort. We have a feast prepared in your honour. It has been some time since we have had a visitor from Dál Riata, and I am eager to hear your news."

The king threw an arm around Conaire's shoulder, and together they walked towards the hall, the warriors following behind. The dog trotted beside them, its long tongue lolling.

Leaving me behind as if I am of no account. She tamped down her anger with effort.

Eanflaed turned to her, sympathy in her eyes. "Do not worry, my lady. Your betrothed is likely tired from the journey. The feast will help to ease the way between you." She took Nona's arm as they made their way towards the hall.

Celyn joined them, his face a dark glower as his eyes followed her betrothed's progress. Nona pasted a look of anticipation on her face to match Eanflaed's, even though Celyn's scowl matched her feelings more closely.

The music and loud celebration in Oswy's hall did not help Nona's headache, but she forced herself to do as her duty demanded, no matter her discomfort. She was thankful that the riotous atmosphere prevented much conversation between her betrothed and herself, although to be polite she forced herself to ask him questions of his journey.

But then he and Oswy's Dál Riatans warriors began a long conversation about how that kingdom fared under the new king, releasing Nona of her obligations. She ate in silence, grateful that she could soon make her escape.

Before she could excuse herself, Oswy turned to her betrothed with a grin. "So then, Lord Conaire, I'm sure you must be eager to depart, but you must stay a few days before you take the Lady Nona back to Dál Riata for the wedding. There is much for us to discuss."

"Of course, my lord king. In fact..." he hesitated. "If it pleases ye, I wish to get married before we go. I ha' waited so long, I do not want to wait any longer. If the Lady Nona will agree, I would say our vows once we can make everything ready. Tomorrow, if possible, but if not, the next day." He turned to her, his face impassive.

Married here? Before we leave? She had thought she would have more time to get to know him. Her tongue froze, and she could not answer.

Oswy snorted, a glint gleaming in his eyes as he clapped Conaire on his shoulder. "Ah, I see. The journey home is long, but with a wife to warm your furs, it will be much more pleasant."

The men laughed, and Conaire smiled, accepting the ribbing. "Aye, so it will."

Oswy turned to her, his eyebrows raised. "Well then, Lady Nona, what say you?"

Nona ignored the hollow feeling in the pit of her stomach and managed a smile. "Of course, my lord king."

Eanflaed smiled at her, excitement sparkling in her eyes. "Ah, do not worry, my lady," she said, giving her hand a squeeze. "The Lord Conaire is right. You have waited long enough."

"Yes," Nona replied, mustering up a smile through her pounding headache. She looked around the table. "If I am to be wed tomorrow, I had better make sure all is ready. Please excuse me."

They nodded at her, and Nona managed a dignified exit from the hall, keeping a pleasant expression on her face until the door shut behind her. It was full dark, and she welcomed the cool air on her heated cheeks and pounding head. She heard the door open behind her when she reached the bottom of the steps.

"Nona."

She turned at Celyn's voice and waited for him to join her.

"Are you well, cousin?"

"Of course." They walked towards the building where she had lived with the other unmarried women.

Celyn grunted, a sound she knew well enough. A sound that said that he did not believe her. "Your betrothed. He..." His voice lapsed into silence, and then he spoke again. "He will do well by you, I am sure."

"As am I," she managed, but the words tasted bitter on her tongue.

He put a hand on her arm, stopping her, and faced her. The moon shone bright enough for her to see the concern in his face. "If you are unhappy with this match, I can speak to your father."

Nona shook her head, gratitude filling her at his concern. She set aside her dismay. What would a few weeks matter? She would wed Conaire, whether tomorrow or after their journey to Dál Riata. "That is unnecessary. You know my father and our king of Gwynedd put this match together for the good of both Dál Riata and Gwynedd. I know my duty and I will not falter."

"As to that, cousin, I know full well that duty can have a cost."

She nodded and squeezed his arm. "But some costs we are happy to pay." She started walking again. "I am glad you will be here to attend our vows. My father sent word that he would meet us in Dál Riata to attend there. It will surprise him when I show up already wed."

Celyn grunted in acknowledgement and glanced at her. "As to that, I will see him as well. Oswy has asked that I go with you back to Dál Riata. He wishes me to bring his greetings to the new king, and to see how he fares."

"To see if Ferchar truly is as hostile to Bernicia as we have heard, you mean."

Celyn's lips twisted in a wry smile. "Aye, indeed."

She twined her arm around his, her heart lighter. "I am glad of it, cousin. It will be good to have you with us. I was not looking forward to saying goodbye to you."

He patted her hand. "Nor I you." The smile faded from his face. "Does the Lord Conaire know I see him as he is?"

As Fey. She shook her head. "No. Not unless we tell him." She let out a breath. "Best not to do that until we know how he might react. Leave it to me."

He nodded, looking uncomfortable, and then let out a breath. "It will be good to see your father. It has been many years since I saw him last."

An icy hand touched her at his words, although she smiled in response. But a sense of looming disaster haunted her. Not only would she have to tell Conaire that Celyn could see the Fey, but she would have to confess it to her father as well.

They had guarded their secret from Celyn all these years. Her father will be none too happy that because of Thomas' actions, the veil had torn from Celyn's eyes.

She would have to tell Celyn first, prepare him. She had warned him to be careful not to react when he saw the Fey, but she knew all too well that it didn't take long for any Fey to realize which of the humans were not only Sensitives but could truly see them.

Her stomach knotted. God have mercy, but somehow her wedding seemed like the least of the problems that faced her.

CHAPTER 22

DIFFERENT

Rocky peaks hemmed the valleys Thomas rode through with Nectan and Domech as they made their way to Nectan's home at Loch Earn. Many valleys held swift streams that sparkled like diamonds as they tumbled over their stony beds. The air was fresh and cool, pine-scented and full of birdsong. Even Missy's steps seemed lighter under the springtime sun. Thomas revelled in the landscape's beauty, enhanced as it was through his embrace of his Fey nature. The sweet thrum of power was a soothing balm to his tattered emotions, blunting the force of Domech's glares and the discomfort of days in the saddle. As much as Nectan's tutelage on being a Fey wore on him, the openness to his Fey nature had some benefits, too.

But the danger they faced always lurked. On the first day, as they rode along a path that snaked its way through a narrow glen, the harsh call from a large raven perching on the top of a pine tree shattered the peace. The reminder of Wulfram's watching eyes pierced Thomas with dread. Suddenly a streaking falcon dive-bombed the raven, its screeching cry keening on the wind. The raven squawked and lifted off from the tree, flapping away heavily as the other bird swooped and dove at it.

The sight chased away the dread that had assailed him. Thomas grinned and looked over at Nectan. "Yours?" He waved at the retreating falcon.

Nectan broke away from his narrow-eyed focus on the birds' flight and glanced at him, satisfaction filling his face. "Aye. Eru will harass Wulfram's birds. 'Twill be harder for him to keep them motivated to follow us." He shrugged. "A small thing, aye, but a distraction for him."

It was like fighting back. His lightened mood at the thought continued throughout the journey, displacing some of the gloom that had settled upon him after his departure from Bebbanburg.

As the days passed, the absence of Odda became more of a dull ache than a sharp pain. But even as the pain of that loss faded, the puzzle of what had happened between them when he broke the Bond persisted. The memory remained elusive, frustratingly out of reach.

Some nights the mist-dream plagued him, casting a pall on his journey, spring-bright though it was. The uneasy sense of wrong haunting him upon awakening after those dark dreams prompted him to return to the disciplines he had learned from the monks. He woke before sunrise each day so that he could recite the *Lauds* prayers at daybreak, seeking spiritual strength along with the invigorating rush of Fey power that came with the sun's appearance. Included with the prayers was his petition that God would provide the way to thwart Wulfram's plans. But, mindful of Aidan's example, he sought the graces of humility and trust, as well.

The journey from Hawkham to Nectan's home on Loch Earn would normally take three of four days, but they took their time, stopping along the way at holdings belonging to people Nectan knew, both Fey and human. Everywhere they went, they heard talk of Oswy— speculation about his ability as king, and rumours of witchcraft and evil deeds besetting Bebbanburg.

Thomas learned not to divulge to the humans they met that he was from Bebbanburg. At one of their first stops, a woman had eyed him with morbid curiosity after Nectan introduced him. *And ha' ye seen the black-haired son o' the Devil plaguing the king's fortress,* she had asked. They had dismissed the rumours, but after that, Nectan named him as distant kin from Eoforwic, who wished to apprentice under Nectan as a jewellery maker.

Nectan schooled Thomas on the various clans and kindred of his family, making his head ache as he struggled to remember where he supposedly fit in. But it was a necessary exercise, for conversations with the humans always began with a discussion of their various kindred groups and where each party belonged. A discussion they all seemed to relish. Thomas endured each one with his heart in his throat, expecting to be caught out.

Indeed, they came across a few who were more suspicious, less trusting of their answers. In those cases, Nectan or Domech would resort to a slight Charm, their Fey power and Speaking Gift smoothing over the questioner's doubts.

Once, Thomas tried a Charm of his own at Nectan's urging, but after that, he left it to the king and his Speaker. Even though he had been successful, he was wary of accidentally Binding another to his will.

The Fey they met posed a different problem. Strang's discontent with Nectan's rule was common knowledge. Although most dismissed the other Fey's accusations, others greeted their king with less than full respect. And one, a young man with flaming red hair, refused them shelter. *I'll no harbour that Unseelie wildin',* he had said, his bright green eyes blazing at Thomas. *I wonder why ye do, my lord king.*

As they headed into the lands of the Picts, the talk among the humans changed from Oswy's embrace of witchcraft to Oswy's summer ambitions. His recent demand for tribute from the Dál Riatans made them speculate if those ambitions would stretch into their Pictish lands, too. Strangers passing through the holdings and villages fuelled these rumours, whispering of dark days ahead. Wulfram's Unseelies doing his bidding, Thomas presumed.

After a week's worth of travel, they came over the crest of a hill that overlooked a large loch. Nectan reined his horse to a stop. He glanced over at Thomas, gesturing at the scene. "Loch Earn," he said.

The path wound down to a small *crannog*, similar to others they had encountered throughout the Dál Riatan and Pictish lands. A wooden pier led out to a small island surrounded by a palisade. Upon the island stood some circular huts and a larger building. Another palisade circled a bigger collection of buildings on the shore near the pier. Cleared fields around the settlement held the green of newly planted crops. In others, flocks of sheep and a few cattle grazed contentedly in the noonday sun.

According to Nectan, the ancestors of the Picts had built these *crannogs*. Thomas couldn't help but be impressed by the sight. The builders had essentially constructed a small island to live upon. It must have been a massive amount of work.

Nectan turned to him. "Dinna forget: to the humans I am not Nectan the king but Nectan the metalworker, and ye my apprentice. This will be another test. To be Fey amongst the humans."

Thomas lifted one shoulder in a shrug. "I've been that since I came here."

"Nay. Ye have been human more than Fey, denying who ye are. Now ye must be Fey, and learn what it means to hide. Not suppress." He looked him over. "In three days hence, ye will play your song at the Gathering. But tonight, in Drust's hall, ye will play for the humans as a bard."

"A bard?" Like the *scop*, the bards were the travelling musicians of the Celtic Britons, who brought entertainment and news from the far-flung reaches of the kingdoms. Thomas had hoped to hide in the shadows, not perform on a stage.

"Aye, but ye'll no play as a Fey, but as a human, else ye Charm them." Nectan turned away before Thomas could protest, urging his horse into motion down the hill. After a hard look of warning, Domech followed.

Thomas kneed Missy forward, anxiety churning at his gut as they grew nearer to the *crannog*. Embracing his Fey nature to keep vigilant against Nectan's and

Domech's Speaking had shifted his perception. Now he saw those who lived there as different from himself. As humans.

Nectan was right. Before, he had ignored his Fey nature. He could no longer do that if he wanted to stay safe from Wulfram's spies. But hiding his Fey nature while also welcoming it might prove a task too much for him.

His fingers gripped the reins tighter, and Missy tossed her head in protest. "I know, I know," he muttered. He took a deep breath, fighting the sense of doom that threatened to paralyze his efforts to do as Nectan had asked.

CHAPTER 23

I RELEASE YE

May 10, AD 643

T he moonlight sparkled on the ebony waters of the loch, a cool sea breeze causing Nectan to wrap his cloak tighter around himself. The settlement was quiet, the *crannog* a black shape against the stars.

Despite the peaceful night, unease touched Nectan like a bitter bite on the breeze. Tomorrow night he would present the wilding to the Gathered Fey.

Thomas' acceptance of his Fey nature had grown, that much was clear. It showed in the ease with which he called upon the power, but also in the subtle shift in how he moved—more in the easy way of the Fey than in the graceless awkwardness of the humans.

The bright, sharp force of his power made the others uneasy, especially because it was in a wilding Traveller. And they all knew of the Binding. Strang had made sure of that.

Nectan's lips flattened into a thin line. When he spoke of Strang to others, he dismissed him as a mere distraction, but he knew full well the wee upstart was much more than that.

Light footsteps distracted him from his gloomy thoughts. He smiled as Eara's glimmering form drew close. He stretched out his hand to her and she took it, leaning close to him as he enfolded her in his cloak.

For a moment, they stood in silence. Eara sighed and stepped away, her gaze roving over him. "Ah, husband. Ye shine like Lugh himself, so ye do. Would that the Seelies would see ye as I do."

He barked a short laugh. "Nay, my heart, ye would scratch out the eyes of any Fey woman who looked at me as ye do."

She smiled. "Ach, away wi' ye, then." She waved a hand, her smile fading. "I only meant I wish they could see the worth o' ye, for I fear many ha' forgotten it."

He studied her as she stood with her arms crossed, looking out over the loch. The muscles of her jaw tightened, and she let out a breath. He knew the signs. She bore a heavy message and struggled to find the words to say it.

His unease deepened, but he kept his voice light as he spoke. "Tell me what troubles ye before ye lose the courage to say it, or me to hear it."

She darted him a sharp look.. "'Tis no your courage I fear lacking. 'Tis your will to do what is necessary."

"And what might that be, then?"

She studied his face for a moment, and then spoke. "While ye were away, many came to me to speak in my ear, hoping I will speak in yours." She made an impatient gesture. "As they do all the time. But this is different. Not requests of small or large favours, nor the whispers of gossip. They all spoke o' the wildin' Traveller whom ye have welcomed into the Court. The wildin' Traveller who is Raegenold's tool, or worse, the Undying's."

Nectan drew back. "Raegenold's—!" He gathered himself. "Words from Strang, carried on the wind." He waved a hand. "When they see Thomas at the Gathering, hear his song, they will know the truth o' it."

"Will they?" Her soft words pierced him. "Ye dinna truly see him, husband. Ye had the Knowing of him, and ye forget we ha' not. I trust your words when ye tell me he wilna cause us harm, but even I forget that when I see the shine o' him. Do ye no remember his first Gatherin'?"

It wasn't the salty breeze that caused the sudden chill that washed over Nectan. Eara's words brought a flash of memory of his first glimpse of Thomas at the Gathering, the wilding Traveller whose power rivalled any of the strongest of them. The fear made his voice sharp. "Aye, and he pledged to us, no to the Unseelies. Ha' they no forgotten it?"

"Oh, they dinna forget it, never fear. 'Tis all they speak of, that ye ha' welcomed a wildin' Traveller into our Court, who ha' Bound a human, who ha' brought the Wild Hunt to us."

"Thomas is not the danger! He is learning the ways of the Fey. He ha' set the slave boy free. The other Traveller, Wulfram, is the one we must ward against. Can ye no feel his stink on the wind?"

Anger flashed on Eara's face. "Oh aye, I feel it. Others do, too. Shadows gather. A dark wind blows. No one denies it. But Strang points to the wildin' as the cause, and our Court believes him."

Nectan blew out a breath. "Then we will show them, tomorrow night. They will hear of Wulfram's misdeeds, of the Binding of Godric the harper. Raegenold himself ha' seen the danger and thrown Wulfram out. They will see Strang's tales as the foolishness they are."

"And I tell ye, they won't."

The words hung between them.

Eara took a breath and continued in a milder tone. "It's gone too far, husband. Strang's words are flying faster than the wind. It's more than idle gossip. A dark force pushes these rumours quicker than we can counter them."

Nectan grimaced. "The Undying."

Fear flashed over Eara's face. "Aye. Too many ha' spoken to me to be anything but. Our Court is riled. Riled and fearful. And what do ye think will happen at the Gatherin' tomorrow night?"

With a sickening lurch of his stomach, Nectan understood. His jaw tensed. "He canna bring a Charge. 'Tis no the Solstice—"

"He will."

The breath caught in Nectan's throat at the conviction in Eara's voice. "What ha' ye heard?"

Her eyes were bleak. "Only that. He is coming wi' a Charge, and wi' enough behind him to succeed."

Nectan's thoughts raced. According to custom, any Charge against a king's leadership happened once a year, at the Solstice Gathering, but occasionally a rival surprised their king by bringing a Charge at another time. Especially in the case of a king who had lost the trust of his Court.

Had it gone that far? His hands clenched into fists. "I set the Gatherin' for tomorrow night. We canna cancel it. And that wilna help, anyway. Strang will just try again at another."

"Nay, ye must no cancel." Eara took a deep breath. "But ye canna do as ye ha' planned. Listen well, husband. The rumours centre on the wildin'. Strang uses your acceptance of him to show your unworthiness as king. Wi' out him, he has no ground to stand on."

Nectan frowned. "What are ye saying?"

"Release the wildin' from his pledge. If he is no longer one of the Court, ye will remain king. There is no other way."

"Release—?" He gathered himself. "Ha' ye lost your senses? Wi'out the Court, Thomas has no protection against Wulfram."

She shook her head. "Traveller business. We should no interfere between them. Step aside and let them work it out. The wildin' talks of the danger to the future. I am more worried about the danger here and now. The danger to ye and our Court. If Strang were king, he would lead us into disaster." She heaved an impatient sigh. "*Ye* must be our king. Not Strang. Help the wildin', if ye must, but quietly. Out of sight o' the Court. 'Tis the only way."

A dog barked once from the settlement and then quieted. Nectan wished his tumultuous thoughts could so easily settle. He'd noticed the hostility towards him among the Seelies in the holdings he'd visited so far. Domech, too, had warned him. But he had ignored it, secure in his position as king. Eara's words had ripped off the veil of complacency that had shielded him from his duty.

Some of his thoughts must have shown in his face, for Eara stepped towards him and put her arms around his neck, pulling him close as she tipped her face up to his. "Ah, husband, dinna fret. 'Tis no only for your good ye must do it. 'Tis for Thomas' sake and all. He will see it."

Nectan squeezed her to him, revelling in the spicy scent that he could never quite identify that clung to her hair. After a moment, he let her go. "Away wi' ye then. I must think on this."

"Dinna think too long. My bed grows cold wi'out ye." She turned and made her way back towards the settlement. Normally he would enjoy watching her graceful form, but he turned back to look over the loch, his gut churning.

The Gathering's bonfire snapped and crackled, throwing up sparks that quickly extinguished. A steady wind blew, bringing with it the smell of rain. The Wards ensured they would not get wet, but they could not hold the rain back forever.

Nectan clenched his jaw. Nor could he put off forever the task at hand. He looked over the Gathered Fey, seeking another solution, but everything he saw confirmed Eara's words.

A curious tension gripped them all, no matter the dancing and feasting that brought laughter. Nectan didn't miss the sideways glances at Thomas and himself, nor the heads bent together in whispered conversations that were too long and too intense for a Gathering.

Nor could he ignore the glittering triumph in Strang's eyes. The cocky upstart thought he had it won already. He assumed he would end the night as king and Nectan, disgraced. Nectan's lips thinned. *Not yet, ye wee bastard.*

His gaze roved over the Fey again. Most were kin, friends, or both. His strongest supporters, those who had carried him on their shoulders when he made his bid to be king last summer. But now he noticed uncertainty in their eyes. Or worse, disdain. Wulfram's Unseelies had been busy indeed. He had hoped to find evidence that Eara's fears were mistaken. But it was worse than she had suspected. And knowing that, he had no choice.

Across the clearing, Thomas sat on a log, sipping at the ale in his mug. Had he noted the empty circle that surrounded him, where the others kept their distance?

Nectan doubted it. The wilding's eyes were far away. No doubt he pondered the song he expected he would perform.

"Now, me love. 'Tis time." Eara, too, had taken in the sidelong glances, the stiff formality of the Gathered Fey towards them. "Before Strang brings the Charge."

A curious calm fell upon Nectan, the same heightened awareness that came in battle once it had begun. There was no turning back.

The wilding frowned at him. Mayhap he sensed something in Nectan's manner. But it was of no account. Nectan gestured with his chin for Thomas to join him. The wilding wiped his hands on his breeches and made his way towards him.

"The way of the Fey comes by doing," he said in a low voice as Thomas joined him. "Dinna forget it."

"What—?"

But Nectan didn't wait for him to finish. He turned to the Fey. "Come, my people, I will have a word wi' ye." His voice rang through the clearing, but he didn't need to raise his voice. The Gathered Seelies had quieted the moment he had spoken.

Strang stood with his arms crossed, a faint smirk on his face. One that would disappear soon enough.

Nectan swept his gaze over the crowd and began. "I ha' Called the Gatherin' tonight to tell ye something that ye must take from here to your *crannogs* and holdings. Ye ha' all felt the shadows gathering around us. Many of ye ha' told me of the dark voice ye hear in the wind. We see the unrest in the human kingdoms. We see it in our own." He paused for a moment, letting his words sink in. "Last summer when I came to the Seelie Throne, I pledged to ye my loyalty and my strength. Ye did the same to me. I swore to uphold the Rule of the Fey, to protect ye and serve ye only. And so I ha' done. Yet in this winter's darkness a tale ha' grown in the telling, a tale of a king who ha' abandoned his people, who rules at the behest of the Unseelie Court, or under the sway of the Undying."

He had their full attention now. They were not expecting him to address their fears head-on. "Many of ye were at the winter Gatherin' near Bebbanburg and met the wilding Traveller, Thomas. The Gatherin' where he pledged to our Court. But I ha' heard from many o' ye that ye mistrust this wildin' even so. Ye see his power. Ye fear his wildin' ways. And ye think I have succumbed to him and led ye astray."

Strang watched with narrowed eyes. Beside Nectan, Thomas stirred, his face flushing. Nectan swallowed back his distaste at what must come and continued. He could not show hesitation. "Your fears are unfounded. This wildin' Traveller, this Thomas mac Cadán, he ha' made mistakes, to be sure. Ye heard o' the Binding. Yet ye see him here free of the human slave. This wildin' is no your enemy. The Traveller Wulfram is the one who creeps in the shadows. He is the one who ha' Bound a Fey, the Traveller Godric, using the Undying. He is the one who spreads mistrust and division amongst the humans, setting them on an ill-advised path."

"And yet this wilding's father brought the Wild Hunt amongst us," Strang interrupted. "You dismiss too quickly your embrace of him. You say he freed the Bound slave and ask us to ignore why he Bound the slave to him in the first place. An Unseelie trick," he added, darting a spiteful glance at Thomas. "Wulfram is a concern, yes. This whole plague of Travellers is a concern. But we know why they are here. Because of this wilding's father. He drew them. And don't forget, it is only the wilding's word that Wulfram means harm. How do we know?"

"Ach, ye wee fool," Nectan spat. "Thomas is no the problem, and ye well know it." He drew in a breath, reining in his anger as he looked over the Gathered Fey. The mood had changed. A brooding tension gripped the crowd, displacing the festive air. Eara was right. Strang had brought enough supporters to turn the tide. He moderated his tone. "Ye lose sight of the true danger by your focus on this wildin'. But I hear your concerns. And so I do what I must do to safeguard the Seelie Court." He turned to Thomas, crossing his arms over his chest. "Thomas mac Cadán, wildin' Traveller and Speaker. Here we be at the Gatherin' o' the Seelie Fey of the North, and here I speak in front of all. By the Earth, the Sky, the Sun and the Moon, I release ye from your pledge to our Court. Go on your way in peace and seek no shelter from this Court."

Silence fell over the Gathering as the power-laced words thrummed in the air and faded away.

Thomas gaped at him. Nectan knew he had felt the subtle wrench of the release of the pledge under the Vow. The same wrench Nectan had felt.

"What...?" Thomas sputtered, and then gathered himself. "My lord king, I—"

Nectan cut him off. "Nay, wildin'. I am your king no longer. Ye will leave this Gatherin' in peace, or be taken out in force."

Thomas' eyes blazed silver, his power snapping to life, but then a muscle twitched in his cheek as he clamped his jaw together. With one last furious look at Nectan, he turned and stalked from the grove, the others parting to let him go.

God help him, but it was done.

CHAPTER 24

NOWHERE ELSE TO GO

By the Earth, the Sky, the Sun and the Moon, I release ye from your pledge to the Seelie Court of the North.

Nectan's voice haunted Thomas as he entered the welcome darkness of the trees. He stumbled and tripped over roots and rocks in the darkness as he fled the Gathering, his normal Fey-footedness abandoning him as completely as Nectan had.

The moment played over and over in his mind. As the shock faded, reason returned. It was easy enough to guess the cause of Nectan's action. Strang must pose a bigger threat than they had thought. Perhaps Nectan had cause to think that Strang would try something at the Gathering, using Thomas as the excuse. And so he had cut Thomas loose, just as Oswy had done. But why hadn't Nectan warned him?

After tripping for the tenth time, Thomas caught himself against a tree and leaned up against it, heaving a breath. *I release ye from your pledge.* The betrayal of that moment lingered, despite his understanding of what led to it. But he also couldn't shake the curious sense that had flooded over him as Nectan spoke. Not just the odd wrenching feel of the release of the pledge. *Déjà vu* had also gripped him, the sudden sense of knowing what Nectan was going to say. It had happened as Nectan crossed his arms on his chest, his figure lit by firelight and Fey power. The feeling stole over him again at the memory, but just as before, was gone before he could chase it down.

He let out a breath. He had bigger concerns. Like where to go now. Rain began falling, adding urgency to that consideration. Perhaps the Fey who had been holding back the rain for the Gathering had been as startled by Nectan's announcement as he was and had lost their hold on the Wards they had set against it. Whatever the cause, he could not dally too long. He needed to be gone before the Gathering ended. He had no desire to run into any of the departing Fey.

A slight movement in the corner of his eye caused his head to snap around. He froze as he saw a large hound standing nearby, its eyes fixed upon him. Fear flashed through him, but he quickly realized it was not one of the Alder King's beasts.

But perhaps not benign, all the same. It must be one of the Gathered Seelie's animals, spying on him. Or worse. Nectan had cast him out of the Court. He was a wilding. Would they rid themselves of him now? Easy enough to skirt the Rule that forbade one Fey to kill another by sending one of their Clan animals to do it for them.

He sank to the ground, keeping the hound in his sight, his questing fingers finding a sturdy branch. He grabbed it and rose to his feet, stepping out to face the dog.

It growled, its canines showing as its lips lifted. Its hindquarters bunched as it prepared to leap.

Thomas lifted the stick, suddenly unafraid as his power filled him in a rush. *Come and get me then.*

The hound flinched and whined under its breath, its ears flattening, and then turned and melted back into the night, disappearing into the forest.

Thomas let out a breath, lowering the stick, releasing the hold on his power. He raked his hand through his hair, and feeling it wet, pulled the hood from the cloak over his head. That was too close for comfort. But at least he had accessed his power without hardly thinking about it.

Thankfully. He would need any advantage he had. Bitterness filled him at the reminder of his predicament. He had to get moving before the other Seelies tried again.

He kept his senses alert for any sounds of pursuit as he hurried through the darkened forest, moving like a shadow through the trees as he approached the holding.

One of the Seelies had Charmed the guard earlier, allowing the Fey to slip out of the night-wreathed holding without challenge. He slumbered still, wrapped up in a cloak, leaning against the wall, and Thomas bypassed him with no trouble. He retrieved Missy and set her nose down the path leading away from the *crannog* along the way they had come two days before. The wind rose, lashing the rain against him as he touched his heels to Missy's side.

He would ride for a time and then seek shelter. In the morning, he would decide what to do next.

Christ before me, Christ beneath me, Christ above me. The words ran through his mind in rhythm to Missy's stride, but they did not drown out the fears that nipped at his heels.

Thomas was more than ready for the dawn's scourging surge of Fey power after a restless night spent huddled under the spreading branches of a pine tree. He held onto his power for a moment after the sun lifted over the horizon, the clean fizz of it bringing energy to his tired body. He had slept little because of the rain and his worries. But the night's wakeful discomfort had given him time to think through his predicament and make a tentative plan.

He couldn't return to Bebbanburg, not yet. And he couldn't survive on his own. He could play the part of a travelling *scop*, much like Godric had done, moving from holding to holding and gathering information along with food and shelter. But he was wary of doing that, especially with the rumours of the dark-haired sorcerer that continued to circulate.

He needed somewhere to hunker down for a while, out of sight. After racking his brain, he decided to seek out Fee's cousin Eachan, the Horseclan Seelie Fey who lived in Dál Riata.

Nectan had told him that the fortress of Dún Duirn, close to where Nectan's *crannog* was located, was on the border between Dál Riata and the Picts. Thomas had likely entered Dál Riatan territory in his flight from Nectan's Gathering the night before. He had travelled far enough westward to make him confident that he had left Pictish lands behind him.

He remembered his father saying that Eachan lived near his own holding in Dál Riata, which he had said was close to the island monastery of Hii. So he would continue westward towards the sea and ask for directions to Hii along the way. He would pose as one of the many pilgrims travelling to the monastery. And as he got closer, he could start asking about Eachan, or go to the monastery and ask the monks there. They would know where Fee's cousin lived. And if worst came to worst he could find shelter with the monks, as he had at Lindisfarne.

Having a plan at least gave him some place to start. So as soon as the sun had risen high enough to give light, Thomas saddled Missy and set off down the path.

The rain held off for the morning, but by mid-afternoon it was spitting down again. Thomas reined in Missy under the shelter of a spreading oak and watched the rain drizzle down, feeling hungry, tired, and cold.

He had met a few people on the path, and they had directed him to continue southwest along the path that followed the loch. But it was becoming clear to him it would be difficult to travel to the coast in a direct line.

He was in the highlands, amid craggy hills and higher peaks that scraped the sky, the valleys between them containing rivers and lochs. Navigating around all these obstacles made it difficult to keep to a steady southward course.

Given the beauty of the rugged landscape, he might have enjoyed the journey if not for the looming anxiety about what was to come. He spent the day second-guessing his decision to head for Hii. Every kilometre took him further away from Bebbanburg. He had to get back there before Solstice. The difficulty of the terrain tempted him to turn around and head back towards Bernicia. Once there, he could find another place to hunker down, maybe at Brorda's holding, near to Oswy's fortress.

With a grimace, he remembered Emma's less than welcoming greeting at the Gathering and dismissed that idea. He heaved a sigh, his rumbling stomach bringing home another pressing worry. He had to find something to eat.

Despair seized him, but he pushed it aside and kept going.

It took Thomas three days to traverse the rugged country between Dún Duirn and the coast and another two to make his way southwards towards the island of Hii. As he had hoped, introducing himself as a pilgrim opened doors along the way, bringing opportunities to offer entertainment by playing for his supper. But the constant strain of hiding who he truly was wore on him. By the time he pinpointed where Eachan lived, he was looking forward to being at a place where he did not always have to be on his guard.

At least he hoped not. When he reined Missy to a halt on the top of a hill overlooking the holding, the urge to hurry to its protection warred with the worry of the reception he might receive. Knowing how quickly news spread along the Fey, the tale of his banishment from the Seelie Court had likely reached the Horseclan Fey already.

For a moment he debated turning around. But reason won out. There was nowhere else to go. If they tossed him out, so be it. As he urged the mare into motion, a longing for his father seized him again. All of this would be so much easier with Matthew to help him.

He let out a breath, trying to ignore the ache in his heart at the thought. After a moment of self-pitying indulgence, he clenched his jaw. *Get a grip, Tommo.* The monks had taught him that bitterness would only make a trial worse. *Christ before me, Christ behind me, Christ above me, Christ beneath me.* As always, the words of the *lorica* bolstered him. It reminded him that he was not alone, despite the voice in his head that whispered that he was.

The holding perched on the edge of a shallow loch that joined up with the sea a few miles to the south. The buildings were arranged in a regular pattern, giving the settlement a tidy look. To the east, a large pasture contained at least a dozen horses.

As he approached the settlement, two women who had been hoeing a small garden straightened at his approach, shading their eyes to see him. Three dogs rushed out to meet him, barking. At their noise a man came around the corner of the house, joined by another who emerged from the large barn. Relief filled him as he got closer and saw that one of the women was Fee, her red curls distinctive.

She recognized him at almost the same time and dropped the hoe, pulling up her skirts to run to meet him. "Thomas!" Her glad cry of welcome galvanized the rest into action as well, and they crowded around Missy as he drew her to a halt.

He slipped off the mare and was enfolded in Fee's arms as she cried and laughed at the same time.

She pulled back and looked up at him. "Sure and I thought ye were your father at first, and me soul gave a shiver, so it did." She reached up a hand to his cheek, her eyes brimming. "Ah, 'tis good to see ye."

He grasped her hand and smiled, his heart easing at her warm welcome. "It's good to see you, too," he managed.

Fee nodded at the man who stood beside her. "This be Eachan mac Flann, me cousin."

The man was short and barrel-chested, his eyes a clear Fey blue under black hair streaked with grey. He nodded at Thomas. "Fee has told us of ye, so she has. We grieve wi' ye at the loss of your da."

Thomas nodded, unwilling to trust his voice to a reply.

Eachan turned to the other man. "This be Thomas, Matthew's son, whom he went to Bebbanburg to meet." He glanced back at Thomas. "This be Senach, of the Ui Neill, kin he is of Dungal of Dún Add, and Eabha, his wife."

He was an older man, with a shock of white hair. A scar marred his temple, cleaving through an eyebrow, and the eye beneath was a clouded white. His other eye filled with wary acknowledgement as he nodded at him. He was not Fey, nor was his wife.

"Ye can speak more later," Fee said, waving a hand at Eachan. "Thomas needs feedin', from the looks of him." She looked up at Thomas. "Come wi' me. There's stew to eat, and salmon freshly smoked."

Thomas threw an apologetic look at Eachan and the other man and allowed himself to be hauled away. But he wasn't that reluctant to escape the inevitable questions. He couldn't avoid them forever, but he'd feel much better facing them on a full stomach.

CHAPTER 25

NO STRANGERS TO TROUBLE

After a hearty supper, Eachan caught Thomas' eye and inclined his head towards the door.

"Come wi' me, lad. I have some words for ye, so I do." He got up from the table.

Time to pay the piper. Thomas braced himself for Eachan's questions as he followed Eachan outside.

The night was cool but dry. They walked down to the dock that jutted out from the coastline near the holding, where two small boats bobbed at their moorings. One dog accompanied them, and it snuffled around the shoreline, digging up interesting tidbits it found on the sandy shore.

Eachan turned to Thomas. "I have heard the Gathering tales, that Nectan released ye from your pledge."

It was as much a question as a statement. Thomas let out a breath. "Yes." He shrugged, embarrassed. Annoyance followed. He had done nothing wrong, but the Fey always made him feel like he had. "Because of Strang. I think. He didn't tell me why." He waved at Eachan's frown. "I think Strang was going to try for Nectan's throne. Bring a Charge against him at the Gathering. Because of his support of me. So Nectan had to show that Strang was wrong by releasing me from the Court."

"Aye, that's how I understood it, too." Anger flashed across Eachan's face. "Strang is a wee fool, so he is, but there are some who like nothing better than to listen to a golden tongue spreading tales. He has those who support his bid."

The dog lifted its head, alert, his ears pricked as he looked back into the holding. Thomas and Eachan both looked back, too, but after a moment the dog resumed its exploration of the sand.

Eachan glanced at Thomas. "What do ye plan, then? Matthew told me his fears of the Traveller Wulfram, and since he left, other Fey have said the same." He paused, giving him a keen look. "The last Fee knew, ye were going to Eoforwic to confront him."

Thomas' jaw hardened. "Yes. My father was right about him. He is trying to force Oswy off his throne, in order to get rid of the monastery. He thinks with Oswy gone, they can drive the monks out. But he knew my father would stand in his way, and so he had him killed. He told me so himself."

"Ah," Eachan hissed, his eyes flashing with anger. "Why did ye no kill him, then?"

"It's not that easy." Thomas grimaced. "He's in league with one of the Undying. He's used it to Bind the harper Godric to his will, and he took me to an Unseelie Gathering to do the same to me. I had little chance against him." He spread his hands. "It's a long story, but in the end, Nectan showed up at the Gathering and Raegenold found out what Wulfram had done to Godric, so he released me to Nectan. And kicked Wulfram out of his Court."

"God has his hand on ye, so he does," Eachan said, his eyes wide. He shook his head. "But now Nectan has let ye go."

"Yeah. Well, like I said, he had little choice."

Eachan gave him a wintery smile. "There is always a choice, young Thomas."

At his words, a faint ripple shivered through Thomas. He shifted his shoulders, uncomfortable. "I suppose," he answered, and sighed. "I'm not sure where to go. Oswy asked me to leave Bebbanburg, too. For now," he added at Eachan's startled look. "Wulfram has gathered some Unseelies around him. They're spreading stories about a sorcerer at Oswy's Court."

Eachan grimaced. "Aye, even here we've heard them. I wondered if that were ye, so I did. A wilding Fey stands out amongst Fey and humans alike."

"Right." Thomas bit back his anger. It would not help him. "They are saying I'm using black magic to sway Oswy away from God." He shook his head. "Oswy was right. My being at Bebbanburg was only playing into Wulfram's hands, making people suspicious of him. I have to stay away for a while. But I have to be back by Solstice. I think that's when Wulfram will do whatever it is he's planning to do."

Eachan's eyebrows raised. "Solstice! Aye, I see it, so I do. The time of changing, when our power will be greatest." His face turned grim. "His, but ours as well. He may not find it such a boon after all."

Thomas gathered his courage. Now or never. "I need a place to lie low. Just for a couple of weeks. Is it—"

"Ach." Eachan waved a hand, interrupting him. "Ye need not ask, lad. Ye must stay here. Your father was a good husband to me niece, and a good friend to me besides. I'll not be sending ye away, and ye in need."

A weight rolled off his shoulders. "Thank you," he managed. "It could be dangerous having me here. If Wulfram finds out—"

"Nay," Eachan said, cutting him off again. "A poor friend I'd be indeed, to refuse his son in his time of need because of fear. Ye will stay as long as you need, so ye will." A wry smile lifted his lips. "Besides, I'd not relish explaining to Fee why I sent ye away."

"Right. Thank you." He shook his head. "Still, he could cause you some trouble." He couldn't help the bitterness that coloured his words. "Or something else could happen. Like you said, I'm a wilding. I attract trouble."

Eachan laughed and clapped him on the shoulder. "Ah, lad, we Fey are no strangers to trouble, wildin' or no. Ye need not worry." The amusement faded from his eyes, replaced by a hard light. "As for Wulfram, I'd like to see him try it, so I would. Do not fret. I'll set a watch. No one will come near wi'out me knowing." He turned to go back to his house, whistling for the dog to follow.

Silence fell in his absence. For a moment, Thomas allowed himself to enjoy the peaceful night, listening to the small splash of the water against the shore and the far-off melody of a blackbird's song floating through the dark.

His father had likely stood in this very place, perhaps thinking about him. At the thought, grief speared through him again. Their time together had been so short. He swallowed, his throat tight. Short as it had been, he couldn't forget that to be reunited with his father again had been an unexpected grace. Nona had pointed that out when Matthew had first appeared. Many who lost loved ones would give anything to have the same opportunity.

He looked up at the sky, where stars were shining through the darkening sky. *Christ stands before you, and peace is on his mind.* The prayer Aidan had spoken over his father's grave came back to him, easing the ache of grief.

The blackbird sang again. Thomas closed his eyes, listening. Psalm 103, the monks' favourite psalm, ran through his mind. *Bless the Lord, O my soul, and all that is within me, bless His holy name.*

A better meditation than to dwell on all the ways he feared he was inadequate to face what might come.

CHAPTER 26

A Fey Wi'out a Court

A couple of days later, Eachan's wife, Binne, returned. She had been away at her uncle's holding, as her cousin's wife had recently given birth. Both mother and babe had been ill, and Binne had gone to give what aid she could. She was not a Healer, but her father had been. She had some knowledge of herb lore and so she went to assist the Healer who was tending to the new mother.

As Thomas helped Eachan repair part of the pasture fence, the Horseclan Fey straightened, a faraway look on his face. Then he grinned, his eyes sharpening on Thomas. "Ah, Binne is coming, so she is! Come, lad, and greet her. She will be glad to meet Matthew's son."

But once Thomas saw the older woman riding into the holding, he had a feeling that *glad* might not be the right word. He recognized her from the Gathering. She must have been close enough to Dún Duirn for her to answer Nectan's Call. The other Fey who rode with her, a young man, had been there, too. He seemed to remember seeing them in the group around Strang, but he couldn't be sure.

By the narrow-eyed look Eachan's wife gave him as she dismounted, she recognized him, too. As did the young man, who slid off his horse, his face hostile as he looked at Thomas.

"Ah, 'tis good to see ye, so it is!" Eachan hugged and kissed his wife and then turned to the young man, his smile fading as he noted the youth's expression. "Was there trouble on the journey?"

"Nay, my lord," the young man replied. "Not on the journey." His gaze darted to Thomas, his face clouding with anger.

Eachan frowned. "Speak, lad."

But before he could answer, Binne spoke up, brushing back a strand of silvery hair that had escaped her head covering. "Nay, Kilian, let me." Her keen gaze swept over Thomas, and she turned back to Eachan. "What ha' ye done, husband? Surely ye know that our king has released this wildin' from his pledge to our

Court. And now I find him here. A wildin'," she added, as if in emphasis. "Or has he not told ye?"

"Aye, of course he has. He is Matthew mac Cadán's son, so he is, and welcome here. Especially now." Eachan spoke firmly.

"Welcome, is it." She fixed her husband with a hard look and turned to Thomas. "Fee has told us how alike ye are to your da, but even so, it gave me a start seein' ye at the Gathering. 'Twas like Matthew himself had come back from the dead." She grimaced. "I had afeared ye might show up here after our king released ye. And here ye be, a Fey wi'out a Court, as your father had been."

"Enough." Eachan spoke sharply. "I will no—"

"No, husband. Ye were not there. The Court is riled up, so it is, and all because of this wildin'."

Eachan's eyes narrowed. "All because of Strang, ye mean."

The young man spoke up, his eyes flashing. "The Lord Strang does what—"

"Nay, Kilian, not now." Binne held up a hand, and the youth stiffened, biting back his words. She turned to her husband. "Strang stirs the pot, aye, but Nectan has given him the spoon. This wildin' brings trouble like a river running downhill, and just as hard to stop."

"Look. I'm sorry," Thomas said, interjecting. He clamped down on the self-pity that had awoken at Binne's words. She was right, after all. It wasn't fair for him to put them in this position. "I will leave. I don't want to cause problems."

Eachan turned to him, exasperated. "Nay, lad, ye will not. I've said there is no—"

"Binne!" Fee's glad cry of welcome cut off Eachan's words. She had been drawing water at the well on the other side of the house and had spotted them as she came around the corner. She put down the bucket of water on the porch and rushed over, enveloping Eachan's wife in a hug. "Ah, 'tis good to see ye. But how are Eithne and the babe?"

Binne pulled back and smiled at her. "Well, both of them."

"Ah, thanks be to God. I have been praying, so I have. But I see ye ha' met Thomas. He's come to be with us for a time afore he goes back to Bebbanburg."

"Aye, so Eachan has said."

Fee did not seem to notice Binne's cool tone. "Come, I would hear all about your journey. Did ye see Faolán, then? He told us he were going to Dún Duirn, so he did." Fee continued chatting as she hooked her arm in Binne's and they went to the house. Binne threw a hard look at Eachan over her shoulder as Fee led her away.

Eachan turned to the other Fey. "Take the horses. Once they're settled, ye can join Thomas and me at fixing the south fence."

Anger flashed across Kilian's face at the older man's dismissal, but he nodded and took the reins, leading the horses away.

Eachan turned back to Thomas, his face apologetic. "I am sorry, lad. Kilian is kin to the Lord Strang. 'Tis no surprise he takes his side."

"And your wife?"

Eachan grimaced. "Ah, well. She has her own mind, so she does." He shook his head. "She loved your da. Give her time. She will see reason."

Thomas ran a hand through his hair, all of Eachan's reassurances from the night before evaporating in the face of Binne's objections. "But she's right, though. I should head back towards Bebbanburg and find somewhere near there to stay." But as before, no inspiration struck as to where.

Fee's uncle once again spared him that worry. "Nay, lad, dinna be foolish. I told ye. I wilna send ye away, not with Wulfram plotting mischief against ye." He heaved a breath. "I will have a word with Binne and Kilian. They will no cause ye trouble."

As if on cue, a horse squealed in the barn. A loud thump indicated a stamping of a heavy foot, following by another piercing whinny.

Eachan's gaze darted to the barn and then back at Thomas, rueful amusement in his eyes. "Ach then, Kilian may take more persuasion. As I said, he is kin to Strang through his ma. But his da, Lonan, is my cousin's son, and being that Kilian is Horseclan, I foster him here. Our ties run through the Fey Court and the human clans alike. Kilian may bluster, but he will no cause ye any grief." He snorted. "If it be any consolation, he didna take to your da, either. Lonan was set to marry Fee. When she spurned him for Matthew, Lonan was no too happy. Kilian's anger burned against Matthew for his father's sake, so it did. It's why he and Fee didna stay here wi' us. Fee had a holding from her first husband, and they made their home there."

As usual, Thomas felt lost in the tangle of family relationships Eachan had described. Thomas had never had the luxury of a large, extended family. Matthew had been estranged from his own. His mother had been an only child whose parents lived in Wales. It was hard to relate to the importance of kinship ties to the people in this time.

The horse whinnied again, followed by more thumps. Eachan winced slightly but kept on talking. "But even so, I ha' been thinking. Fee wants to go to her holding where she lived wi' your da. Her nephew and others in her family are coming to help her with sorting things out there, but they canna come until after the crops are planted. Perhaps ye should take her. It's not far away, not even a day's journey. Ye need not stay long. It will give me a chance to remind Kilian of his place here."

His father's holding. Thomas wasn't sure he wanted to go to a place where Matthew's absence would be so keenly felt, but what else was he going to do? "Of course. We can leave today, if you like."

"Nay, lad, not today. We wilna let Kilian think he has driven ye away. Tomorrow will be soon enough."

Another thump sounded from the barn. Eachan looked over, irritation filling his face. "I will meet ye back at the fence, so I will." He strode towards the barn, his mouth set in a grim line.

Thomas watched him enter the barn, trying to ignore the feeling that he was being bandied about like a hot potato. First Oswy, then Nectan, and now Eachan. He sighed, resigned. He supposed going away for a couple of days was not a bad idea. Perhaps by the time he got back, the young man's anger would have cooled enough that he wouldn't have to worry about getting brained by an errant horse's hoof.

But perhaps not. He grimaced as he started towards the pasture again. The Fey treated the Rule against spilling another Fey's blood more like a suggestion than a Rule. Since he was a wilding, and without a Court, they probably didn't think it applied to him at all.

Where there's a will, there's a way, he thought. And judging from the heated words from the barn that faded as he headed towards the pasture, Kilian's will was very much set against him, no matter Eachan's assurances.

He hunched his shoulders against the sharp tones that followed him as he strode across the pasture. Tomorrow couldn't come soon enough.

Chapter 27

Diarmud's Pillar

After Thomas saddled Missy the next morning, he gave her one of the withered apples left over from the last summer's hoard as an apology to the mare for the unexpected journey.

She took it with a snap of her big teeth, munching the tasty treat with relish. Her ears perked up as Thomas rubbed her nose affectionately. "Sorry, girl," he murmured. "It won't be too far today."

She nudged him, her nostrils quivering as she snuffed at him in search of another apple. He laughed and pushed her head away, giving her neck an affectionate pat as Fee came out of the barn, leading a dainty grey mare.

Eachan waited, holding the lead rope of a donkey that was laden with the belongings Fee was taking with her. She had decided she would stay at her holding for the summer, and no persuasion from Binne and Eachan could make her change her mind.

"Now then, Fee, I will send Mellan along to ye once he arrives," Eachan said as he tied the donkey's rope to Missy's saddle. "But if ye wish, ye can look over the holding and then come back wi' Thomas in a couple o' days. Once Melian comes, ye can go back wi' him."

Fee shook her head. "Nay, cousin," she said again, as she had said every time Eachan brought it up. "'Tis time for me to go. There is much to tend to there. Eieramhon does his best, but the slaves will work better when I'm there." She embraced her cousin, holding him to her in a long hug. "Ach, ye ha' been a blessin' to me, so ye have. Ye and Binne ha' eased me heart."

Eachan's arms tightened around her. "We will pray for ye, lass. Go wi' God, and may all the angels watch over ye. Binne will come to ye after Thomas comes back, to see how ye fare."

The morning sun cast sharp shadows as they mounted their horses and started towards the holding, donkey in tow. According to Fee, they would get there by mid-morning. The holding was Fee's property that she had brought to her first marriage. According to local custom and laws, she kept control of the land when her husband died. Her parents were both dead, but a distant relative managed the holding on her behalf. Marrying Matthew, a stranger and a man with no property, had been a scandal. But Matthew had won over most of her family after their marriage. He established a name for himself as a maker of fine musical instruments, earning him respect in the community.

Thomas was both eager and apprehensive to see where his father had lived with Fee and built his new life in the aftermath of his escape to this time. A place where they were happy, from all accounts. That thought did not bring as much bitterness as it used to, but it still rankled if he dwelt on it.

But the landscape they rode through helped to dispel any gloomy thoughts. Lofty peaks interspersed with rounded hills surrounded them, and the deep glens held lochs and rivers that mirrored the clear blue sky. The water sparkled under the morning sun, and a fresh breeze brought not only a salty tang from the sea but also a sweet coconut scent from the flowering gorse bushes that spread their bright yellow flowers along the path and in every crook of the hills.

It was not only the gorse that added colour. Many spring wildflowers bloomed in the meadows, along the lochs, and in the marshes. Frothy white mead wort, delicate pink orchids, and purple butterwort thrived in the bogs and watery marshes, while small pansies and rusty red sheep sorrel peeked out among the grassy areas.

For the first time since his father's death, a deep contentment settled in Thomas' heart as they rode along the narrow track that angled south towards the coast. It sprang from the dazzling beauty of the highlands, the warmth of the bright spring sun and the birdsong that filled the silence between their words. He had grown accustomed to allowing his Fey nature to hold sway, which enhanced his reaction to the natural world. The unhurried ride through this spring-bright morning made him feel freer than he'd felt in a long time.

Fee's holding was inland, near the south end of Loch Nell, so they angled eastward, away from the sea. After they had travelled a couple of hours, they came to a spot where the path divided into two, with one track continuing south and the other eastwards. Fee reined in her mare and looked over at Thomas. "Ye canna see it here, but the loch is ahead, past those trees. But I have something to show ye afore we go there. I think your da would ha' liked ye to see it. 'Twill no take long."

Curious, Thomas nodded, and Fee turned her horse's head eastward along the intersecting path. After about fifteen minutes, Fee stopped again. "There."

Up ahead, an ancient standing stone stood next to the path. Thomas had seen many of these monuments in his travels across Britain. They always stirred a sense of deep mystery within him, and a feeling of time's long passage.

The stone itself was tall, around fifteen feet. It was old, covered in lichen, worn and craggy. The sun had gone behind clouds that had scudded over the hills in the last half hour, and a misty sheen covered the rock. A small tingle crept up his spine as he studied the stone. There was something about it that set his teeth on edge. He glanced at Fee. "What is this place?"

She smiled slightly. "It is called Diarmuid's Pillar. My ma told me long ago that it marks the grave of Diarmuid Ua Duibhne, he who stole away Gráinne, the wife of Finn Mac Cumhaill. When a boar gored Diarmuid, Finn refused to heal him, and Diarmuid died." She dismounted, looking up at Thomas. "Come."

Thomas slid off Missy, and he and Fee looped their horses' reins over a branch of a tree that stood on the other side of the path, opposite the standing stone. As they approached the stone, his heartbeat quickened. He looked around, trying to pinpoint the vague sense of danger that gripped him.

Fee seemed unaffected, striding towards the stone and laying her hand on it affectionately. "I came here as a child, and me and my brothers would play at being Diarmuid and Gráinne."

Thomas' gaze snagged on a circle of large boulders which was slightly north of the monument. The mist grew more substantial even as he looked at the stone circle, and he frowned, taking a few steps towards it.

An odd feeling passed over him, a drawing sensation pulling him towards the stones. He froze as sudden realization crashed down on him. This was a Thin Place. A Crossing spot. That pulling sensation felt exactly the same as the other two he had encountered thus far. But suddenly the mist increased, thickening so that he could barely see the stone. He whirled around, searching for Fee. But he couldn't see her. "Fee!" His shout got swallowed up in the fog, and there was no answer. "Fee!"

He spun around the other way. It was like being dropped into the dream that had plagued him since he had first Crossed here, complete with the ghostly mist and the sense of impending doom clutching at him with invisible fingers. He froze, afraid of stepping into the circle and getting swept away as he had when he had Crossed to this time. His father had told him that was highly unlikely to happen again, and his one attempt at Crossing back home had not worked when he had placed himself deliberately in the right spot. But he didn't want to risk it all the same. He curled his hands into tight fists, accessing his Fey power almost without thought. The strong flood of it brought warmth and beat back the dread that had seized him.

Suddenly, a lengthy, eerie howl wafted through the fog, and his blood ran cold. The Hunt. Had Wulfram set it on his trail, hunting him down as he had hunted down his father? Or was it Fee whom the Alder King was after? Had he already taken her?

Fright broke his paralysis. He spun around, his hands reaching out. She had been right there. "Fee!"

"Thomas!"

Relief flooded through him as he heard her voice, even though it was muffled in the mist, like she was speaking to him from behind a door. But in the next second, she was there, in front of him, frowning. "Thomas, what is wrong? Are ye sick?"

"No," he stammered, trying to calm his thundering heart. He looked around, disoriented. The mist was gone, the horses and the donkey munching on the new green grass contentedly. They showed no sign of alarm, or of having heard the Hound. Nor did Fee, and she surely would have reacted if she had. "It was…" He trailed off, not sure how to explain. What had happened? He shook his head. "I don't know. I'm all right."

"Your da said this is a place of the Old Ones. I should ha' warned ye. He would come here a time or two. But he said it gave him peace. I thought ye might find it the same."

He took a steadying breath. The eerie feeling faded as the sun came out from behind the clouds. The stone no longer seemed menacing, radiating only the same timeless aura as previous ones he had seen. An old place, ancient. A wren trilled its song, followed by another. *Peace.* He let out a breath. "I'm fine. There was something strange for a moment. But it's gone, now."

Fee frowned slightly. "Ye had a queer look on your face, so ye did."

"I couldn't see you. Did you not hear me yelling your name?"

"Nay. Ye were just standin' there, staring." She peered up at him. "Are ye sure ye are all right?"

Thomas felt slightly embarrassed. "Yes, I'm fine," he repeated. He walked towards the stone circle, the slight pull of it increasing as he approached it. At its edge he hesitated, then stepped inside.

The same extraordinary awareness swept over him that he had felt when he returned to where he had inadvertently Crossed before. But as before, it was not menacing. Quite the contrary. The last of the fear leeched out of him under its benign weight, and a smile lifted his lips as he slowly turned around.

Fee joined him, her face lighting in a smile even as tears gathered in her eyes. "Ye look so like your da," she whispered, one hand reaching up to cup his cheek.

Pain squeezed his heart as he saw the grief in her eyes. "I miss him, too," he said, his voice cracking.

Fee drew him in for a hug. Then she pulled back, wiping at her eyes. "I feel close to him here," she said with a watery smile.

"Me too," Thomas said, his throat aching. This must have been the place where his father had contemplated Crossing back. He could imagine him there, battling the desire for his family and the necessity of keeping them safe.

He would never know what might have happened if his father had made a different choice and came back to them. Matthew's absence had shaped Thomas differently than his presence would have. So much would have been different, and it was too difficult to even try to imagine all of it.

"He was happy here, wasn't he?"

"Oh aye," Fee replied, wiping a tear from her cheeks and crossing her arms as she looked away from him.

"If he hadn't come to see me, he would still be alive," Thomas said, pain piercing him.

Fee turned to him, shaking her head. "Ye must not think that. I tell ye true, I loved him something fierce. But when he heard ye were here, I never saw such joy in him as I did that day."

Her words eased the pain in his heart, and he managed a nod. Fee squeezed his arm, and then without further words they left the circle and went back to the horses.

They rode back the way they came in silence, which gave Thomas time to puzzle out what had happened. In some ways, the experience had felt like the strange *déjà vu* that had grasped him the night of the Gathering when Nectan set him free. Perhaps it had something to do with being so close to the Crossing.

But it was more than that. It was almost as if something had wrenched him out of one place and into another, and then just as quickly brought him back. What caused that odd dislocation? It was as if he had been transported to the strange Otherworld he had encountered before, when freeing Odda. *A place of mist and shadows*, Nectan had said. But Fee had seen him the whole time, it seemed. Or had she? Perhaps the peculiar magic of the place had Charmed into thinking he was there.

And what about the Hound? He dared not tell Fee of it. The last thing he wanted to do was to disturb her with the memory of the fearsome Alder King, who had caught her in a nightmare the night he chased Matthew and her down.

He had heard it. He was sure of that. But was it in the Otherworld, or here? He wrestled with the puzzle as they rode back to the path leading to Fee's holding, but could come to no conclusion.

CHAPTER 28

A Dangerous Place to Be

*May 18, AD 643, Loch
Nell*

Fee's holding lay in a wide valley at the south end of the loch, hemmed in by hills. Ferns bordered the path that led to the holding, nodding their shaggy fronds at them in the breeze as they passed. The holding itself was small, with just a few buildings surrounded by pastures holding sheep and cattle.

Fee's kinsman Eireamhon was a young man of seventeen who greeted Thomas with a wide-eyed look of wonder, his even younger wife standing beside him, curiosity sparking in her almond-shaped blue eyes. "Matthew's son and no mistaking it," he said to Fee.

"Aye, as I have said," Fee replied with a laugh, and turned to the young woman as she untied one of the bags from the donkey and hoisted it up. "Aoife, I ha' brought some flour and honey from Eachan, as well as a new spindle to replace the one ye broke. Come wi' me, and we'll make some honey cakes for our supper tonight, so we will." She turned to Eireamhon. "I ha' brought some other things as well, but ye can take them to the storage shed for now."

As the two women disappeared into a house, the young man watched them go, his gaze following his wife.

"How long have you been married?" Thomas asked, amused at the other's ardent gaze.

Eireamhon glanced at him, a blush filling his cheeks. "Since Christmas," he said. His face grew solemn. "Your father played us a fine song at the weddin'. I was sorry to hear what happened to him. May God rest his soul." He crossed himself. "Matthew was a good man, so he was, and he made Fee very happy." He cleared his throat. "But we will ha' plenty o' time to speak of your da, so we will. Ye can put your animals in the pasture, there, wi' the others. I must see to the sheep. There is one which is poorly."

"I will unload Fee's stuff if you show me where to put it. Once I've seen to the horses, I'll come help. I tended the flock with Brother Seamus at Lindisfarne. I can have a look if you like."

"Oh aye, and thank ye. I've put her in the small pen in the north field." He gestured with his arm. "The shed is behind the house."

Thomas watched him go for a moment, and then looked around, drinking in the sights. This is where his father had lived during the years of separation from his family. By the quirks of Travelling it had been eleven years for Thomas but only a few for his father. But Matthew had made a life for himself in this spot, with these people. A good life, from his accounting of it.

With a sigh, he grabbed both the horses' reins and led them towards the barn, with the donkey plodding behind. He could never forget the pain that Matthew's absence had caused his mom, but it was strangely comforting all the same to hear of Matthew's life here.

Aiofe's parents also lived at the holding, along with her grandmother, a small, wizened woman whose black beady eyes and white fluffy hair reminded Thomas of the ewe he and Eireamhon had tended to that afternoon.

When she entered the larger hall where they gathered for the supper meal, she fixed her eyes upon Thomas and cackled in laughter, hanging onto her daughter-in-law's arm as she wheezed in delight. She wiped her eyes as her laughter faded and then patted Thomas' cheek. "Oh aye, a bonny one ye be, young lad, and the image of your father." She chortled again as she gave Fee a sly look. "Ach, Fee, 'tis a canny woman, so it is, to find a younger version o' her husband to share her bed."

Fee laughed and waved away the old woman's insinuation. "Ach, Gran, away wi' ye then, and none of your foolishness. Here now, Eireamhon has brought us a fish for our stew tonight, and Aiofe ha' made honey cakes. Sit down, will ye no?"

It had been a long time since Thomas felt so relaxed. Here, in this remote holding, the cares that burdened him ever since he had arrived in this time melted away. He laughed with the rest as the old woman teased not only Fee, but the rest of them as well.

After supper, though, as the sun grew low on the horizon, he excused himself to go outside, to go for a walk alone. His odd experience at the standing stone was still bothering him. He was pretty sure he had somehow slipped into the Otherworld under the Crossing's peculiar influence, but before he turned in for the night, he wanted to walk around the holding and make sure all was well. Make sure the Hound wasn't around.

He went first to the pasture closest to the holding, where shaggy cows bunched together, chewing their cud. He watched them for a moment, listening for any sign of the Hound or the Hunt. But there was nothing. Nor did he sense them.

He began a slow circuit of the holding, and as he did, the *caim* prayer came to mind. He murmured its phrases as he walked.

O mighty Three
Thy protection be
Encircling me

His fear of the Hunt faded under the comfort of the prayer and of the quiet, settled night. Once he returned to the house that Fee had shared with Matthew, he lay down on the gathered furs by the hearth fire and fell asleep in an instant.

He woke up, startled, certain someone had touched him. But he was alone except for Fee. Her even breathing and the slight rattle of the shutter over the window from a small breeze were the only sounds.

He was drifting off again when he felt it again. His eyes snapped open. Someone *had* touched him, but not physically. A Fey was attempting to Speak into his mind. Nectan had taught him how to recognize the slight pressure before it happened, like the knocking on a door. He had a choice to open the door or not. In this case, the decision was a firm no.

He scrambled out of bed, grabbing for his knife, and he froze as he spotted Fee. A faint shimmering light lay upon her. A Charm.

The questing invitation prodded at him again. Someone wanted to talk to him, but who? He doubted Wulfram would bother with the niceties. Godric, perhaps? Nectan?

He stood up, gripped with indecision, and then stalked to the door and slipped outside.

The holding slumbered under the stars. He stood by the door, looking around carefully, but could see no one in the faint moonlight. Then a sharp, chittering sound erupted above him that almost made him jump out of his skin until he recognized the call of a peregrine falcon.

His lips thinned, and he let out a breath. *Nectan.* The falcon swooped down and settled on the roof of the house. It emitted its *kek-kek-kek* cry once again and then took off, flying towards the barn and disappearing in the dark around the corner.

Thomas followed it, rehearsing all the things he wanted to say to the king. But he stopped short when he rounded the corner and saw who stood there. Not Nectan, but Cadán Longshanks, his ancestor. Speaker to Raegenold, King of the Unseelies.

Missy squealed in the barn, sensing his alarm. *Stupid mistake,* he chided himself. Nectan wasn't the only Eagleclan Fey bonded to a falcon. Cadán must be another.

"Let it be, lad," Cadán said, one hand out. "I'll no hurt ye. I'm just here to have a word wi' ye."

Thomas didn't know what Cadán meant until he realized he had drawn on his Fey power without noticing it in the shock of seeing the Unseelie. Access to his power had become more automatic as he let his Fey nature come to life. He wasn't sure if that was good or bad, but at that moment, he was glad of it.

He held onto it a moment longer, looking for any signs of deception in the other Fey and seeking the sense of any others around. But the night was quiet, and they were alone, so he allowed his power to subside. "Why are you here?"

Cadán smiled slightly, spreading his hands. "As I told ye, I ha' some words for ye. From Raegenold, king of the Unseelie Fey of the North."

"Really." He didn't hide the skepticism he felt. Cadán seemed sincere, but Thomas couldn't imagine why Raegenold had directed one of his Speakers to seek him out.

"We heard of Nectan's release of ye, so we did. Ye are wi'out a Court, and that is a dangerous place to be."

"Not like I have much choice," Thomas countered. "What's it to him?"

Cadán cocked his head. "Ah, but ye do. Raegenold sends me to tell ye that if ye would but pledge to his Court, he would take ye."

"Pledge to his—" Thomas broke off, shaking his head. "Right. The last time I saw him, he first threatened to Bind me to his Court, and then he was more than happy to get rid of me once Nectan showed up."

"Aye, 'tis true. But ye forget. Raegenold first offered ye a place in his Court if ye would but pledge to him. Only if ye refused were he prepared to Bind ye. But ye did not answer him. Now that the Seelies have sent ye away, he bids me to tell ye that the offer still stands."

"And the threat? Does that stand, too?"

Cadán's eyes narrowed. "Ach, dinna be a fool. Raegenold ha' no desire for that. He wouldna ha' done it that night. He merely walked down that path with Wulfram to see how far the Traveller would go. Ye were in no danger."

Thomas snorted. "You'll forgive me if I don't believe you."

Cadán chuckled. "Well, I suppose I dinna blame ye." He spread his hands. "But think carefully, wildin'. Your da was Unseelie. Your blood is tied to ours. Nectan has no need of ye any longer. But a Fey without a Court is like a bird without wings." He shrugged. "Look what happened to Matthew."

Anger flashed through Thomas, and he clenched his jaw to bite back the retort that sprang to his lips. "An Unseelie ordered him killed is what happened to him. And Raegenold thinks I'll go running to him for help? No thanks. His kind of help I don't need." He shook his head. "He's not offering this for my sake. What's in it for him?"

Cadán barked a laugh. "Ye are learnin' the ways o' the Fey, I see." The amusement faded from his face. "'Tis true, our king has his reasons. But they are no for me to tell ye. Meet wi' him and he will explain them himself." He took a step closer. "Do ye think ye can stop Wulfram on your own? Ye need a Court to back ye, or he will sweep ye away. Like your father was." He held Thomas' gaze a moment longer and then shook his head. "Ye dinna have to decide now. I'll give ye two days." He gave Thomas a hard look, and then turned, raising his hand in a dismissive farewell as he walked away. His retreating form shimmered slightly in the darkness until he faded away, leaving Thomas alone. The faint cry of the falcon came to his ears and then silence fell again.

He let out a long breath. Raegenold could not be serious. He remembered the bright power of the Unseelie King. Cold sweat pooled under his arms at the thought of pledging to him and of the Knowing that would follow. That had been bad enough at the hands of Nectan. He didn't want to imagine what it would be like with Raegenold.

But Cadán was right about one thing. He needed help to vanquish Wulfram. And without the help of the Seelie Court, his chances of stopping Wulfram were slim.

Frustration filled him. Wulfram wanted the monastery gone. Toppling Oswy off his throne was a first step. To do that would involve political manoeuvring and influence among Oswy's allies and enemies alike. But Thomas had no way of doing the same to counter Wulfram's influence.

The only influence he had, which was slim, was among the Fey. His status as a Traveller and the strength of his power were enough to cause them to consider his words. But the fact he was a wilding blunted much of the status he might have otherwise enjoyed.

And with his ouster from the Seelie Court, he had lost even that. As much as it disturbed him, he had to at least consider Raegenold's offer. The Unseelie King would have some influence over those who followed Wulfram, and more influence over those who did not. Perhaps the best way to undermine Wulfram's influence was to steal away his followers, cripple his ability to act. All the plans in the world did no good without boots on the ground to implement them.

There were so many layers to it all that it left his head spinning. The Fey Courts were one thing. But they were also part of the human world. Raegenold himself was Deirian. Getting rid of Oswy would help his king, Oswine. Did that not matter to Raegenold? Nectan was a Pict and therefore neutral in the affairs of the Saxons, as far as Thomas could glean. But every king looked for ways to expand their power and wealth. This would be the perfect time for the Picts to strike against Bernicia while Oswy was still consolidating his power.

Perhaps it wasn't just Strang who had forced Nectan's hand. Perhaps Nectan didn't want Thomas to stop Wulfram because of his Pictish king's ambitions, and he had banished Thomas to keep him from persuading the other Seelies to help.

Thomas took a breath and reined in his wild speculations. Both Nectan's and Raegenold's anger and disgust at Wulfram's use of the Undying and the Binding of Godric had been real. Neither king would want to allow Wulfram to succeed for that reason alone. Wulfram brought many more dangers with him than just political ones.

He leaned back against the barn, looking up at the stars intersecting the inky carpet of the sky. *God, help me. What am I supposed to do?*

The words had no sooner left his thoughts when the *caim* ran through his mind again. *O Sacred Three. Encircling us.*

They felt like a reply, but what did it mean? To trust in God? What was it that Aidan had said? *Go where God leads ye, trusting that He will provide the answers ye seek.*

Was this an answer? To commit to the Unseelies? The thought of it curled his fingers into fists. There must be something else. He just wished he knew what it was. He sighed as he pushed himself away from the barn and walked back to the house, meditating on the prayers. *Encircling us. Christ above me, Christ below me, Christ before me, Christ behind me.*

He had no more answers, but when he lay his head back on the bed, he found that the questions that threatened to overwhelm him had quieted. In their place, he saw a circle of light encompassing the holding, repelling all evil.

Despair fled in the light of that vision, and he dropped off into a dreamless sleep.

CHAPTER 29

UNSETTLED

*May 21, AD 643, Loch
Glashan*

Nona sat on the bench outside the house she shared with Conaire, looking out over the misty fields. Hills brooded as dark shadows at the edge of the valley, mainly obscured by the falling rain and low-hanging clouds. The early morning sun was barely over the horizon and cast little light in the grey, misty sky. The damp leached into her bones, it seemed, and she pulled her cloak closer with a shiver. But no matter the chill, she cherished this moment alone, the first since she and Conaire had arrived at his holding three days ago. The first since she left Bebbanburg nearly two weeks ago.

Several families, all of whom belonged to the nGabrain, the ruling *cenél*, or clan, of Dál Riata, lived at the holding. As he was the head of the holding, Conaire lived on the *crannog*, the small island constructed in the loch itself. It also held the main hall and a few other buildings.

She had been intending to collect some eggs for their breakfast, but the invitation of the empty seat and a time alone to think had proven irresistible.

The grey, gloomy landscape mirrored her feelings. She felt lost, adrift in this new place with a husband who was a mystery to her. Who seemed to have no interest in her other than carnal ones. Her throat tightened, and before she could stop it, the memory of the stricken look in Thomas' silver eyes when she told him of Conaire's arrival pierced her. She shifted on the bench. She suspected that she herself had looked much the same. As if she had been cut to the heart.

She had tried to suppress the powerful pull that drew her towards Thomas, but still it remained. No matter his wilding ways, no matter the storm of danger he brought with him. She had used anger to deflect the spark of attraction that flared between them, but it hadn't worked, and they had both succumbed. She hadn't forgotten his kiss, sweet and wild, that had nearly brought her to her knees.

She flushed, guilt sweeping over her. A married woman could not indulge in such thoughts. She knew her duty, both to her husband and to God. Vows now bound her and Conaire; vows that she intended to keep, no matter the difficulty.

Conaire. The flush deepened as she remembered the intimacy they shared the night before. From the very first night, passion had flared between them, surprising them both. But still she struggled to understand her husband. At the wedding, he spoke his vows without looking at her, and during the days as they travelled to Dál Riata, he held himself with a cold aloofness that made her think she displeased him. But at night, when they were alone, he treated her with unexpected tenderness. Though he spoke few words, she sensed an openness in his touch that gave her hope that perhaps she could win his affection. She sighed. It was also possible that he would tire of her quickly and look elsewhere for the pleasures found in the marriage bed.

Conaire was not the only one she needed to win over. From the moment she arrived, Elatha, the widow of Conaire's father, had shown her no regard. Equally clear was the hostility in the Fey woman's manner towards Conaire himself.

It was not Conaire, but Tynan, her husband's most trusted warrior and friend, who had helped her understand Elatha. Tynan was a Sensitive, and he had been a welcome companion on the long days of travel. He had answered her questions about her new home, filling the silence that stretched between her and her new husband.

Tynan told her that Conaire's uncle had fostered him at his holding some ten miles away from Loch Glashan. Conaire had gone there when he was but four years old. His mother had died giving birth to him, and his father had blamed the boy for her death, for he had loved his wife dearly. Once Elatha became Lady of the *crannog,* she had not been eager for Conaire's return, preferring to have her husband to herself. His death, and Conaire's marriage, had brought Conaire back to take his rightful place. A place Elatha was loath to give up.

Aside from Elatha, the people seemed cautious of Conaire, but not overtly hostile. Her husband would have to prove himself an able leader to win their hearts. From what she had seen of him so far, Nona believed he would. His men obviously respected him, which was a good sign.

She wished she could speak of these things to Conaire. As his wife, she could help smooth the way between him and his people. But he had not given her any opportunity to do so. On their journey, he left her and Celyn to keep each other company while he rode with his men. In truth, he had shown more attention to his wolfhound, Liath, than to her. Since they had arrived, he left her to get settled as best she could. They had only been alone at night, and then he was not interested in talking. Except for two nights ago, when he had brought up Nectan and the difficulties he faced with Strang, and almost in passing had mentioned that he had met Thomas at a Gathering before he came to Bebbanburg.

Which had opened up many questions in her mind, but she did not ask them, for at that moment he kissed her fiercely and all thoughts fled. Afterwards, wrapped in his arms, she was reluctant to break the fragile peace between them.

The door opened and her father exited the house, a welcome distraction from her thoughts. "Ah, *fy ngeneth*. Here you are," Albanwyr said, smiling. He settled beside her on the bench.

She smiled back. His calm acceptance of missing the wedding had mollified her regret that he could not be there. He understood she had no choice. Their message announcing their marriage had not reached Gwynedd before he left, so he was at Conaire's holding to greet them when they arrived. He and Celyn brought a touch of warmth she sorely needed in this new place, even with the worries she had about her father discovering that Celyn knew about the Fey. She had yet to find the courage to disclose that news.

So far, Celyn's normal reticence had been a strong enough shield to hide his reaction from her father. Hope had blossomed that she would not have to confess to her father after all, for he planned to leave this day to meet with Ferchar, and go from there back to Gwynedd. It was cowardly of her to feel so relieved that she could avoid the conversation. All the same, if she could put it off, she was happy to do so.

She set aside her tangled thoughts and smiled at him. "Good morn, Father."

He squinted out at the grey and misty landscape and grunted. "Good for fish, perhaps." He turned to her, his eyes keen. "Would you take a walk with me?"

"Of course." She stood and picked up the basket she had set at her feet. "You can accompany me as I collect the eggs."

As they headed towards the barn where the chickens sheltered overnight, he took her arm companionably. "Ah, 'tis good to have a moment alone with you." He looked at her, his face solemn. "Truly, you are well?"

It was not an idle question. She bit back the automatic assent that had risen to her lips. She sighed. "I hope to be. But as for now, I am—" She wanted to say *homesick,* but supplied another word. "Unsettled." She saw the flash of worry in her father's eyes and spoke again before he could. "As is my husband. You have seen it, too, I am sure. He is now lord of the holding, but the people here seem wary of him."

Albanwyr grunted. "Aye. Well, 'tis not surprising, perhaps. He was here but a few months before he journeyed to Bebbanburg. They don't know him."

"No. And his father's wife resents him. That much is clear."

Her father nodded. "Aye, I have seen it." He sighed. "Conaire is a good man, from all accounts. He'll make a place here, for him and for you. Give him time."

She smiled faintly. "Aye, Father." She shook off her gloomy thoughts. "I will be fine, truly. You must not worry."

His lips twisted in a slight smile that didn't quite reach his eyes, but he shook his head. "As to your husband, *fy ngeneth,* I am not worried. 'Tis another matter that brings me concern."

A young woman approached, carrying a bucket of water, preventing Nona from asking her father what he meant. But a quick glance at him as the woman passed showed her the depth of his concern. His face was solemn, his eyes worried.

Ice touched her. *Now what?*

CHAPTER 30

FOUND OUT

Before Albanwyr could speak, another person approached. A young girl, this time, smiling shyly at Nona as she slipped past them and into the barn, likely on the same task as them.

Albanwyr's lips tightened. "I wish to speak without ears to hear," he said in a low voice.

Fey business, then. Had Celyn gone against her wishes and revealed what he knew? She forced down the spike of fear that pierced her. Her father would be much more upset if that was the case.

Aye," she replied and steered them towards the path leading to the causeway that connected the *crannog* to the shore. Nona looked up at him, steeling herself. "Is there something wrong?"

Her father grunted. "Wrong? I am not sure. You can tell me. I have heard of the unrest in Nectan's Court, and of the wilding Traveller. And of the other one in Eoforwic, who has been wooing Raegenold's Court with some foolish scheme."

She let out a breath. Bad enough, but she didn't have to speak of Celyn just yet. "Not just foolish. Dangerous."

Albanwyr shot her a skeptical look and lapsed into silence. They reached the midpoint of the causeway, and he stopped, looking out over the loch. The misty rain obscured the far shore, but the landscape held a quiet beauty all the same. He turned to her. "What have you to say of this wilding Traveller? The tales we have heard have brought much alarm."

She forced back the memory of their kiss for the second time that morning and strove for a casual tone. "When he first came to Bebbanburg, he had little knowledge of the ways of the Fey. I gave him some guidance until he pledged to the Seelie Court and Nectan gave him a Teacher." She sighed. "There has been much that happened since I left Gwynedd, but I have never been in any danger."

His face darkened. "Never—" He sputtered and then gathered himself. "A Fey facing the Ordeal, rumours of the Undying in the Unseelie Court, the Wild Hunt riding down yet another Traveller, who turns out to be the wilding's father. All the tales centre around this wilding. And, they say, a Fey Healer from Gwynedd has been giving him aid. Any one of those hold great danger, my daughter, and yet you were involved in all of them, or so I hear. Are the tales wrong, then?"

She lifted her chin, reminding herself she was a married woman and not a small child in her father's house. "Thomas has pledged to Nectan. This Wulfram, the Traveller in Eoforwic, is dangerous. He must be stopped. I have only acted at the behest of our king, who also sees the danger."

Albanwyr raised an eyebrow. "Does he indeed? Then why has he released the wilding from his pledge to his Court?"

Nona stared at him, the blood draining from her face. "What? I have not heard thus." She gathered herself. "Wulfram's Unseelies are spreading many lies about Thomas, to cause trouble both in Bernicia and amongst the Seelies. It was likely—"

Her father cut her off. "I heard it from your husband."

"What?" Nona choked out again. *Conaire?* "When did he tell you this?"

Albanwyr looked apologetic. "I am sorry. I thought you knew. He told me last night."

Nona's thoughts whirled, trying to come up with a response. How had Conaire found this out? And why hadn't he told her? "When did this happen?"

Albanwyr shrugged one shoulder. "A few weeks ago, it seems, but I am not sure."

"He left Bebbanburg before Conaire arrived. With Nectan," Nona said, trying to think it through. "Nectan planned to take him to his holding at Dún Duirn and hold a Gathering there."

Albanwyr opened his mouth to reply, but closed it again as Bronwyn approached.

Nona managed a smile as her maidservant stopped in front of them. Like Celyn and Tynan, Bronwyn was a Sensitive, but Nona was careful not to share too many details of the Fey with her. Too dangerous for them both.

"My lady, your husband has need of you and your father. He sent me to find you when I went out to fetch the bread."

"Ah. Thank you, Bronwyn." She handed her maidservant the basket she carried. "You might as well get the eggs, too."

Bronwyn dipped her head, accepting the basket, and then turned and went back towards the *crannog*.

Once she was out of earshot, Nona rounded on her father. But before she could speak, he held up a hand.

"I will tell you what I have heard." He took her arm again as they walked back over the causeway. "Strang, son of Siric, is seeking to wrest the throne from Nectan, as I am sure you have heard." He glanced at her, and at her nod, he continued. "He tells the Court that Nectan's embrace of this wilding is foolish at best and dangerous at worst. As you said, Nectan Called for a Gathering at Dún Duirn. The word is that Strang planned a Charge that night."

Ice pierced her. "He planned to take the throne that night? Not to wait until Solstice?"

Albanwyr shrugged slightly. "That is being said. But because Nectan released the wilding, he cut Strang's ambition at the knees. He will have to wait until Solstice now, as is proper."

Dismay filled her at her father's words. "But what has happened to Thomas? Where did he go?"

Her father shrugged again. "I do not know."

Nona bit back her frustration at the answer, but it only fed the anger that grew as they approached the house. Why had her husband kept this from her?

As they entered the house, they found Conaire alone, studying a scroll spread out on the table. He gestured at them to sit and carefully rolled the scroll up, storing it on a shelf along the wall, and sat down across from them. "Lord Albanwyr, I have decided that I and my lady wife will accompany ye today when ye go to visit Ferchar at Dún Add. He wished me to bring him news of Bernicia when I got back, so he did. Now seems as good a time as any."

"You did not think to ask me of this?" Nona couldn't help the edge of anger in her voice.

Conaire raised an eyebrow. "Ye dinna wish to go?"

"Of course. That is not the point."

He stared at her a moment, his eyes narrowing. "Ah. Your father must have told ye the news of the wildin'."

"Why did you not tell me yourself?"

Conaire eyed her, anger flashing in his eyes. "I wondered perhaps if ye might tell me."

"I don't know what you mean." Her cold voice hid the fear that spiked through her. What was this about?

His jaw clenched, but he ignored her and turned to her father. "I told ye I attended a Gathering before I came to Bebbanburg. And that I met this wildin' who has set the tongues of the Court afire. I heard him speak of Wulfram, the Traveller in Eoforwic. Tell me, my lord, is the Court of the Southern Seelies aware of this Wulfram?"

"We have heard some tales. There seems much unrest in the Fey Courts of the North, Seelie and Unseelie alike."

"Aye." Conaire's gaze shifted to Nona. "Nectan told me of the aid ye ha' given to the wildin', this son of Matthew of Dál Riata, the Traveller who is now dead. The wildin' seems to know much of this Wulfram's scheme. And it seems ye knew him better than most. I wonder why ye did not know that Nectan ha' released him."

She drew back. "How would I know? I have no—" The words choked off as a sudden realization froze her blood.

Better than most. The words echoed through her mind, explaining Conaire's anger, his coldness towards her.

Somehow, in his interaction with Thomas at the Gathering, Conaire had gleaned the attraction that had flared between them.

God help her, but he had found her out.

Chapter 31

We Cannot Forget

Nona swallowed back her panic. She had done nothing wrong. She glanced at her father, who looked at her through narrowed eyes. She would much prefer to have this conversation with her husband without her father's presence. Why had Conaire only brought it up now?

"I have had no contact with Thomas since I left Bebbanburg." She forced her voice to stay level. "Nectan must have had no choice but to release him because of Strang's ambitions. Whatever the cause, this is ill news. 'Tis likely Wulfram had a hand in it."

Nona braced herself for Conaire's accusations, but to her relief, he merely waved a hand.

"Strang ha' held ambitions for the throne since Nectan gained it. Long before this Wulfram was known."

"Yes. But separating Thomas from the Seelie Court will only help Wulfram."

"Help him do what?" Her father looked skeptical. He looked between the two of them. "I have only heard warnings and vague murmurs of disaster."

"Wulfram means to interfere in the affairs of Deira and Bernicia. He seeks to change events now in order to alter the future. He says the Fey are much diminished in his time, but that he can change that by what he does now." She grimaced. "He wishes to take Oswy off his throne and to rid Bernicia of the monks."

"The monks?" Her father frowned.

"Yes. It seems he fears their influence over the Fey in the future." She waved a hand at their skeptical looks. "As to that, only God knows. What *I* know is that here, now, Wulfram is dangerous. He has called an Undying and with it has Bound Godric, the Unseelie gleeman Traveller, to his will. That I have seen myself. Wulfram seeks ill, I am certain."

A muscle in Conaire's jaw tightened. "So our king ha' said." He studied her through narrowed eyes for a moment and then turned to her father. "An Unseelie

Fey lurks at Ferchar's Court. Grith ap Ethernan, whom they call Ulchabhán. A Healer. Kin to Ferchar, so he is. It seems he ha' gained the king's ear. No doubt Raegenold uses him as his mouthpiece when he sees the need."

"Do you have any influence with Ferchar?" Albanwyr asked. "Perhaps we can find out what this Ulchabhán tells him."

Conaire grimaced slightly and shook his head. "My uncle was close with Domnall, but now that Ferchar has gained the throne I ha' no standing at Dún Add. Ferchar hails from the Cenél Comgaill and is no friend o' Cenél nGabrain. My father extended a hand towards Ferchar, so I heard, but I dinna know how far he got."

"Wulfram has been banished from the Unseelie Court, but there are some Unseelies who follow him, all the same. It would be good to know if Ferchar's counsellor is one of those," Nona mused.

"Aye. It would aid Nectan to know if he speaks Raegenold's words or Wulfram's in Ferchar's ears." Conaire's fist clenched, and he shook his head, looking over at Albanwyr. "Do ye know anything about this Ulchabhán?"

Albanwyr shook his head. "Only what you have said: that an Unseelie Pict has wormed his way into Dál Riata's Court."

"Ach." Frustration flashed over Conaire's face. "I asked our king about him, but Nectan doesna know him. Ulchabhán married into Cenél Comgaill many years ago." He paused, thinking. "Ferchar was no friend of Domnall, and he ha' no ties with the *athelings* of Bernicia as Domnall did. The Comgaill will be pressing him to break with Oswy." He straightened, his jaw hardening. "So, as I said, me wife and I will go wi' ye to Dún Add. We may see where Ferchar seeks to lead Dál Riata. And I wish to meet this Ulchabhán. Perhaps between us, we will get a sense of where his loyalties lie."

Albanwyr nodded. "As to that, it is a good idea, my Lord Conaire. We will have to be wary, though, of Celyn. We will have to speak to Ulchabhán without him."

Dread washed over Nona. How had she ever thought she could avoid this? She heaved a breath, her stomach knotting. "As to that, there is one thing more. While I was at Bebbanburg, Celyn found out about us. I was forced to tell him I am of the Fey, and you both, as well. He sees all of us now."

Both men jumped up from their seats as if bees had stung them, looking down at her in shock. Albanwyr was the first to recover. "Knows of us? You have told him—?" He collected himself with an effort. "Forced by whom?"

Too late, she saw her error. She stood, her thoughts racing, her hands twisting together to keep them from trembling as she met her father's glowering gaze. She had asked Celyn not to speak of this until she told her father, but now she wished she had let him break the news. *Mother Mary, aid me.* "Not forced, exactly. But I had no choice. Thomas had told him of us."

"The wildin' *told* him—"

Nona ignored her husband's choked exclamation and focussed on her father. "Celyn told you he and Thomas tracked down the Saxon who slew his family. They found him in a Wild Place, in a *coed*. But Celyn would never have found him except for Thomas. And Thomas could only lead him through the *coed* using Fey power. He had to tell Celyn that he was Fey." Her mouth went dry at her father's thunderous expression, and she hurriedly continued. "He didn't understand the risks of it. We cannot forget that he is a wilding."

"Oh, I dinna forget, never fear," Conaire muttered, his eyes burnished silver.

Shock, fear, and anger chased over Albanwyr's face. Reluctant sympathy tugged at Nona. She must have looked the same when Thomas told her what he had done. "Please, Father. The thing is done. Celyn has accepted it. We must protect him as best we can, that is all."

Her father's eyes narrowed, but he shook his head, controlling himself with an effort. "We will speak of this later," he snapped at her and turned to Conaire. "Celyn is a man of honour. You need not fear him."

But Conaire ignored him. His silver eyes focussed upon Nona. "Ye tell us this only now? I wonder how many other secrets ye keep from me, so I do." He clamped his jaw shut against further words. With a hard glare at both of them, he pushed between them, Liath at his heels as he left, shutting the door with a rattle behind him.

Albanwyr swung to her, his eyes flashing. "Are you mad, daughter?"

She swallowed and sat down again. "Sit, please," she said, gesturing at the seat across from her. "I will explain."

He sat, his eyes hard. "Speak."

Nona took a deep breath and gave him a quick summary of all that had transpired since she had arrived at Bebbanburg, leaving out only the attraction that had grown between her and Thomas.

When she finished, her father regarded her for a long time in silence, his hands steepled under his chin in a look of concentration she knew so well. She waited in an agony of tension for him to speak.

Finally, he sighed and placed his hands on the table. "I sent you to Bebbanburg for safety. But it seems you faced more danger there than at home."

Her tension dissolved as she saw the exasperated affection in his eyes. She shook her head. Her entanglement with the Unseelie Court of the South that had led her to her journey to Bebbanburg seemed so long ago that she had almost forgotten it. "I have never been in any real danger."

His eyebrows raised. "No? Finding a wilding? Almost taken by the Redcap? Facing the Wild Hunt?" He let out an exasperated breath. "Conaire was likely not expecting a wife as headstrong as you." He eyed her, and it was all she could do not to squirm under his keen, hawk-like scrutiny. "All of this has come between the two of you, I fear."

Nona flushed and shook her head. She could hardly tell him she and her husband had hardly spoken. And now she knew why Conaire had rebuffed her attempts at conversation. He knew how Thomas felt about her. How she felt about Thomas. She pushed aside her dread at the thought. "We will be fine. It is just—" She broke off and tried again. "How was it between you and my mother when you first wed?"

He smiled faintly. "Ah, as to that, her beauty captured me the moment I saw her." His smile faded. "You are much like her. I had hoped your husband would feel the same." He shook his head. "I mourn your mother every day, but now I especially feel her loss. I have not the words that she would have for you."

She swallowed down the lump in her throat. "Conaire and I will make our own way." She spoke with more firmness than she felt. "Do not worry about me, father."

"Ah, that is impossible, *fy ngeneth.* 'Tis a father's lot to worry." He sighed. "I will always come if you need me."

Tears pricked her eyes. "Of course."

"Your husband is a good man. You will win him over, I am sure. Give him time."

She nodded, wishing she had her father's certainty.

He squeezed her hands once and let them go, rising from the table. "And so I must speak with Celyn, it seems." A cloud covered his face. He sighed, closing his eyes briefly. He opened them and looked down at her. "I will see you soon."

She nodded again, distracted by her thoughts as he turned and left.

Albanwyr, as Eagleclan, shared the focus and laser-sharp attention of the birds of prey. But her husband was Wolfclan, valuing loyalty over all. Despair filled her. She had broken his trust before she even met him. How could she ever mend that break? Her thoughts skipped again to the last time she had seen Thomas, the anguish in his face as she told him of Conaire's imminent arrival. If she had told Thomas then that she would leave Bebbanburg with him, he would have welcomed her presence. Part of her wished she had, truth be told.

She shook her head, angry at the thought. He was a Traveller. He intended to go back to his own time. That had not changed. And she had her duty to her father, her family, and the Seelie Fey of the South. She was married now. She had to make the best of it.

But still, Thomas' face haunted her. She closed her eyes, grief piercing her. This would not do. *Thomas. I must let you go. God calls us down different paths. I cannot hold on to you and move forward on the way set before me.* In her mind's eye, she lifted a hand to his face, just as she had done before, and, just as before, he caught her hand in his. *I must let you go,* she said to him again.

She opened her eyes and dashed the tears from them, letting out a breath and setting aside her tangled feelings with an effort. The past was done. Her task now was straightforward: to mend the rift between her and Conaire, and better now than later.

Before she lost her courage.

CHAPTER 32

MORE THAN STRANGERS

Nona found Conaire in the hall, speaking with Elatha. She faltered as she spotted the disagreeable older woman, but then composed herself and kept going. She was the lady of the holding now, whether the wife of her husband's father liked her or not.

As she approached, the woman broke off what she was saying to Conaire and turned to her, one eyebrow arched, her usual expression of cool disdain on her face. Nona's skin pricked, reminding her that this woman was a powerful Fey. Her main Gifting was in Glamour, but as with many who shared that Gift, she was also a powerful Speaker.

Nona forced herself to speak civilly. "Greetings, my lady."

Elatha nodded and turned back to Conaire, dismissing her. "I say again, wait. Your father would not want the good he did in building his ties with Ferchar to be undone by one ill-timed visit. We Fey must not be too eager to dance to the human's songs."

Lecturing him like a child. Nona's ire rose at the woman's condescending tone.

"I will keep that in mind when I speak with him, my lady," Conaire said, his voice cool but his jaw set in a stubborn line.

Elatha's eyes narrowed. She turned to Nona. "Gwynedd would prefer that Dál Riata frees itself from Bernicia's embrace, I am sure. Your husband would do well to remember that." She raked her gaze over Nona's form. "As would you."

"As to that, I will trust my husband's judgement in the matter, my lady." Nona ignored the glint of anger in Elatha's eyes and continued. "I came to speak to Lord Conaire. Please excuse us."

Elatha's nostrils flared, but she spun on her heel and stalked away, her back rigid.

Conaire's lips pressed together as he watched her depart. He turned to Nona. "We must prepare for the journey to Dún Add," he said before she could speak. "Gather what ye need. We will leave by noon."

He turned, but Nona put a hand on his arm to halt him. He turned back, impatient.

Nona ignored his scowl. "I must speak with you." She glanced around the hall, where the slaves replaced soiled rushes on the floor and a knot of men sat at a table, engaged in a lively conversation. "Alone. Would you walk with me?"

He let out a sigh but took her arm and led her outside. He marched her towards the pastures, and when they reached the fence, Conaire turned to her. "There is no much time. Speak and be on your way." Liath flattened her ears at his tone and looked up at Conaire, but he ignored her, his gaze hard as he glared at Nona.

Stung, Nona drew herself up but spoke in a mild tone. "I am your wife. I ask that you not order me around like a slave." She paused, collecting her thoughts. "There are things to discuss. Things you have avoided ere now," she added. Conaire's flush emboldened her. "And as to that, I will not tiptoe around my husband, fearing his outburst. Please speak plainly, and I will do the same."

"I dinna think ye want that, wife."

"I say what I mean," she said, exasperated, and heaved a breath, her heart pounding. This was not the best time for this conversation. But if not now, when? "I wish to speak of Thomas."

Anger flushed Conaire's face. He stiffened, but he did not speak.

He wouldn't make this easy for her, then. Nona pressed her hands against her skirt, willing them not to tremble. *I have done nothing wrong.* "You accused me of keeping secrets from you. But you give me no encouragement to speak to you. Of Celyn or Thomas or of anything else. You spent the time on our journey here surrounded by your men, and it is the same since our wedding. If it were not that you share my bed, I would think that you regret our marriage."

His eyes flashed. "I will no be tied to my wife's strings and led around like a puppy."

"Don't be ridiculous," she said through her teeth. "I do not ask for that. But we could be more than strangers to each other. 'Tis what I wish." She searched his face for a glimmering of fellow-feeling, but seeing none, she gathered her courage and continued. She may as well find out where she stood. "Thomas was at Bebbanburg when I arrived last fall. He had little knowledge of the Fey. Indeed, he had Travelled here without even knowing that he was Fey. It was only by God's grace that Celyn found him right after he Crossed." Fear touched her again at the memory of Thomas' tale. What had it been like to jump from one time to another without knowing what had happened, or why? She pushed the thought away and continued. "I told you that Celyn is a Sensitive. He saw the Undying that chased Thomas here. He had already half-believed Thomas to be one of the Fey when

Thomas told him. 'Twas no stretch for him to accept it. But that left me no choice but to tell him of me. You know how it goes with the Sensitives. Once they see one of us as we are, they know us all."

Conaire's jaw bunched. But he remained silent.

Emboldened, Nona continued. "Thomas and Celyn met Godric as they journeyed to Bebbanburg. From what Thomas said, I suspected the harper was an Unseelie, up to their usual tricks. By God's good mercies, Celyn stopped Thomas from rejoining Godric. The harper would have taken him straight to Wulfram." Conaire frowned, and Nona waved a hand. "But never mind that. I will tell you all of what conspired in Bebbanburg between then and now, if you have not heard it. You've said you met Thomas at the Gathering and heard his story, did you not?"

But Conaire ignored her question. His eyes flashed. "All? Indeed, wife, I am most interested in all that happened."

"If you wish to insult me, then at least use my name, *husband*," Nona snapped in reply before she could stop herself. She let out a breath, seeking calm. "Tell me what happened between you and Thomas at that Gathering. For something did."

Conaire's lips thinned. "'Tis more what happened between ye and the wildin' that is the point." Liath whined in the sudden silence, hushed by a look from Conaire. He looked back at Nona, silver fire edging his eyes, his Fey power rising on the heels of his ire. "It was a surprise, so it was, to hear the Call to a Gatherin' as I came to Bebbanburg. But a welcome surprise. I thought ye might be there, and looked forward to seeing my betrothed at last, in the company of the Fey. But instead, our king introduced the wildin' Fey I ha' heard about. Thomas of Bebbanburg. Nectan urged him to play a Gatherin' song for us."

A Gathering song. A song that laid bare a Fey to those Gathered. "I see."

"Do ye now?" His lips twisted. "Imagine hearing a song of love, beautiful and haunting, so it was, and having the slow dawnin' that it is about your own betrothed. I told myself not to be hasty, but I had a word wi' him afterwards and he couldna deny it. It saw it in his face. He loves ye. And I canna help but wonder, so I do, if ye feel the same."

His words were clipped and angry, but for a moment Nona saw fear flash in his eyes, and it stopped the hot words that wanted to spill out. She understood his fear. His mother died birthing him and his father abandoned him. And now he was afraid she would abandon him, too.

Her heart softened, and she reached up to touch his cheek. His jaw bunched, and she dropped her hand. "Conaire. Listen well. I will not deny that Thomas was drawn to me." She forced the words out, her heart pounding. "And I to him. But I always knew my life was here. And he knew it, too. I am here, now, married to you. I have sworn vows to you I intend to keep. If I had not, I would not be here." Her mouth was dry, but she forced out what she wanted to say. "You must intend to keep them, too, for after that Gathering you could have returned to Dál Riata and sent word to my father to break the betrothal. Yet you continued on to Bebbanburg."

Another flash through his eyes. Guilt, this time. He had considered it. The thought pierced her.

"'Tis no that easy, and ye know it well." He looked out at the pasture. When he turned back to her, the cool distance had returned to his eyes. "I ha' told the wildin' to keep away from me and mine. I will tell ye the same, so I will. Ye will have no contact wi' him." He spun away from the fence and stalked away from her.

Liath gave her an almost apologetic look and loped after Conaire.

Nona let out a trembling breath. *God, help us.* She forced her scattered thoughts into order. She could think on their conversation later. It was a beginning, at least. For now, she must get ready for the upcoming visit to Dún Add. She would prove her loyalty to her husband and set aside all thoughts of Thomas.

"My lady?"

Bronwyn's voice caused her to turn. Her maidservant joined her at the fence. She had a full basket of eggs hanging from her arm, a fresh loaf of bread balanced on top. "I saw your husband with thunder in his face." Her eyes searched Nona's. "What is it, then?"

Nona forced a smile. "I am well, never fear."

"Hmm."

Bronwyn's skeptical look was one Nona had seen a thousand times. She sighed, her shoulders slumping. "He is angry at me," she admitted. "He thinks that Thomas and I—" she waved her hand. Bronwyn knew most of what had transpired between her and Thomas, except for the kiss, although she knew Bronwyn half-suspected something like that had happened.

Bronwyn's eyebrows raised high. "You told him?"

"Of course not. He met Thomas on the way to Bebbanburg. They spoke about me."

"Spoke—" Bronwyn sputtered, alarm on her face. "That must have been interesting."

Nona couldn't help a snort. "Yes, I suppose it was, the two of them circling each other like dogs fighting over a bone."

Bronwyn snorted too, a rueful smile lifting her lips.

Their eyes met, and suddenly they both laughed.

But the memory of Conaire's cool manner towards her returned, and her laughter faded. Would anything she say to him make a difference? She sighed. "Nothing of significance happened between us. I've told you that. But I am not sure I can convince my husband."

Bronwyn pulled her into a hug, the basket bumping against Nona's back. "Never mind then, my lady. Give him time. Think you, Master Thomas will soon leave us. You have said so yourself, that he plans to return to his home in Byzantium."

Leave. A pang went through her. She pulled herself away, dashing the tears from her eyes with her fingers. "Yes, of course."

Bronwyn linked her arm in Nona's. "Lord Celyn has said ye are going to Dún Add with him and your father. Ye had best get ready."

"You can come too, if you wish."

Bronwyn shook her head, grimacing. "Nay, my monthly courses have come. If you please, my lady, I will stay here. Lord Celyn said you would not be gone long."

"I will leave you a draught for your pains, if you like."

Bronwyn nodded. "Thank you, my lady."

They walked in companionable silence. As much as Nona appreciated her friend, she longed for someone with whom she could share all parts of her life. Which was all the more reason for her and Conaire to come to an understanding. She could only pray it would come in time.

Hir yw pop ymaros. Her aunty used to say that when Nona grew impatient. *All waiting is long.* And unavoidable. She had no alternative but to wait. For Conaire to get over his anger, for the shape of Wulfram's plot to be revealed.

But in the meantime, she did not have to be idle. Perhaps their journey would serve to further both those aims.

CHAPTER 33

DÚN ADD

They travelled to Dún Add by boat down the River Add as the fenland around the fortress was difficult to traverse by foot or horse, especially in the spring. The river wound its way right to the Dál Riatan stronghold, making it the better method of travel. After a couple of hours on the river, the rocky outcrop upon which the fortress was located was close enough for Nona to see details.

It was impressive. Four levels of stone walls snaked around it in a spiral, concluding in an enclosure at the very top. Smoke rose from the small walled settlement at the bottom of the outcrop, and from the buildings at the top, also hidden behind a stone wall. With the surrounding fens on the landward side and the sea loch on the other, it would be difficult to conquer.

At the base of the fortress, a small wooden pier jutted out into the river, and they fastened their boats there. A pathway led to the base of the hill where two armed guards stood by a wooden gate built into the stone walls that enclosed the bottom of the fortress. They had sent word of their coming, so the guards were prepared to greet them.

"Hail, lords of Gwynedd and Bernicia," one of them said. "Our king, Ferchar mac Connaid, brings greetings, so he does, and asks that ye join him in the hall." He gestured at the other guard. "Cellach will lead the way."

They followed Cellach through the gates and began climbing up the path that snaked to the summit, intersecting through the walls. Seagulls and other ocean birds wheeled above, their cries loud and piercing.

It was not an easy path. The steep pitch and the rocky boulders they had to navigate around meant she needed Conaire's help more than once to continue. The wind snatched at her skirts and played with her head covering, and her hair came out from under it under its assault. Dark clouds scudded towards them from the west, blowing in over the sea loch.

The path ended with a narrow passageway hewn through massive boulders that led to an imposing gate. Strong stone walls stretched out from either side of the gate, from the top of which a blue and white banner flapped in the sea breeze, displaying an embroidered golden boar. A wooden platform running along the top of the inside of the walls gave the guards a bird's-eye view of any who approached the fortress.

Dún Add was imposing from the outside, and once they passed through the gate, the impression of strength and wealth only increased. To the right of the gate, a handful of buildings clustered against the massive wall. To the left, a larger building that Nona recognized as a metalworker's workshop snuggled up against the corner of the wall, which continued on past it towards the highest part of the outcrop. A cookhouse leaned against the wall further towards the top.

At the very top, the hall of the kings of Dál Riata perched like an eagle overlooking its domain. The Dál Riatan boar fluttered on a banner on a pole fixed over its massive carved doors. In front of the hall, just off to the right, a platform of raised rock marked the site where the Dál Riatan kings pledged their oaths to God and their people. Nona had heard it said that St. Columba himself was present when the great Dál Riatan king, Áedán mac Gabráin, took the crown in this very place. A footprint carved in the rock was where a newly crowned king placed his foot and swore allegiance to the land and its people.

The legend said the hero Fionn mac Cumhaill had left the rocky footprint behind while leaping away from his enemies. Fionn was not only a hero to the humans but to the Fey as well. In Fey tales, he was a king of the Seelie Fey of the North who had a strong Gifting of Glamour and Speaking.

Dál Riata's reputation as a powerful kingdom had been tarnished under the hapless Domnall Brecc. But as Nona looked around the prosperous fortress, she sensed they were biding their time before showing their might again.

To the right of the gate they had just entered, steps led up to the platform that ran along the length of the wall at the top. Conaire gestured to the steps. "Come," he said. He led the way up and the rest followed, eager to see the view.

They were not disappointed. A vast expanse met their eyes. To the east, the River Add wound its way through the fenlands, called the Moine Móhr in the Dál Riatan tongue. Mountains rose beyond the trees that edged the Móhr. To the west, the waters of the sea loch tossed in the stiffening wind. An impressive number of ships rode at anchor in the loch, a reminder of Dál Riata's sea-faring strength. Far above, her father's falcon screeched as he soared above them, catching the updrafts from the sea breeze that blew against them. She took in a deep breath of the brisk salty air and allowed her Fey power to enhance her senses.

Immediately the weight of time pressed on her, a sense of the generations of people who had lived here with their struggles, griefs, and joys. Their fierce pride and confident security in the fortress' strength and in its people flooded through her. The rugged land expected much of those who lived here. But it rewarded them for their efforts and gave them beauty as a bulwark against the harshness of life.

She closed her eyes, revelling in the tingle of power as it swept through her before letting it go. She opened her eyes to see Conaire looking at her, but he turned away to speak to her father. But not before she had seen a brief spark in his eyes, the same spark of desire that lit them at night when they were alone. She ducked her head, hiding her heated cheeks.

"Come," the guard said, gesturing at the hall. "Our king awaits ye, so he does."

Even as he spoke, the threatened rain fell. They hurried down from the platform and across the grassy expanse to get to the welcome shelter of the hall.

Two large fires blazed inside, and a couple of smaller ones lined the walls. Tapestries, shields, spears, and other weapons and finery hung from the walls. Expertly carved designs swirled over the posts which held up the roof. Gold, bronze, and silver glittered from the tapestries and weapons. Nona had hardly seen such abundance, not even in Bernicia's hall. A wealthy kingdom, indeed. No wonder Oswy wanted a share of its wealth.

The hall was full. They wound their way through the crowd to where Ferchar mac Connaid sat on a raised platform at the end of the hall, surrounded by his trusted war band. Curious gazes followed them, but on the whole, the people seemed friendly enough.

As they approached, Ferchar stood, a faint smile on his face. Dál Riata's king was tall and bulky, wearing a blue tunic edged with silver that strained at the front to encompass his stomach. His small black eyes almost disappeared into deep-set eye sockets, and black hair poked up from under the thin gold band he wore that marked him as king.

He reminded Nona of the boar that she had seen on the banner: large and hairy—and noting the cunning that flashed in his eyes as his gaze raked over them, dangerous.

She spotted Grith, Ferchar's Fey counsellor, right away. Even without the tingle of Fey power that swept over her when she saw him, his large, wide-set eyes and spiky grey hair showed why others called him Ulchabhán, the Owl. A slight narrowing of his eyes was the only sign that he recognized the Fey among their group.

The guard stopped in front of the king. "My Lord King Ferchar, I give ye Albanwyr ap Bledri of Gwynedd, and Celyn ap Wynn of Bebbanburg. They come with the Lord Conaire mac Alpin."

The king spread his arms. "I bid you welcome, my lords." Ferchar's voice was high and thin, in stark contrast to his form.

"Thank you, my lord," Albanwyr said, inclining his head in respect. "My lord king, Cadwallon, bids me to bring you greetings on his behalf."

Celyn bowed his head as Ferchar turned his gaze to him. "And I bring the same from my lord king, Oswy of Bernicia, foster-son of Dál Riata."

Celyn spoke the tongue of the Dál Riatans better than Nona, who, although she had some knowledge of it, still stumbled over her words. Celyn had spent some time with the monks on the holy isle of Hii after he left his brother's side and had gained fluency in the tongue. But his words still held traces of his homeland. It was no mistaking that he did not hail from Bernicia.

As Ferchar noted. His eyes narrowed. "Ah. Tales ha' reached us of this Celyn ap Wynn who forsook Gwynedd to take root in Bebbanburg's hall."

Celyn stiffened, but before he could speak, Albanwyr smiled. "Ah, my lord, as to that, Celyn and I are kin, and a more worthy man I do not know. I am proud to stand with him, no matter the differences in our loyalties."

Conaire stepped up beside Celyn. "My Lord King Ferchar, the Lord Albanwyr and the Lord Celyn ha' both come to Dál Riata to celebrate my wedding to the Lady Nona, daughter of Lord Albanwyr." His smile didn't reach his eyes. Conaire was as disturbed as she was by Ferchar's discourtesy. "I ha' come with them to present to ye Lady Nona of Gwynedd, my wife."

He gestured at her, and Nona sank down in a curtsey. "My lord king."

Ferchar's gaze swept over her, and he turned to Conaire. "A fortunate match indeed, Lord Conaire. Our ties with Gwynedd serve us well, so they do. Rise, my lady. Ye are welcome here." His gaze shifted back to Celyn and barked a short laugh. "Ach, dinna fret, Lord Celyn. Everyone who comes in friendship is welcome in Dún Add. I am eager to hear your news about Oswy of Bernicia, so I am. And I will have words for ye to take back to Bebbanburg as well."

Although Ferchar's mouth stretched in a smile, Nona heard menace under those words. Judging by Conaire's expression, so did he.

But Celyn ignored the subtle threat. "As to that, Oswy will be glad to know how ye fare as king."

Ferchar snorted. "Indeed, I am sure he will."

"My lord king, we await your word on the feasting. All is ready," the Owl said, interjecting.

Ferchar held his gaze on Celyn a moment longer, then turned to his counsellor. "Aye, of course. 'Tis time! Let us be friends at the table, together." He waved at the hall. "Come, my lords. Join me at the feast."

Nona followed Conaire, her stomach twisting in knots. There were undercurrents in this hall that could drown them all if they were not careful.

163

CHAPTER 34

STRANGE TALES

Nona thought Ferchar might join them right away, but in fact, it was much later before the king appeared by the table, with Ulchabhán lurking behind.

"Ah, my lords, I trust ye are well fed?" He looked from one to another, his small eyes glittering under his heavy brows.

"Of course, and we thank ye, my lord king," Conaire said.

"Good, good," Ferchar said, settling himself down on the bench beside Conaire, across from Celyn and Albanwyr. Ulchabhán sat down beside him. Ferchar glanced at his counsellor. "But perhaps we shouldna have been so free with our welcome, do ye no think, Ulchabhán? 'Tis better perhaps for the Lord Celyn to take a tale of Dál Riata's poverty rather than of our riches back to Bebbanburg, eh?"

Ulchabhán smiled thinly in response but did not reply.

Ferchar chortled as if he had spoken a funny joke and lifted the silver goblet he held in his hand, looking around for a slave. "Ale!"

A serving girl hurried over with a jug and poured into the king's goblet, and at his gesture, filled up the others' goblets as well. Ferchar took a drink and wiped his lips. He waved a hand. "Ach, forgive me, Lord Celyn. I canna seem to resist funnin' wi' ye. Take no notice of me foolishness. Truly, I am most eager to hear the news from Bernicia, so I am. How fares your king?"

"He looks forward to the summer, when he may meet with you in person."

Ferchar snorted. "Aye, I'm sure he does." All humour fled from his face as he leaned on his elbows towards Celyn, his eyes narrowing. "From what I hear, he will come wi' his hand out, seeking tribute."

Celyn's face was impassive. "As to that, he has not said such to me. But Dál Riata and Bernicia have close ties. Domnall Brecc was always Oswy's friend, and has shared of Dál Riata's bounty, as has Bernicia with Dál Riata."

Nona took a sip of her ale, seeking to look unconcerned, but her heart skipped a beat. She had heard from Tynan about the controversy the expected demand for tribute had sparked in Dál Riata.

"Aye, but Domnall is dead now, isn't he? Killed while fighting a battle on Oswy's behalf. Your king should have thought better of sending him against the Alt Clut in the middle of winter. I tried to counsel Domnall thus, but he didna listen." Ferchar leaned back and shrugged. "Much ha' changed. Oswald and Domnall both now haunt Heaven's halls. As I recall him, Oswy was ever in his brother's shadow. Time will tell whether he can step out from it and make his own path."

Although Ferchar's voice was mild, there was no mistaking the antagonistic undercurrent drifting below his words.

Ulchabhán spoke up. "Perhaps ye should ask the Lady Nona how things fare in Bernicia. From what I hear, she has been there for some time, awaiting the Lord Conaire."

Ferchar turned to her, his eyebrows raised. "Have ye now? So far away from Gwynedd?"

Her father came to her rescue. "Nona went to Bebbanburg to see Celyn when we heard he had been very ill last summer. Then winter came early, as you know. It was safer for her to stay there and await her betrothed."

Celyn glanced at her, his eyes narrowing at her father's half-truth. But she ignored him. She had not told him the complete story of why she came to Bebbanburg, and she never would, seeing as it involved her misadventures in the Unseelie Court of the South. The less her cousin knew about that, the better. She hoped he would not ask about the necessity of inventing an illness to explain her visit.

"We have heard strange tales from Bernicia, so we have," Ulchabhán continued. "Perhaps the Lady Nona or the Lord Celyn can tell us the truth of them. Tales of a sorcerer who consorts with the Devil himself, so he does. 'Tis said he faced the Ordeal but escaped the holy trial when one of the Devil's Hounds spirited him away in the night. None can say where he's gone."

Ulchabhán's round eyes fixed on her in curiosity. His act did not fool Nona. He was stirring the pot. But for what purpose? She forced herself to answer mildly. "The tales are strange indeed, but that is all they are. Tales around a winter's hearth, with no substance. There is no sorcerer at Bebbanburg."

"Indeed? I heard from the monks at Hii themselves that there was an Ordeal, so I did."

Celyn rescued her before she could answer. "As to that, 'tis true there was an Ordeal. They accused the bone carver at Bebbanburg of devilry, saying he was involved in the disappearance of Deorwald, *thegn* of Oswy. Some say they saw him riding past their holdings during the night Deorwald went missing." He shrugged. "But God judged him innocent, so there is none to accuse him otherwise."

Ferchar regarded him with narrowed eyes for a moment and then laughed. "Aye, who indeed would accuse him?" He shook his head. "I am glad to hear of it, for these tales of witchcraft in Bebbanburg's hall are causing tongues to wag across Dál Riata, so they are. Good to know there is no truth in them." He slapped his hands on the table and rose. "I must depart, ere the ale makes me weak as an old woman. In the morn, Lord Celyn of Bebbanburg, we will have further words, so we will." He waved a hand at them as he rose and departed, joining another group at a different table.

Celyn's eyes narrowed as his gaze fell upon Ulchabhán, who had stayed seated at the table, and then he looked back at the rest. "I have a need for some fresh air and to find the latrine," he said, rising. He nodded at them and made his way to the door, weaving through the crowd.

He'd left them so that they could speak of Fey matters, Nona knew, and her heart swelled in gratitude for a moment towards her cousin. After his initial upset, he had accepted the Fey's existence with his usual stoic manner, but it could not be easy on him, even so.

"What are ye playing at, ye wee shite?" Conaire hissed at Ulchabhán once Celyn was out of earshot. He leaned across Nona towards the Unseelie, his voice low. "Do ye wish to stir up the humans against us?"

The Unseelie chuckled. "Ah, just a bit o' fun, that's all. Apologies, my lady, but it were too good an opportunity to resist." He nodded at her, but there was no apology in his eyes.

"Opportunity for what?" Albanwyr said, scowling. "Lord Conaire has asked a question, and you have not answered. Unseelies are the ones who spread these tales against Oswy. Unseelies—who have thrown in with the Traveller, Wulfram. Are you one such, then? Do you dance to Wulfram's tune? Are you whispering lies in Ferchar's ears, pitting Dál Riata against Bernicia?"

Ulchabhán drew back, his eyebrows raised, and he put a hand on his heart in mock outrage. "I am but a loyal servant of both my Lord King Raegenold and my Lord King Ferchar, so I am. It just so happens that their purposes align. The Cenél nGabrain are none too happy with Oswy's ambitions, and Ferchar is beholden to them if he wishes to keep the throne. And my Lord Raegenold is Deirian, as ye well know. His king, Oswine, would benefit if Oswy were gone." His eyes hardened. "I ha' no need to tell ye the difficulties of being under the thumb of the humans. If Raegenold's human king benefits from Oswy's demise, Raegenold benefits. And what benefits Raegenold benefits the Unseelies." He shrugged. "Ye all should ask yourselves why it is ye listen to this wildin', Thomas mac Cadán, and his tales of woe. He admits the Fey are sorely diminished in his time. Why should we not change the tide in our favour now if we can?" His tone rose as passion seized him, and a few heads turned at the tone of his voice.

"Calm yourself, Unseelie," Albanwyr said. He continued, his voice low and urgent. "Think you. You know full well why. The Rule forbids it, for one. That should be enough. But if it is not, do you not see the danger Wulfram puts us all in? Do you want to end up like the harper Godric, Bound to Wulfram and chained to one of the Undying?"

Uncertainty flickered through the Owl's wide eyes, but then he shook his head, a sneer creasing his face. "Ach, the harper has made his own trouble, so he has. As does the wildin'. He had best be careful, or he might find himself in the same boat." He stood, giving them an angry glare, and then stalked off, shaking off the hand of someone in the crowd who tried to slow him down.

That person, an older man, gave them a wary look before he turned away.

The flash of fear in the man's eyes was not unusual. Even humans who were not Sensitive to the Fey could have an instinctual reaction to them. But seeing it only deepened Nona's unease, coming as it did after Ferchar's thinly veiled hostility towards Bernicia and the conversation they had just had with the king's Unseelie counsellor.

What had Ulchabhán been whispering into Ferchar's ears? And more to the point, where did those words come from? Whether it was from the Unseelie Court or from Wulfram, the forces gathering against Oswy were gaining momentum and strength, fuelled by rumours and fear.

Ferchar. Nectan. Strang. Oswy. Too many little fires burning. No matter how hard they tried to stamp them out, new ones sprang up every time they turned their backs.

How long before they would join into an unstoppable conflagration that would burn them all to the ground, Seelie and Unseelie, Fey and human alike?

After a night's rest in the fortress, they took their leave of Ferchar and made their way down the winding steps to the dock. Although Albanwyr had intended to go on to Gwynedd from there, he decided to come back with them for a few more days. Their unsettling encounter with Dál Riata's king and his counsellor had left them with questions they wished to puzzle out.

Nona thought it likely he also wanted to make sure she and Conaire were settled before he left, but whatever the reason, she was glad he would not be leaving her yet.

Nona, Conaire, Albanwyr, and Celyn took one boat, and Tynan and her father's two men occupied the other. Celyn and Conaire spoke of Ferchar as they navigated down the River Add.

"He is set against Oswy and eager to be free of Bernicia's influence. That much is clear." Celyn's gaze darted from Albanwyr to Nona. "Is the Pict who speaks in Ferchar's ear one of yours?" Unease flashed over his face as he spoke of the Fey.

Conaire answered before she could. "Aye. In a manner of speaking. Ye know of the Courts?" He, too, looked wary. Sensitives could often be helpers to the Fey, but the Fey had to be careful about who they trusted.

"Nona has spoken of such."

Conaire nodded. His muscles flexed as he pushed the long pole against the river's bottom, fighting to propel the boat against the current flowing towards the sea. "Ulchabhán is Unseelie. We cannot trust those of that Court to speak truth. They twist and spin a tale into one that will cause the most calamity, especially amongst the humans. He seeks to bend Ferchar against Oswy. And from what he said to us last night, he does this to aid Wulfram."

Fear squeezed Nona's heart. "He can aid him a great deal if he turns Ferchar away from Bernicia. Oswy needs Dál Riata to hold on to his throne."

"As to that, I think not, *fy ngeneth*. He can survive without them," Albanwyr said, throwing an apologetic glance at Conaire. He and Celyn both stood at the opposite end of the boat, aiding Conaire in poling the boat upstream. "Forgive me, Conaire, but Domnall Brecc did Dál Riata no favours. Too many ill-advised battles lost. Wolves nip at Dál Riata from without and traitors plot from within. These are the waning days of Dál Riata, with or without Oswy. If Oswy was wise, he would seek a stronger ally in the North. But the real question is, if Ferchar abandons Oswy, who does he run to?" He grunted as he planted his pole and pushed. "The Alt Clut? The Picts?"

Conaire frowned. "The Picts ha' no been willing to set themselves against Bernicia. Their king, Talorc, fosters Oswy's nephew, Eanfrith."

"Yes, but Eanfrith is a Pict through and through from all I've heard, with no love lost for his uncle. Think you, what if the Owl persuades Ferchar to seek after Talorc, and to get his sword aligned with those gathering with Penda against Oswy?"

Conaire's face was grim. "Oswy canna stand against them all."

"Can you not speak to Ferchar, warn him away from Ulchabhán's lies?" Nona asked.

"Oh aye, I can speak all day long. But he will no listen to me. I am not that important to him." Conaire's hands tightened on the pole. "My father had his ear, though." He glanced back at Nona. "As does Elatha. But I dinna think she will help us, do ye now?"

Considering Elatha's disdainful treatment of Conaire, Nona could only shake her head. "Is there nothing we can do then?"

"I will seek what I can learn from Cadafael. I will get word to you of anything I learn," Albanwyr said, nodding at Celyn.

Celyn's face was grim. "I will leave for Bebbanburg in the morn," he said. "Our king needs to know that Dál Riata's support is uncertain." He shook his head. "But as to that, I am not sure he will believe me. He is loath to believe ill of Dál Riata. His ties here run deep."

"Perhaps no as deep as he thinks," Conaire mused. He planted the pole and gave it a hard push. "We will keep our eyes on Ferchar and his Owl." He grunted as he pushed at the pole again. "Seems all we can do is watch and wait."

Frustration seized Nona, but she knew her husband was right. She heaved a sigh of her own and settled back in the boat.

Hir yw pop ymaros. All waiting is long. Her aunty's words seemed truer than ever.

Chapter 35

Wi' God's Good Hand to Guide Ye

May 31, AD 643

Thomas looked out over the sun-dappled loch and took a deep breath, allowing the peace of the early evening to fill him. The beauty of this place was a bulwark against the fears that haunted him. Not for the first time, he reflected that Fee's holding must have suited his father well. Even in a land of remote and rugged beauty, this place seemed untouched by human hands: a tiny, tucked-away corner that could hide a solitary Fey with little difficulty. Thomas thought Matthew must have found some peace here; at least he prayed it might be so.

Ripples touched the smooth surface of the loch, where the fish were rising to feast off the dragonflies and other insects that skimmed across the water. Occasionally, a bright flash of scales and water would glint in the sun as a fish leapt to catch one, and a small splash would reach his ears. The soft *baas* of the sheep, an occasional bellow from the few cows in the pasture, and the incessant twitter of the birds in the trees were the only other sounds.

As it had been his practice every evening, he quested with his Fey-sense for any taint of the Hound, but as had been the case every time, no hint of it marred the peace of the holding. Nor was there any sense of another Fey nearby. The two days Cadán had promised until his return had come and gone over a week ago, and still there was no sign of the Unseelie.

There were too many unknowns for Thomas to speculate why. Whatever the cause, he could no longer tarry at his father's holding. Tomorrow, he would leave for Bebbanburg.

At best, it would take him ten days to get there, but he wanted to give himself plenty of time to arrive before Solstice. He would be alone, which carried dangers of its own. Even with no complications on the journey, the weather could cause delays at any point along the way. As much as he was reluctant to leave this place and the connection he felt with his father here, he had no choice. He could delay his leaving no longer.

Soft footfalls behind him caused him to turn around. Fee approached, a shawl wrapped around her shoulders, carrying a leather satchel. She joined him at looking out over the slate-blue waters of the loch.

"Ach," she said, glancing at him with a smile. "Your father loved to stand and look out over the waters here, too, so he did. I almost thought ye were him when I spied ye." She waved a hand and smiled. "But enough o' that. I ha' come to give ye a gift." She held out the satchel to him.

He took it, curious, and opened it up. His heart constricted. His father's lyre lay inside, the one Fee told him he had made for himself. He pulled it out of the bag, running his hand over the smooth wood.

"He would want ye to have it, so he would."

Thomas glanced at her, his throat tight. "Thank you," he managed. Silence fell, and then he spoke again. "Will you be all right here?"

A faint smile tugged at her lips. "Oh aye, never fear." She looked out over the waters. "I feel close to him here, so I do. 'Twill suit me well to stay. At least for the summer." She turned to him, wistful. "Are ye sure ye must go? Ye are welcome here, ye know that."

"Yes, I know," Thomas replied, thrusting aside the sudden longing that seized him to give in. "But I have to be back in Bebbanburg by Solstice." He sighed. They had discussed this before. "You know why."

She shivered and drew her cloak closer. "Aye, I know it, so I do." Her face grew troubled. "I know I canna change your mind. But I ask ye to be careful, so I do. The one who killed your da will no stop at killing ye if ye stand in his way."

"I will."

"And will ye let me know? When it's over?"

"I'll send word," he reassured her. "Or get someone else to, if—" His throat closed. Now that the time drew near, he couldn't help the fear that stalked him at the thought of what might come.

She reached up and touched his cheek. "Nay, dinna say it. Ye will prevail, with God's good hand to guide ye. And I will see ye again, so I will, that I promise ye. If no in this world, then in the next."

She pulled him into a hug, and for a moment they stood quietly, until Fee pulled away and smiled up at him. "Now then, Gran asks that ye play a song this eve, so she does, and I dinna want to tell her ye refused."

He smiled and linked her arm in his as they walked back up to the hall; the satchel bumping against his back.

Chapter 36

Happy

*June 1, Loch Glashan,
Dál Riata*

*C*ome, Seelies, come!

Nona woke up with a gasp. The Call to a Gathering faded in her mind, leaving behind the details of time and place. Solstice. At a location near Bebbanburg. The reminder that the time was so near was a rude awakening in more ways than one.

Conaire rolled over, facing her. She could just make out his face in the gloom, as the Call had come as dawn broke. "Ye heard it, then?"

She took in a deep breath to calm her racing heart. "Yes. We must make ready to leave."

"Aye. Our king will need our support."

"Yes. For the Charge. But we must also be ready to help against Wulfram." She dared not say Thomas' name, but the flash of anger in Conaire's eyes showed he understood full well what she meant.

He rolled over onto his back, blowing out a breath. "The wildin'." Irritation tinged his voice.

She gathered her thoughts before replying. She and Conaire had forged an understanding between them, and it had seemed best to avoid this topic. For days, as they awaited the expected Call, they'd danced around the subject of the upcoming Gathering. But now she had to tackle it. "Nectan told you of the danger that Wulfram poses. He wants us to stand against him, for the good of all the Fey. But most of the burden falls on Thomas' shoulders. He understands the threat better than any of us. We must help him. For all our sakes, not just his."

Conaire's jaw clenched, and then he exhaled. "We will see what we have to do once we reach Bebbanburg. We'll stand for Nectan at the Gatherin'. As for the wildin', I make no promises now."

As if in emphasis, the roosters sounded their morning alarms, followed by the harsh caws of the rooks from their rookery at the edge of the barley field that lay between the loch and the surrounding hills to the south.

Nona bit back further words on the subject and spoke instead of another worry that niggled at her. "And Lady Elatha? Will she accompany us?"

"Nay." The word was clipped and angry. "She ha' told me that she will stay here to manage the holdin' while we are gone."

Of course she will, Nona thought, half angry, half amused. Elatha would relish the opportunity to undermine both her and Conaire in their people's eyes. But Nona could deal with that, if it meant she and Conaire could travel to Bebbanburg unhindered by Elatha's cold presence.

"And what of Ferchar? Will he attend the *witenagemot* as friend or foe of Oswy's?"

Conaire made an indistinct sound in his throat that was almost a growl. "From all I hear, our king hasna chosen a path to follow yet."

Without further words, he rose from the bed, threw on his breeches, tunic and cloak, and went outside into the early dawn light.

Nona lay in bed for a moment longer, casting aside her uncharitable thoughts of Elatha and her worries about Ferchar's loyalties with an effort. Her biggest concern was the upcoming Gathering. Conaire hadn't forbidden giving aid to Thomas, she was careful to note. It was also heartening that he said they would both attend. She suspected he might have preferred to keep her away from Bebbanburg, or more to the point, from Thomas, but Nectan's need of support meant that he had to allow her to come.

And she dared to hope that maybe he desired her presence as well.

Regardless of his motives, she thanked God that he hadn't opposed her attendance at the Gathering. She would have gone with or without his approval, but at least this way she didn't have to face the difficulties that defying him would bring, especially if her suspicions were correct.

Her hand rested lightly on her still-flat stomach. There was nothing yet to confirm her belief that she carried their child. Her monthly courses were late, but she had not always been regular. Yet the conviction that she carried a new life within her womb had only grown the past few days. Joy and fear speared through her at the thought. Conaire would never allow her to come if he knew. She prayed she could keep it secret until they reached Bebbanburg.

She also added a prayer for Thomas. The question of where he had gone after Nectan had released him from his pledge had been a constant worry. If Conaire had heard any news, he had not mentioned it to her, and she hadn't wanted to ask. She could only pray, as she had daily, that he was safe.

Wherever he had gone, she knew he would be at Bebbanburg for the Solstice Gathering. Over these last few weeks, even in this remote holding, a sense of menace had grown. An unsettling feeling of unrest and unease blowing in on the wind. The disturbances caused by Wulfram were rippling away from him like waves on the loch disturbed by the fish. Solstice would bring a confrontation between the two Travellers, that much was certain.

Nona prayed her husband and the other Seelies would see the need to stand with Thomas. She was afraid that he would need all of them before that night was over.

A week later, Nona woke to another dawn, listening to the gathering chorus of birdsong as the night faded, as she had every morning since they began their journey to Bebbanburg.

She gritted her teeth and sent a quick prayer heavenward that this morning she might feel better, but she already knew it was of no use. Experience taught her that ignoring her roiling stomach through sheer force of will would not work. Dread seized her, making her gut even more touchy. She had to get up, and soon, or risk spewing last night's supper in the tent she shared with her husband.

Thinking about it only made it worse. Groaning, she threw back the furs, ignoring her husband's startled reaction, and staggered outside. She barely made it before her stomach rebelled.

Conaire jumped up behind her and followed, reaching her in time to hold back her hair. She had a moment's gratitude before her gut spasmed again and she leaned over, retching.

Tynan appeared, thrusting a container of cider at her, but she shook her head, the faint scent of it making her heave again. "Nay," she managed. "Water." He exchanged a glance with Conaire and sprang up again to do her bidding.

She had brought up everything that had been in her stomach, and she sat back on her heels, already feeling better. She could just make out Conaire's face as the dawn light strengthened, so she saw the exact moment when he realized the truth.

His face changed from worry to sudden understanding, and his eyes narrowed. "Tell me, wife, just how long ye ha' known that ye carry our child."

There was no point in lying. In fact, she was glad to get it off her chest, for the secret had been weighing on her. She opened her mouth to reply, but Conaire saw the answer in her face.

"God's blood, wife, ye came on this journey knowing ye are with child? Ye should never ha' come, and ye know it full well." Anger darkened his features.

"I do not know it," she answered, trying to keep her voice level. "Which is why I did not tell you, for I knew this would be your reaction."

"My reaction—" He sputtered in outrage for a moment and then gathered himself. "Ye behave recklessly and condemn me for wanting to keep ye safe? Ye risk the life of our child—"

"Conaire!" She held up a hand, stopping his words, searching for what to say next. She loathed to break the bond that had formed between them. His fierce passion for her had woken the same in her. And besides the pleasures of the marriage bed, other feelings had grown. She admired him for his dedication to her and for the care he took in building a place for them at Loch Glashan, even in the face of Elatha's meddling and disapproval. But it was a fragile peace. She prayed that this disagreement would not cause him to revert to the stiff manner he showed towards her at the beginning.

She took a breath. "Please. Stop. Be angry if you like later, but as for now..." She leaned forward and grabbed his hand. "God has blessed us with a child. Can we be happy together about that first?"

Conaire's jaw clenched. He held her gaze, his eyes hard, and then his face softened. "Happy." He snorted. "Ach, wife, ye try me sorely, so ye do." He sighed, the anger draining from him as his gaze travelled over her face. He lifted a hand to cup her cheek. "Ah, *mo ghràdh*," he breathed, and he leaned forward, his forehead touching hers. His eyes closed. "I could never have hoped to be so happy, as God is my witness. A child. Praise God and all the saints, a child." His other hand caught hers.

Tears pricked Nona's eyes as relief filled her. *Mo ghràdh.* My love. She treasured his words of endearment, for he was not prone to speaking much of his feelings. She intertwined her fingers with his, content. The burgeoning chorus of the birds filled the air even as Fey power swirled around them with the sun's emergence over the horizon.

They sat up straight and pulled apart as Tynan returned, with Bronwyn close on his heels. The commotion must have roused her, too.

"My lady," she said, dropping to her knees before her. "Are you all right?" She darted a glance at Conaire, worry in her eyes.

Nona smiled faintly. She had told Bronwyn of her secret, and of her fears of Conaire's reaction. "I am fine."

Tynan handed her a dripping leather bag. The icy water, fresh from the nearby burn, washed the foul taste from her mouth.

Conaire helped her up, catching her arm in his as he faced his friend. "Tynan, my lady wife is wi' child."

Tynan's grin nearly matched Conaire's own. "Ach, me lord, that is grand news indeed. A great blessing from God Himself. I suspected as much. My mother was much the same when she carried a babe." He turned to her. "She always said the sicker she was, the healthier the babe."

Conaire's grin dimmed, reminding Nona that his own mother had died giving birth to him.

"Then this babe is as healthy as a horse, so it is," she said, squeezing her husband's arm.

"Will we continue, then?" Tynan looked at Conaire, hesitant. "We are more than halfway to Bebbanburg."

Nona answered before Conaire could speak. "Of course. There is no need to turn back. I have some sickness in the morning, that is all. I am well, truly." Her nausea lingered past the morning, but he didn't need to know that right now.

Conaire's lips tightened, but to her surprise, he did not put up an objection. "Aye. We will continue," he said to Tynan, and looked at her. "Are ye wanting to eat, then?"

"Nay, not yet." She shook her head, her stomach lurching at the thought of food.

Conaire nodded and then turned to Tynan. "Come, let us ready the horses. We will stop in a little while for breakfast, once me wife is up to it." He looked at Bronwyn. "I would have Nona rest while we prepare to depart. Please see to our bedding and your own."

"Of course, my lord," Bronwyn said, bobbing her head and hurrying off to do his bidding.

Conaire glanced at Nona, his eyes hooded, and then went with Tynan to where the hobbled horses munched on the green grass.

Nona let out a breath, her hand pressing her stomach as she watched him. She knew him well enough now to know what that glance meant. He would have words with her before this day was over.

She could not blame him for his anger, but she was not sorry. She had to be at Bebbanburg for Solstice. For Thomas' sake, and for Nectan's. Conaire, who valued loyalty, would understand.

Eventually.

CHAPTER 37

GET IT BACK

June 19, AD 643,
Lindisfarne

A cold spray wet Thomas' face as he came to a halt at the northern tip of Lindisfarne. The churning waters at the base of of the cliff where the pounding waves met stone were as chaotic as Thomas' thoughts. Despite the bright morning sun, the lingering remnants of the misty, menacing dream that had plagued him since his Crossing clung to him like a shroud. Even the morning prayers had not brought the peace he sought, driving him to take a walk along the coast to try to calm his agitation.

Fear had stalked him since his arrival three days ago. Solstice was tomorrow. Even now the *ealdormen* and *thegns* and other high-ranking members of Bernicia's and Deira's aristocracies were heading towards Yeavering for the *witenagemot.*

Thomas' conviction that whatever Wulfram might do at Solstice would cause dire consequences for Oswy at the *witenagemot* had only strengthened since his arrival back at Lindisfarne. Potential scenarios nearly drove him to distraction, marring the serene sense of order he usually experienced at the monastery. Perhaps the gathered nobles would rise against Oswy in armed rebellion. Or an assassin would strike down the king. Or something less drastic would force Oswy to vacate the throne. However it happened, Thomas was convinced that Wulfram would disrupt that meeting.

Yet Thomas was helpless to dissuade Oswy from holding the *witenagemot.* The rumours of sorcery in Oswy's court still flew through Bernicia on dark wings. They had chased after him all the way from Dál Riata to the king's fortress, following as relentlessly as the crows and ravens that had stalked his journey. Even some monks had looked at him sideways upon his return from Dál Riata. A few of them had made the sign against evil when they had thought he wasn't looking.

Thomas did not dare to go to Bebbanburg to confront Oswy and risk putting fuel on the fire. His presence there would confirm the rumours, making people even more convinced that the king was collaborating with the powers of darkness.

So he kept away. Instead, Aidan and Celyn had both tried to counsel Oswy against the meeting, but their words fell on deaf ears. Oswy saw the danger, but he dismissed it. Celyn told him of Ferchar's hostility. The king knew there were others, like Owain of the Alt Clut, whose support was uncertain. And Oswy knew their fears about Wulfram. But he was confident the *witenagemot* would prove his supporters outnumbered those who opposed him, and thus the dissenters would fall in line. He felt secure against any danger in the company of his trusted warriors and allies.

Thomas didn't share the king's confidence. But the only thing he could do about it was to go to Yeavering himself, keeping out of sight unless he was needed. If others knew he was there, his presence might tip the balance towards the very outcome he feared.

But the more immediate worry was Solstice, when Nectan, too, faced a dangerous meeting. Strang would bring his Charge against him at the Gathering tomorrow night. Nectan would have his hands full with Strang, and no means to help Thomas even if he wanted. Which Thomas doubted. All he could do was to ignore the Calls to Nectan's Gathering and the anxiety they brought.

Frustration seized him. Aidan kept telling him that God had brought him here to prevent Wulfram from succeeding. So why was he so helpless? The bishop's words haunted him still. *Raise your sail, Thomas.* Hard to do that when he didn't know where to go. A stiff breeze blowing from the ocean caused his cloak to flap behind him, and he pulled it shut, his thoughts spiralling around and around the same questions that had haunted him since he left Loch Nell.

A more immediate decision pressed upon him. Celyn had sent a message two days before that Nona and Conaire had arrived in Bebbanburg. He should have gone to see them right away. He needed to know if they had gleaned anything about Wulfram's plot while they were in Dál Riata. But his fear of being spotted at Bebbanburg had kept him at the monastery.

His fears of facing Nona had also played a part. He grimaced, angry at himself for his cowardice. Facing Nona couldn't be any harder than coming to Lindisfarne knowing Odda was here.

But glimpsing Odda in the dining hall the day before had elicited only a twinge of unease, not the raging fire of need he had feared. Odda had glanced at him but had not approached him. Thomas suspected the boy was just as wary as he was of being together. He hoped that once he dealt with Wulfram, he and Odda could make peace with each other.

He hoped for the same between himself and Nona. *Even in this, God, help me see the truth of myself. Help me give her up.* The piercing screech of a seagull riding the air currents high above gave a fitting voice to his heartache. He squinted against the dazzling sunlight as he watched it, envious as always of its freedom.

Below, the tides retreated, leaving the way open to Bebbanburg. He heaved a breath, settling himself to the tasks at hand. First, he would go to Bebbanburg to find out what Nona and Conaire knew of Wulfram's plans. He would keep away from the king so as not to rouse suspicion. Then he would decide whether to stay at the king's fortress or to come back to Lindisfarne for Solstice.

Neither choice felt right. If he came back to the monastery, he risked becoming trapped by the tides if Wulfram attacked Bebbanburg. But if he stayed on the mainland, the opposite could be true. He could be stuck at Bebbanburg, unable to help if Wulfram orchestrated some disturbance at the monastery. *The way of the Fey comes by doing,* he reminded himself. For once, the Fey proverb provided some comfort. Taking action would be better than this fog of uncertainty that gripped him.

What action to take would depend on what Wulfram would do. He saw the noose tightening, but the way forward remained murky. He sighed, remembering Aidan's words in the dining hall that morning. *Anyone who seeks truth must understand what hides it and what discloses it. Truth hides itself from those who despise it and shows itself to all who go all the way with it.* Perhaps the reason he couldn't discern Wulfram's plan was because he was unwilling to see every possible shape of it. What was he missing?

Thomas. The slight nudge in his mind came just before the voice, interrupting his anxious thoughts. He spun around, his heart in his throat, blocking the Fey from his mind. A tall, spindly figure approached, one hand lifted in greeting. Cadán Longshanks.

Thomas' lips thinned, frustrated. He had been one step too slow to block out the other Fey's Speaking, which didn't bode well for him had it been Wulfram, instead. Being too wrapped up in his own thoughts had allowed his careful alertness to slip.

Cadán joined him at the cliff's edge. Thomas eyed him, wary. The other Fey had never contacted him again after his offer. Thomas assumed either Raegenold had thought better of it, or that Cadán had. He hadn't decided whether Cadán had been acting on Raegenold's behalf or on his own.

"Ach, this place," Cadán said, grimacing as he waved a hand southward, where the monastery buildings lay out of sight from where they stood at the most northward tip of the tidal island. "Being this close is bad enough. How ye stand to live wi' the monks, I canna understand."

Thomas shrugged. "I prefer it here." He studied the other Fey. There was a glint in his eye he didn't like. "Why are you here? The last time I saw you, you said you'd come back in a couple of days."

Cadán shrugged. "Aye, well, there seemed no point. Ye didna seem likely to change your mind. Were I wrong?"

"No."

"Well then. Besides, Raegenold had need o' me."

"For what?" That shrug seemed too casual. There was more to this than Cadán was letting on.

The Unseelie laughed. "I'm hardly likely to tell ye the doings of the Unseelie Court now, am I, seeing as ye refused our invitation." His face grew solemn. "But my king's interest in ye has no waned. We ha' watched ye from afar."

Of course. He suppressed a sigh. "So, what do you want now?"

"I crossed the sands just behind a messenger from Bebbanburg who carries dire word to the bishop, and I bring ye the same. Oswald's arm was stolen from Bebbanburg's church last night, and they lay the blame at Oswine's feet."

"What?" Thomas gaped at him. "Oswine took the arm? But—" He sputtered to a halt, trying to think. This must be part of Wulfram's plan, but what did it mean?

Cadán grinned. "Nay, wildin'. I said they blamed Oswine. I didna say he took it."

"Wulfram. Pointing the blame at Oswine." The shape of it tumbled together in his mind. "Oswine is on his way to Yeavering to attend the Solstice meeting. He'll deny he had anything to do with it. But how does this help Wulfram?"

"Oh, Oswy wilna wait that long to confront him. Think, lad! 'Twas said far and wide that the restoration of Oswald's arm was a sign from God of His approval of Oswy as king. Oswy was happy to let that tale spread. So how will it look if the arm disappears? Ye can be sure that Wulfram has another tale ready. A tale of judgement against Oswy for dabblin' in the dark arts. A sign of God's favour removed and given instead to the good King Oswine of Deira." He gave a sideways glance at Thomas. "Oswy must act quickly. Get it back and come triumphant to the meetin', with the arm in one hand and Oswine's head on a spear in the other. Proof of Oswine's treachery and of Oswy's supremacy over Deira and Bernicia alike. Just like his sainted brother. He ha' sent his men out to search for clues. But the king's ire is roused and he will no wait long. They will ride out today to meet Oswine, of that I am sure."

Ice speared through Thomas. Is this what he had been unable or unwilling to see? What might happen if Oswy rode out from Bebbanburg with his war band to intercept Oswine? The alliance between the two was an uneasy one. Everyone knew it would not last forever. Would this be the straw that broke the camel's back?

He reined in his thoughts and focussed on Cadán. "Why are you telling me this? Why are you here?"

A wicked grin split Cadán's face. "Because you and I, wildin', are going to get it back."

Shock pierced him. "Get it back? What do you mean?" He gathered himself. "Why would you help? What's Raegenold's stake in this?"

Cadán hooted with laughter, his eyes watering. "Ach, wildin', your face!" He wiped his eyes, the grin fading. "Raegenold is no fool. He sees the danger this Wulfram poses. And besides, he himself hails from Deira. He has no wish for Penda's foot on his neck, for surely Mercia will come marching in if Oswine loses his head to Oswy."

"And then Penda will turn against Oswy," Thomas said, dread clutching at his gut. It could work. With Oswine dead at Oswy's hand, there would be unrest in Deira. They would reject Oswy as king. They might even welcome Penda with open arms. He forced his thoughts back to the matter at hand. "Who took the arm, then? Wulfram's Unseelies?"

Cadán shook his head. "Nay. Wulfram enjoys using humans for his work. In this case, a couple of Mercian younglings. Losing the arm to Oswy has been a burr under Penda's saddle, so it has. I'm sure it were no hard for Wulfram to whisper in their ears how taking it would make their king verra happy indeed."

"But how did they take it?"

The Unseelie shrugged again. "It were no guarded. They snuck in last night over the wall and took it from the church wi' no one the wiser. The priest found it missin' this morn."

Thomas eyed him. "You seem to know an awful lot about it."

Cadán waved at the sky. "I ha' eyes on Bebbanburg, so I do." The Unseelie grimaced at Thomas' scowl. "A storm follows ye, wildin'. Ye canna blame us for wanting some warning for when it will hit."

"Seems to me that if you are so worried about it, you should be watching Wulfram instead. If you knew this was going to happen, you could have stopped it."

"And ye think we havena tried to discern his plan?" Cadán held Thomas' gaze until Thomas had to look away. "Dinna be a fool. His paths are shrouded. As ye ha' told us, he is no acting alone."

"The Undying."

"Aye," Cadán said, his face grim. "It sheilds him from our eyes." He shook his head. "Raegenold has asked me to keep watch, and to step in if I had to. He has no love for Wulfram nor for Oswy. He has no wish to see Oswine lose his head because of Wulfram's scheme. If we get the arm back, we can prevent that." He made an impatient gesture. "But we must go now. My hawks watch the Mercians. They travel southeast towards Mercia, and Oswy will head south to meet Oswine on the road. I'll direct one o' me birds to watch Oswy. Once we retrieve the arm, we can meet Oswy on the road, or take it back to Bebbanburg if he hadna left yet."

Thomas didn't trust Cadán as far as he could throw him, but he didn't see how he could refuse the other Fey. But he had to be careful. This could all be a ruse by Cadán. Or Raegenold. He thrust aside the thought with an effort. "Fine. Let's go."

CHAPTER 38

DARK AND LIGHT

June 19, AD 643,
Bebbanburg

"Can ye no eat?" Conaire's face was a mask of worry as he glanced at Nona's untouched bowl. "Ye must keep up your strength, for the sake of the babe."

The smell of the hot porridge caused her gut to wobble, and she pushed it away. "No, not now. Maybe later." Another whiff of porridge undid her, and she leapt up, holding her stomach with one hand and her mouth with the other. She barely got outside before she had to double over.

Conaire followed her out. He rubbed her back and made soothing noises as she retched. Once the nausea had passed, she accepted the cloth he handed to her and wiped her mouth before straightening.

"Is this normal?" he asked, gesturing at the mess on the ground. "Every morning the same, and some nights, too. Ye are wasting away, wife!"

The anger in his voice stung, even though she knew it came from worry. She was worried, too, although she would never admit it to him. She had cared for a few pregnant women, and none had been as sick as she was. It was a never-ending misery, a roiling stomach that never settled, except for brief moments when it became too much and she had to heave.

But she couldn't express this to her husband lest he become even more worried. She swallowed back her fear, wishing that Bronwyn was with her to deflect the full force of Conaire's concern. But her maidservant had left before breakfast to collect herbs, as Conaire had refused to let Nona do the task herself. "I am fine. As I've told you, many women are sick when they are with child, especially at first. This will pass. The baby is strong. Do not fear."

He stepped closer to her, his voice lowering. "Ye know full well my fear is no for the babe. We should find a Healer to aid ye. Is there any here, do ye know?"

"No. Not when I was here last. But it's likely to be at least one at the Gathering." She thought for a moment. "Perhaps I should go to the bone carver's workshop. Some of the Fey are staying with Torht and Hilda. I'll ask if anyone there knows of one." She saw his uncertainty and laid a hand on his arm. "There is no need to worry. 'Tis not far. Bronwyn and I can walk there in an hour." Conaire had forbidden her to ride since they had arrived the day before, which had been fine by her. The long journey had taken more of a toll on her than she wanted to admit. The last thing she wanted to do was to get back on a horse.

"I will go with ye, so I will."

She sighed. While she appreciated his concern, his protectiveness was grating on her. She named it over-protectiveness to Bronwyn, but she dared not say it to him. "Of course," she replied. "Perhaps later today—"

She broke off as a young lad came barrelling towards them—one of Father Colm's novices.

He skidded to a halt in front of them, looking flushed and scared. "I must speak to the Lord Celyn."

Something was wrong. She exchanged a glance with Conaire and saw the same unease she felt mirrored in his face.

"Come in then, lad. The Lord Celyn is inside," her husband said, opening the door and gesturing for the boy to go in.

Celyn and Tynan were still eating and looked up in curiosity as the boy entered, followed by Conaire and Nona.

The boy wasted no time in blurting out his news. "Lord Celyn, Father Colm asks that you come to the hall. The arm is gone, taken during the night."

Silence fell for a second after this pronouncement, shock freezing them in place, and then Celyn jumped up, the stool clattering behind him as it fell. "Oswald's arm? From the church?"

The boy nodded. "Aye. Come to the hall. The king is there." He bobbed his head at them and then rushed out to take his message to others.

"This is Wulfram's doing," Nona said, conviction seizing her.

The others exchanged grim looks.

"Aye," Conaire said. His fists clenched.

"But to what purpose?" Celyn frowned.

"At the very least, to cause confusion, I suppose," Nona said. "We need to know what happened."

"Aye, we must go to the hall," Conaire said. He looked at Tynan. "My lady wife will go to the bone carver's holding today. Ye will go with her."

Tynan nodded. "Of course, my lord."

"Is that necessary?" Celyn asked. "Safer if she stays here, with Master Tynan to watch."

"Nay," Nona said before Conaire could agree. "I will be fine. Tynan and Bronwyn will come with me. And perhaps Torht and Hilda will know something about this. Don't worry about me if I don't return tonight. If I am up to it we will return before nightfall, but if not, we will stay there and come back in the morning."

Conaire pressed his lips together, but he nodded. He held her gaze for a moment and then turned to Celyn. "Come then, let us go."

Nona let out a breath as the door closed behind them. Hunger pains assailed her. She cast a wary eye at the cooling porridge on the table. Maybe her traitorous stomach would allow her to have a bite.

"Will we leave once your maidservant returns, my lady?" Tynan asked.

A slight flush tinted Tynan's cheeks at the mention of Bronwyn. Nona had noticed the tendency of her maidservant's eyes to follow the tall, soft-spoken Dál Riatan. His blush told her Tynan might harbour warm feelings for her friend, too.

Satisfaction filled Nona at the thought, resolving to speak to Conaire about it later. She sat and pulled the bowl towards her, lifting the spoon tentatively to her lips. The only response was another hunger growl from her gut. She took a cautious bite. "Perhaps. I think I will eat first, and then see how I feel."

He smiled at her and sat across from her. "Ah, your husband will be glad to hear it."

She sighed and took another bite. "He worries overmuch."

The smile faded from Tynan's face. "Because he cares for you, my lady."

She saw the sincerity in his eyes and dipped her head in acknowledgement before taking another bite.

She couldn't help the glad response of her heart, even as worry gripped her. *Dark and light, dancing together. May God have mercy on us.*

CHAPTER 39

ARE YE FEY OR NO?

Thomas and Cadán doubled up on Cadán's horse, as there was no time to fetch Missy and saddle her. Thomas wished he could have sent word to Nona at Bebbanburg, but if they had any hope of retrieving the reliquary and getting it back to Oswy before he confronted Oswine, they had no time to waste. As it was, the tide lapped at the horse's hooves as they reached the mainland.

Although he pressed Cadán, the Unseelie only shrugged in response to Thomas' questions about how they were going to get the arm back. Finally, Cadán looked over his shoulder at him and snapped, "Are ye Fey or no?"

Cadán's question struck home. The Unseelie was right. Thomas had been thinking as a human. But they were Fey. They could use their power to Charm the men into giving them back the reliquary. Anxiety pierced him at the thought. A Charm was just a milder version of the Binding.

Maybe there's another way. But he couldn't see one. Unless they were to injure or kill the men, which he didn't want to do.

The thieves' route had taken them across country and on little-used pathways to keep out of sight, which slowed them down. But Cadán set off on the quickest route south along the ancient Roman road, planning to angle across land to the Mercians once they were close enough.

Despite their need for haste, the weather didn't cooperate. Soon after they started out, dark clouds scudded in on a sudden wind, bringing fat raindrops that quickly turned into a deluge.

Cadán hauled his horse to a halt with a curse. "Can ye feel it? A Ward has changed the weather against any who follow."

"Yes," Thomas said, putting up his hood against the downpour. The slight buzz of Fey power in the air was unmistakable.

"'Twill be hard for Aoibh to track them in this," Cadán waved at the rain.

Dismay pierced Thomas. If Cadán's falcon couldn't find the Mercians, this whole exercise was for nothing. "We'll never find them in this without her."

Cadán looked over at him, grinning. "I said hard, but not impossible. 'Twill just take a wee bit longer."

Indeed, they had to stop a few times, huddled in their sodden cloaks under the shelter of a tree, waiting for Cadán's falcon to seek the thieves out. Thomas hoped that the rain might cause the Mercians to shelter somewhere as well, but their quarry pressed on, heading south.

Despite the delays, they began to catch up. Soon, Cadán reined his horse to a stop, looking up at the sky and holding up his arm as a small speck barrelled at them through the rain, growing larger as it approached. As she neared, Aoibh slowed, landing elegantly on his leather-wrapped arm with a small chirrup.

"Ach, me beauty, ye ha' done well," Cadán crooned at the bird, adding other Gaelic terms of endearment as he rummaged in his bag with his other hand. He came up with a small piece of meat, which the bird devoured. "Away wi' ye then. Ye've earned a rest." He lifted his arm in a boost as the bird gathered her wings and flapped up to roost in the branches above, ruffling her wet feathers.

Cadán slipped off the horse. Holding onto the reins, he led it into the woods until they arrived at a rushing stream, where he tied the horse to a nearby tree, gesturing for Thomas to do the same. He turned and spoke in a low voice. "They are no far, now. There are three of them. When we get close, lay a waking Charm on them. I'll do the rest." His eyes sparkled. "A wee bit o' fun, no?"

Thomas remained silent as he followed the Unseelie through the woods along the edge of the stream. A waking Charm. Just like Matthew had done to Celyn when they had first met. He knew how to do it, thanks to the Knowing. But his earlier fear remained. What if he Bound them instead?

Get a grip, Tommo. He took a deep breath, seeking calm. It had to be done. A Binding took far more power than what he needed for the Charm. He had more control now, thanks to Matthew and Nectan's tutelage. There was no danger. Or so he told himself.

Cadán soon turned to him, one finger raised to his lips, and waved Thomas ahead, pointing past a stand of ash trees. Thomas peered through the trees and saw the Mercian warriors on the banks of the stream. They had dismounted and were filling their water containers as the horses took a drink.

"Go on." Cadán gave him a little push. Pure glee radiated from the Unseelie's face as he motioned with his hands for Thomas to go.

God, help me. Thomas gathered his courage, drew on his Fey power, and stepped out from the trees. The horses startled, alerting the men, who spun around, surprise on their faces as they spotted him.

Thomas crooned a melody threaded with tendrils of power. Just enough to freeze them in place, subdue their fears. A subtle connection to their minds tugged at him, and he almost lost the thread of the Charm. He forced back his fear, concentrating on holding his power to a mere trickle. And to his surprise, it worked.

The men stood watching him in slack-jawed interest. *You are safe,* the song said. *Nothing to fear, nothing to see.* The melody wrapped around them and washed through them, creating a waking dream of quiet surrender and peace.

A surge of Fey power from behind him nearly broke his concentration as Cadán brushed past, approaching the men. Thomas expected the Unseelie to snatch the brightly jewelled box the men had left lying in the grass, but Cadán had another idea. He strode towards the Mercians, glowing with Fey power that made him shine like the sun come to earth.

The effect on the men was immediate. They stumbled back, raising their forearms to shield their eyes.

"I greet ye in the name of the holy God and in the authority of Michael, the chief of the host of Heaven." Cadán's voice throbbed with Fey power, sounding impressive to even Thomas' ears, but to the men, the effect was twofold, and they covered their ears, cowering before the apparition.

One of Cadán's Gifts was Glamour, which was especially effective combined with the Charm Thomas held over the men. Thomas was immune to Glamour, but as he squinted at the Unseelie, the glow of Fey power surrounding Cadán morphed into a ghostly figure that sported impressive wings spreading out from his back.

Dismay pierced him. This explained why Cadán's reluctance to explain the details of his plan. He had suspected Thomas wouldn't approve of him impersonating an angel. And he was right. Thomas ground his teeth together. Nothing he could do about it now.

While the men cowered at his feet, Cadán looked back at Thomas and winked at him, and then turned back. "Ye have done a great evil today, men of Mercia. Ye have disturbed the holy arm of God's servant Oswald, he who brought my servant Bishop Aidan to Bernicia and gave him the lands for his mighty house of God. Your king defiled this righteous king's remains, offering it to the Devil himself in thanks for his victory. Shame!"

Cadán was getting into the part, his voice reverberating around the men. They moaned in terror and pressed their foreheads to the ground.

"But Oswy rescued his brother's arm from such evil and brought it back to his people, as a sign of God's favour. A sign of hope. But ye stole it away in the dead of night, O foolish men. Ye are cursed, I say, cursed of God—"

That's enough! Thomas Spoke into Cadán's mind, instinctively turning a thread of his power towards the Unseelie while still holding on to the Charm. It cut off the Unseelie in mid-sentence. It was bad enough to Charm the men. He wanted no part of this ridiculous show of Cadán's.

The Unseelie froze, startled, and then gathered himself and continued. "This wickedness will no stand. I am taking the arm back to Bernicia, and ye will go to your king and confess your failure. Go now, before God gives me league to char ye to cinders!" He made a flourishing motion with his hands, as if he were conducting an orchestra, and at the same moment Thomas released the Charm.

They staggered back and turned tail and ran, the sounds of their passage through the trees fading before long.

Cadán released his Fey power and turned back. His eyes blazed with anger. "Ye will no Speak at me again, wildin', am I clear?"

Thomas saw the fear lurking under the anger in Cadán's eyes with some satisfaction. *Serves him right.* "Maybe if you had told me what you were going to do, I wouldn't have had to."

The Unseelie scowled. "And ye would have objected, no?" He drew in a breath, his anger clearing from his face and amusement taking its place. "Ach, did ye see their faces? I thought they would piss their breeches, so I did." He doubled over, wheezing with laughter.

Thomas' anger wasn't so eaily shed. He stalked past him, picking up the reliquary. "Come on, let's go. Before they come to their senses and realize we've tricked them."

Cadán straightened up, wiping at his eyes. "Oh, they'll no stop until they reach Mercia, I guarantee." He grinned. "Ye did your part well, even though ye overreached wi' the Speaking." He wagged a finger at Thomas. "A true Unseelie surprise, that was. But to be a true Unseelie, you need to ha' more fun."

Thomas bit back the words he wanted to reply. "So where is Oswy now?"

Cadán's eyes grew distant as he focussed on the bond he shared with the falcon that watched the king. After a moment his gaze sharpened on Thomas. "He hasna left Bebbanburg yet. If we make haste, we can get there afore he leaves."

CHAPTER 40

CONFUSION AND DISCORD

Cadán pulled his horse to a halt. "Now then, wildin', we part company."

The pouring rain hid Lindisfarne from sight. The wet pathway disappeared into the misty distance, unobscured by the tide, as the waters had receded while they were pursuing the Mercians.

Thomas couldn't see the sun, but he guessed it was shortly after midday. The tide wouldn't come in again until evening, so it would be safe to cross. As long as he didn't wander off course in the rain and head towards the ocean instead of the tidal island. There were good reasons why the monks didn't cross in foul weather. They had set up rocky cairns in the sands between the tidal island and the mainland, to mark the way when the weather was bad, but still, it was dangerous. The cairns often got knocked down when the waves were rough and so they couldn't always be relied upon.

Thomas slid off the horse, glad to be getting away from the Unseelie. They had decided Cadán would take the reliquary to Oswy because if Thomas did, speculations about his part in the theft would follow.

But to his surprise, Cadán tossed the reliquary box to him, and only his quick reflexes prevented it from hitting the ground.

"What are you doing? Aren't you taking it to Bebbanburg?"

"I've had a better idea, so I have." He scowled at Thomas' expression. "Think. They will know me as a Pict as soon as I speak. As much as ye wish to avoid questions about how ye got the arm back, I do as well. I dare not drag my Lord King Talorcan into this. But if the good Bishop Aidan brings the arm to Oswy, there will be no questions. Take it to him. He can bring it to Bebbanburg."

Thomas wanted to object, but he could see Cadán's point. "But what if Oswy leaves before Aidan gets to Bebbanburg?"

"Aoibh shows me he still meets with the war band. Once they decide on their plan, they will ha' to get ready. The bishop will likely find them there when he arrives." He shrugged. "And if not, he can ride after them and catch up afore Oswy reaches Oswine, ha' no fear." He grinned. "But standing here wagging our tongues will no help. Off wi' ye then, wildin'. Go wi' the wind." Without waiting for Thomas to reply, he wheeled his horse around and urged it into a gallop down the road they had just come.

Thomas watched him go. As always, the encounter with the other Fey unsettled him. He was never sure of Cadán's motives, or whether Raegenold was behind his actions.

His lips tightened. There was no point in speculation. He clutched the reliquary box to his chest and walked onto the sands, heading towards Lindisfarne.

Come, Unseelies, come!

Domech's Call echoing through his mind froze him in his tracks, reminding him of Nectan's difficulties. Thomas suspected Wulfram, and the Undying, had fuelled Strang's ambitions. But the other Seelies may not have recognized their influence. He hoped Nectan had enough supporters when the time came.

He heaved a breath and began walking again, squinting against the Fey-created rain that drove against him. With an effort, he set his mind away from the enigma of Cadán and his motives and Strang's Charge against Nectan. What to tell Aidan was a more immediate problem.

Thomas exhaled a sigh of relief once he reached the shore. His boots were soaked from the tide pools he had splashed through instead of avoiding in fear of going off course. His cloak was just as sodden. He was looking forward to drying off.

He hid the reliquary under his cloak as he hurried to the church, where Brother Barach had told him Aidan was in prayer. Grim humour filled him as he imagined Aidan's reaction when he came with the answer to his prayers under his arm.

When he slipped inside the candle-lit interior of the church, he discovered Aidan wasn't alone. Several other monks prayed with the bishop, their voices rising and falling as they recited Scripture and the prayers.

Aidan led the brethren, his arms stretched to heaven as he prayed the Breastplate prayer, the one that had given Thomas comfort and courage since Aidan had taught it to him. Peace washed over him at the familiar words.

"This day we call God's strength to direct, God's power to sustain, God's wisdom to guide, God's vision to light, God's ear to our hearing, God's word to our speaking, God's hand to uphold us, God's pathway before us, God's shield to protect, God's legion to save us from snares of the demons, from evil enticements, from failings of nature, from one man or many that seek to destroy us, near or far."

Aidan continued, but Thomas could not focus, his mind distracted once more by worries of what Wulfram was planning.

Soon the bishop drew to a close and Thomas added his *amen* to the rest. Aidan nodded at Brother Seamus to recite a psalm while he took his place among the brethren.

Thomas moved up to stand beside Aidan as the monks began their singsong chant of the psalm. "Forgive me, my lord bishop," he said in a low voice. "I must speak with you. Now. It's very important."

Aidan's keen gaze swept over him, no doubt noting his soaked cloak and muddy breeches. He nodded once and then murmured into Father Donal's ear, who stood beside him, before turning and following Thomas out of the church.

He turned to Thomas once they got outside. "What is it, me son?"

Thomas shook his head. "Not here. In private."

Aidan's eyes narrowed. He led the way to his small cell, ushering Thomas inside.

Once Aidan shut the door, Thomas drew the reliquary box out from under his cloak.

Aidan's eyes widened, and he stared at Thomas in shock. "Praise God and all the saints! But how—" His words sputtered to a halt as emotions chased across his face, from surprise to confusion.

Thomas took a breath. "I can't tell you everything. I got word this morning that the arm was missing. The person who told me said that he knew who took it and where it was. We got it back."

Aidan frowned as he digested Thomas' words. "It was Wulfram, no? He took it to set Oswy against Oswine, just as we have feared. I suspected as much." His gaze swept over him again. "Did ye confront him, then?"

Thomas shook his head. "Wulfram was behind it, but he directed others to do it. Three of Penda's warriors."

"Penda! But we heard it was Oswine who was behind it."

"Yes. Wulfram is sowing confusion and discord. As you said, he wants conflict between Oswy and Oswine, but perhaps between Penda and Oswine, too. Penda will not be too happy if he hears Oswine is taking the credit for getting the arm back." He shrugged, dismissing the puzzle. "Whatever he hoped to gain from stealing the arm doesn't matter. We got it back."

"Ach, 'tis true. But who assisted ye?"

Thomas's cheeks flushed. He hated keeping secrets from the bishop, but he had no choice. "Not anyone you know. I can't tell you who. I'm sorry, my lord bishop."

Curiosity flared in Aidan's face, but then he shook his head. "Ye have your reasons, I am sure. But why did ye bring it here, and not to Bebbanburg?"

"I can't. What would people think if I showed up with it?"

Aidan's eyes narrowed. "Ah. I see. You're afraid they'll say ye got it back using sorcery. Perhaps directed by Oswy. It will only increase their suspicion of our king."

"Yes. The only thing I could think of was to ask you to take it to him."

The bishop's eyebrows raised. "But how shall I explain it?"

Good question. He gave the only answer he had come up with on his walk across the sands. "Say that God revealed to you where it was." His jaw clenched at Aidan's expression. "I know I'm asking you to lie. But what else can we do?"

Aidan frowned. "The brethren at the church saw ye speak to me, so they did. They will suspect that ye had something to do with it whether ye take it back there or no." His voice trailed off, and then resolution filled his face. "I will no invoke the name of God in a lie." He held up a hand before Thomas could protest. "I can say that ye crossed the sands this morn for a walk, afore we got news of the theft. Ye found it alongside the road to Bebbanburg and brought it back here, thinking it belonged to us."

It was a thin story, but time was running out. He grimaced. "All right. They'll likely still suspect I conjured it up out of thin air, or something. But that can't be helped." He sighed. "Wulfram isn't done yet, I'm sure. But getting the arm back to Oswy before he confronts Oswine might put a block in his path."

Aidan nodded. "We will pray that it might be so." He eyed Thomas. "What will ye do now?"

"I'll stay here and keep an eye out. Wulfram's plans are coming to a head. He might try something here—I don't know what," he added at Aidan's questioning look. "And maybe he won't. But I don't feel right about leaving Lindisfarne if you aren't here."

Aidan nodded, thoughtful. "Aye, I see. I'll come back afore the tides come in if I can. Tomorrow I will go to the *witenagemot*. Ye planned to go to as well, no?"

"Yes. I'll go with Celyn. Just in case Wulfram tries something there."

"So perhaps I should not attend, if ye think the brethren here are in danger."

Thomas shook his head, frustrated. "I don't know. It will depend on what happens tonight."

Unease touched Aidan's eyes. "Aye." He heaved a sigh. "Our Lord tells us not to worry about the morrow, for the day holds enough trouble of its own. Today, I must take this to Bebbanburg. Let us focus on that." He placed a hand on Thomas' shoulder. "God will protect us. Dinna fear, me son." He hefted the reliquary box. "He has foiled this plan. Ye must not worry."

Thomas wished he had the bishop's confidence. He still couldn't shake the feeling that they had missed something. The stealing of Oswy's arm had been unexpected. What else did Wulfram have planned?

CHAPTER 41

COME ALONG QUIETLY

Nona, Bronwyn, and Tynan left Torht's holding in mid-afternoon to return to Bebbanburg. Despite the upcoming Solstice, Nona's heart was lighter than it had been in weeks. By God's good grace, she had found an experienced Healer at Torht's holding who had given her ideas for draughts to help her nausea. The Healer reassured her that although Nona's symptoms were more severe than most, she and the babe were in no danger. The relief Nona felt surprised her. She hadn't realized how worried she had been.

They knew nothing about the theft of the arm, nor had seen anything unusual on their journey from Deira. Although they agreed that they, too, felt the same unease that had been plaguing Nona and Conaire: the sense of an ill wind blowing against them, pushing dark clouds before it.

A light drizzle began as they started out right after lunch. Nona hardly noticed it, wrapped up as she was in her concern for what was happening at Bebbanburg. She also worried about Thomas, wondering for the hundredth time what he was doing or whether he knew anything more about what Wulfram planned. She had heard nothing from him since she and Conaire had arrived, even though Celyn had told her he was at the monastery. Her cousin had explained his reluctance to come to Oswy's fortress because of the rumours that swirled around him, but his silence worried her. She sighed. She hoped the reliquary's disappearance would bring him to Bebbanburg. Solstice was fast approaching. They needed to hear from him.

A flush warmed her cheeks at the thought of seeing him again, despite her best effort to control it. She reminded herself of her earlier resolution to let him go. She must put aside childish things.

"My lady." Tynan's voice broke into her thoughts as he placed his hand on her arm, halting her.

She looked over at him, startled, and then heard what her speculations had caused her to ignore. A faint melody that sparked and buzzed against her drifted to them through the drizzly rain. Tynan looked around, curiosity and wonder filling his face. Beside him, Bronwyn stood stock still, a small smile lifting her lips. "What..." she managed, a breathy sound, and then she lapsed into silence, delight wreathing her face.

A Charm. Nona whirled around, seeking the source, but the road was empty in both directions. The road cut through a small copse of trees. The music, and a faint tingle of Fey power, came from those on the right. "Tynan! You—" She whirled back to him, but her words died on her tongue. He stood vacant-eyed, lost to the Charm as rain pattered around them with increasing force. *A Ward, too?* She concentrated, and her lips twisted. The slight hum of power as a Weather Ward did his or her work was only noticeable once she sought it. There was more than one of them. At least one for the Charm and one as a Ward. *Christ, have mercy.*

She forced away the sick feeling in her stomach and gathered her courage. "That's enough!" Her voice echoed in the odd cocoon made of rain and melody that wrapped around them. "Leave them be. What do you want?"

A slight chuckle came in answer, drifting through the song, and Godric stepped out from the trees.

Nona's tongue dried to the roof of her mouth at the sight of him. He was thin, his cheekbones jutting out of his face in sharp angles, his colourful robe tattered and dirty. His familiar sardonic grin stretched his mouth as he stepped towards her. But dark shadows roiled in his eyes, and Nona's stomach heaved in rebellion as her heart quickened in fear. It was obvious the Undying had almost completely swallowed him.

Bile rose in her throat, and her gut revolted. She had no choice but to bend over and retch, pulling her knife in her belt out as she staggered back from him and waving it in front of her to ward him off.

But she only got a few steps when she bumped into something hard. Strong arms wrapped around her, one hand wrenching the knife away. She fought against her captor, but she may as well have been fighting against a stone statue for all the good it did her.

"Enough now, my lady; be still. We don't want to hurt you." The words in her ear held exasperation but no malice, which gave her some courage that her captor spoke the truth.

Godric stopped in front of her and gave one of his flourishing bows, the smile still on his face as he straightened. "We meet again," he said. His shaggy eyebrows lifted in mock surprise. "A little bird told me you are pregnant. Congratulations are in order, I suppose."

Nona's skin crawled at the sound of his voice. A slight dissonance distorted it, a strange echo that held another voice, deeper and malevolent. She shivered. They had told no one of her pregnancy. She dared not think of how he had found out.

Behind Godric, two other Fey emerged from the woods. One, a weaselly looking fellow, took the unresisting Tynan by the arm and the other, a slight woman sparking with Fey power, took Bronwyn's hand, darting a triumphant glance at Nona. The two Fey led the humans into the trees.

Anger sparked within her. "Let them go! They have nothing to do with this!"

Godric cocked his head. "Don't worry; they'll come to no harm. We have an important job for them, but they'll need to rest first. A long, satisfying rest." He waggled his eyebrows at her. "I'm afraid we can't offer you the same."

She struggled against her captor, fear surging through her. Did he mean to kill her?

"Don't worry; we won't hurt you. Unless you make us," Godric said. "There's nothing you can do. Just come along quietly, and you'll be all right." He snorted. "Come along quietly. I've always wanted to say that!" He laughed, snorting and wheezing as he slapped his thigh.

Had he gone mad? "Godric! You must stop this!"

Godric's hand lashed out, quick as lightning, and grabbed her face, his bony fingers cold and hard.

"You'll not call him by name, little Nephilim." The words were a low growl, unlike Godric's usual voice. His eyes were completely black.

Nona squeaked in terror, but just as quickly as it had happened, he let go and stepped back. His eyes were blue again, or at least as blue as they had been.

"Cooperate, and you won't get hurt. Please." The harsh whisper that emerged from his mouth differed from both the Undying's growl and his earlier voice. With a jolt, Nona realized she was hearing Godric's true voice. His eyes held hers and her heart squeezed in pity as she saw the panic and desperation within them.

But in a flash his eyes darkened again, their normal clear blue alternately obscured and revealed by churning shadows.

She forced herself to stay calm. "You've taken the arm, haven't you? What do you want with it?"

Godric grinned at her, tapping his beaky nose with one finger. "All will be revealed soon enough. You'll just have to be patient. You'll see your husband tomorrow when we deliver you to him, safe and sound. Until then, you'll be our guest. It will be up to you how comfortable your stay with us will be." The grin faded, and he shrugged.

All will be revealed. The words echoed around them. A shudder crawled up Nona's back. Her jaw tensed. "Fine."

Godric nodded at the Fey behind her, and he released her, shoving her into motion. She joined Godric as he entered the woods. They passed Tynan and Bronwyn, who lay hidden in the crook of a large oak's roots, slumbering. The other two Fey stood watch.

She gritted her teeth, biting back her anger and committing her companions to God. She dared not provoke her captors too far. *Mother of God, aid us.*

They led her to where their horses sheltered from the rain. She was directed to mount one of them, and the Fey behind her mounted behind her, wrapping a large arm around her stomach to keep her anchored in the saddle.

Fear speared through her as she thought of her helpless babe lying nestled against that hard arm, and she closed her eyes, saying a prayer to strengthen her resolve. She had a duty to protect her child. That was all that mattered, now.

CHAPTER 42

END GAME

As the afternoon grew long, Thomas found himself where he had begun the day, walking once more along Lindisfarne's beach. The day's events had done nothing to ease the fears that crashed through him like the waves upon the shore as high tide approached. He brushed his hair out of his eyes and blinked through the streaming rain, trying to pray. An ominous sense of impending doom ticked closer with every second, disrupting his concentration, and he soon gave up his attempt at prayer.

The slight buzz of Fey power in the rain had ceased. But that hadn't stopped the rain. Nature had taken over, and there were no signs of it relenting. It was going to make for a difficult journey for those on the way to Yeavering for the king's *witenagemot*. Thomas prayed it would also slow Wulfram's pawns. Although, since one of them likely started this storm on his orders, it was not likely to be a surprise for Wulfram.

He clenched his hands into fists, frustrated at his impotency. There was still no word from Bebbanburg. Aidan had left with the arm shortly after Thomas gave it to him. Since then, there had been no sign of him, and the tide would soon be in. Aidan must have missed Oswy, or else surely the bishop would have returned.

He was two steps behind Wulfram and falling further behind with every moment that passed. But what could he do?

He had been cautioning himself to patience, but it wasn't working. The intermittent Call to Nectan's Gathering didn't help. Each time it speared him like a lightning bolt, a reminder of yet another thing he was helpless to change. At dusk on the longest day of the year, the Fey would revel in the surge of Fey power and celebrate not only the turning of the season but either Nectan or Strang as king. A few days later, Oswy would be at Yeavering.

Wulfram would strike tomorrow, using the heightened Fey power at Solstice. Thomas knew it in his bones. Something that would disrupt the upcoming *witenagemot* and weaken Oswy's position as king. Or remove him. Somehow.

Something. Somehow. He gritted his teeth as frustration boiled up within him. *God, I need to know what he's going to do. Why won't you help me?*

Another splat of wind-lashed rain against his face was the only answer. He heaved a sigh and started towards the monastery. He may as well get dry and go to the church to pray with the monks, who were keeping vigil as they awaited the news from Aidan. Tomorrow, as soon as the tide receded, he would go to Bebbanburg to talk with Nona. And her husband. Another thought that brought anxiety.

But he had only taken a few steps when a rider on a galloping horse came around the curve of the beach. A large dog ran alongside the horse, dodging the clods of sand thrown up by the horse's hooves as it ran.

Fey-sense tingled along Thomas' nerves as dread washed over him. As if conjured up by his thoughts a moment ago, Nona's husband rode towards him, bent low over the horse's neck. Thomas knew in his gut that whatever had brought him here was bad news.

Conaire yanked his horse to a stop in front of him. The horse fought the bit, its head bobbing as it danced on its hooves, breathing hard. Conaire's face was a mask of anger, his eyes a cold silver. "He has Nona." He spat the words at Thomas like daggers.

Thomas' blood turned to ice. He didn't have to ask who Conaire meant. *Wulfram.* "What? How?"

Conaire jumped from the horse, catching hold of the reins. The wolfhound circled them, tongue lolling out, narrowed eyes fixed on Thomas. It growled at him, and the horse tossed its head, its eyes showing white. Conaire shushed the dog with an absent-minded hiss and a flick of a finger, and the beast settled on the wet sand, its ears back.

"Oswald's arm were taken from Bebbanburg's church this morn, ha' ye heard?"

"Yes." His cheeks flushed.

Conaire's eyes narrowed. "What do ye know of it?"

Thomas made an impatient gesture. "I'll tell you later. Tell me what happened to Nona."

Conaire's lips thinned. "She went to the bone carver's holding after we heard the arm were missing to see if he or any of the Fey at his holding knew anything about it. I couldna go with her, as Oswy was much disturbed at the arm's disappearance and called me and his warriors together to decide what to do. But I sent my trusted man, Tynan, with her, and her maidservant." His lips twisted. "But I didna feel easy, even so. Oswy directed us to ride out around Bebbanburg to see if there were any traces of those who had taken it. So I headed towards the bone carver's holding, to stop by there first. On the way, I met Tynan and Bronwyn heading towards Bebbanburg. Without me wife."

The wolfhound whined as it stood up, its stringy tail whipping back and forth.

Anger flooded Conaire's face. "Tynan didna know what ha' happened. He said they were walking and heard strange music that sent them into dreams."

Thomas breathed out, dread gripping him. "Godric. He Charmed them."

"Aye, I fear so," the other Fey said, his eyes bleak. "Him or another Unseelie, to be sure. When they woke up, Nona was gone." He held up a crumpled and muddy piece of parchment. "He found this clutched in his hand and ha' but one thought in his mind, to give it to Thomas of Lindisfarne. We returned to the place where he woke up, but the rain had washed away all the signs. There were no trace of her. I sent him back to Bebbanburg to find Celyn and begin a search and came here to find ye. I canna read the letters. Do they make sense to ye?"

Thomas took the parchment from him and scanned it, frowning. He looked up at Conaire. "Yes. He's written it in the language we both speak in our own time."

Conaire's nostrils flared, and the dog growled, canines showing.

Thomas bent his head over the parchment, trying to shield it from the rain as he read the note.

Thomas.
End game. I have the girl. I propose an exchange. You for her. I will meet you at sunset on the night of the Solstice, at Merton's farm near the Crossing. It is best if you come alone, but if you bring others, Fey or human, no matter. It just depends how many deaths you want on your conscience, for I assure you, all of them will die. If you come before sunset, I'll kill her.
Wulfram

Thomas looked at Conaire. "He wants to meet me at dusk tomorrow night, to exchange me for her."

Conaire's eyes narrowed. "Exchange ye? Why?"

"He doesn't say. I suppose he still wants to Bind me to him, to use me for his plan. Whatever that plan is." His lips thinned. "Or he just wants to kill me to get me out of the way. Like my father."

Conaire's jaw tightened. "Where?"

"At Merton's farm. East of here, across the sands, between Goswick and Berwick. There's a Crossing spot on his farm." That had to be significant. But why?

"This Merton is Fey?"

"No. He must have thought of a way to get him and his family out of there."

"Or Charm them," Conaire said, his mouth twisting. "But even a harper enslaved by the Undying would find it difficult to Charm so many."

"He has other Unseelies with him. Other Speakers. They would help him."

"Ach," Conaire said, irritated. He blew out a breath and eyed the rising water along the shore. "We must go afore the tide comes in." He put a foot in the stirrup to hoist himself back on his horse.

Thomas put a hand on his shoulder to stop him. "Not now. We can't. We don't have enough time. Not in this weather. Crossing so close to the tide coming in is dangerous enough on the best days. On days like this..." He waved a hand at the rain-lashed landscape, frustration filling him. "But even if the weather was perfect, we couldn't go yet. He said in the note that if anyone came before sunset tomorrow, he would kill her."

Conaire cursed, his face darkening. "He wouldna dare."

"He might. We can't risk it." Thomas held his gaze. "There's something else. He wants me to come alone. No one else. He says anyone who comes with me will die."

Conaire snorted. "If ye think I will tarry here like a fearful child while ye get her back, ye are mistaken. I will go with ye. I'm no afraid of this Wulfram's threats."

"I didn't expect you would be," Thomas snapped back, Conaire's condescending tone rousing his anger. He raked his hand through his hair. "Look. I can't stop you from coming. But I know what Wulfram's capable of, better than you. I understand him. You have to follow my lead. The fate of the monastery, of the future, is at stake."

Conaire's eyes narrowed. "She is me wife," he said, his voice a low growl. "She carries our child."

Shock pinned Thomas to the spot. *Pregnant.* He collected himself. "All the more reason for us to be extra careful."

The Ward stepped closer, his Fey power infusing him in a bright surge that snapped against Thomas. "I will no have a wildin' endangering her life and the life of our babe. I will do what I must to keep her safe. *She* is me future. I'll no let her be a sacrifice for yours."

Thomas allowed his power to rise in response, the clean sharp tang of it adding warmth and energy. The wind gusted, whipping their cloaks around their ankles, spraying the salt water from the crashing waves over them. "I won't risk her. Trust me. As she does."

"Trust!" Conaire snorted, his eyes snapping with frustration and anger. He stiffened and then swung away from Thomas, looking out into the storm-tossed ocean. After a moment, he turned back. "Only God can help ye if ye cause her death, wildin', for after I deal with the whoreson Wulfram, I will tear your throat out, and there will be none to stop me. This I promise ye."

Their gazes clashed for a moment. Thomas' jaw clenched. "I understand." He couldn't blame the other Fey. He would feel the same himself, if Nona was his wife.

If. But she wasn't. Dread snaked through him. He hadn't been completely honest with Conaire. He might end up having to sacrifice Nona to save the future. But he thrust that thought aside. He would deal with that if it came. And pray that it wouldn't.

The rain drove against them in increasing fury. "Look, let's get inside. We can talk about this later."

Conaire's lips curled, but he mounted his horse and extended his hand to Thomas to get on behind him.

Thankfully. At least Conaire wasn't willing for him to drown out here.

Yet.

With a touch of his heels on the horse's flank, Conaire set the horse galloping into the wind towards the monastery, the rain slapping against them with every stretch of the horse's legs, the dog a silent shadow coursing beside them.

CHAPTER 43

SHADOWS UPON SHADOWS

When they got back to the guest house, they discovered that Aidan had returned from Bebbanburg.

"He just arrived," Brother Barach said to Conaire as he arranged the blankets on the bed. The lightning-fast news network on the island had reported Conaire's arrival, and the Guestmaster came with extra bedding just as they were stripping off their soaked clothing. "I'm surprised ye didna see him on the crossing."

"'Twas hard to see anything in the rain," Conaire said, pulling on one of Thomas' extra tunics.

It was small for him across the shoulders. *Of course.* Thomas squelched the jealousy, irritated at himself.

"Oh aye," the prior agreed. "'Tis the Devil's own storm this eve. Ye were fortunate ye didna lose your way on the crossin', so ye were." He sighed, setting his worries aside as he eyed their bedraggled appearance. "There is some stew over the fire in the dinin' hall, if ye are hungry. But the Bishop bade me to tell ye that he wishes to speak wi' ye. He ha' news for ye, so he does."

"The arm?" Thomas asked. "Did Oswy get it?"

Brother Barach didn't notice Conaire's startled look at Thomas' question. The monk shook his head. "Nay, I'm afraid not. The bishop said the king was already gone when he got to Bebbanburg. But he sent the reeve, the Lord Aethelwin, after him. We can only pray he can catch the king." He waved a hand. "The bishop was most insistent that ye come to see him right away. You'll find him in his cell. I'll send a novice with some oatcakes and cider for ye all. Brother Llew has been hard at work preparing for the Midsummer's Eve feast, but I'm sure he'll no begrudge ye something to warm ye." He smoothed the furs over the bed and straightened. "If ye need anything further, send someone to fetch me." His face darkened. "These are evil days. May God ha' mercy."

After the monk left, Conaire swung to Thomas. "What is this? The arm is returned? How?"

Thomas cast around for an explanation that wouldn't make him look worse than he already did in Conaire's eyes. But try as he might, there was none. *Honesty is the best path*, Aidan had said. Thomas doubted that would be the case now, but he had no other choice. "I had a visitor. An Unseelie Fey. He told me the arm had been taken by Mercians. We got it back. I gave it to Aidan to return to Bebbanburg."

"An Unseelie—" Conaire's jaw snapped shut, his eyes blazing as he drew himself up to his full height. "And ye ask me to trust ye wi' me wife's life? A wildin' Fey who ha' been cast from the Seelie Court, who deals wi' the Unseelies?"

"I don't *deal* with them. He sought me out." Thomas set aside his rising anger with an effort. "Look. I'll tell you the whole story. I swear. But later. Aidan may have news of Nona."

"I look forward to hearin' it, so I do." Conaire scowled at him for a moment before relaxing his fists and heaving a breath. "What are ye to tell the bishop? We canna speak of the Fey."

Thomas' lips tightened. "He already knows. Not everything, but he knows about Wulfram. That he is Fey. He knows Wulfram plans to destroy both Oswy and the monastery."

Blood drained from Conaire's face as he gaped at Thomas, wide-eyed. But anger quickly replaced the shock. "Ye told him all this? A human?"

Even though he had expected it, Thomas couldn't help his irritation at the other Fey's reaction. "He guessed Wulfram was one of us. I think he suspects me, too. He might be a Sensitive."

Conaire gathered himself. "Ye take risks no true Fey takes, wildin'," he growled, his gaze raking over him. "I'm no surprised Nectan released ye from your pledge. 'Tis a wonder he accepted it in the first place."

Thomas flushed at the insult. "I had to make things up along the way. The *true Fey* have been little help to me." Scorn crept along the edges of his words, despite his efforts to keep it out.

Conaire snorted. "No? What of Nona? All I've heard is how the Healer at Bebbanburg has been helping the sorcerer."

"That's not what I meant. She—" He bit off his words. He didn't want to get into a conversation about Nona with her husband. The less he said, the better. He heaved a breath, fighting down his anger. "We can't help Nona if we are at each other's throats all the time. Like it or not, I am the best hope you have for getting her back. Believe me, I wish it were different. But it's not."

Conaire's jaw hardened, but he made no reply.

Thomas braced himself, but the expected explosion didn't come. *At least he hasn't hit me yet. That'll probably come later.* "Come on. Let's go find out what Aidan knows."

But Conaire didn't move. "Be careful what ye say. Nona's life is at stake. No good comes of involving humans in Fey business. First Celyn, now the bishop.... I fear where this may lead."

Thomas feared it too, but he kept that to himself.

As it turned out, they didn't need to tell Aidan of Nona's kidnapping. He had encountered Tynan and Bronwyn just outside Bebbanburg on his way back to the monastery. They told him of their strange experience and that they gave the note to Conaire. It was this news that Aidan wanted to pass on to Thomas.

After Thomas read him the note, Aidan paced in front of the fire, his long face filled with grief. "Shadows upon shadows fall upon us, so they do. But we must not despair." He stopped pacing and looked at Conaire, compassion filling his gaze. "Your wife is in God's hands. She will return unharmed, of that I am sure."

Conaire nodded in response, his face stony.

Aidan turned to Thomas. "Do ye mean to meet this Wulfram at Master Merton's holding?"

"Yes. Wulfram will harm her if I don't. I'm sure of that."

"He seeks to press ye into his service, so he does. The *sidhe* dinna like to give up what is theirs. But what does he wish to do wi' ye, I wonder?"

Use me to destroy you. Thomas thrust the thought away. "It's hard to say." Beside him, Conaire shifted on his feet, his hands clenching. Thomas hastily changed the subject. The last thing he needed was for the Dál Riatan to chime in. "But what about Oswy? Can Aethelwin will catch him before he meets up with Oswine?"

Aidan lifted one shoulder in a half-shrug. "I hope so, but this rain..." He heaved a sigh. "All we can do is watch and pray, and trust that God has us in His hands." He looked over at Conaire. "Dinna despair, me son. Ye said that the Lord Celyn has started a search for his cousin. Perhaps he will find her before the sun sets tomorrow. But if not, will ye go wi' Thomas?"

"Aye," Conaire said, his face grim. "I am no fearful of Wulfram's threats."

"I am glad to hear it. But ye must be careful. Dark forces bend towards us. A foul voice on the wind." Aidan frowned, as if he were catching a hint of that voice.

"I will keep vigil in the church this night with the brethren. We would welcome your prayers added to ours."

"Of course, me lord bishop. But I confess I wish I were huntin' the one who took me wife instead."

Aidan nodded. "I understand, me son. God sets a challenge before us, but it may be not the challenge ye think. The *sidhe* are dangerous, so they are, untrustworthy and cunning. Ye will need to take care. But there is harder work before ye than raising a sword against those who ha' harmed ye." He paused, his eyes steady on Conaire's. "The desert Fathers spoke often of prayer, and Abba Zeno's words on it have been much on my mind. He said a man must pray with all his heart for his enemies afore he prays for anything else. Through this, God will hear everything he asks." He stretched out his hands, looking at them both. "This is our first task: forgiveness. The rest will follow." Silence fell, and then he continued. "I will join the brethern at prayer. May God preserve us from all who seek to do us harm."

After he left, Conaire exhaled, his face bleak. "Forgiveness," he mused. "If that is required there is little hope for us, for I ha' nothing but hatred in my heart for Wulfram. If he harms Nona—" He broke off, his hand curling into fists.

Thomas didn't blame Conaire for his anger. He felt the same way. He sighed. "I know. But Aidan isn't wrong, either."

Conaire grunted in response, sounding as unconvinced as Thomas felt, despite his words to the contrary.

Conaire decided to eat before he joined the monks at the church, but Thomas skipped the dining hall. The monks had often counselled that fasting added weight to their prayers. He figured that if ever there was a time to make sure God heard him, this was it.

Relief washed over him as he entered the church. Conaire's glowering tension was a barrier to the calm resolve he sought. Theirs was an uneasy alliance. It would only survive if they did not strain it too far during these hours of waiting.

Inside the church, it was gloomy and cool. He stood by the door, breathing in the faint scents of incense and beeswax, allowing the peace that permeated the place to settle his jangling nerves. With an effort, he tore his mind away from his fears and focussed on the psalms that the monks were chanting together, their voices rising and falling in harmony.

Bless the Lord, O my soul, and all that is within me, bless His holy name.
Bless the Lord, O my soul, and forget not all His benefits:
who forgives all your iniquities,
who heals all your diseases,
who redeems your soul from destruction,
who crowns you with lovingkindness and tender mercies,
who satisfies your mouth with good things
so that your youth is renewed like the eagle's.

The chanting was a soothing sound that eased his anxiety. They recited this psalm every time they met for prayer, so it was one he knew well. He joined in with them, the familiar words and the presence of the others a comfort.

After they finished, Thomas' thoughts drifted back to Wulfram. *Forgiveness.* Aidan's admonition caused his jaw to harden, peace leaching away from him. How was that possible?

For him, it's personal. That was Matthew's conclusion of Wulfram's motives. A conclusion confirmed when Thomas met Wulfram in Eoforwic and heard Wulfram's story of his twin, who died in the 9/11 attacks. Wulfram was there, on the ground, Speaking with his brother, when his twin jumped from the towers on that terrible day.

Thomas shied away from the thought, the horror of it too great to contemplate. Despite his anger, a small seed of compassion for Wulfram's plight took root in his heart. If he had seen Danny die like that, what might he have done? If he could prevent it, would he?

Wulfram had asked him much the same thing. *If you could have prevented your father from dying, would you?*

Thomas understood all too well what drove Wulfram. Love for his brother. A desire to negate the terrible emptiness of grief. Revenge on those who had killed him.

But then he remembered Odda and the terrible, hollow thump of the axe when he had cut his own finger off at Wulfram's behest. And now Nona was in Wulfram's hands, the hands of a Fey whose obsession had led him to being dangled like a puppet on the strings of a demon, causing chaos and destruction. Anger flooded through him again.

Forgiveness would have to wait.

CHAPTER 44

THUNOR ONE-EYED

June 19, Bernicia

Celyn squinted through the gathering twilight, seeking for the lights of the holding. He hoped not to spend the night outside if he could help it. He and Tynan were already soaked to the bone, and the rain showed no signs of stopping.

"This holding ye tell of," Tynan said. "Are we close, do ye guess? The rain is getting worse." Weariness shadowed his face, matching the same exhaustion Celyn felt. They had been on the road for hours, searching with no success for news of Nona and the arm.

"It cannot be much further. But as to that, I've not been here myself, only heard tell of it."

Tynan grunted. He hadn't been keen to go to this remote holding. Celyn didn't blame him. The stories of Thunor One-Eyed had spread far and wide, and not all of them good.

But there was no better source of information about travellers on this road. Thunor might know something about the stolen arm or Nona's disappearance.

If so, it would be their first good lead. He suppressed his frustration with an effort. The search around Bebbanburg did not yield any sign of the relic. Once they and the rest of the men returned, Oswy ordered them to prepare to go to Eoforwic, hoping to catch Oswine on the road as he travelled north towards Yeavering for the *witenagemot*.

Tynan and Bronwyn had arrived during Celyn's preparations to leave. Anger and fear assailed him again at the recollection of the Dál Riatan's tale. Nona's disappearance had to be linked to the theft of the arm. Wulfram must have directed both.

Celyn tried to dissuade the king from riding out to meet Oswine, but to no avail. Oswy insisted Oswine had sent his men to steal the arm, and no argument against that belief would shake him out of it. He had no patience for words of caution.

Both Oswy and several others reported tales of Deirians in Bebbanburg. Others heard of men spotted going south, either last night or early in the morning. But pressing the men on these rumours did not glean any details, just a strangely stubborn certainty of the tale.

Celyn shifted on his saddle, disturbed again by the thought of the odd light in Oswy's eyes when he questioned the king about these reports. *The work of the* tylwyth teg *and no mistake,* he mused. The king and his men had come under an evil influence to make them believe these accounts.

At least Oswy permitted him to search for Nona instead of accompanying him and the other men. Celyn couldn't help but wonder if that was part of the reason Wulfram had seized both Nona and the arm. To separate Celyn from Oswy, and to take the king and his warriors away from Bebbanburg.

He sighed. There was no point in speculating. For now, he had to focus on finding the holding or risk bedding down under whatever scanty cover they might find.

That might be as God willed, depending on their welcome. He set aside his gloomy thoughts and peered ahead through the trees. Relief flooded over him as he spotted a glinting light in the distance, obscured at once by the wind-tossed branches.

"There it is!" Tynan pointed ahead at the light.

"Aye. We'll have a place to sleep inside, God willing."

The Dál Riatan's blew out a breath. "Thank God for His mercy. I didna wish to spend the night in the open, where any might find us." Fear flashed in his eyes. "Those dreams," he added, his voice low. "They were like ale to a thirsty man that only made ye thirsty again. But in a new way, like ye had never had ale before..." He lapsed into silence, his eyes haunted. Frustrated longing filled his face.

Fear trickled down Celyn's spine. "As to that, 'tis best not to speak of it now," he said, gesturing at the growing shadows. As he now knew, the *tylwyth teg* did not need the open doors between the worlds at Solstice to walk among them. He had no wish to gain their attention.

St. Michael, guide my arm. Celyn pushed away his fears and urged Arawn on towards the holding.

The path took them through a winding valley amongst shrouded hills empty of human habitation. They spotted goats scampering away from them and heard the thin cry of a hawk far above, but saw no other signs of life. The wind gusted around them in erratic bursts that drove the steady rain into their faces.

A brooding, dreary place. Celyn was glad they would shelter indoors that night. They soon came to a knot of trees which stood sentinel around a cluster of buildings. Smoke drew upwards from the roofs of the buildings, and chickens roosted in the trees. Dogs barked, rushing towards them on stiff legs as they turned their horses' heads down the path towards the settlement.

There was no sign of people. That was not surprising, given the weather, but Celyn's warrior instincts screamed danger. He exchanged a glance with Tynan and saw the same unease reflected in his eyes.

A flickering shadow caused him to haul on Arawn's reins, and the stallion reared up with a protesting whinny just as an arrow thudded to the ground in front of them.

"That's far enough, now, my lord, if ye please!"

Celyn drew his sword, whirling Arawn around to find the speaker. Tynan, too, drew his sword as his horse pranced underneath him.

The archer was up in the spreading branches of a large oak tree. The leaves hid him from view but for the bow that held another arrow aimed at Celyn's heart. "We be a peaceful people here and want no trouble. Ye be on your way, now." The voice was firm but not hostile.

Celyn looked over at Tynan and nodded before sheathing his sword. Tynan grimaced, but followed suit.

"Look you," Celyn said, speaking loudly enough to reach any others hidden around the holding. "We come in Oswy's name, the king for whom you hold these lands. We do not come bringing harm. Come down from there, Thunor One-Eyed, and tell us why you greet us in such a manner."

The arrow did not waver. "Ye are from Bebbanburg? What brings ye here, then?"

"This morn the arm of the blessed King Oswald was stolen from Bebbanburg's church. My cousin, the Lady Nona, was taken by force near Bebbenburg later in the day by unknown men. We are seeking her and news of the arm. You have no fear of us, unless you have a part in these deeds."

"The Lady Nona?" A young woman stepped out from her hiding place behind a building. She put her knife into the holder on her belt and addressed the archer. "Thunor, put down your bow! These men haven't come to harm us."

"Know that for certain, do ye?"

The woman made an impatient gesture. "The Lady Nona came when Aethel had the pox! Do ye not remember? She were kind—"

"Enough, Glytha! I remember well! But how do we know this man tells the truth?"

"Do not be foolish, husband! He has the tongue of the *wealas*, as did the Lady Nona." The woman turned to Celyn, her eyes troubled. "The Lady was taken, did ye say?"

Celyn nodded. "Aye. Near Bebbanburg. We seek to find her before she comes to harm. I know you keep watch on the road for the king, and so seek any news you may have."

"I understand." She glanced up at the tree. "Do come down, husband. These are the king's men."

The bow lowered and, with a rustle of branches, a young man dropped from the tree, eyeing them with hostility. He had black hair and a stubble of a beard. He would have been handsome but for a long scar marring one side of his face. It ran from his chin, across his cheek, and disappeared under an eye patch that covered his left eye. The scar continued up his temple, disappearing behind the hair that hung over his forehead. "And who are ye, then? I'll have your name, if ye please," he said in a growl.

"I am the Lord Celyn, of Bebbanburg, and this is Tynan, who serves Lord Conaire mac Alpin of Dál Riata, the Lady Nona's husband."

"Ye pledge to Oswy, king of Bernicia, then?"

"As to that, I would think it obvious," Celyn said with asperity, growing tired of the other man's suspicion. "I have said we were from Bebbanburg and told you our errand. Now either welcome us in or allow us to go on our way without the threat of an arrow in our backs so that we might find more hospitable shelter elsewhere."

"There's no need for you to depart," Glytha said. She looked at Thunor in entreaty. "The Lord Celyn is right. 'Tis a poor welcome we are giving them, and this the Lady Nona's cousin!" She turned to them. "I am sorry, my lords." She bobbed a small curtsey. "Earlier this day, a band of armed men on horseback rode past here. My husband did not like the look of them, see. We were afeared ye may be more of the same."

"Men?" Celyn sat up straighter, his weariness forgotten. "Tell me of these men!"

The man scowled, casting a dark glare at the sky as the rain spattered down. "Ye best come down off your mounts and come inside." He turned to the small settlement. "Brun! Bosa! Come see to the horses! It be safe!" There was no response, so he pitched his voice louder. "Come then, all of ye!"

Two youths came out from behind a shed. One carried an axe, the other a sturdy stick. Other than that, they were exactly alike; identical twins. Tynan crossed himself and made the sign against evil surreptitiously as they approached.

But the one-eyed man noticed, and his face darkened even more. He opened his mouth as if to speak, but then shook his head and spun on his heel, marching towards the largest building. He yanked the door open and stalked inside, the door clattering shut behind him.

A wizened old man came around the corner of another building, followed by a small grubby girl and a young woman. She held a long, sharpened stick, and a baby nestled in a sling against her. A swirling pattern beginning on her hand and disappearing under her sleeve marked her as one of the Picts. A few more people appeared, slipping out from their hiding places among the buildings, all carrying rudimentary weapons, all with suspicion written on their faces. And none of them, Celyn noticed, were whole. A youth with a twisted leg walked with the aid of a stick, and another had a missing hand—a thief, by the looks of his shifty eyes. An older man joined them, twitching like he was being stung by bees.

Tynan took in this odd assortment of people and glanced at Celyn, his eyebrows raised in a silent question. *Leave or stay?*

It was a strange crowd, but it was nearly dark and the downpour gave no hint of stopping. Besides, they needed more information about the armed men. Celyn shrugged at the other man and dismounted, leaning against Arawn as he stretched his legs and adjusted to standing after the day's ride.

"Oh, he's a big 'un, m'lord!" One twin stood at a respectful distance, eyeing Arawn with open admiration. The stallion responded with a snort, pawing the ground. He was as eager to be rid of Celyn and his saddle as Celyn was to be done with riding. He patted the horse's neck, feeling Arawn's muscles quiver under his hand.

"Softly," he murmured to the horse. "None of your wicked ways." He glanced at the boy. "Look you. Come over here and let him get your scent."

The boy inched closer, his eyes wide, coming to a halt close enough for Arawn to stretch out his neck and nose at him. After a moment, the stallion blew through his big nostrils and nickered, stomping a foot as the boy's twin took Tynan's horse and led him towards the barn.

Celyn handed him the reins. "Take him, lad, and rub him down. But be careful. He has a quick temper, but it looks like he'll put up with you."

The boy nodded, eager. He clicked his tongue and followed his twin, looking up at the horse as if for approval. Arawn walked into the barn with him as if he were a docile mare and not a seasoned warhorse.

Celyn shook his head, mystified. He didn't understand why Arawn would occasionally allow someone to handle him without giving them difficulty, when most of the time he was an ill-mannered beast.

The other people followed their leader into the hall, leaving him and Tynan alone.

"I dinna like this place, my lord." Tynan looked around, his lips tightening. "A den of thieves, or worse, I reckon."

"As to that, I am not sure. But either way, we need to hear more about the band of men they saw."

"Aye, if they are not lying, to fool us into trusting them." Fear tightened the other man's eyes as he gazed at the settlement.

Celyn clapped him on the shoulder. "The good Christ is with us. Have no fear. These are not the *sidhe*. Thunor One-Eyed has lived here for many years. I know of him from the king. We must be wary, but I do not think they will harm us."

Tynan frowned. A sudden gust of wind blew a cold splat of rain against them, and he eyed the worsening weather with resignation. "I suppose ye are right, my lord."

Another gust got them moving towards the main hall. Celyn was grateful they would not have to shelter outside, but despite his confident words to Tynan, he would keep his sword handy, just in case.

CHAPTER 45

SOLDIERS THEY BE

They dried off, warmed up, and ate before the young man would answer any of their questions. During the meal, a tasty stew, Celyn observed the motley group of people and came to some conclusions. Conclusions which were confirmed when the one-eyed man saw Tynan looking at the twitching man with some distaste.

Their host slammed down his fist, his dark eye sparking with anger as he caught Tynan's look.

The baby gave a startled squawk and began to cry. The Pictish girl soothed it with soft pats and murmurs.

Glytha frowned at her husband. "Calm yourself, my lord. There is no need for this."

The man scowled, the scar lending his face a fierce cast. "Oh, aye?" He pointed at Tynan with his knife. "This one is wondering, see. He thinks we be a nest of cutthroats and thieves, or worse, I reckon!"

Tynan flushed at the man's accurate assessment.

Their host turned to his wife. "We do just fine here wi'out strangers, I told ye! More trouble than they be worth!"

Glytha threw Celyn an apologetic look. "I am sorry, my lord. We do not have many visitors. Most avoid us," she added self-consciously.

"As to that, I can't blame anyone for not wanting to get an arrow in the chest as a welcome," Celyn said, keeping his tone mild. But his hand closed on his knife handle. Celyn had seen men like Thunor before. He had the air of a cornered dog about him, and Celyn knew he was just as dangerous. *But just as loyal to his pack as well*, he mused, looking at the faces huddled in the gloom beyond the hearth fire, their eyes watchful.

"It's more welcome than most deserve." Thunor growled at his wife, and then turned to Celyn. "Tell me, my lord." A mocking emphasis on the last two words reminded Celyn uncomfortably of Godric. "How would ye have us greet strangers when most come seeking to burn us out as a nest of witches?"

Witches. Suddenly, the reason for the man's hostility became clear. These gathered misfits were outcasts. Some Christians would consider the twins, the malformed, and even the fierce Pict as being in league with the Devil. Those who followed the pagan ways would say their gods rejected them. Christian on pagan, their lives would be miserable, and likely brief, unless they found a protector powerful enough to shield them. One such as Thunor. But why would he take these outcasts under his protection?

A niggling thought surfaced—a passing remark from Brother Frithlac some months ago, spoken under his breath to Aidan when Thomas first came to Lindisfarne. *He belongs with the Saxon at the* weald's *edge.* The monks were obviously well-acquainted with Thunor's holding. Oswy, too, had mentioned it in passing. But neither Aidan nor Oswy would speak much of him, and Celyn had never pressed either of them on it.

He eyed the fierce Saxon. "As to that, I would protect my people."

The other man glared at him for a moment longer, then blew out a sigh. "Aye. There be no one else, and most are but children." His jaw worked, anger flaring up in his eyes again. "Children and old ones, and they should starve because of that which they cannot help? Nay," he said, shaking his head. "I am more of a Christian than that."

"And some are not?"

The man turned and spat onto the rushes on the floor. "What do you think, *wealas*?"

Celyn's ire rose at the insult, but then he understood. He himself had faced the same suspicion and contempt as an outsider at Bernicia's hall as these outcasts faced. People feared what they did not know.

Grudging admiration filled him. Thunor accepted the burden of caring for those who had no one else, who would die without his protection—die of neglect, or cruelty, or loneliness. Celyn knew full well the despair that loneliness brought.

He nodded to show the man he understood. "Surely the monks do not neglect you?"

"They be kind, mostly," he acknowledged. "Bring us food for the young 'uns. I take in those who aren't at home with them. Not all are suited for prayers and books." He waved a hand. "They help when we have someone sick or injured. As Glytha said, they sent your lady cousin here for Aethel. I have no quarrel wi' them." His dark eye challenged Celyn. "But I have no love for the rest," he stated, waving his knife in the air. "They would kill me as soon as help me, and I feel the same for them."

"But there is only one of you, and all these mouths to feed," Celyn said. "I saw no fields for crops. How do you—" He broke off, the truth dawning.

The other man saw it and grinned, his eyes fierce. "Oh aye," he said. "I not be too proud, see."

Tynan glanced at Celyn, discomfort on his face. "My lord, he is the disturber of the king's peace we ha' heard of, who sets upon good men travelling through here. He and his band o' outlaws." He glanced around at the elderly and the gathered misfits. His face flushed. "Or so they say," he muttered.

"They no be *good*," Thunor stated. "Those I took from would ha' done the same to me and mine—or worse, given half the chance. I make no apology and swear so before God."

Celyn eyed the man, troubled. There was more here than met the eye, but he wasn't here to untwine the lies from the truth. Oswy and Aidan both knew of this man and used his particular skills for their own purposes. For Aidan, this was a place of shelter for those who would not take to the monastery. He could direct them here instead of leaving them to the harshness of life on their own.

As for Oswy, he had reasons of his own to keep people wary of travelling the path bordering the holding. A path where spies from Deria or Mercia could enter Bernicia unseen. If Oswy had trustworthy eyes and ears here to bring him news, he would be happy to turn a blind eye to the occasional outlaw raid against those who came asking for trouble. An arrangement that worked for Thunor and Oswy both.

He sighed and turned to Tynan. "Peace. None of this is our concern. Master Thunor has given us a place out of the rain for the night. The rest is the king's business, not our own. We are here to find my cousin."

Tynan gave him a black look but made no comment.

Celyn turned back to Thunor. "Tell us of these armed men. Are you sure they did not have the Lady Nona with them?"

Thunor turned to those gathered around the hearth fire behind them. "Old One, come tell your tale, as you told me this afternoon," he commanded.

The wizened old man rose to his feet, helped by one of the twins. He shuffled to the table and lowered himself onto the bench, wincing as he did so.

"My lord," he said, his voice a thin rasp as he tugged at his forelock in respect. "No lady with them, no. Soldiers they be, armoured, and weapons aplenty. One had a sword like your own—a fine one, by its look."

Celyn frowned. "Did you recognize any of these men?"

"Nay, m'lord, they be strangers to me. But I'd know 'em again, that I would. Especially the big one."

"Big?" Tynan asked. "What do ye mean?"

The old man glanced at him, aggrieved. "I mean as I say. Big black-haired one 'e was, and his grey, high-stepping horse a thing to behold. Much like yours, my lord," he said, turning to Celyn.

Celyn's blood froze, the truth hitting him like a hammer. Much like Arawn indeed, for if he was not mistaken, that horse was a full blood-brother to his own, even as its rider was a brother to him. Griffith. *Tell Celyn I will see him again. Soon.* Thomas' words echoed through his head. It seemed the time had come. But why now?

Tynan must have seen something in his face. "You know this man, my lord?"

Celyn swallowed, his mouth dry. He gathered his scattered thoughts. "As to that, I suspect it was my brother Griffith, who serves Penda of Mercia."

Tynan drew back as if struck. "Penda!" He recovered quickly, his eye narrowing. "Ye know more than we, then. We ha' heard that many are uncertain of our king. Mayhap ye ha' invited your brother to Bebbanburg to open the way for Mercia to walk in." Steel glinted in Thunor's good eye, and his hand tightened on the knife. This man had few loyalties other than to his band of misfits, but it seemed he held another towards Oswy of Bebbanburg.

Celyn held up a hand. "I haven't seen my brother for a good many years. He bears no love for me." A pang pierced his heart, but he forced himself to continue. "He has pledged to kill me when he saw me next."

Thunor eyed him but seemed satisfied with his answer, for the dark suspicion left his face. "He's come looking for ye then?"

"As to that, it's hard to say." It seemed too coincidental for his brother to appear now. This, too, must be part of Wulfram's plan.

Deira. Mercia. Was the dark *sidhe* bringing men from both kingdoms against Oswy and those loyal to him at the *witenagemot*?

Tynan interrupted his speculations. "Your cousin? Would those who have taken her be in league with these Mercians?"

Celyn set aside his other worries and forced himself to consider the question. "Nay. That is a different matter." He would not speak of the *tylwyth teg* in front of Thunor, but the flash of unease over Tynan's face told him the other man had understood his meaning. "There is no reason for Penda to anger Dál Riata. He would want them as allies, more like." He thought for a moment, but he could not make it all fit together.

"Penda ha' no love for Oswy," Tynan mused. "And Deira is tied to his leading-strings. But I wouldna think that Mercia is powerful enough, just yet, to make a bid for the Bernician throne." He grimaced. "My Lord Conaire worried that Ferchar was abandoning Oswy and turning to others to band against Bernicia. If that be the case, perhaps Penda ha' decided now is the time to strike."

"Aye. 'Tis more likely that Penda is behind the theft of the arm than Oswine, no matter what our king believes of Oswine's treachery. At first light we must return to Bebbanburg to tell Oswy this news."

"Aye," Tynan said, his face grim. "And mayhap my lord will be back from Lindisfarne as well."

"Yes. We need to know what that note said."

Curiosity flared over Thunor's face, but before he could ask questions, Celyn stood. "We thank you for your hospitality, Master Thunor. But it has been a long day and we must leave early in the morn, so we will take your leave and bed down with the horses."

Glytha sprang up. "I have extra blankets, my lord. I will bring them to ye."

Celyn nodded his thanks at her and escaped the hall with Tynan, pondering what they had learned.

The disappearance of the arm, the rumours of Deira's involvement, the *witenagemot*, Griffith and his Mercians roaming Bernicia, Nona's disappearance. These were all connected, he was sure of it. All part of whatever scheme Wulfram had planned for Solstice. What was their small strength against the evil that bent towards them in such a relentless tide?

Celyn fought back the fear that filled him at the thought of the morrow. God would not leave them at their time of need. They would not be defenceless against Wulfram's plots, no matter the form they took.

CHAPTER 46

THE DREAMS OF THE FEY

June 20, AD 643 Solstice

Missy danced sideways, pulling at the reins, preventing Thomas from putting his foot in the stirrup. She obviously sensed his anxiety. He stoked her neck to soothe her and took a deep breath, trying to let his tension go. He didn't fancy getting bucked off the second he sat in the saddle.

Father Gaeth approached, holding up a hand in greeting. "The bishop bid me to see ye off. God go with ye, Master Thomas. We will pray for ye both, to be sure."

Conaire nodded at the monk, his horse also fidgeting underneath him. His hound paced around them in a circle, whining under her breath. The Ward's patience had stretched to the breaking point. It was time to go.

Thomas mounted Missy, who swished her tail and pinned her ears back, but kept her feet on the ground. "Thank you, Father. God be with you."

Before the monk could reply, Conaire touched his heels to his mount's side and the gelding leapt into motion, followed by his dog with its tongue lolling in a long-legged run. Thomas threw an apologetic look at the prior and leaned over Missy's neck as she surged into a gallop, catching up with the Ward. By unspoken assent, they allowed their horses to run full out for a few minutes, the pent-up frustration of having to wait soothed by the pounding of the horses' hooves underneath them. But soon Conaire drew back on the reins, slowing his mount to a walk. He peered towards the horizon, his face stony.

A shimmer of Fey power surrounded the Dál Riatan like a nimbus, sparking with a faint tingle against him. It wasn't an unpleasant feeling but a comforting reminder that between the two of them, they would sense any attempt that Wulfram or another Unseelie might take to come upon them unaware.

The receding tide exposed a long expanse of wet sand bordering the island. Here and there, the last of the spring bloom of pink thrift showed in a bright display against the marram grass. Orange and black butterflies flitted among both these and the marsh orchids that also dotted the grassy dunes. Birds swooped and dived over the exposed sands, their cries a counterpoint to the constant sound of the waves. And as always, the wind blew, spraying them in occasional mists of cool, salty water.

It was impossible to ignore the beauty of this bright day, washed clean by the previous day's storm. Especially since Thomas knew that this could be the last morning that he experienced, depending on how things went later that night. He breathed in, holding all the beauty—and his reluctance to leave it—as an offering on the altar of his hopes. *Help me do whatever it takes.*

The tides had turned a couple hours past midnight, and the way would be clear until mid-morning. They planned to go to Bebbanburg, followed by Aidan, who would come before the tides came in, despite Thomas' pleas to the contrary. They hoped Celyn would come back to Bebbanburg with news of Nona before they had to leave for Goswick. If not, they could fill him in with what they had learned.

Thomas doubted Celyn would find any trace of his cousin. The Fey held her, and they knew how to keep hidden from humans, even the Sensitives. Which meant that the Welshman would insist on accompanying them to Goswick, no matter the warning in Wulfram's letter.

They all will die. His jaw tightened. He knew Wulfram meant what he said in his note, but he saw no way of dissuading either Conaire or Celyn from coming with him.

As if conjured by his gloomy thoughts, a faint sense of *wrong* touched him. He hauled on Missy's reins, scanning the horizon. *There.* The disturbance emanated from the point ahead of them where the grassy land ended and their trek across the sands to the mainland would begin. Fear struck him. Had the Hound returned?

Conaire hissed and drew his mount to a halt. "A Ward lies ahead. Can ye feel it?"

Relief flooded over him at Conaire's words. A change in the weather he could handle far easier than one of the Alder King's beasts. "More rain?" He glanced up. The only clouds in the sky were high and thin, scudding along the blue dome of the sky.

"I think not. Calling up a mist would be easier this morn, with this sun."

Mist. Missy tossed her head up and down, her eyes rolling in response to his tight grip on the reins. His earlier dread returned twofold. Of course.

Conaire's gaze sharpened on him. "What troubles ye? Do ye sense something else?" He scanned the empty landscape around them, looking for trouble.

Thomas swallowed. "The mist. I—" He gathered himself and continued. "It's a dream I've had, ever since I Crossed to this time. A dream of walking through the mist towards something bad."

Dismay flashed across Conaire's face. "The dreams of the Fey make the world," he muttered. "I dinna suppose your dreams tell us anything helpful about what to do?"

Thomas shook his head. "Can you undo it? Whatever weather he throws at us?"

Conaire grimaced. "If there were only one Ward, mayhap I could. But there's likely more than one if they seek to create a large weather pattern." His wolfhound whined, eager to get going. The Dál Riatan's jaw hardened. "For now, there is nothing we can do. But the two of us, together, are no helpless." He set his heels to his horse without waiting for a reply.

Thomas urged Missy into motion, cold sweat pooling under his arms. Conaire's words would have been more heartening if it weren't for the reminder that pounded through his mind with every step the mare took.

In his dream, he was always alone.

As they drew near to the place where they would cross to the mainland, they saw a figure standing at the edge of the island. The mist that uncurled above the wet sands like the dread blossoming in Thomas' gut obscured the distant line of the mainland. A faint tingle of Fey-awareness identified the figure as Fey.

He was small and wiry, but his shoulders were broad. He leaned on a crude crutch, as he had a club foot. But his power snapped against them, disabusing them of any thought that this Fey was weak. Beside him a large brindled dog rose to its feet, growling as it spotted Conaire's wolfhound. She returned the growl, her ears pinned back.

Conaire's hand fell on his sword, looking around with a keen gaze. But there was no one else in sight, nor could Thomas sense any other Fey. He wasn't sure if this Fey was the Ward, or if another was in control of the mist. But as Conaire had said, it was likely that more of Wulfram's Unseelies were nearby.

"Welcome, welcome! We are long parted, my brothers!" The Unseelie had a deep voice, unexpected for his small size.

Conaire answered with a snarl that echoed his dog's growl. "Out of our way, Unseelie!" He nudged his mount closer, causing the other Fey to step back.

"Ah, Wolfbrother, do not be hasty. Without me you will never find your heart's desire, that I promise you." He held up his free hand. "I mean you no harm. But it pains my neck to look up at you. Dismount, and then we can speak more easily."

Seeing their hesitation, he shook his head. "Come now, Lord Conaire. Do you want to find your wife or not?"

Thomas and Conaire glanced at each other, but there seemed no choice but to do as the Unseelie asked. They both dismounted, holding their horses' reins in their hands.

The mist grew behind the Unseelie, the feel of it sparking against Thomas' skin. An odd sensation flashed over him, just like the one he had experienced with Fee. *Déjà vu. I've been here before—*

"Where is she?" Conaire's abrupt question snapped Thomas back into focus. "Tell me, afore Liath tears your throat out."

The other Fey smiled, but his eyes remained cold. "Come now, we both know I'm in no danger from your beast." His gaze shifted towards Thomas. "I cannot say the same of this wilding. He is the one bringing danger in his wake. I am surprised to see you with him. He is to blame for your wife's discomfort. He is the one who stands in our way, who will doom the Fey to obscurity and defeat." His eyes blazed. "Wulfram is not the enemy."

In one smooth motion, Conaire stepped forward and grabbed the other Fey's tunic, yanking him forward so that they were nose to nose. "I grow impatient with this conversation, Unseelie," he snarled. "Tell us where she is."

"Unhand me, *Seelie,* or your wife dies now." He glanced up, and Thomas and Conaire followed his gaze. A crow circled overhead.

Conaire looked back at the Ward, his eyes hard. He released the other Fey with a shove.

The Unseelie staggered back, clutching at his crutch to keep himself upright. He scowled. "The Healer is not with the Lord Wulfram." He looked at Thomas. "The Ward will come with me. They will be our guests until Lord Wulfram tells us otherwise. You will go on alone. But I warn you again: he is watching." He gestured up at the circling crow. "If either of you do anything except as I have said, he will Speak to those who hold the Healer, and she will die."

Thomas clenched his jaw. "Fine."

"This is foolishness!" Conaire erupted, turning to him with fury in his eyes. "We canna be certain this Unseelie speaks the truth. Giving yourself to Wulfram is exactly what he wants."

"What choice do we have?"

Conaire glared at him but did not answer.

"The wilding is right," the Unseelie said. "There is but one choice if ye want the Lady Nona back. Come with me and she won't be harmed."

Conaire gave the Unseelie a fierce look, but then he let out a breath and shook his head. He looked at Thomas. "Nona will have my hide if ye dinna return. Be careful."

The Unseelie stepped closer to Thomas and held out his hand. "I'll take those reins. The Ward will get to his wife far sooner if we both ride." He gestured at his foot. His eyes flashed. "From here you will go alone."

Thomas wondered if he had imagined the slight emphasis he heard on the word *alone*. It echoed through him as he handed over the reins. He hated to put Missy in the other Fey's hands, but he didn't have a choice. He patted her neck. "Go with him, girl. I'll see you soon."

The mare blew on his shoulder, her big brown eye regarding him solemnly, and then nudged him with her nose. Thomas rubbed her between the eyes, resigned. The dream had never shown him on horseback. He should have known he would have to leave her behind, too.

The Unseelie adjusted Missy's tack and then mounted. "Wulfram bids me to tell you he is as eager for your meeting as you are, but if you value the Healer's life, you will not come to Merton's holding until evening. Your friends await in Bebbanburg. Go there, if you like." He smirked. "I'm sure you'll find it an interesting journey." He clucked and touched his heels to Missy's side, urging her into motion.

But Conaire held his horse still for a moment as he looked down at Thomas. "Go with God, wildin'. I'll come to ye when I can."

Thomas nodded, and without further words the Ward swung his horse's head around. He caught up with the Unseelie and they soon disappeared into the thickening mist, their dogs loping beside them, leaving Thomas alone.

A faint caw met his ears, and he looked up. The black silhouette of the crow still spiralled above him. He sucked in a breath, trying to dampen down the fear that bubbled through him, eyeing the mist with dread. He felt poised on a precipice, as if stepping forward would send him into the abyss. The thought froze him in place.

From far off, the faint sound of ringing bells drifted to him, their bright peals striking back the fear. The monks were going to their mid-morning prayers. He closed his eyes for a moment. *Christ before me. Christ behind me, Christ above me. Christ beneath me.* The Breastplate prayer, as always, bolstered his courage. He was not alone, no matter how it looked.

It had taken him over an hour to cross by foot the other day, when he had the reliquary. But the mist would add an extra challenge. Remembering his soaked boots after the previous crossing, he pulled them off, shoving them under his belt at the waist to avoid carrying them. As a final precaution, he rolled up his breeches.

He heaved a breath, crossing himself as he took a step, and then another, heading into the mist.

CHAPTER 47

VOICES

Odda pulled the blanket over his head, trying to escape the voices. But it was no use. He had been trying to drown them out for two days, but still they continued, swirling inside his head on and off during the day like a *scop's* melody.

He scowled, wishing he had gone with the other novices to the kitchen as they had asked. Preparations were underway for the meal for the upcoming feast. Father Donal would give them a treat, perhaps even one of the sweets baking for the celebration. St. John's Eve, they called it, but everyone knew it was Midsummer's Eve, for all that the monks tried to bring their god into it.

Guilt poked him at this errant thought, and he said the *Pater Noster* once under his breath as penance. He liked the monks well enough. Their kindness was a sweet balm that soothed his troubled heart. They fed him well, for another, even with the fasting days that came around with too much frequency for his liking. And, for the first time in his life, he had found friends among the other novices. He would be happy at the monastery, except for the memories that haunted him. And now, the voices.

He twisted and turned in his bed and gave up with a frustrated cry as he threw back the blanket. He sat up and pulled his knees up under his chin, thinking, and then scrambled off the bed and dug his hand under the straw mattress. His fingers soon found what he was seeking, and he pulled it out.

He had hidden the knife two days ago when the voices started. That day he thought the dark *aelf* himself had come back to claim him. Odda suppressed a shiver at the thought and crossed himself, as the monks had taught him to do to ward against evil. But he was not sure the monks' dead god would be of any use to him if Wulfram wanted to make him his plaything again. The solid presence of the iron blade brought more reassurance, and he stroked it, comforted. Iron warded against the mischief of the *aelfas*. Its cold weight in his hand felt a more effective deterrent than the monks' mumbled prayers.

His thoughts scattered as the insistent need surfaced in his mind again, along with Wulfram's command. *Now! The time has come! Now! Come to me!* The voice was so clear that Odda could see his face, his golden eyes glowing. Odda ducked and covered his head, his heart pounding in fear. He expected to see his former master materialize in front of him, but the connection faded, slipping back into the restless desire that had begun haunting him two days ago.

His eyes flew open. It was the strongest Call yet. But his heartbeat slowed as the quiet of the monastery filled the building where the novices slept. The golden-eyed *aelf's* command was not specifically directed to him. Not like before, when he was chained to Wulfram's will.

This Call was more like when he was a small child, falling asleep at night with his parents' murmured conversations in his ears. It was only because of his former Bond with Wulfram that Odda could hear him at all.

Odda had puzzled this out over the last couple of days after the voices started, for it wasn't just Wulfram's voice that he heard. Another voice Called first, bringing with it an excited, restless feeling that caused him to squirm and fidget in Father Donal's schoolroom. A heightened anticipation which lingered even when the voice was silent. This voice also brushed against him on the way to its actual targets, the *aelfas* who followed Wulfram.

He was glad that he had worked that out before he heard Wulfram. But even though the Call was not directed at him, knowing the *aelfas* were close by seized him with fear. He had run to the kitchen and stolen the knife just as soon as Father Donal wasn't looking. Best not be foolish, after all.

His hand closed on the knife's handle. He took it as a means of defending himself should Wulfram try to enslave him again. He would bury the blade in the *aelf's* wicked heart before he knew what was happening. But over the last couple of days, as the different calls wove in and out of his thoughts, a new plan had taken shape. The final piece had fallen into place last night.

The sharp blade of the knife shone silver in the light coming through the chinks around the shuttered window, reminding him of Master Thomas and his *aelf*-eyes. Odda had hated him at first, as he had hated Wulfram. But the link between he and Master Thomas had shown him that this new Master was not the same as Wulfram. Instead of cruelty, he brought kindness. And in the end, he had given him the choice and set him free.

Odda frowned at the memory. The time enslaved to Wulfram and then to Thomas was a time of shadows, of fear and despair. He remembered Master Thomas offering him freedom. And then the memory faded into mist. The next thing he knew the Lady Nona was bending over him, stroking his hair and telling him he was free.

Free. Master Thomas had saved him from Wulfram's cruel grip, and from his own gentler one. For that, Odda would always be grateful. He still feared the silver-eyed *aelf*, but he knew Master Thomas wouldn't harm him.

He also knew Wulfram feared Thomas. The chill snaking down Wulfram's spine at his first sight of Master Thomas had given Odda hope that the newcomer would destroy his evil Master.

Even when Wulfram commanded him to hold the knife to his own throat, he hoped that Master Thomas would prevail against Wulfram and the *sceadugenga*. Guilt touched him. Perhaps if he had not been there, if Master Thomas had not had to free him, he could have struck Wulfram down. He couldn't help but think it was his fault Master Thomas hadn't succeeded. That Wulfram still lived, and even now sought Master Thomas' death. Or worse.

Now Wulfram called more of his kind to him, or maybe more of the *sceadugenga*, calling them to him to aid in his scheme to destroy these monks, and to destroy Master Thomas.

But last night, in his dreams, the angel had shown him the way to be free forever.

His fingers closed over the hilt of the knife, feeling its hard edges bite into his palm, seeing the space where his finger once was. He knew where to find Wulfram, thanks to the Call. And Wulfram didn't know he was listening.

Oh, he would be careful, say his prayers, and set his wards against evil. There was more to fear than the *aelfas* this Solstice eve. A shiver ran through him at the thought, but then resolution filled him again. He knew he could do as the angel had bid. Sneak up on Wulfram, plunge the knife right into his heart and watch him fall dead. He would erase his debt to Thomas *Aelf*-Eyes, cause those nattering black birds to fall right out of the sky, and silence that hateful voice in his head forever.

Come to me now! The Call pushed him to his feet, excitement pulsing through him. He pulled on his cloak, opened the door, and stepped out into the rain, the knife hidden under his cloak.

CHAPTER 48

ILL PURPOSES

Nona started awake, her eyes flying open. Rain pattering down on her face had woken her. For a moment, she couldn't work out where she was until it all flooded back.

Godric.

Somehow she had slept, but the dull, throbbing pain in her arms, shoulder and hip testified to the discomfort that came from lying trussed on her side on the hard ground with her hands tied behind her. She did not know where she was. They had walked northwards for some time yesterday after her abduction until coming to a halt under the shelter of a small stand of ash. Godric had tied her hands together behind her back and left her propped against a tree in the company of two other Unseelies before melting off into the deepening twilight.

Nona was glad to see the back of the harper even though his departure meant that she was alone with two disagreeable Unseelies who were as ill-mannered as they were dirty. But she couldn't forget the Undying revealing itself in Godric: the low hiss of its voice, the eyes as black as night. Her flesh crawled with remembered horror. No, she would far rather face an army of Unseelies than that creature again.

She pushed herself to a sitting position, thinking of Thomas. He would not avoid the harper quite so easily this day. Godric was likely with Wulfram now, preparing for whatever mischief they had planned. Her abduction, and the theft of Oswald's arm, must be part of it, but to what end Nona could not guess. Easier to guess was Conaire's reaction when he realized she was missing. Of course, he may not know yet. She had told him not to worry if she didn't return until today.

"So you are awake." One of the Unseelies, a shifty-eyed fellow, crouched down before her, interrupting her thoughts. He held up a waterskin, his forearm bulging at an odd angle. It had obviously been broken and healed without anyone setting it properly. "Are you thirsty?"

Nona was desperate for a drink, but she didn't want to reveal anything they could use to torment her. She prayed that her queasy stomach would not rebel and alert them of her condition. "I would drink if you would untie me."

The other Unseelie, a hulking older man with stringy grey hair and more gaps than teeth, snorted as he looked over at her from where he tended a small fire. He rose and strode over to her, hauling her to her feet and yanking her against him as he stood behind her, one arm wrapped around her waist. With his other hand, he grabbed her hair and forced her head back. "Master Godric told us to watch you carefully, my lady, and by no means to free you." His putrid breath wafted over her face as he spoke into her ear from behind, causing her stomach to roil. "We would not want to be disappointing Master Godric now, would we?" He looked over at the other Unseelie. "Give her the water, then."

The other Fey stepped over, and with a sly smile, lifted the skin to her mouth. "Drink up."

Nona tried to sip at it, but he poured it too quickly and she gasped and choked as it ran down her throat, spilling down her dress. The other man released her, and she bent over, coughing and retching.

Their chuckles ignited her temper. She straightened up, leaning against the tree. "You had better be far more worried about what my husband will do to you when he finds me than about Master Godric.

They exchanged a knowing glance, and then the younger one spoke, smirking. "Oh, I don't think so. But we'll find out when he joins us, won't we?"

An icy chill washed over her. "What do you mean?"

But they did not answer. They pulled out some food from their bags and began to eat. Hard bread and dried fish, it looked like. They didn't offer her any, but that was of no account; she doubted she could keep it down, anyway.

She lowered herself to the ground and sat down, leaning back against the tree. Worry assaulted her. What had happened to Conaire? The way the Unseelie spoke, it was almost as if he knew her husband was coming as a prisoner, too. She swallowed back her despair before it overwhelmed her. There was no point in worrying until she knew for sure. In the meantime, she would set her prayers against Godric and Wulfram and against all who worked for ill purposes on this day.

CHAPTER 49

CLOSER TO DOOM

Even with the mud squelching underfoot, Thomas had every intention of walking quickly until he crossed the sands, but those intentions evaporated after only a few paces. The fog swirled around him, caressing him with its clammy fingers and reducing his vision to only a few steps ahead. The glimpse of the mainland had vanished.

But he only needed to see as far as the next cairn, which loomed ahead as a grey shadow. He pushed ahead to it, and then the next.

Even on sunny days, it could be dangerous to cross these featureless sands if a storm blew up, as it often did. But the hardiest of monks would not dare to cross in the midst of the sea fogs that were common here, not even if the tide would not come in for hours. It would be too easy to lose your way and end up being claimed by the waves.

The thought niggled on the edge of his mind until it bloomed full force, stopping him in his tracks as a horrified realization swept over him. It had been too long since the last cairn. He squelched down the burgeoning panic and the impending sense of doom, so familiar from his dreams. *Think, Tommo.*

A seagull cried, the call muted by the suffocating fog. Thomas cocked his head, listening, and then he had an idea and he focussed on the noise of the waves instead. He marked a scuff in the sand before turning slowly around, listening. If he was going the right was the ocean would be behind him, and to the right. But the sound of the surf was strongest when he faced the scuff mark. Fear washed over him. He had been heading straight for the waves. *Christ, have mercy.* He oriented himself and walked forward. To his relief, the shrouded shape of a cairn emerged minutes later. That was too close.

He slowed his pace, ignoring his overwhelming desire to get across the sands as quickly as possible. The mainland was a long way off. He couldn't risk getting off course again. Plus, the footing was uncertain. Some tide pools were deeper than others. Other times, the mud caused him to slip and slide if he went too fast.

He picked his course cautiously, setting his mind on the next step and the next, praying the Breastplate, trying to fight the fear that haunted him.

The fog muffled most sounds except for those closest to him. He heard the splashing of his feet through water, or his own voice saying the prayers underneath his breath. Occasionally, the cries of seabirds came as if from far away. Once, the harsh chortle of a raven stopped him in his tracks. He looked up but could see nothing but billowing fog, and so he continued.

The monks had taught Thomas the value of reflection, and this trek was as good a time as any to practice that discipline. This journey through the featureless mists felt like a metaphor for this whole crazy adventure. He walked in uncertainty, shadowed by doubts and fears, with only his will pressing him onwards.

A strange feeling crept over him. A sense of unreality, as if he had left the world behind, much like the odd dislocation he had felt at Diarmud's Pillar. Had he once again slipped into the Otherworld? Solstice, like Samhain, was said to be a time of turning, when the walls between the worlds were thinnest. Thomas would have dismissed that as nonsense before his inadvertent leap between this time and his own. He had learned the hard way those tales held more truth than he knew.

He forced his fears aside and pushed on. Cocooned in the mist, it was easy to get disoriented. Even the persistent sound of the waves faded under the suffocating fog. The clouds of mist swirled, but not in tandem with the sea breeze that lifted his hair from his face. Once he thought he saw lights twinkling, but when he squinted at them, they disappeared. His breath came more quickly as he fought against the fear that had so often accompanied the mist-dreams that had plagued him since his arrival in this century.

He could not shake the feeling that each step took him closer to doom.

Thomas stopped again to take his bearings, raking his hair back from his face. He had gone off track twice, and that, along with his slower pace, had made the journey longer than normal. The water pulled at his feet as the tide raced in to cut off the island. He swallowed back his unease and allowed a trickle of Fey power to fill him, flooding him with warmth and a renewed confidence.

A sudden disturbance caused him to leap to one side and duck as a black shape whooshed out of the fog above him, erupting in a harsh croak. The big raven landed near him, its black eyes glittering as it cocked its head and squawked at him with its harsh voice.

Come to me now! Come! Wulfram's voice speared through him. Thomas whirled around, thinking that the other Traveller was there in the mist with him. But his heartbeat slowed as he realized it was a Call from Wulfram to his Unseelies.

The raven croaked again, tilting its head as it pierced him with its unblinking gaze. Thomas scowled. He had instinctively grabbed his knife from the holder on his belt, but he squashed the urge to throw it. If he missed, he would lose it in the tide pool stretching between him and the raven. Instead, he sheathed it and stooped down, his fingers curling around wet sand. He threw it at the bird as he rose from his crouch.

The bird hopped away with an indignant screech, ruffling its feathers.

"Tell your master I'm coming and he had better be ready," he growled at it. He stooped and threw another clump of sand at it. This time the bird rose into the air with a few ungainly flaps and soon disappeared into the mist. Thomas watched it go, noting the direction. Ravens were not sea birds. It would head towards land.

And then he wondered if Wulfram had sent it to lead him off course.

He blew out a sigh through his nostrils, dismissing the thought. He splashed through the tide pool and kept going. Suddenly his toe caught on a clump of grass, and he stumbled up a slight rise, coming to a halt on firmer ground. Relief washed over him. *Thank God.* He had made it across the sands. He stood for a moment, savouring the sensation, but then the pressing question of what to do next returned.

Wulfram had told him not to come to him until closer to sunset. Which is what the Unseelie had told him, too. The raven was a reminder, if he had needed it, that the other Traveller still watched.

But Thomas wasn't sure about the Unseelie's casual directive to go to Bebbanburg. A little too casual. Was it a good idea to do what he said?

He hesitated, uncertain. He had to assume that both Conaire and Nona were being held as prisoners, their lives dependent on Thomas' actions. Sunset would be close to midnight, so he had plenty of time to get to Bebbanburg and find out if Celyn was indeed there. He looked up out of habit to check the time by the sun's position and noticed that the mist was dissipating, along with the faint sense of a Ward.

Thankfully. It would be easier going, and quicker, without it. He wiped his feet against the marram grass in the dunes along the shoreline to clean the mud off, and then sat and pulled on his boots. After he was ready, he stood up and started towards Bebbanburg, praying that he was making the right choice.

He walked along the beach, the grassy dunes of the mainland at shoulder height beside him. A path wound its way through those dunes towards Bebbanburg, but on the beach, he felt less exposed to anyone coming along the path. If he spotted anyone, he could at least hide among the dunes until he discovered who they were. No point in taking any chances.

It didn't take long for the mist to disappear. Its departure revealed a grey, gloomy day, the earlier bright sunshine dimmed by clouds. But at least it wasn't raining.

It would take him about two hours to reach Bebbanburg. He wondered idly if Aidan had left from Lindisfarne yet, but he quickly dismissed the thought. The bishop would walk, as was his custom. He would wait until the mist cleared. He also wondered what was happening with Nectan, and if Conaire had been reunited with Nona yet.

All these worries threatened to overwhelm him, and so, with an effort, he set them aside. They were all distractions from his upcoming confrontation with Wulfram. No matter what else happened, the success or failure of Wulfram's plan depended on the outcome of that confrontation. Otherwise, why had the other Traveller gone to such trouble to make sure it would happen? It felt like he was being led as a lamb to the slaughter. But he couldn't give in to fear. He had to have faith that God was the one leading him, not Wulfram, and that for His good purposes. If not, why was he here at all?

These thoughts occupied his mind as he walked, and he lost track of time. But his speculations scattered when the hairs on the back of his neck rose, and the eerie feeling that someone was watching him swept over him. He spun around, scanning the beach behind him, but the only beings in sight were the skittering sandpipers busy along the edge of the waves. Up ahead, a crumpled slump of dunes cut off most of the beach.

He clambered up the dunes, staying low, and peered over the edge. It was hard to see far from his angle, but strain as he might, he could see no one else ahead or behind him along the path or on the beach. But Thomas had learned to trust his instincts, and his Fey senses. Someone was watching him. Most likely that someone was Fey. He concentrated, frowning. *There.* His gaze sharpened on a dune on the side of the path ahead of him, catching a slight movement. The sense of another Fey swept over him at the same time, confirming his hunch.

He sucked in a breath. Now what?

CHAPTER 50

BURN, YE WILL

Thomas started towards the dune where the other Fey was hiding, seeking to flush him out. Whether it was one of Wulfram's underlings or Nectan's Seelies; or Raegenold's lackey, Cadán, he or would not go any further with this Fey shadowing his steps. He was sick and tired of being watched. He drew on a little of his power, its sharp tang of it giving him confidence.

But he had only moved a couple of steps when a faint sound of voices from behind caused him to whirl around. A group of humans came into view around a curve in the path along the way he had come. At almost the same time, a flash of movement out of the corner of his eye made him spin around again, and he saw a Fey leap up from behind the dune, quicksilver in his movements, covered with a shimmering glow of power. He darted away into the rumpled dunes, gone before the humans had seen him.

Thomas dove for the dunes as well. He peeked around the knoll he was hiding behind and his breath caught in his chest. A hand lay curled and unmoving against a clump of yellow stonecrop beside the dune where he had spotted the Unseelie. A human hand, not one belonging to a Fey. A woman, judging by the graceful curve of the fingers.

The club-footed Fey's voice snaked through his mind. *I'm sure you'll find it an interesting journey.* He had assumed the Unseelie had been referring to the mist, but with a sinking heart he realized Wulfram had planned more surprises for this day.

A breathless chortle reached his ears. His head snapped around, but he saw no one. He scooted forward on his stomach so he could see further along the path.

His breath caught. Five men approached, carrying weapons. Axes, two scythes, a *seax*, and a spear bristled from their hands. The presence of the Fey, the woman, and the humans was not coincidental. The men must be searching for the woman who lay motionless ahead. They would stumble upon her within minutes. And then upon him, if they investigated further.

Cold sweat pricked his brow. They would blame him for the woman's plight. Which was likely the point of this little drama.

But if he made it to her first, he could make it look like he was trying to help her. A thin plan, but it was the only one he had. He prayed under his breath as he scurried over to the other dune, hunched over so as not to be seen.

A young woman lay on her side with her eyes closed, pillowed on her outstretched arm. Her features held a delicate beauty. Her tunic, although plain and patched, was clean enough, and her blonde hair combed under the scarf wrapped around her head.

He saw no injury. She seemed asleep. But the problem was obvious. The Unseelie had Charmed her. A faint shimmering net covered her, and his hand tingled when he shook her shoulder, trying to wake her. "Miss?" he asked softly, so as not to startle her. "Miss? Wake up!"

But the Charm held her fast asleep. Thomas scanned her supine form. The scuffled footfalls of the humans drew closer. He had run out of time. He raised his power, brushing his hand against the net that covered her.

The Charm broke with a small *tick*. The girl took a shuddering breath, her eyes fluttering open to meet his. Her eyes flared in shock and she screeched in fright, pushing herself away and scrambling to her feet. She tried to back off but staggered; her face a mask of fear.

Thomas caught her before she fell. "Hush now, it's all right. You're all right."

Shouts rose from the men, and they broke into a run.

The girl struggled against him. "Da!" she screamed. "Help! Da!"

Thomas had no choice but to release her, and she lurched into the group of men as they churned to a halt. One folded her in his arms as she collapsed, weeping, against his chest.

The others ringed themselves around Thomas, their weapons held at the ready, their faces hard and wary.

The man patted his daughter's back. "There now, lass, be not afraid. What has he done to ye? Tell me."

"I've done nothing to her," Thomas interjected, striving to sound innocent despite the wild tripping of his heart. "I found her here, asleep."

The father's eyes narrowed, and he looked back at his daughter. "Maida, is this true? What possessed ye to leave your bed in the middle of the night?"

The girl sobbed, unable to speak. The man pried her fingers from his tunic and gripped her upper arms, his face stern. "Speak, girl, and be quick!"

The girl gulped back her sobs at the look on her father's face. "I don't know! It were the music I heard, so sweet. I thought it a dream."

Her father glanced at Thomas, dark speculation in his eyes.

The girl continued. "I went to find out where it came from, and I..." She stopped, frowning. "It were beautiful, Da, like the song of angels..." A dreamy look crept over her face as she spoke. Her eyes fluttered as her voice trailed off.

Alarm filled his eyes. "Maida!" He shook her once, hard.

Her eyes snapped into focus, and she looked at her father in confusion. "Da! Why are you here?" She looked around at the men and noticed Thomas. She shrieked and scrambled behind her father. "I saw him, Da, in my dreams!" Tears coursed down her cheeks.

Great. Thomas' heart sank. This was Unseelie mischief, a plot that he had walked right into. A plot set in place by Wulfram. But he had no time to puzzle out the reason.

One man looked over at the father. "Witchcraft!" he hissed.

There was a mutter of agreement, and some made the sign against evil.

"No, you are mistaken!" Thomas said, holding up his hands. He looked for a sign that one of them might believe him, but all of their faces were hard and angry. He spun back to face the girl's father again. "She was sleeping. I swear it by all that's holy. I woke her up just before you appeared."

A burly fellow with a bristling black beard spoke up. "This is he! I've seen him, at the bone carver's Ordeal. This is the one who has brought corruption amongst us. 'Tis obvious he has wicked intent against Maida. Perhaps he seeks to steal her away in to the Otherworld. We cannot listen to him lest he ensorcels us all!"

Fear flitted from face to face as the man's words hit home.

Thomas lifted his hands in supplication, hoping to appeal again to reason. "No, wait, I—"

A tremendous whack to the back of his head cut him off. He staggered, and blackness rushed over him.

Thomas woke with a groan, his head pounding along with each heartbeat. *The mist. Going to Bebbanburg. The girl—*

An icy hand of fear seized him as memory rushed back. He lay on his side, in dim light, with his hands tied behind his back. A rough cloth tied over his mouth restricted his breathing. A buzz of excited voices came from outside the shed, but the thudding headache made it hard to concentrate on anything else.

He was in a small, windowless building that smelled of leather and horse. A storage shed for tack, likely. He did not know how long he had been out, and the dim light that filtered through the chinks in the wattle and daub walls gave him no clue.

He sat up, gritting his teeth as he leaned back against the nearby wall. He struggled against his bonds, but to no avail. Frustration filled him. There was nothing to do but wait. He shut his eyes, seeking calm. Aidan would counsel him to pray. He began the Breastplate, and followed it with the *caim* and Psalm 103, reciting them in a low murmur.

The opening of the door interrupted him, revealing the shape of a man against the grey outdoors.

"He's awake," the man said over his shoulder to whomever else was outside, and then stepped aside.

The girl's father strode in, his face set and hard. Thomas shrank against the wall, but there was nowhere to go. The father did not say a word as he lifted his hand with a sneer. A hand that held a knife. "Not yet," he snarled.

Adrenaline kicked Thomas into action and he propelled himself to his feet, but he was a split second too slow to dodge the blow. The knife handle connected with his temple, and everything winked out.

Consciousness returned slowly. Bits and pieces of himself swooped and fluttered like bits of paper in the wind, each holding a different bit of memory. *The mist. Conaire. The girl. Nona.* Nausea and dizziness swept over him as he tried to sit up, and he retched, sinking down again. He breathed in through his nose to settle his gut. He still wore the gag. The last thing he wanted to do was vomit.

Urgency speared through him. He had to get to Goswick by sunset. He pushed himself to a sitting position, supported by the wall. After a moment the dizziness faded, allowing him to think more clearly.

Wulfram must have orchestrated this diversion. Perhaps to stop him from arriving at Merton's holding before the appointed time. And to weaken him before their meeting. He had to figure out how long he'd been out.

But before his addled brain could work that out, the door opened, causing him to squint against the sudden light.

A man stood in the doorway. "He's awake, my lord! Be careful!"

Another man stepped in, a *seax* in his hand. He paused and then strode towards where Thomas sat propped against the wall.

Thomas would have pressed himself *through* the wall if he could, for the newcomer was Raedmund, whose brother Deorwald disappeared the night the Alder King chased Thomas' father back into his life.

This was not a good development. Neither was the appearance of the *coerl* Dunn on Raedmund's heels, a nasty grin on his broad face.

Raedmund crouched before him, fingering the edge of the *seax* as if testing it for its sharpness before he grabbed Thomas' hair and forced his head up. He pressed the blade against Thomas' throat. "*Sceadugenga,*" he hissed, anger flaring in his eyes. "Now, at last, I shall avenge my brother."

Muted by the gag, Thomas could make no reply. Not that anything he said would help. Once Torht had been judged innocent through the Ordeal, Raedmund's suspicions had fallen upon Thomas. Clearly, he had not changed his opinion.

"Oh aye," Dunn said. He stood beside Raedmund, his fingers hitched in the belt that spread across his wide form. "Burn, ye will, and with none to save ye this time!" His small piggy eyes glittered with malicious delight.

Thomas' blood ran cold at this pronouncement. Panic flared as they reached for him and hauled him to his feet. He struggled against them but his efforts weren't enough to stop them from dragging him out of the shed.

CHAPTER 51

CHRIST GOES BEFORE US

Celyn and Tynan rode up to Bebbanburg's gates, their horses snorting as they slowed them to a walk. They had ridden hard after leaving Thunor One-Eyed's holding, propelled by their eagerness to get to Oswy's fortress. But even with their urgency, it was a little past noon when they reached Bebbanburg.

As they approached the village at the bottom of the outcrop, the guard on duty stepped out to greet them. Celyn recognized him as one of the young men who fostered at Bebbanburg and trained with Oswy's war band. The youngling, Dudwine, nodded to him and opened the gate, standing aside for Celyn to pass. "Lord Celyn," he said, lifting a hand in greeting.

But instead of entering, Celyn drew Arawn to a halt. "Any news of the king?"

Dudwine shook his head. "Nay. But after you left yesterday, Bishop Aidan came to Bebbanburg with the arm. By God's grace, Master Thomas had found it and the bishop brought it back." The guard grinned, excitement lighting his eyes.

"Master Thomas—?" Celyn sputtered.

Before he could gather his thoughts, Dudwine continued. "The bishop had hoped that our lord king would still be here. But he sent Lord Aethelwin after him in hopes he could catch up with the king."

Celyn bit back his frustration. In the meantime, his brother was leading a group of armed men into Bernicia. And for what purpose? Were they coming to attack Bebbanburg when the king and his warriors were away? Or had Griffith decided it was time at last for their confrontation?

He set aside the questions that haunted him and focussed on the guard. "Be wary, Dudwine. Four of Penda's men have been sighted south of here. They are armed and on horseback. There may be more."

Alarm filled the young man's face. "Penda's men! 'Tis an evil day, to be sure! First Oswine takes the blessed arm, and now Mercia assails us." Fear lurked in his eyes.

"Take courage. The blessed arm is returned. And the men I describe were heading east, away from Bebbanburg. But we must be cautious. I will send out another to stand watch with you."

Dudwine took a deep breath, composing himself. "Thank you, m'lord."

"Now look you, has Master Thomas come from Lindisfarne?"

"Nay. But the bishop has returned, not one hour hence."

"Bishop Aidan? Here?"

"Yes, m'lord. He came alone. He went to the church to pray and told me to tell you where he was if you arrived."

Celyn swallowed his disappointment over Thomas' absence. Aidan might know the reason. He picked up the reins. "God be with you. Keep your eyes open."

Dudwine nodded. "Yes, m'lord."

Celyn glanced at Tynan. "Let's find out what brings Aidan here." He urged Arawn forward, stifling the questions swirling around his mind. The answers would come soon enough.

Aidan was on his knees before the cross in the church, but rose to his feet as they entered. After greeting them, the bishop recounted all that had transpired while they were gone, including Thomas' discovery of the arm.

"But how did he find it?" Tynan asked, suspicion on his face. He shared his lord's distrust of Thomas. Not that Celyn could blame him. Aidan's tale was thin, at best.

Aidan frowned. "I am not sure. He wouldn't tell me." He sighed. "'Twill be a tale for another time. 'Tis no matter now. When I returned to Lindisfarne last eve I discovered the Lord Conaire was there, and had told Thomas about his wife's disappearance. The note you were given was from Wulfram, telling Thomas to meet him at Merton's holding at sundown today."

"Merton's holding? But why there?" Celyn had been to the holding. He couldn't guess why Wulfram chose that spot.

"Thomas did not know. He and the Lord Conaire set out for Bebbanburg this morn, afore me. They hoped to hear news of Lady Nona. I am much disturbed, so I am, that they are not here."

Ice filled Celyn's gut. "Something has happened to them."

Aidan grimaced. "Likely. I saw no sign of them on the journey from Lindisfarne, but I did not look for them, even so."

"Has Wulfram taken them, too, do you think?"

Aidan grimaced. "I fear it, so I do."

Celyn took a breath, trying to think. "Wulfram's spies must be watching. Mayhap they saw Thomas and Conaire and took them to Wulfram right away. Or are holding them, preventing them from seeing him until later."

"Or perhaps they were ensorcelled, as I was," Tynan said, his face grim.

Fear snaked down Celyn's spine, but he ignored it. "Either way, I must follow. This Wulfram has my cousin. I will not leave her in his hands."

"I will come too, my lord." Fear lurked in Tynan's eyes, but he lifted his chin. "'Tis my fault she was taken. I must get her back."

"As to that, 'tis Wulfram who holds the blame. But I will be glad of your sword even so." Celyn gripped Tynan's shoulder and then turned to Aidan. "But I ask for your blessing, my lord bishop. We will need God's help in our task. You know what we fight against."

"My blessing ye both will have, so ye will, but more than that. I am coming with you." A stubborn glint lit Aidan's eye.

Alarm pierced Celyn. "Nay, my lord, you must not. Thomas warned us that Wulfram seeks to destroy the monastery. What better way than to destroy you, the bishop? You cannot go to him like a moth to the flame!"

Aidan squared his shoulders, his face resolute. "It became clear to me as I prayed over this matter. God asks me to go. I have heard Him, and I dare not disobey."

Celyn eyed him with exasperation. How could he take Aidan with him to the very person who thirsted for his destruction? "My lord bishop," he said, striving to make Aidan see reason. "Please. Stay here and pray for us, I beg you. But you cannot come. Think you! This *sidhe* means you harm. God would not want us to be foolish and put you in harm's way."

"The call I had was as unmistakable as the one that brought me out of Hii to begin the work here. I must go. If you do not wish to be burdened with me, I understand. I will go alone. But I confess your companionship would ease my heart." The bishop paused, his eyes softening as he put a hand on Celyn's shoulder. "We must trust that God guides our steps even now."

Celyn gritted his teeth. He could think of no argument that would sway the bishop. "As to that, I confess your faith is stronger than mine. But I will protect you with my life, I swear it."

"And I, my lord bishop," Tynan said in agreement.

"I am sorry to lay the burden of my safety on your shoulders." Worry clouded the bishop's face as he looked at them, but then he straightened, drawing himself up to his full height. "But we will not walk alone. Christ goes before us, and the victory will be His."

Victory. The word rang hollow in the light of all they faced. Celyn cleared his throat. There was one more piece of ill news to impart. "As to that, we will need the help of Christ and all His angels. It is not just the *sidhe* we face. My brother Griffith has been seen going eastward into Bernicia, along with three other Mercian warriors. More may follow." He took a deep breath and spoke of the fear that had haunted him since the old man revealed what he'd seen. "It is no coincidence he is here now. He is being driven by the same evil that seeks both Oswy's destruction and Lindisfarne's. He and I will meet this day, that I know. And one of us will die."

A shadow crossed Aidan's face. When he spoke, it was in the language of the *Scotti*, and it took Celyn a moment to understand him. "As thy bishop would say, God's will be done. But as thy friend, I pray thy life will be spared."

Tears pricked Celyn's eyes, and he answered him in the same tongue. "O thou my friend, I can assure thee I will pray the same."

CHAPTER 52

UNTIL THE DEED IS DONE

After a brief respite, by mid-afternoon the rain fell in a steady downpour that drummed against the earth. With her hands tied, Nona could not wrap her cloak around herself, and she became soaked to the bone and chilled. The only thing that made it tolerable was that the others were just as miserable as she. The ash trees gave minimal shelter from the rain, and the fire had long since gone out. Her two captors huddled under a tree opposite her, their hoods up against the rain.

Nona pretended to doze but kept a careful eye on them. If they dropped off to sleep, she would take her chances and run. At least the exercise would warm her.

But they did not cooperate. The weather was as much a barrier to sleep as it was to comfort. They muttered together and cursed the rain. Occasionally, one would stand up and disappear through the stand of trees along the path they had taken and then come back looking disappointed. They were obviously waiting for another to arrive.

Which forced her to wait in mingled fear and anticipation of who that might be. Even if it wasn't Conaire, any prisoner of these would be an ally of hers. But if they expected Godric—or Wulfram—that was another story.

A horse's whinny brought her alert. The other two scrambled to their feet, facing the path. A large dog burst from the trees, streaking towards them. Nona had no time for fear as the dog veered around her captors and scrambled to a halt before her, emitting high-pitched whines as it licked her face and pranced around her.

Liath. Tears pricked Nona's eyes as Conaire's wolfhound nuzzled at her with her shaggy head, panting. Nona could only wish her hands were free so that she could give the hound a hug. A moment later, another dog burst through the trees, followed by two men on horseback. Conaire, and another Fey who sat awkwardly upon a bay mare. Nona's joy dimmed as she recognized Thomas' horse. *What had happened to him?*

Conaire spotted her at once. With a curse, he leapt from his horse and rushed over to her, falling to his knees and enveloping her in his arms, muttering curses and endearments in his own tongue, too fast for her to follow. Nona leaned into him, the tears that she had kept at bay wetting her cheeks. "I am sorry, my husband. I should have been more careful. Tynan and Bronwyn were Charmed. I had to leave them—"

"Hush." Conaire pulled away. "Dinna fear, *mo ghràdh*. They are well. I went to Torht's holding last eve and found them coming to Bebbanburg to tell me ye had been taken." His gaze swept over her, anger making his eyes silver. "Are ye hurt? I—"

"That's enough." The Unseelie who had arrived with Conaire hobbled towards them, hampered by a twisted foot and leaning on a wooden staff. "Step away from your wife, my lord. You can see she is unharmed, as I promised."

Liath stiffened, whirling to place herself between them and the gap-toothed Unseelie, who joined the newcomer with a *seax* in his hand. A low growl issued from her throat, matching the growl from the newcomer's dog, also standing stiff-legged at its master's side with its hackles raised.

Conaire rose to his feet, his hands curling into fists. "I wilna leave her."

The newcomer waved his free hand. "Nor do we wish that. We are to wait together until the deed is done tonight."

"What deed?"

"That will depend on the wilding's cooperation," the shifty-eyed Unseelie said, a sly smile lifting his lips.

The newcomer rounded on him. "That's enough. You'll keep your mouth shut unless you wish to explain to Master Godric why you did not."

The other man's face blanched, and he knuckled his forehead in a gesture of respect. "Nay, nay."

The lame Unseelie fixed him with a hard glare for a moment longer and then turned back to Conaire. "Now then. I will remind you that Master Wulfram has his eyes on you." As if on cue, a crow perched nearby erupted in a strident *caw*. "Do as we say, and you and your wife will live to see another day." He gestured to the crooked-arm Unseelie. "Bind him."

For a horrified moment Nona thought the Unseelie spoke of Binding by Fey power, but her fears were relieved as the Unseelie advanced on Conaire with a rope in his hands. Her husband glared at him, his arm muscles bulging as his fists clenched. The other Unseelie raised his *seax* and took a step forward, his eyes narrowing.

Nona struggled to her feet to stand beside Conaire. "Enough. You hold us here to make sure that Thomas does what Wulfram wants. If we die, that only harms Wulfram's cause. Your threats are meaningless. You remind us of Wulfram's eyes. Very well. He sees you, too. You kill us and you risk his wrath. Cease your empty talk. You have the means to hold us captive for now. So be it. But think you: when word gets out that we are missing, my cousin will search for us, as will our king, Nectan. Are you meaning to hold both of them as well?" She wasn't sure if Nectan *would* search for them, but they wouldn't know that.

The lame Unseelie's eyes hardened for a moment, and then he snorted. "Other matters occupy your cousin and your king this day. There is no help coming for you, I assure you." He looked at Conaire. "But your wife speaks truth, even so. Your deaths are not in the plan. Harm, however, is something else. Wulfram has given us leeway to do what we must to get you to cooperate, short of your deaths. How much pain do you want to cause your wife before you give in?"

Fear snaked through Nona's gut at the malicious glint that lit the gap-toothed Unseelie's eyes. He would hurt her and enjoy it.

"*Go dtachta an diabhal thú,*" Conaire growled under his breath, his eyes bright points of silver as his power rose within him. Nona knew enough of his tongue to understand the words. *May the Devil choke you.*

The crow squawked again as a sudden gust of wind almost unseated it, and it flapped its wings to keep its balance.

The lame Unseelie staggered against the gust, causing the shifty-eyed one to grab him to keep him upright. But the other was unmoved, his own power increasing in response, his blue eyes shining like sapphires.

Horrified realization struck Nona like a blow as her earlier fear returned. He was a Speaker. This one would Bind Conaire with Fey power if Conaire persisted. And she, too, for the fun of it, she suspected. His power snapped against them with force. She suspected he could do it. Her own power rose in response, and she reined it in with an effort. She did not want to gain his attention.

"Hold, my husband," she said, striving to make her voice even. "He is right. There is no need for this."

Conaire glanced at her, his eyes narrowed into silver slits. She prayed he would see reason. She wished she was a Speaker and could tell him privately what she feared.

But after a split second, his power subsided, and he looked back at the others. He crossed his arms on his chest. his gaze hard as iron. "Ye are lucky me wife has a clear head or I would call up a wind to toss ye all into the sea, and Wulfram be damned." His jaw bunched. "If we are to be held until sunset, I suggest ye find somewhere out o' the rain."

Seeing his capitulation, the one with the rope stepped behind him and bound his wrists. Liath growled again, but Conaire quieted her with a soft word.

"I know of a place," the lame one said. "Never fear. We will wait in comfort."

They walked for some time in the misty rain, Nona getting colder with each step. Occasionally the fog would thin enough that she could try to get her bearings. They were heading north, as far as she could tell. Away from Bebbanburg.

Eventually, the Unseelie led them to an abandoned holding that lay inland from the coastal path. It wasn't exactly comfortable, Nona reflected, but one building had a roof that was mainly intact. Once the hearth fire was lit, Nona began to thaw, aided by Liath curling up on one side of her and Conaire sitting beside her, leaning against the wall.

There was nothing to do now but wait.

CHAPTER 53

DEVILISH WORK

Arawn snorted, pulling on the reins. Celyn kneed him forward, but the horse tossed his head and whinnied shrilly, dancing sideways. Aidan and Tynan were having the same trouble with their mounts.

"'Tis this mist, m'lord," Tynan said as he patted his horse's neck, calming it. Fear lurked in his eyes as he glanced at Celyn. "'Tis unnatural, like the breath o' the Devil himself. They will no enter it."

Celyn grimaced. Tynan was right. Arawn rarely disobeyed him, but this strange fog made the stallion uneasy. And truth be told, Celyn could not blame the animal. He had never seen such a thick fog in the middle of the day, especially not when the winds were blowing off the sea as they were today.

Aidan glanced at him. "The mist of the *sidhe*," he said in a low voice so that Tynan could not hear. A chill went up Celyn's spine at Aidan's words, but before he could comment, the bishop spoke again to them both. "The horses will go no further. We will have to walk from here."

"Nay, surely not," Celyn said, and tried again to get Arawn to advance. The stallion took a few steps but once again balked, his eyes rolling. Celyn felt him gathering his haunches underneath him and wheeled the horse around to rejoin the others. He had no desire to be thrown off Arawn's back. "It seems you are right, my lord bishop. But it will take us at least two hours to walk to Merton's holding from here. Longer, if this mist slows our pace." Impatience bit at him. "If they have taken Thomas and the Lord Conaire, they will likely be at the holding by now, along with my cousin."

Aidan nodded. "Aye, so ye say. We must press on."

"But where will we leave the horses?" Tynan looked around at the empty landscape, his face drawn with fear. "I dinna wish to be on foot in this mist."

Celyn understood his fear, and held others he dared not share. Thomas had said that Wulfram would have others of the *tylwyth teg* with him tonight. They would likely encounter some of them. And if the stories of the fair folk were true, what else might they find in the cursed mist?

"Do not fear, me son." Aidan's comment to Tynan brought Celyn back from his fearful imaginings. "God goes with us. Let us not lose courage." The bishop thought for a moment. "If we press the horses, we can get back to Torht's holding within the hour. Perhaps he will come back with us, so as to take them back when we set out on foot from here."

It seemed as good a plan as any, so they turned their horses' heads back the way they had come. Touching his heels to Arawn's flank, the stallion leapt into a gallop, eager to leave the haunted mist behind.

Celyn couldn't blame him. But for himself, he chafed at the delay. Nona and Thomas needed him. He could only pray that his sword would reach them soon enough to make a difference against the evil that threatened them.

"It seems thicker," Celyn said as they approached the misty barrier once again upon their return. Torht had not accompanied them but had exchanged their mounts for some of his own and told them to let the horses go once they reached the mist. He was confident that they would find their way home. Celyn thought it odd, especially when the bone carver whispered in the beasts' ears before they set out from the holding. The work of the *tywlth teg,* he thought, with a slight shiver.

The fog curled eerily in movements unrelated to the ocean breeze. The hairs rose on the back of his neck. He turned to Aidan. "My lord bishop, are you sure you must come with us? Tynan said it true. This is devilish work."

A grim smile crossed Aidan's face. "A poor bishop I would be, to let the Devil roam unchallenged through these lands. Nay, we have your swords, and all the saints and angels beside. We do God's work, and He will help us. Have no fear."

Celyn tried one more time. As much as he understood the bishop's desire to face the evil head-on, he could not easily set aside his concern for Aidan's safety. "Of course. I pledged you my sword. But I do not know how much use it will be against that," he said, gesturing at the mist.

"Ah, Celyn, your sword arm is not your only asset. We need your courage, your faith, your constancy. And not just I, but the Lady Nona, and Thomas as well. Do not forget that." He turned to Tynan. "Me son, none would fault ye if ye came no further."

Tynan squared his shoulders, swallowing back his fear. "Nay, me lord bishop. I ha' pledged to me lord to keep his lady safe, her and the babe. I failed her once. I will no do so again."

Aidan nodded. "As you wish." He dismounted, and the others did the same. They quickly stripped the tack from their horses and left it hidden in the marram grass edging the path. Torht had said he would come back in the morning to retrieve it.

As soon as the horses were unencumbered by their saddles and bridles, they tossed their heads and, almost of one accord, turned and headed back.

Aidan watched them go and then looked back at them. "We must not delay any further. God be with us," he said, his jaw tightening. He gripped the cross around his neck with one hand, and with the other he took a firm hold of his bishop's staff and stepped into the swirling, veiling mist.

Celyn had taken this path before. Usually, the walk was a pleasant one, especially in high summer. To their left would be verdant fields, dotted with white sheep, the rolling hills on the horizon a pleasing counterpoint to the view. Songbirds would flit among the hedgerows and dunes, their melodies filling the air.

But now all colour and sound were muted, except for the occasional harsh caw of a crow and the squelch of their feet as they walked the sodden path. A drizzly rain fell, or perhaps it was the constant mist that dampened their skin. They could see only a few paces ahead.

An unspoken eagerness to get to their destination hurried their pace. Aidan prayed in an indistinct murmur, his voice rising and falling in time with their steps.

It was a comforting sound, easing Celyn's fears, and his grip on his sword loosened slightly under its benign effect. In the mist, the passage of time was hard to judge, and Celyn began to lose the sense of how long they walked, or even where they were. The measured rhythm of one foot in front of the other mirrored his heartbeat; the shadowy forms of his companions were his only contact with the others. It was hard not to let his thoughts drift.

Celyn forced himself to concentrate on Aidan's murmured prayers, but there was something odd about those. Was the bishop singing? A spike of alarm pierced him. Celyn stopped. Where was Aidan? Tynan? He peered through the billowing mist but could see no one. His call to the others stuck in his throat as the chanted prayers melted into a low humming song accompanied by a pipe playing a light, dancing tune. The notes dipped and wove around him and his thoughts fled as he listened, admiring the skill of the player.

A ghostly shape appeared, but he felt no fear, only a piercing longing, for the graceful outline was surely none other than Murieann, and he reached for her, aching to enfold her in his arms again. The sweet haunting melody that accompanied her brought joy and sorrow in equal measure. *Ah, fy nghariad—*

She faded away, along with his longing, as the complexity of the music captured him. He tried to commit it to memory, but it was as ethereal as the mist and could not be grasped. Everything else dropped away, lost to the siren song. He stopped walking, but his spark of alarm at doing so quickly faded under the spell of the pipe. They were the most intriguing harmonies he had ever heard, the rhythms exotic but familiar and beguiling.

Words drifted towards him. Celyn frowned, trying to hear.

I summon today all these powers between me and those evils, against every cruel and merciless power—

A cold shock of recognition brought his wits back. "Aidan!" He gasped and opened his eyes.

The bishop loomed over him, his face wreathed in mist. "Celyn! Are you well, me son?" He grasped Celyn under the arms and hauled him to a sitting position.

Celyn's head swam. He couldn't make sense of where he was, what had happened. He looked at Aidan. "My lord bishop," he managed.

Aidan smiled, relief blooming in his eyes. "I thought I'd lost ye, so I did."

The music. It all came back with a cold rush of fear. A Charming, just as Tynan had described. A hint of the melody reached him and his heart contracted in yearning.

"Celyn!" Aidan shook him. "Do not listen! They seek to steal thy soul, *mo cara.*" In his urgency, he had reverted to the tongue of the *Scotti.*

The words brought back the memory of the time he had spent at the great monastery of Hii, of the prayers and songs the monks spoke in their own language and that he had grown to cherish. The last of the mist-spell dissipated under the memories, and anger filled him that he had been so easily tricked.

He stood up, looking around. "Where is Tynan?"

Aidan grimaced and gestured behind him. "I cannot wake him."

Celyn turned and saw the Dál Riatan sprawled on the side of the road, asleep, a faint smile on his face. He knelt beside him. "Tynan," he said forcefully. "Wake up! Tynan!"

But the man still slumbered, no matter how much he shook him. Celyn looked up at Aidan. "This happened to him yesterday, when Nona was taken. Perhaps hearing it again so soon strengthens its hold." An echo of music tickled against his ears, and he stood up, speaking to drown it out. "As to that, I am not sure I would have been any different if you had not been here. But how did you escape its power?"

Distaste crossed the bishop's face. "I did not. I was lost, as you were. But for the good Christ, I would be lost still. I heard His voice, calling me away."

"Thank God for His mercy," Celyn said, a thrill of awe creeping over him. He let out a breath. It was impossible to tell where they were, but it seemed darker. "It's growing late. This spell has delayed us. We must hurry."

"Aye." But Aidan crouched down beside Tynan and placed a hand on his forehead, saying a quick prayer before rising again. "God will shield him from the worst of this evil. We must not fear. Christ walks before us."

Celyn clenched his jaw, seeking courage that was as elusive as the mist. "Aye," he managed. He began walking down the trail, his hand firm on his sword hilt, Aidan striding at his side. *Christ, have mercy. St. Michael, guide my arm.*

Some time later, they rounded a hill and spotted a man lying motionless by the road. Aidan knelt beside him while Celyn stood watch. The man was a warrior, dressed in mail and with a fine sword in a wooden sheath at his belt. He was fast asleep.

"He has fallen under the spell o' the *sidhe*," Aidan said. He shook the man, but it was no use. Like Tynan, they could not rouse him.

Celyn scanned the landscape, but the clinging mist did not allow him to see far. "We must be careful. 'Tis likely that this is one of the Mercians the old man spotted. My brother and the rest of his men must be close." He drew his sword, the weight of it in his hand a comfort.

They had not gone far before they found the next man, Charmed like the other. Two more lay further down the path. But there was no sign of his brother. *Yet.* An icy chill chased up Celyn's spine. This mist would obscure anyone who wished to creep up on them and attack. His shoulder blades twitched at the thought.

The shadows deepened around them. It would soon be sunset. And then what? He couldn't bear to think of the other evils that might be unleashed upon them. And where was Thomas, or Nona?

The road ahead climbed up a slight hill. If Celyn remembered right, there was a hill just before an intersection with the path that would lead to Merton's holding. He glanced at Aidan. "The holding is just ahead. Stay close."

As they got to the top of the hill, Celyn saw another figure ahead. But this man was not asleep. He stood upright, his sword unsheathed, looking up at him. He couldn't see his features in the gathering misty dusk, but Celyn didn't need to.

"It is my brother," he said, over his shoulder, but then there was no time for anything else as Griffith ran towards him, his sword in hand.

Celyn lifted his own sword, waiting.

CHAPTER 54

A SUBTLE HAND

The men herded Thomas down the path, his hands bound behind him. The gag was still in place. That, and the knot of anxiety that had settled in his chest, made it hard to breathe. Mist curled around the dunes, lifting its shadowy fingers from the ground in long tendrils.

Thankfully, his captors had not burned him to death on the spot. Thomas had gleaned enough from their conversations to know Raedmund wanted a larger audience for his revenge. But they headed north, to Goswick, not south towards Bebbanburg. Raedmund did not want to risk a repeat of the Ordeal and the chance for Thomas to be declared innocent.

The *thegn* led the group, grim-faced, his eyes glittering with feverish anticipation. Dunn tromped beside Thomas, occasionally poking at him with his spear to make Thomas go faster. His eyes, too, were lit with an unholy light, his smile even more malicious than normal. In fact, all the men seemed driven along by something more than anger or fear. They occasionally muttered to each other in low voices that he heard as smattered snatches of words: *free Maida*, or *sorcerer*, or *blood*. Thomas sensed the stink of the Undying's influence as a miasma that surrounded them along with the mist. The dark shadow of the Undying had fallen over them; a subtle hand directing their will.

Thomas had no intention of being burned to death, but he didn't see a way to stop them. And time was running out. Most of the day had passed while he lay unconscious. At least they were heading in the direction he needed to go: Merton's holding was north of Goswick, along a river that emptied into the sea.

I will do it. Thomas stumbled as Odda's voice whispered through his mind. A vivid flash of memory jolted through him.

Odda sat beside him, his face frightened but determined. Horror filled Thomas, a frantic denial springing to his lips.

He gasped as the memory disappeared, and no matter how he strained, he could not retrieve any more.

It was part of the lost time between when he had freed Odda from the Binding and when Thomas had woken up afterwards. That time had remained a blank in his memory. Why, now, had this piece returned? And why not all of it? What had Odda meant to do? He gritted his teeth against the helplessness that grew as the mist thickened and the growing darkness as the sun dipped towards the horizon.

The men cast a fearful gaze around them as the fog swallowed them, muffling all sounds and blotting out their vision.

Raedmund turned. "Pick up your feet," he snarled. "It's not far."

The men glanced at each other. Maida's father gave Thomas a shove from behind as they quickened their pace to follow the *thegn*.

Thomas fought down the fear that grew with every step. *Christ before me, Christ behind me.* He wielded the prayer like a weapon against his creeping despair and forced himself to think. There was about an hour to dusk, as far as he could tell. He had to keep focussed. All this was just a distraction. A pretty major distraction, granted. There was still time, if he could just get free of the humans—

The thought acted like a handful of ice water dashed in his face, waking him up. *If he could just get free of the humans.* That was the problem. He had forgotten who he was. What he was. Humanly speaking, it would be difficult to get himself out of this situation. *But I am Fey.*

He could use his Gifts to escape. Not Travelling, but Speaking. An icy lump formed in his stomach at the thought, but he ignored it. He had learned much since he had inadvertently Bound Odda. He had more control.

As they rounded the next dune, the mist thickened, billowing around them and blotting out all but their own shadowy forms. It was now or never. Thomas gathered his power to him in a dizzying rush and lowered his shoulder, barrelling into the man ahead of him. Surprised, the man stumbled forward, colliding into Raedmund with a startled yell. As a minor scuffle broke out, Thomas spun around to Maida's father, who held a spear at his back.

He lifted the spear to shoulder height, his face twisted in a snarl as he prepared to attack.

NO! Thomas' command was as forceful as he dared to make it.

The man froze in place.

You'll let me go.

Thomas felt the man's confusion and fear as his grip on the spear slackened. He took his chance, pulling on more of his power as he dodged through the milling group of men, the surge of power making him more nimble than usual. One man grabbed at him, but he avoided him, skipping away and fighting through their grasping attempts to stop him. With a final effort, he wrenched free and plunged into the mist.

He is gone, he threw at them, the contact with all of their minds, overwhelming him for a panicked moment until he roped in the power and withdrew.

He ran blindly, trusting that God would lead his steps.

The mist parted before him and closed behind him as he pounded away from the men. But he couldn't run blind forever. After a few moments he stopped, panting. He strained his ears to hear any sounds of pursuit, but there were none, only muffled sounds of alarm through the mist.

They wouldn't follow. He had disappeared into the mist, and it would take a stronger man than any of them were to plunge into it after a sorcerer on this Solstice eve. They would go home and barricade their doors against him and the other *sceadugenga* who might lurk in the dark, seeking their blood.

Triumph sureged through him, and he almost laughed aloud. *Feel the Force, Luke. Hah.* But his glee at his trick quickly faded at the memory of their fear. He grimaced, squelching his guilt. They would have killed him without hesitation if he hadn't taken matters into his own hands.

Dizziness swept over him as his headache pounded in time with the furious beats of his heart. He felt wrung out. The slight use of his power and the blows from the men had taken a toll. Which as probably the point of all this. Wulfram and the Undying had ensured that Thomas would either be dead and unable to stop them, or weakened and more easily conquered. But he couldn't dwell on that now. He had to get going.

He looked around, straining to see through the thick fog. A spike of panic pierced him. *Come on, Tommo, think.* The answer came immediately. Once again, he was thinking as a human. He didn't have to see. He could find out where to go, even in this blinding mist.

He closed his eyes, seeking Wulfram's Call. At first, he heard only a jumble of confused voices, both Domech and Wulfram Calling the Fey to their Gatherings. He concentrated, blocking out Domech, and soon Wulfram's voice flared in his mind. *Come to me. Come, my brothers!*

Thomas' eyes snapped open, recoiling from the Unseelie Call. But as he had hoped, it left behind the exact location. It would lead him like a beacon, even through the mist. But not just him, of course. Others would come.

Thomas set that thought aside. He had accepted that he might not survive this night. If it came to that, he could only pray his sacrifice would not be in vain.

I will do it.

Odda's voice, again. Thomas whirled around, but he saw nothing. Odda was not there. Why did he keep hearing him? Why this memory, now? He shut his eyes, searching for more, but there was nothing. He heaved a breath through the gag. First things first. Cut his bonds with a rock or something else he could rub them against. He tried to push the gag off with his shoulder, but gave up in frustration.

He forced himself into motion, straining to remember if there was another holding before Goswick. If he could find one, it would be easy enough to use a sharp-edged tool and free himself without being seen, thanks to this fog.

Thomas felt cut off from everything and everyone, a growing sense of dread enveloping him. So many times in his dreams he had been walking towards his doom, fighting fear. Now the odd sense of *déjà vu* that had haunted him since leaving Bebbanburg returned full force.

But something else other than *déjà vu* assailed him. A sense that he had left this world entirely and had stepped into another. Much like when he had been at the standing stone near his father's holding and the mist had rushed in. Or when he had sought Odda out when he freed him from the Bond.

It was hard to gauge the passage of time other than the shadows growing as the sun went down. But he didn't need that outward sign to tell him that sunset was approaching. Power awakened around him, gathering for the surge that would accompany the day's disappearance into night.

He recited the *lorica* under his breath to the pace of his steps, concentrating on the words to dispel the unease that crept around him on questing fingers like the mist. *God's hand to guard me, God's shield to protect me, God's—*

A sudden chittering noise startled him out of his thoughts, and he looked up to see a shape swooping towards him out of the mist. He ducked instinctively, and a sense of another Fey prickled over his skin. He whirled around.

A shape materialized out of the fog. His heart slowed as he recognized Cadán Longshanks, his golden armband muted by the swirling fog. Relief and fear rushed through him at the sight. As always, he wasn't certain if Cadán was friend or foe.

"We are long parted," Cadán said with some amusement as his gaze travelled over Thomas. He held up a hand. "I wilna hold your lack of reply against ye, wildin'."

He stepped forward quickly, drawing his knife, and Thomas stumbled back, fear piercing him. But the other Fey deftly cut the gag and stepped behind him to cut his bonds.

Thomas sucked in a breath, relieved as he rubbed his sore wrists. "Thanks," he muttered. "What are you doing here? Did Wulfram send you?"

Cadán snorted faintly. "Ach, he has no hold on me. I told ye before. I serve Raegenold."

Thomas studied him. More than likely he spoke half-truths, indulging in the game that all the Fey, Seelie and Unseelie alike, loved to play. "So Raegenold wants you to help me?"

"I wouldna have freed ye, else wise," Cadán retorted. "My king has no love for Wulfram, ye know that full well."

Thomas wasn't sure he *did* know that, but he kept that thought to himself. No use antagonizing Cadán. "Fine. Let's go then."

Cadán fell into step beside him. "What do ye plan to do?"

Thomas glanced at him. The question seemed sincere. But he wasn't sure how much to reveal, especially since he wasn't sure of Cadán's loyalties. He might be loyal to Raegenold. But he also might be playing both sides, and in league with Wulfram, too. He couldn't risk having the Unseelie communicating everything he said to either of them. "I guess you'll find out."

"I canna help ye if ye dinna tell me more," Cadán protested. "Come now, wildin'. There are more than a dozen Unseelies gathered with Wulfram. Do ye think ye can vanquish them all by yourself?" He scowled. "Powerful ye may be, but not that powerful. Especially since the foul sense of the Undying hangs over the holding like the breath of hell." He blew out a breath, exasperated. "Nectan is no comin' to rescue ye this time. They'll be none to stop Wulfram from snarin' ye and Bindin' ye to his purposes, not with the Solstice power and the Undyin' to help him."

"So why are you here? Are you going to help me?" A thought struck him. "Is Raegenold nearby? Is his Court coming against Wulfram?"

But before Cadán could answer, a muffled shout from ahead suddenly broke the mist-wreathed silence, followed by the unmistakable steel-on-steel sound of blades clashing. A fight had broken out on the path ahead.

Thomas halted in his tracks, straining to hear. A sudden premonition seized him, and he broke into a run towards the sounds, slapping away the hand Cadán had held out to stop him.

CHAPTER 55

HARBINGER

With a muffled curse, Cadán caught up with him just as Thomas spotted a slumped figure lying by the trail. Another human caught in a Charm. Thomas knelt beside him. A warrior, judging by his sword. Not one he recognized from Bebbanburg. In fact, by his clothing, the man was one of the *Scotti*.

"Celyn!" The muffled shout came from ahead. Thomas' head snapped up. *Aidan.* What was he doing here? He jumped up to go to the bishop's aid.

But Cadán stopped him with a hand on his shoulder. "Dinna be foolish," he hissed. "Ye may be a powerful Fey, but ye'll bleed to death like any human."

The words checked Thomas' urgency. Cadán was right. Rushing in blindly was a good way to get killed. "That's the bishop up ahead. I have to help him. Wulfram wants to destroy the monastery. What better way than by killing him?"

Cadán's eyes snapped with impatience. "Think! If that is his plan, then ye walk into his trap. Who will be blamed for his death if ye are there? For certain Wulfram will no be seen. Ye alone will carry the blame, and to be sure the story will go that ye did it wi' Oswy's blessin'."

A chill touched him. The Unseelie was not wrong. That could be what Wulfram had planned. But maybe not. Aidan believed God had brought him here to use him to thwart Wulfram. Now, more than ever, he had to believe that, too.

Aidan's shout came again, over the top of the sounds of clashing swords, but this time Thomas could not hear the words. He seemed further away. He turned to Cadán, shaking off his hand. "I have to go," he said. "Come with me or not. Just don't get in my way."

He shoved past the Unseelie and ran down the path, slowing as he got closer to the noise. He scanned ahead for any of the Fey, but the prickly feeling of the Fey-mist obscured the sense of their presence. A quick glance behind him revealed only the fog. Cadán had vanished as quickly as he appeared. If Raegenold indeed had sent him to aid him, where was he now?

But there was no time to think it through. A low, guttural cry reached him, and another shout, and a clash of steel. Cadán was right about one thing. This could be a trap. He swallowed and walked cautiously towards the sounds, his nerves screaming danger at every step.

Two figures emerged as shadows in the fog. One was Celyn, the other his brother Griffith. They circled each other with weapons raised. Thomas saw no sign of the bishop or of anyone else.

"Traitor!" Griffith snarled the word at his brother in the language of the Cymry. He thrust at Celyn and then leapt back, dodging the circling, swinging sword of his brother. "My blade is thirsty for your blood. These crows—" he gestured grandly to the black audience assembled on the branches above—"are hungry for your flesh."

The horrific, cawing assent of the birds drowned out the clash of steel as the brothers leapt to engage each other again.

They had not spotted him. Thomas crouched behind a clump of gorse on the path, his heart in his mouth as he watched.

Celyn and Griffith fought in a deadly dance, striking at each other and leaping back. They were well matched, each so versed in the other's fighting style that it was clear this fight could last some time. Griffith had an advantage of height and bulk on Celyn, but Celyn moved with a quicker grace, his sword swooping in elegant, efficient arcs in his attempts to get past his brother's defences.

The sun was sinking. As sunset approached, power intensified, making Thomas' blood sing. His jaw clenched. He could not help Celyn. In fact, he might be a hindrance. And time was running out. Whatever Wulfram planned, he was going to use his heightened strength at sunset to do it. As the bishop was nowhere to be seen, Thomas had to assume Aidan was now in Wulfram's clutches.

But how could he leave Celyn now? The Welshman had stood by him from the beginning. It felt like a betrayal to abandon him. He half-stood, preparing to leap out at Griffith to provide a distraction, but then Wulfram's Call pierced through him again. *Come NOW!*

There was no time. Sunset was coming. He could not tarry here. His part lay elsewhere. He grimaced and crept away from the gorse, committing Celyn to God. Wulfram had drawn him here for a purpose. He had escaped the trap of the humans, which would have ended in his death. But Wulfram surely had a Plan B. He had to assume it the same as before: to use the enhanced power of Solstice to Bind Thomas to himself or, more likely, to the Undying. Or to both.

And to then send him to Lindisfarne to destroy it, or to the *witenagemot* to disrupt it. Or to do both. It was foolish to put himself in the other Traveller's hands, but what choice did he have, with Nona's life at stake? And Conaire's. And now Aidan's as well.

He didn't know how to prevail against the joint threat of Wulfram and the Undying. He had considered one idea after another and rejected each in turn. The only remaining idea was a wild and crazy one, holding many dangers of its own. A last option, to be used only if there were no other choice.

Suddenly he felt an odd resistance, an odd pressure against him, and he stumbled, jerked out of his thoughts. He squinted through the fog, searching for landmarks. A hollow, eerie feeling crept over him, as if the world beyond the mist had vanished, leaving him in an unfamiliar wasteland. In the shadowy dusk, even the ground beneath his feet felt alien.

The strange *déjà vu* sense that had haunted him earlier crashed upon him. Dread filled him. This was the place of his dreams: the misty darkness, full of terrors unknown, his doom waiting to fall on him with rending claws. He breathed in shallow gasps as he fought the fear that tripped his heart into overtime. *Get a grip, Tommo,* he scolded himself. *Get moving.*

He forced himself to take a step, and then another. Better that to being frozen in place, waiting for something to tear him to pieces. The holding still pulled at him. But it felt more distant, as if he had shifted locations.

His headache returned full force. He drew a deep breath. Bad idea. The mist filled his lungs, causing him to choke and retch as if he had inhaled noxious gas. He suppressed his coughs as best he could. The sound was a come-and-get-me invitation to whatever strange beasts occupied this mysterious place. As if conjured up by that unwelcome thought, a low, rasping snarl sounded behind him and he whirled around, drawing his knife from his belt. But nothing met his eyes except the swirling fog, and he lowered the knife and wiped a trembling hand over his face.

Just keep going. Christ, have mercy. God, help me.

Thomas had not gone far when a long, sobbing wail pierced the mist. A female's voice. For a split second, he thought it was Nona, but then it came again, closer this time, and he realized it wasn't. Nothing human made that sound. He clapped his hands over his ears as it continued. He would prefer to hear Nona screaming for help over the sound of this voice. It throbbed with sorrow and aching loss, its wails containing the grief of every mother weeping over a child, every lover bereft by death.

He whirled around, seeking the source. Muffling the sound didn't help. The voice soaked into his soul, bringing with it the overwhelming grief of his losses, as sharp as a knife scraping against his heart. His mother. His father. The weight of their absence was so heavy he could hardly breathe.

The voice cut off, leaving him on his knees, wracked with sorrow. He took a shuddering breath as reason returned, but froze as he glimpsed a shape floating through the fog ahead. Long wisps of hair floated around its head in strings. It turned towards him, its face a shadowed oval.

A banshee, harbinger of death, spoken of in folktales and legends. Thomas lifted a shaking hand to keep it away. "Please no, God no, don't let it..." If it wailed again, he would be lost.

But it made no sound. They stared at each other for a heartbeat until the fog boiled up in front of it. When it had subsided, the banshee was gone.

Thomas got to his feet, shaken. He rubbed the tears from his face, trying to calm his heart's furious pounding. The banshee's wails meant that someone's death was near, or so the stories went. He exhaled, fighting the lingering sorrow that remained, wishing with all his heart that his father was with him. His throat tightened.

Christ before me, Christ behind me, Christ above me, Christ below me. He was not alone, he reminded himself, and starting walking again. But one question kept whirling through his mind as he drew closer to his destination.

For whom did the banshee wail?

CHAPTER 56

GOD'S INSTRUMENT

Odda gripped the knife, trying to ignore the strange mist. He focussed instead on Wulfram's voice. As much as he hated it, it was the only thing that could lead him through this unnatural fog. But he had to be careful. If he paid attention to his former Master for too long, he felt strange inside. Hollowed out, as if the golden-eyed elf were trying to get inside him once more and steal his soul.

Come, Unseelies, the time is now! The voice broke through his thoughts and he concentrated on it, chasing down the sense of which way to go. But it was maddening, like the mist, and difficult to pin down. He frowned, seeing a light bobbing ahead. His steps slowed as he squinted at it, fascinated by the patterns the light made in the fog.

A sudden screech of a seagull startled him, bringing him alert. He stood still, staring at nothing. His knife lay at his feet. Fear seized him. He must have dropped it, although he had no memory of doing so.

After that, he tied the knife to his wrist with a piece of rope he had in his satchel and was careful to only consult the voice in small snatches. Thoughts of using the knife to stop Wulfram kept him moving through the mist-wreathed landscape.

Not only the fog haunted him. Soon after he crossed the sands and reached the mainland, a movement out of the corner of his eye caused him to drop to the ground, clutching the knife to his chest. A slight breeze shifted the fog aside, and he glimpsed a shadowy figure. He froze in place for many long moments, barely breathing, until he was certain that the shadow figure had not seen him. By the queasy feeling in his stomach, he recognized it was another of the *aelfas* answering Wulfram's Call.

He crossed himself twice for good luck. He had not thought about others of Wulfram's kind being there, following the same Call that led him on. Surely, they would fight him when he attacked Wulfram. How could he vanquish them all? He lingered for a few long moments, torn by indecision and fear.

But then the Call pulled at his mind, bringing the memory of the knife's edge against his throat and the utter terror he had felt at his own helplessness. After Master Thomas had freed him, he vowed never to be a slave again. But there had always been the possibility that the wicked *aelf* could find him and force him to serve him once more.

Odda straightened up, his resolve renewed. This was his chance to rid himself of that threat. He could not forget the angel's words: *you will be God's instrument, young Odda. Take courage.*

He would just have to be extra careful. Besides, he could sense them, another leftover from his tie to Wulfram, but he did not think they could sense *him*. It was a slight advantage, but a useful one.

He crossed himself again and rubbed the iron blade for luck. Squaring his shoulders, he continued on, keeping a wary eye out for any more shadowy shapes.

CHAPTER 57

A Willing Victim

Thomas walked on through the eerie landscape. The banshee had disappeared, but other strange creatures roamed, hidden from his sight by the fog. Pattering footsteps followed him, but when he turned around, they stopped. An odd hulking shadow ghosted through the mist beside him for a time, but he couldn't figure out what it was, or if it was just a trick of the swirling clouds. Lights winked in the distance, but he didn't see any buildings.

Nor did he see Cadán. He spared no attention for the other Fey's motives. If the Unseelie would not help him, he hoped he would not stand in his way.

He came to a wide, rushing river that tumbled over large rocks, white foam gleaming in the dusky light. The water looked oily black in the twilight. He frowned. A placid stream edged Merton's holding. Not this powerful torrent. Nor was there an arching bridge spanning the stream as he saw now, which dissolved into the fog on the other side. Yet he knew he was heading in the right direction. The lodestone of the Call drew him on. He was almost there.

Foreboding seized him as he eyed the bridge. What was waiting to pounce upon him when he crossed?

But he had no choice. He dared not risk the river, so he gritted his teeth and stepped onto the bridge, ignoring the strange quiver that ran through the solid structure. It reminded him uncomfortably of the vibration of a web when a fly became ensnared in it.

Once on, he did not want to linger, in case the wooden surface became sticky, freezing him in place as an unknown horror descended. Fear from that unwelcome image quickened his steps, but he resisted the urge to break into a run. Once he started running, he might never stop.

The rushing water murmured and whispered. Once or twice, he thought he heard a word sighing through the sound, but he ignored it, and it soon faded.

The crossing took longer than he expected, considering the width of the river, but at last he caught sight of the other side. He slowed, scanning the shore, but there was nothing there, and he stepped off the bridge with relief.

The gathering of power spurred Thomas onwards. He stumbled suddenly as the mist swirled thickly around him, clutching at him, but he pushed through it, and it lessened. He looked around. A familiar landscape revealed itself through the fog. Wherever he had been, he was back now on the path leading up to Merton's holding.

He swallowed, his mouth gone dry. *This is it.* Images flashed before him—the monks at prayer, Aidan's long face, his eyes filled with love—and fear squeezed his heart at the thought of what would be lost if Wulfram succeeded. He had been brought through time and space to this very moment, hurled by God to stand against another of his kind who sought to undo history. *I'm here. Please—* His prayer stuttered and died, but he gathered himself. *Help me.*

Now or never. He sucked in a deep breath and continued on, his senses alert. There seemed to be no one around, but as he approached, glowing figures slipped out from behind the buildings. Wulfram's Unseelies who had answered his Call. He counted at least seven of them, but how many more still hid in the shadows? Cadán had said a dozen or more were here. Where were the rest?

But he hadn't come this far to stop now. He kept going, fuelled by shaky courage and dogged determination. And faith that God would see him through.

The Unseelies stood silent and watchful. A few dogs stood beside those of the Wolfclan, but they too regarded him silently, unthreatening. *Wulfram wants a willing victim.* The errant thought stole through his mind, bringing a grim smile to his lips. He was willing, but not for what Wulfram had in mind.

The gathering power increased as every second ticked by and with every step he took. It washed away his weariness and the lingering pain from his headache. Even so, he was no match for all of them if they rushed him, but he wasn't worried about that. This was all intimidation.

He dismissed the Fey, studying the building instead. Along the roof, a row of black birds ruffled their feathers, their beady eyes sharp upon him. But it was the house itself that drew more of his attention.

The mist roiled sluggishly around it, exposing and obscuring its details. His gaze kept skittering away from it and then jumping back. He couldn't look away, yet he didn't want to see it. Much like the same compulsion that caused people to slow and stare as they passed a traffic accident.

The Undying was inside that house. He knew it in his bones, in his soul. An icy trickle of sweat dripped down his back, and he wiped his palms against his tunic, clenching his jaw. Surely the bishop was inside, too, another hostage to Wulfram's plans. The thought spurred him onwards.

The huddled birds muttered and croaked as they watched him approach, black eyes alert. It was creepy. Fear crept over him, each step forward becoming more difficult. The Unseelies began a low, murmuring, discordant song. He couldn't make out the words, except for the handful of times he heard *wilding*. His head buzzed, and he felt slightly dizzy. The song murmured in his ears, questing deeper into his mind, probing past his defences. Panic surged. He raised a little power, keeping the voices out.

He reached the door, feeling like he'd run a marathon. He leaned against, gathering his thoughts, reciting the Breastplate in a low murmur as a shield against the evils arrayed against him. *Don't forget who you are. Thomas McCadden. Thomas mac Cadán. Seelie Fey and human both. Christian. Traveller. Wilding. Use it all.*

He crossed himself and opened the door.

CHAPTER 58

BEYOND REASON

Celyn lost himself to the fight, moving instinctively as he dodged his brother's blade, striking when he could. They had done this so often, practicing together to hone their skills, that he could almost believe that the years had fallen away and that they were skirmishing again in front of their father's men at their *crenef* in Gwynedd.

But instead of the good-natured jeers of an audience, he heard only the caws of the crows. The stings from Griffith's blade where he had cut through Celyn's defences were a reminder that this was no practice fight.

Celyn was a better fighter. He always had been. Griffith had stopped their practice fights when Celyn got old enough to beat him. Griffith relied on brute force; Celyn used his lighter size and quickness to his advantage.

And so it was no surprise to find himself in a position to take the killing blow. Griffith had swung with vicious strength at Celyn's midsection and Celyn had swung around, his sword in a long arc. He could have taken his brother's head off right there, but at the last second he checked himself, spinning away again as Griffith recovered and swung at him.

"Coward," Griffith spat at him, blood flowing into his eyes from a gash in his temple. He panted heavily as he circled around, his blade rock-steady in his hands. "That was your chance."

"Griffith," Celyn managed, keeping his eyes steady on his brother. Griffith's muscles gathered and Celyn skipped away from the feint, bringing his blade up to counter his brother's blow. Their blades strained against each other, and for a moment they were almost nose to nose. "Stop this, I beg you. This is not—"

Griffith snarled and pushed back, and then advanced again, his eyes sparking with a crazed light. "Traitor. Coward." A step punctuated each word.

Celyn gave up on speech. Whatever drove his brother was beyond reason. He parried Griffith's blows, steeling himself against emotion. Griffith's furious attack left room for nothing but the will to survive. He didn't feel the pain of the blows.

None were a killing strike. He shifted his weight as Griffith leapt forward and saw his moment. Saw his brother's exposed side and swung his sword to cleave him.

But at that second, a crow erupted from the branch of the nearby tree and swooped at him, screeching, causing him to hunch and dodge in reaction. His blow connected, but his balance was off, and Griffith had his chance. Celyn's sword dropped from suddenly nerveless fingers as Griffith's strike hit his shoulder, even as his brother dropped to his knees, blood gushing from his side. With a vicious cry, he thrust at Celyn again with his last strength.

Celyn dodged, but the damnable bird flew at him again, obscuring his sight. White-hot pain erupted as Griffith's sword struck home, piercing his gut, and Celyn fell to the ground. Dimly he was aware of Griffith falling over, too, and grief seized him. *My brother...*

But then he could think no more. He heard a crow cry as if from a distance. Regret pierced him for an instant before blackness smothered him with ebony wings.

CHAPTER 59

DEFIANCE

Thomas paused in the doorway, scanning the interior of the house. It was dim inside, despite the hearth fire and the flickering candles on the table pushed up against the back wall. Wulfram stood before the table, his eyes gleaming in the dusky light, a faint shimmer outlining his form. Godric stood beside Wulfram, wreathed in shadows, a sardonic smirk twisting his lips.

And Aidan stood to his left with a Fey behind him, holding a knife against his throat.

There was no sign of Merton and his family. The Unseelies must have drawn them away from the holding. At least he hoped so. The other possibility didn't bear thinking about.

Thomas drew on his power to give him more energy. He didn't want to reveal how tired he was, how close to the end of his strength. *Just give me enough. Please, God. Just enough.*

Wulfram clapped, the sound breaking the silence as he walked towards him. "Ah, Thomas, look at you," he said, admiration in his voice.

The strain around Wulfram's eyes belayed his nonchalant manner. He had been in close contact with the Undying for months now. Thomas couldn't imagine what that had cost him.

Wulfram's gaze travelled over him. "My God, but you are a prize!" He shook his head. "You've learned some things since the last time we met. How do you like it? The power, dancing in your blood, a sweet mistress that beguiles you with her charms!" He leaned closer. "Oh, I can see you like it very much." He smirked. "Don't you see? This is what it means to be Fey! We are creatures of spirit and song and power, far above the humans in worth and ability. They know nothing. And yet we Fey are content to let them rule over us, kill us—"

Wulfram's words choked off, his fist closing tightly at his side. His golden eyes blazed. "I have the means, now, to undo the deaths of our people that are coming. *We* have the means! You and I, Thomas, will be the saviours of the Fey, our names celebrated throughout the ages. It is perfect, can't you see? You were brought here to finish the work your family started. Don't let your father's weakness taint you. You have greater potential than even he had! Stand with me, Thomas! Join me!"

Power wove through Wulfram's words, dancing along the edges of his resistance. Thomas let it wash past him, steeling himself against its potency.

"The world will be different when we return to our time," Wulfram continued, anticipation glowing in his face. "Beauty celebrated, the joy of the dance, the freedom to be Fey without having to hide—"

"You waste your breath," Godric interrupted, his voice a low growl that scraped against Thomas' ears. Another voice overlay Godric's normal tenor voice. A voice of shadows, of blood and hatred and need. It filled the room like a poisonous fog. Thomas blinked as the room wavered around him.

He ran, dark shapes pursuing him. Their hard claws on his arm, the jolt of pure longing—

The room snapped back into focus. *Jesus, Jesus.* For a split second, he didn't know where he was, but then he saw Aidan. The bishop gazed at him, his lips moving in prayer. It bolstered Thomas' courage, and he gathered his own burgeoning power around him as a shield.

Wulfram flinched as the demon spoke, and his mouth snapped shut. A slight tremor ran through him, and one eye twitched. But he remained silent, even taking a step back as Godric pushed away from the table and stalked up to where Thomas stood.

The harper looked terrible. He was thin, his cheekbones prominent in his face, his beaked nose more pronounced than ever. His soiled and ripped tunic hung loosely on him. Judging from the smell, he had not bathed himself in some time. But the worst was his eyes. His clear blue Fey-eyes were now a flat black. The demon had taken over.

Thomas shivered when those coal-black eyes rested on him. He avoided the demon's gaze. He couldn't bear the thought of seeing what was in the depths of that inky stare. In fact, it was hard to look at Godric at all, although his gaze kept skipping to the demon-thing before recoiling. Just like the house, Godric held a horrible fascination, a whirlwind that kept sucking in his attention no matter how much he did not want to look at it. The others in the room were having the same trouble, their gazes skittering away from the harper and then sliding back as if drawn to a magnet.

All except for Aidan. The bishop's eyes were closed, and although a thin sheen of sweat had broken out on his brow, his lips continued to move. For a moment,

Thomas concentrated on him, trying to hear what he said over the pall that the demon's presence threw on them all.

"God, hear my prayer; hearken to the words of my mouth. For haughty men have risen against me and fierce men seek my life; they set not God before their eyes."

One of the Psalms. The words broke through like a bright wash of sunlight. For the first time he wondered why Aidan was being restrained by a knife and not reduced to a mere Bonded slave by Wulfram. The answer came in a flash as he noted the quick sideways glance Godric gave Aidan.

They had tried, but they had failed. Aidan had withstood their attempts to overcome his will. But Thomas didn't have a chance to savour the thought.

"He can't help you," Godric said in his demon-altered voice. "His resistance will not last. Nor will yours. You have spent much power already, little Nephilim. Soon your feeble grasp on it will break, and you will be mine, along with the priest." The word came out as a hiss. "His faith will shatter, for God will not help him, not when he seeks to aid you, demon-spawn that you are. But do not fear. We will not reject you. I will send you both back as my tools, and oh, what mischief we will work!" Godric chortled.

Thomas gritted his teeth, feeling nauseous, fighting the despair the demon's words brought. The laughter was worse than the voice, something that normally expressed human pleasure twisted in Godric's mouth into a celebration of darkness and death. He dared a glance at Godric's eyes and tore his gaze away before his soul froze in his body and shattered. Nothing remained of Godric there. His hope of unBinding Godric as he had Odda evaporated. Godric was buried too deep. Thomas could not pull him out without going through the demon, and if he attempted that, he would have no hope of resisting its will.

"Yes," Wulfram breathed, his eyes glazed as he looked at the Undying, his face twisted in longing. The demon had harnessed Wulfram's obsession in avenging his brother's death for its own purposes. But it did not possess the Traveller as it did Godric. Maybe he could reach Wulfram, break his Bond?

"Pay attention!" Godric snarled.

Thomas' gaze shot back to the harper, his thoughts dissolving. Desire to obey blossomed to life within him, his fragile control slipping under the strength of the Undying's command.

The door flew open, and another Fey rushed in. Thomas got a reprieve from the demon's black gaze as Godric looked over at the newcomer, who scrambled to a halt, his face pale.

"My lord," he gasped, looking at Wulfram. "You wished me to report—" He broke off in confusion when he saw Thomas, glancing between Wulfram and Godric.

"Tell me," Wulfram demanded.

"Penda's man is dead," the messenger blurted out. He leaned over and rested his hands on his knees, panting.

"And the other one? Speak, fool!"

God, please—

The messenger straightened. "Gravely wounded. He is dying."

Celyn! Thomas stood rooted to the spot, despair crashing over him.

Wulfram nodded, a smile of satisfaction wreathing his face as he flicked his fingers at the messenger, who bowed and left. In his haste, he left the door open, and some tendrils of mist snaked inside, glimmering in the candlelight.

A dark cavern opened within Thomas that left no room for light. *Celyn. My fault.*

"There is no hope for you, little Nephilim," Godric said, the words tolling in the dark space inside Thomas like a dissonant bell. "There is none to help you. This defiance is foolish."

Wulfram whispered the same words along with Godric. *This defiance is foolish.*

The demon continued. "You are alone, as you have always been alone. Neither human nor Fey. You do not belong in either world." The words were low and caressing. "But it doesn't have to be that way. We can use you without your cooperation, but it is far better to have you willing. Come with us, half-blood. We will destroy the Church, make no mistake. But if you help us willingly, I will spare some. I will allow a remnant in return for your submission to me. And I will give you all you desire."

Images flitted through Thomas' mind: Nona, standing in the moonlight with stars in her eyes; Celyn, smiling one of his rare smiles as he rode beside him; his father, wrapping his arms around him and his brother as they wept for joy.

Godric raised his hand, reaching for him. Thomas stood frozen as a wave of anticipation roiled through him, bubbling up from the darkness. It could all be his.

Aidan spoke, alarmed. "Thomas! No! Ye must not—" The Fey holding Aidan scuffled with the bishop, cutting off his words.

But it was enough. Aidan's voice snapped him back to himself. Horror filled Thomas as he realized how close he had come to giving in. The restoration of those he loved would come at a terrible cost to countless others. And he would be beholden to the dark forever, chained in bonds of fear and loathing, guilt and regret. Even if what the demon showed him came to pass, his bliss would not last, and it would mean ruin for the world he knew.

Fear spurred him to action. He dove to the side, crashing into the Fey that restrained Aidan, who went down under Thomas' weight. Aidan pushed himself away from his captor, who struggled against Thomas.

Don't move! Thomas just barely stopped the command from slamming into the other Fey's mind. He was a young teen, scared and way out of his depth.

The Unseelie ducked and held his hands up in front of his face, but Thomas felt the slight click as the command froze him and he knew he had succeeded. He scrambled to his feet, his heart pounding as he yelled at Aidan. "Run, my lord!"

But the bishop ignored him. He stood in front of the harper, one hand lifted, the other clutching his staff. He looked upward and prayed in Latin. "I call on Your holy name in fear and trembling, asking that You grant me, Your unworthy servant, pardon for all my sins, steadfast faith, and the power, supported by Your mighty arm, to confront with confidence and resolution this cruel demon. I ask this through You, Jesus Christ, our Lord and God, who are coming to judge both the living and the dead and the world by fire."

At his words, the harper snarled and crouched in front of the bishop. His midnight eyes fixed on Aidan, an unearthly howl intermittently breaking through his snarls.

But Thomas could not focus on the bishop's struggle. Sunset was close, and power surged through him.

And not only through him. Wulfram shone brightly with it, almost blinding Thomas, the force of it snapping against him painfully. Confidence shone in his eyes.

"Wulfram. Stop. It's not real." Thomas gasped out the words, trying to reach the other Traveller through the misguided desire the Undying had used to Bind Wulfram to it just as thoroughly as Wulfram had Bound Godric with Fey power.

But Wulfram ignored him, advancing on Thomas with measured steps. "You will help me Bind this bishop and we will send him as a wolf among the sheep to rend and tear. He will be ours. We will destroy this monastery. Their prayers will be useless against us. The Church will bleed and fall. There won't be anyone to stand against the Fey. The humans will be swept away." Unholy glee lit his eyes. "And when I return, Bran will greet me with open arms."

"Your brother is dead!" Fey power edged Thomas' words. It caused the words to ring through the dwelling, and Wulfram flinched, stopping in his tracks. "He's gone. You can't change it. You'll just destroy everything that is good. That's what the Undying wants. Stop this. Please."

For a moment, Wulfram's eyes cleared, and Thomas' heart was pierced with pity at the grief in them. He had almost succumbed himself to the same temptation a moment ago. He understood all too well what Wulfram had been promised.

"You can't change it," he said, urgent. "Do you really think your brother would want all this?"

But it was too late. The Undying's grip held Wulfram too tightly. Rage lit his eyes, erasing the grief as if it had never been.

"You're a fool," he snarled, his hands curled into fists. "You know nothing. All those you love are dead. Your chance to save them is gone. You have lost, wilding! There is nothing you can do!" Wulfram's words drowned out both Aidan's prayers and the demon's snarls. A manic grin stretched over the other Traveller's face as he spread both arms wide and closed his eyes, preparing for the moment of sunset.

Thomas grasped at his power, trying to let it loose to join with the wild rush of power that was building to almost painful strength. But he couldn't grab onto it. The power stayed stubbornly elusive, just out of reach. He backed up, his heart pounding. His grasp on power was too sporadic and uncertain to defend himself from what was coming. He wouldn't be able to resist.

He was out of options. Except for one. The wild plan he had come up with as a last resort. He didn't know what good it would do, but he had no other choice. "You forget," he snarled. "A wilding never does what you expect."

As the sun slipped under the horizon, power blazed around them, washing away his fear. The surge tore open the door holding back his own, and he put it all into a command that he screamed in defiance. "JACK REDCAP!! COME TO ME, NOW!!"

The Call erupted out of him in a wild torrent, his words laced with fire. He put everything he had into it, even though he risked being burned to a cinder under the onslaught of Fey power. But it didn't matter. He would rather be dead than enthralled to Wulfram and the demon, if it came to that.

Wulfram staggered, caught off guard by Thomas' Call as it seared through his mind like a white-hot poker. The cries of the Fey outside came to them through the open door.

But Thomas had no attention to spare for them. The sweet ride of Fey power was a careening horse he struggled to control. He wrestled it and focussed it into the Call, his words blazing with power. "REDCAP! UNSEELIE TRAVELLER. HE WHO WALKS BETWEEN THE WORLDS! COME!"

And white fire exploded.

CHAPTER 60

TIME RUNS ON AND RUNS AGAIN

The flare cut off his torrent of power. He staggered as much as from its sudden cessation as from the flash, his knees gone weak under him as he collapsed to the wooden floor. As the flash faded, he blinked, trying to see, feeling as if the mist outside had invaded his head.

Wulfram huddled against a leg of the table, clutching his head. His mouth contorted in an open scream, but Thomas could hear nothing over the ringing in his ears. Nor could he get his muscles to work or his eyes to focus.

Aidan. He squinted at the bishop, who still prayed fervently, his words a low drone in the background. Godric crouched before him, his eyes fixed upon Aidan with hatred blazing in them. Thomas' Call had not affected them. Thomas tried to get up, but it was as if his limbs were tied to anvils. He had nothing left.

The room spun and wobbled around him; the figures wavering as he blinked his eyes. Something tickled against the back of his mind, something important, but he couldn't focus on it. His head dropped, too heavy for him to hold up. Nausea roiled his gut, and he fought it, gasping. He lifted his head again and froze.

Redcap crouched before him, squatting on his haunches, a wild light in his eyes and a feral grin on his face. "Young shepherd," he said in his melodious voice. "You have Called me, and here I am. Jack o' the Wisp, Jack-be-quick."

There was no threat in his manner. Thomas squinted at the other Fey, his head spinning. Were there two Redcaps? No, the images wavered and then coalesced into one. He opened his mouth to speak and then stopped, interrupted by that insistent tickle in the back of his brain, but it evaporated like fog when he turned his attention to it.

Wulfram lifted his head, a look of horror on his face that turned to rage as he pushed himself up. But his movements were weirdly slow, as if he were caught in molasses.

Slo-mo, Thomas thought, bemused. But that was as far as his scattered thoughts could go. The effort of figuring out what was going on was too much. The Calling of Redcap had been his last resort, a wild card to throw on the table to buy himself a little time. He was surprised that it had worked. What to do now was anyone's guess.

He gathered himself. "What's happening?" His words sounded odd in his ears, as if he were in a deep hole.

Wulfram launched towards them. But he was moving so slowly in the strange time distortion that he was no imminent threat.

Aidan advanced on the demon with his hand raised, his words unintelligible.

Redcap stood up and extended a hand to Thomas, and after a moment he accepted the other Fey's help, surprised his legs held. But he wobbled a bit as he looked around, trying to figure out what was happening. Except for him and Redcap, everyone else was caught in a time warp. Looking at them for too long made his stomach flip unpleasantly.

An odd sound erupted from Wulfram's lips. A scream, distorted just like the other sounds.

"Did you do this?" Thomas asked, waving at the others.

The wilding crossed his arms, delight in his face. "Ah, youngling, you flatter me, you do. Not I, but you. You did this—and well done too, I say! Well done indeed!"

Me? "But what..." Thomas shook his head, not knowing what to ask. The movement caused him to stagger as the room whirled around him. He steadied himself against the wall. *Bad idea. Move carefully.*

Redcap shrugged. "Two wildings, two Travellers. One of them raw in need and desire, Calling the other. Oh, such a Call, youngling shepherd!" He giggled. As quickly as the laugh began, he stopped. Jack leaned closer to him, his green eyes aglow. "Time works differently for Travellers, yes, indeed. Only the most experienced Travellers can create this." He waved at the surrounding figures.

Wulfram was two steps closer, his knife raised in the air. Thomas felt the power cresting in him. His eyes blurred, and dizziness swept over him again. He felt bone-weary and fragile. It was as if he were removed from himself, powerless to act.

"Or a wilding, yes." Redcap continued. He chortled again. "But beware, youngling, the decision comes. This will not last long."

A spike of alarm went through him at Redcap's words. A glance around showed what the other Fey meant. Things were speeding up, second by second, events catching up with them. Soon this moment would end, and Wulfram would be upon them.

"What decision? I can't stop him. I used up all my power Calling you. You have to help me!"

But Redcap just laughed. "I have come, but for my own purpose. There will be blood and blood again. My own purpose. Another comes with his own, and then we shall see."

Another comes. The words froze his blood. With a sudden jolt, they unlocked the meaning of that odd feeling in the back of his mind. He should have recognized it sooner, for indeed he had felt it before. *Odda.*

As if summoned by the thought, the boy entered through the open door, a knife in his raised hand.

Thomas' breath caught in his chest. The feeling of *déjà vu* swept over him again and everything faded—Wulfram, Aidan, Godric, even Redcap.

Thoms and Odda sat side by side in the dark, the golden rope that bound them together casting a glimmering light. "He hurt you. I hurt you. But you can be free."

Odda's eyes met his. And something odd happened. Suddenly a kaleidoscope of images swirled around them: Thomas facing Nona, his heart breaking; Nectan, standing before him with his arms crossed, resolution in his face; Fee, her eyes shining with laughter; Cadán, shimmering in the dark; Conaire, galloping towards him on a horse, clods of sand flying from his horse's hooves; the banshee's eerie cries.

The visions swirled and faded, dissolving into another scene: Odda rushing through an open door, a knife in his raised hand as Wulfram leapt towards Thomas.

"Odda, no," he whispered, horror seizing him as the vision dissolved. "You can't. He'll kill you!"

"He will take you if I don't," Odda said, his face frightened but resolute. "I must do it."

The vision returned, but more than just a vision. This time Thomas was thrust into it, living it.

Wulfram leapt towards Thomas, a knife in his hand. Panic speared through Thomas as he scrabbled at the door to his power, but it was too late. Wulfram reached him just as the power of the Solstice sunset flooded through them. Aidan's prayers increased in volume, but with no effect.

"You're mine!" Wulfram snarled, his knife at Thomas' throat as his mind speared into Thomas' like a hot knife through butter, Binding him.

All of Thomas' will disappeared under the onslaught, and he could only watch, helpless, as Godric rose from his crouch before the bishop, his face lit by unholy glee.

Mingled horror and exquisite pleasure swept through Thomas as he saw the moment Aidan realized he was lost and the prayers stuttered on his lips.

Godric threw out a hand towards Wulfram, who raised his hand. An odd wrench shuddered through Thomas as the other Traveller and the Undying harnessed his power, bringing it to bear upon Aidan, who collapsed under the onslaught, weeping.

Thomas felt the bishop's will break, felt the despair and terror of it, but the savage delight of the Undying's triumph smashed his horror and grief into ashes, leaving only glee.

Aidan rose, staggering slightly, but when he lifted his face to Godric, a small smile curled his lips. "My lord," he said, bowing. "What is your pleasure?"

"Please. Free me, Master Thomas."

Thomas gasped as Odda's words kicked him out of the future and back to the odd Otherworld with a wrenching twist of his guts. He turned and retched, his body trying to expel the lingering feeling of corruption from Wulfram's Binding.

"Christ," he gasped, panting as he rubbed at his face, trembling. He crossed himself hurriedly. "God, save us."

Odda held up his hands, determination filling his face. "I don't want to be a slave anymore. And if I'm free, I can help."

Once again, Odda's words threw Thomas into the future.

Dismay speared him as Odda came through the door, the knife in his upraised hand glittering in the candlelight as Wulfram leapt towards Thomas.

"Odda, no!"

Wulfram saw Odda coming and turned, his own knife flashing down to defend himself, a split second before Thomas tackled Odda, knocking into Wulfram, and they crashed to the ground. Blood flowed—

And then Thomas was again jerked out of the future and thrown back into the mists.

He sucked in a breath, disoriented, grasping at the last tendrils of what he had seen, but they dissolved into fog. Frustration filled him. Two futures had been presented. In one, Odda wasn't present. In the other, a freed Odda had confronted Wulfram with a knife.

Right now was the fork in the road, the place where one scenario would prevail. But how could they decide? What had happened next?

Odda gaze met his gaze. His face was pale but resolute. "You'll be there. You will save me."

"I don't know. I can't tell, can you?" No matter how hard he tried, he could not see past that last terrible moment.

Odda shook his head, but conviction filled his face. "You will."

Thomas sought for another solution. "Look. This happens if I free you now. Maybe if we wait—"

"How long?"

The despair in Odda's voice pierced Thomas' heart. How long, indeed? It had been hard enough to get to this point. Could he turn back now and bring himself to it again? He wasn't sure he would be strong enough. In fact, he was pretty sure he wouldn't be.

He would be just as bad as Wulfram if he kept Odda Bound. Wulfram wouldn't need the Undying to corrupt him. He would do it to himself. But if he freed him now, events would play out as he had seen. Either Wulfram would be triumphant or Odda would end up confronting Wulfram. Likely, the boy would die.

But maybe not. Now that Thomas knew what would happen, he could do things differently. Sudden hope flared but was quickly dashed. That was what he was trying to stop Wulfram from doing: changing events now to alter a disastrous, known future. What horrors might erupt if he did it, too?

There was no way out. He had thought that Odda would make the choice to be free, but instead, the choice was before him. Free Odda and condemn him to death. Or keep him Bound against his will.

"Master?"

Thomas closed his eyes. The boy's voice was both hopeful and frightened. Did he understand what he asked? He opened his eyes. Odda looked up at him, his hands outstretched, his chin trembling. But he met Thomas' gaze without flinching, determination filling his eyes. He understood.

"I'm sorry," he choked out. "I'll do what I can."

The boy nodded, and before he could change his mind, Thomas touched the rope.

Thomas gasped as the memory winked out, thrusting him back to Merton's holding. Nausea swelled. Skipping through time had made him disoriented and dizzy, his thoughts in a jumble between past and present, what might be and what was.

Motion snagged his attention. Ahead, Wulfram caught sight of Odda and twisted around—

The same scene he had seen played out before.

"Decision," Redcap whispered. "Time runs on and runs again. Time-shepherd, Traveller on the wind. One more time the choice is yours. Stop him, or no?"

The horror of being Bound, and of what came after, froze his blood. But how could he let the boy die in front of him without lifting a finger? Even to save the future?

Wulfram moved faster now as time sped up, as did Odda. The boy's face contorted in a scream as he thrust the knife forward, just as Wulfram's knife slashed at him.

All considerations fled. This moment, right now, had been given to him. To save this boy. The rest of it, the future to come, was as insubstantial as the mist. With a desperate prayer on his lips, he launched himself at Wulfram, seeking to tackle him before his knife could strike the boy. As he did, time snapped into place with an odd whooshing sensation.

Thomas crashed into them both, causing them all to fall in a tangled heap.

He grabbed Odda in his arms and rolled off Wulfram. The other Traveller lay unmoving, Odda's knife jutting out of his chest, his eyes dimming as quickly as his power. "Fool," the dying man gasped. "You—" But there was no more. He was gone.

Redcap laughed. "Blood! You chose blood, as Redcap did, and does again! Wilding shepherd, I claim him!" He darted forward and crouched beside Wulfram. "He is mine!" He placed his hand on the Unseelie's chest, into the blood that was flowing. "Blood!" he screamed, and a white flare erupted around him, obscuring his form.

Thomas stretched himself over Odda to protect him from the blinding flash. When it had faded, he straightened up again. Redcap and Wulfram were gone. Sounds of alarm erupted from the Unseelies who had Gathered outside. With Wulfram's death, the compulsions that had tied them to him were gone, and they fled. Likewise, the young Unseelie that Thomas had commanded to stay in place leapt up and ran through the door with a panicked glance at him.

But Thomas had no thought to spare for the others. "Odda!" He laid the boy carefully on the floor, horror filling him at the sight of his slight form. "No, no, no..."

He had been too late. Blood pumped from a gash where Wulfram's knife had struck home, right at the junction of the boy's neck and shoulder. He pressed his hands against the flow, trying to stop it. But there was so much blood. *Christ*

Almighty. Too late. Too late. My fault. Thomas scanned the room, seeking help, but the only ones left were Aidan and Godric.

The bishop held his staff high over the harper. "Begone, Satan, inventor and master of all deceit, enemy of man's salvation!" Aidan's voice rang through the room as Godric crouched at his feet, hissing and spitting, his face contorted.

Thomas dared not disturb Aidan now. He looked back at Odda just as the boy's eyes fluttered open.

"Master Thomas," he whispered. "I heard him. I followed..."

"Shhh, Odda, just rest." Thomas shrugged off his cloak with one hand, keeping the other one clamped on Odda. So much blood.... He pressed the cloak against the wound to help staunch the flow.

"He's dead." Satisfaction filled the boy's face. "I did it."

Thomas forced himself to speak. "Yes, you did. He's gone. He won't hurt anyone again." His gut tightened. The blood was slowing. With a choked sob, he gathered the boy in his arms. Guilt crashed over him. "I'm sorry. I tried...." But his throat was too tight to continue.

Odda's face was pale, so pale. "My choice." The words escaped him in a soft breath.

For a moment, time shifted again. They were back in the place of mists. Odda lifted his bound hands to Thomas, asking to be free, his face determined. And then they were back in the darkened room, the flickering candlelight casting jumping shadows around them.

Thomas managed to nod. "I know." Odda had known then that his choice for freedom would bring him to this moment. Yet he had chosen freedom. And Thomas had honoured that choice and freed him from the Bond.

Choice. The consequences from that moment had rippled away from it, finally catching up with them again. Thomas had given Odda the choice then, saving them both from the Binding's corrupting influence. And Odda had saved Thomas, and by extension, Aidan and the monks, from a worse corruption now.

But why hadn't Thomas been able to save Odda? If he had been a split second sooner...

Wulfram would be alive. Thomas' thought stuttered and died, lost in the whirling possibilities of what could have happened. He would have a lifetime to ponder it all. But Odda had only a moment left. He swallowed down the lump in his throat as he met Odda's gaze. "You saved the monks. You saved us all."

A small smile lifted the boy's lips. "An angel told me I could do it." His eyes widened as his gaze shifted slightly, and he looked over Thomas' shoulder. "Look..."

And then he was gone.

"Odda," Thomas choked out, gathering him to his chest. He bent over him, his tears falling on Odda's hair, rocking the prone body of the boy as he wept.

CHAPTER 61

ALL GONE WRONG

Nona woke from an uneasy slumber as sunset approached and power gathered along with the deepening shadows. Conaire glanced at her, his eyes wary as he motioned with his chin at the Unseelies, who stood huddled against the door, peering out. A sense of nervous anticipation wreathed them, their Fey power sparking in response to the coming sunset.

"How will we know, do you think?" Eagerness edged the voice of the shifty-eyed Unseelie.

"He said he would tell us. Now shut your hole." The lame one looked back at Nona and Conaire, and then back at the other Unseelie.

He glanced at them, too. "They're awake. How are we supposed to—"

"Shut up, idiot," the other hissed, shifting on his crutch.

The third one did not speak, but the look he gave Nona over his shoulder held anticipation and malice in equal measure.

Nona fought down her fear. Their usefulness was fading as fast as the sun went down. The older one would think nothing of killing them once Wulfram had Thomas in his grip, she was certain. There was something twisted about him, something off. Maliciousness held him in its grip. He was not Bound to an Undying like Godric, but its influence had poisoned him.

With a low voice, Conaire spoke in her ear, distracting her from her thoughts. "Be ready."

She nodded in reply. She would do what she could to save their lives, and the life of their babe. Her heart twisted, pierced by grief that she may never know her child. But she could not think of that now. She breathed in, allowing the power to wash over her as she opened the door to her own power. The clean strength of it cleansed her aches and pains and took away the last of her tiredness. *May God give us strength*, she prayed as the power reached its zenith as the sun dipped below the horizon.

JACK REDCAP! COME!

The unexpected Call, unmistakably in Thomas' voice, tore through her in a torrent that took her breath away. And not only her. Conaire stiffened in shock. The Unseelies staggered back into the building, holding their heads.

REDCAP! TRAVELLER! UNSEELIE! HE WHO WALKS BETWEEN THE WORLDS! COME!

The second Call knocked the others off their feet, but Nona hardly noticed in her fight to hang on to herself. The power flaring through the Call nearly ripped her apart. For a panicked moment, she thought she might die.

"Nona!"

Conaire's voice came to her through the fading reverberations of the powerful Call. She gasped for air, trying to speak, but the Call had knocked the breath out of her. *Redcap*, she thought, fear piercing her. *Merciful Christ.*

Two of the Unseelies clambered to their feet, but the bigger one lay unmoving. "He's Called the Redcap." The lame Unseelie massaged his temple. Fear flashed in his eyes.

"Wulfram?" The crooked-arm one, too, rubbed at his head, looking dazed.

"No, not Wulfram, you idiot!" He leaned on his staff, gasping. "The wilding. God's Blood, he Called the Redcap." He shook his head, as if to dislodge the thought.

The gap-toothed Unseelie stirred, pushing himself to his knees, but he looked groggy, and didn't attempt to stand. Nona supposed that being a Speaker meant he had felt the effect of the Call even more keenly, and she almost had sympathy for him. Almost.

"Are ye all right?" Conaire's eyes shone slightly in the dimming light. He whispered so that the others could not hear.

Nona finally got her breath to work, and she nodded. "Yes. But—"

The lame Unseelie lurched towards her, interrupting her. "You! You know the wilding better than most. What connection does he have with the Redcap?" He pointed his staff at her, scowling as he advanced.

Liath snarled and launched herself at him, causing the lame one's dog to leap to his master's defence. The two dogs erupted into a snarling, snapping melee, and in their single-minded fight, knocked over the Unseelie again.

Conaire jumped to his feet and looked down at her. "Now! Come!"

Nona didn't need Conaire's prompt. She recognized as well as he that this distraction might be the only chance they had to escape. She was on her feet before the words left his mouth. They both leapt for the door, Conaire barrelling into the shoulder of the crooked-arm Unseelie first and knocking him down, Nona on her husband's heels.

But although the Call had affected the gap-toothed Unseelie more than the others, he had enough wits about him to reach out and grab Nona's foot as she flew past.

She fell hard and lay stunned, her breath knocked out of her once again.

"Nay, bitch," the big man wheezed, his eyes clouded by dark shadows. He yanked her towards him. "You'll no get away this night."

Conaire turned and kicked at the man in one smooth motion but somehow the Unseelie saw it coming and he dodged, getting hit in the shoulder instead of his head as he rose to his feet, drawing the *seax* from the holder on his belt and launching himself at Conaire.

Nona could only watch, helpless, as her husband dodged one strike and then another. With his hands bound, he had no means to defend himself. She looked around, frantic. Surely there was something she could do to help? She pushed herself off the ground, her surrounding swooping around her unpleasantly. Her head had hit the ground hard when she fell.

But before she could do anything, an odd tremor rippled through her, like the expanding circles in the water after someone tossed in a rock. For a split second, time stood still. But almost as soon as she noticed it, it was over.

The gap-toothed Unseelie staggered once again, his face a comic mask of shock, and he wheeled around, crashing into the wall. He rebounded off the wall, a wail erupting from him as he shoved past Conaire and dashed out the door. They heard his moans fading as he ran away.

"He's dead," the lame Unseelie hissed at the other one. "It's all gone wrong." He whirled around and half-ran towards the door, hampered by his halting steps. His hound broke away from Liath and bounded after him, and the two of them fled into the night.

The other Unseelie gaped after him and then swept a wide-eyed gaze over Conaire and Nona. Without a word, he, too, ran through the door and disappeared into the night.

Conaire rushed over to her. He looked around and spotted the *seax* lying on the ground. He crouched down, grunting as he scrabbled at it, finally snagging it, and then stood behind her so that they were back-to-back. "Be still," he said, looking over his shoulder. Frustration edged his words. "I canna see. Tell me if I cut ye." He awkwardly sawed at the ropes holding her wrist. It only took a moment to cut them, and only a moment longer for Nona to do the same for him.

"What happened?" Nona rubbed her wrists, her fingers prickling as blood flowed more freely into her hands.

"I canna say. That Call…" Conaire's voice faded as he grimaced. "The Redcap. Why would the wildin' Call him?"

Nona's skin crawled at the thought of the odd solitary Fey with his blood-soaked cap. "As to that, I cannot say. But it seems Wulfram is dead. Perhaps that is why Thomas Called him. To kill Wulfram."

Conaire's mouth twisted in distaste. "Aye, perhaps." His gaze sharpened on her. "Are ye well, *mo ghràdh*?" His fingers skimmed over her brow, and Nona hissed as pain flared. His eyes darkened in anger. "Ye hit your head when the whoreson tripped ye. The babe…" Fear flashed in his eyes as he darted a glance at her stomach.

Nona took a breath. "Nay, do not fear." She grabbed his hand. "I am fine. The babe is fine. I would know if it were not."

Relief washed over his face, and he reached for her, enfolding her in his arms. "Ah, lass, I am sorry ye had to suffer this, so I am. I shouldna ha' let ye leave Bebbanburg."

Nona closed her eyes, revelling in the embrace of his brawny arms. "It's not your fault." She took a deep breath and leaned back, looking up at him. "We must find Thomas. He may be hurt."

Conaire's jaw tightened. "He canna be that far, for us to hear the Call as we did. Wulfram bade him to meet at the holding of Master Merton, so he did. Do ye know where that is?"

"Yes. He broke his leg last winter. I set the bone." She paused for a moment, putting together what she remembered of the gruff *coerl's* holding together with where the Unseelies had taken them. "You are right. I don't think we are far."

Conaire grimaced. "I should take ye to Bebbanburg first. We canna know for certain Wulfram is dead. And even if he is, the Undying may still lurk."

Nona stepped away from him, shaking her head. "I must go. There may be a need for a Healer. I will be fine."

Conaire's lips thinned, but then he sighed and stooped over to pick up the *seax*, thrusting it under his belt. "Come, then. The Unseelies fled on foot. We can take the horses." He fixed her with a hard look. "But ye will do as I say. Ye wilna rush in until I say it is safe."

"Of course." She would not risk their babe unnecessarily. She followed her husband outside, praying under her breath that they would find Thomas unharmed.

CHAPTER 62

BEGONE

*B*egone...

The word floated past Godric. More echoed in the surrounding darkness, but he couldn't make sense of them. They were such a long way away, and the effort was too much.

He was tired. So tired.

Begone, now!

Odd that he could feel the words, not just hear them. They reverberated through him like a hammer striking a stone. He didn't know where he was, but he felt comforted by the voice, despite its stern and commanding tone. He had been alone for a long time. It was good to have company.

The thought brought sadness. Where was he, anyway? His brain felt stuffed with wool. He couldn't make sense of anything.

There. Ahead, a light. So far away, he wondered if he was imagining it. But no, it got closer; the words getting louder as it approached. Which was weird, wasn't it? He tried to focus on what they said, but they slipped away, dancing past him before he could pin them down.

He snagged one. *Serpent.* He only had a moment to puzzle over that when he snatched another. *Unclean.*

The words came faster now, but an accompanying song distracted him. A song weaving complex counterpoints of melodies he couldn't capture, no matter how hard he strained to listen. But he couldn't stop himself from trying, humming under his breath as the golden light grew stronger. The words fell around him, becoming clear.

You might delude man, but God you cannot mock! It is He who casts you out, from whose sight nothing is hidden.

Sudden pain pierced through Godric, and he cried out, twisting away from the words that cut and the light that became too bright, but the voice was relentless. The song swelled over and around the thundering words, tumbling Godric around like a leaf in the wind.

It is He who repels you, to whose might all things are subject. It is He who expels you, He who has prepared everlasting hellfire for you and your angels, from whose mouth shall come a sharp sword, who is coming to judge both the living and the dead and the world by fire.

At the word *fire*, Godric's eyes snapped open. A voice screeched in agony—the Undying, who ripped itself out of Godric with a tearing, wrenching sensation that made him feel like he was being torn inside out.

Sensation returned. He was on his hands and knees, his hair hanging over his face as he panted in great gulps of air. *Where...* He looked up and saw Aidan, the Bishop of Lindisfarne, kneeling beside him. At the sight, it all tumbled into place in Godric's mind: Wulfram, Thomas, the demon. *It's gone.*

Deep compassion warmed Aidan's long face. "Come now, me son, ye are free."

He reached towards Godric to help him up, but he recoiled in horror at the fire snapping from the bishop's fingers. He scrabbled away, not wanting to get burned. "Get away from me, man, don't touch me!" His voice was a harsh croak. Thankfully, Aidan let him go.

He pushed himself upright, scattered impressions flitting through him. He was in a house. It was dark.... *Thomas?* His blood froze as he saw Wulfram stretched on the floor next to the wilding, a Fey crouching over him. A Fey wearing a red knitted cap, who placed a hand on Wulfram's chest.

"Blood!"

The single, triumphant screech was following by a bright, white flare that knocked Godric down. For a moment, he thought he was dead. He gasped, shuddering as the voice echoed through him. *Blood!*

The Redcap. *Gotta get out of here.* He scrambled to his feet, lurching around Thomas towards the door. *Get out. Get out.* He had almost made it when another voice cut through him, freezing him in place.

KILL HIM.

The Undying. Aidan had freed him from the creature, but he had no resistance to that command. He reached down and in one motion drew the knife from his boot, twisting back towards the bishop and letting it fly. But he had regained enough of himself for defiance, to adjust the trajectory in the last second before the knife left his fingers. He would not kill the bishop this night at the Undying's command.

But his satisfaction was short-lived.

"NO!" Thomas' howl burst through the darkness as the wilding launched himself towards Aidan, seeking to knock him out of the way of Godric's dagger.

No, you idiot, it's fine! It's fine! But his frantic thoughts were not enough. Godric could only watch, horrified, as the dagger struck Thomas in the thigh just as he crashed into Aidan.

Oh, Christ. Gotta get out of here. He turned and fled into the night.

CHAPTER 63

RIDE

Godric stumbled away from the house, his legs wobbly, trembling from head to foot. Only two thoughts ran around and around in a loop through his tattered excuse for a mind.

I'm free. I gotta get out of here.

The litany helped to suppress the memory of the Undying leaving him; of that awful, wrenching feeling like his soul was being torn out of his body. He had thought he was going to die. He must have come close.

Memories of all that happened over the past few months whirled like a kaleidoscope. But the past few days were a black hole. He had been nearly lost to the Undying's presence. Words had brought him out. *Begone and stay far from this creature of God.*

He puzzled over them. Was he a creature of God? He had never thought about it much before. The Fey of his time were eclectic in their religious beliefs, happy to adapt to any that fit their purposes.

As they were here, the only difference being that having no belief in anything had not occurred to them, unlike in his own time.

Begone. Fire had seared through him at that word, fire that burned off the chains holding him fast to the Undying. Like Fey power, but stronger. Purer.

And that song. He remembered it now. He'd heard it before, when he was released from Wulfram's grip to run with the Hunt. The song of the other Undying, whom some called angels. If he listened hard enough, he could just about recall it.

Distracted by the song, he stumbled and flopped to the ground. *Gotta get up. Gotta get out of here.* But those were fleeting thoughts. He was so tired, and it felt good to lie there in the peaceful night, seeing the thin crescent moon piercing the sky. He strained after the faint melody, elusive as starlight but just as beguiling.

Another memory dropped into his mind. There was a Crossing spot near here. Hope speared through him, but quickly faded. He couldn't face the wrenching horror of the jump, not now when his Fey power felt as remote as the stars. But maybe if he rested for the night, laid low, he could attempt it in the morning.

Suddenly, another sound split the night. A long, throbbing howl.

Fear pierced Godric, and then he laughed. Of course. Saved from the clutches of the Undying, only to be torn apart by the Alder King's beasts. He saluted the heavens. *Well done.*

He couldn't outrun them. He knew from experience that didn't work, even if he was at his peak strength, not this washed-out shell of the man he'd once been.

The sounds ripped apart the peacefulness of the night. He closed his eyes, resigned, but another thought struck him, and his eyes flew open again. *They're not here for me. I was just a tool in this whole thing. The wilding is the prize.*

Wulfram must have bargained with the Huntsman again to bring him here tonight. But why? A little insurance plan in case Thomas was too much to handle? But even as the thought crossed his mind, Godric rejected it.

Then he had it. The bishop. The Undying's all-consuming hatred for the monks, and Aidan in particular, had filled him for months. Like him, Wulfram had been but a tool in its hands in its quest to destroy the monastery. The demon's last command had been for him to kill Aidan, so it was not surprising it would have prompted Wulfram to send the Hunt on a mop-up operation, just in case.

Godric closed his eyes again, fighting against the urge to do something, to care. He could feel the vibration of hooves through the earth. He couldn't draw them off, nor would they take the bait, if their ultimate prize was the bishop. Or Thomas. Or both.

But then he remembered something else from his time with the Hunt. Remembered those who stood and faced the darkness instead of running in terror. Those who survived. Could he not do the same?

He owed the bishop something, surely, for his freedom? And Thomas, too. He winced as he remembered the spinning dagger striking home. Not to mention that Wulfram had used Godric to draw Matthew to his death. Shouldn't he at least try?

He wanted to ignore those thoughts, to leave the others to their fate. Hadn't he suffered enough? The weight of the decision pressed down on him.

But then he let out a breath. He was tired of running, tired of being a pawn. He had a chance, now, to do something. Make a difference. He clambered to his feet as the Alder King, on his horse the colour of ashes, thundered around the corner of the path, the Hounds like rippling shadows at his heels. Their baying froze the air.

But oddly, he felt no fear, just a sense of the vast, solemn regard that he remembered from before.

Creature of God. Do not be afraid. Aidan's words or those of another?

But he had no time to ponder it as the Huntsman drew his horse to a halt and regarded him, his face a black shadow under his horned helmet.

Step aside, Traveller. I have no business with you.

Godric gritted his teeth against the unpleasant feel of the words as they slithered through the air and through his mind.

The Hounds milled around the horse, whining and growling, eager to finish the Hunt now that they were so close. Godric couldn't stop them for long. But what could he do? He had nothing to offer in exchange that the Alder King wanted, except maybe his blood. And he wasn't feeling *that* generous.

Another idea struck him. He caught his breath. Could he do it?

No time to think it through. He put on his performer's face. "Look, man. I know you're on a mission here. But I have another proposal." He spread his hands. "Let's face it. The bishop will be no easy prize. Do you really want to take him on? Wulfram's dead. The Undying is gone. Aidan is no pushover."

The Alder King made no comment. Emboldened, Godric continued. "This is a dead end." He waved at the silent house, wondering for a moment what was happening inside. *Dead end.* Was Thomas dead? What was Aidan doing? He could only hope they wouldn't come outside. He forced the thought away and continued. "I know your Hounds are hungry. And you need something to show for this night's work." He heaved a breath. "So take me with you. I'll ride with you again. You and me, man." He stopped himself before he said, *Together again.* That was laying it on a little too thick. And he doubted the Alder King would appreciate the sentiment.

He wasn't sure if he did, either. Did he want to be tied to the Huntsman, when he had just been freed from Wulfram's tether? But this would be different. It was his own choice. A sacrifice of sorts. That had to count for something. Besides, it would provide him a way to get out of here. He was too feeble to attempt the Crossing, or to go very far. If Thomas was alive, he would no doubt track him down, demand a reckoning for all he had done. And he wasn't sure he could face Aidan again, nor his words of fire.

This way he would repay his debt to the bishop, save Thomas' life in compensation for taking his father's, and get a ticket out of here, in case the Undying came back, looking for revenge. He knew all of his resolution would fade to nothing under its inky gaze.

Riding with the Hunt held dangers of its own, of course. But he wouldn't stay long. Just long enough to get his strength back, to get back home.

All these thoughts flashed through his mind as he waited for the Huntsman to answer.

After a long moment, the Alder King nodded. *I accept. Come; ride.* He gestured with a hand and a sudden blast of wind whirled around them, knocking Godric off his feet.

When he picked himself up, another horse stood there, saddled and ready. The same horse he had ridden before, Godric assumed. *Cool. Gotta learn how to do that.* He had barely settled himself in the saddle when the Alder King lifted his horn to his lips, blowing a piercing note that shuddered through him.

The Huntsman whirled his horse around. With a touch of his heels they were away, Godric hanging on for dear life as his own horse followed suit.

A fierce grin stretched over his face as excitement gripped him. But he still had time for one wayward thought before the thrill of the Hunt filled him completely.

Do not be afraid.

And strangely enough, he wasn't.

CHAPTER 64

HE WANTED YE BOTH

"Thomas." Someone shook him urgently. "Wake up."

Thomas gasped as consciousness and memory flooded back, and he opened his eyes. Cadán Longshanks bent over him. "What…" He tried to work out what to ask. "Aidan," he managed, trying to sit up, but everything whirled around him, white sparks running through his vision.

"Nay, not yet," Cadán said, keeping him from rising. "Lie still. The bishop is here, but he's hit his head on the table."

Thomas turned his head and saw Aidan lying still, a trickle of blood seeping from his temple. "He's all right?"

Cadán's face was grim. "Oh aye, he'll be fine. But ye are hurt."

Thomas remembered the knife spinning end on end towards him, the impact of it hitting him as he tackled Aidan. "My leg…" He couldn't feel any pain. Maybe he had just imagined it? He steeled himself and raised himself up to look.

Godric's knife stuck out of his left thigh, buried to the hilt, blood flowing black in the flickering candlelight. Everything went white around the edges again, but he looked away before he passed out. *That can't be good.* "What are you doing here?"

"Gettin' ye out of here." Cadán glanced at him as he tore a piece of cloth into strips. "The—" He froze as a long, ghostly howl split the night, followed by more. His lips thinned as he continued his work. "They're comin' for ye, or the bishop. Or both."

The Hunt. *Great.* Another chorus of howls broke the silence, closer this time. But strangely, he felt no pain or fear, but only a remote interest. Shock, he supposed. "Wulfram called him?"

"Likely," Cadán said. "Leavin' nothing to chance. He wanted ye both. Dead or Bound, and it seems it didn't matter which." He looked at Thomas, fear touching his eyes. "But he wasna countin' on ye Calling the Redcap."

The howls erupted again, closer this time, and then cut off abruptly.

Cadán shook his head. "No time to talk, wildin'. We must hurry." He tore another piece.

He wanted ye both. The truth of it struck home. "Take the bishop and get out of here. I'll distract them."

But Cadán just shot him an impatient look and kept on ripping the cloth.

Thomas tried again. "We both know I'm likely to die either way. But we have to save the bishop. Otherwise, all of this is for nothing. Go!"

Cadán's lips twisted. "Dinna be foolish," he said, bending over him. "I canna carry him fast enough to outrun the Hunt."

Thomas wanted to protest again, but soon as Cadán touched his leg to get the tourniquet on, a red wave of pain hit him, leaving him panting and moaning as the Unseelie worked.

"There," Cadán said, straightening up. He opened his mouth to speak again when a long, piercing blast of a horn vibrated through the night, so loud it was almost unbearable.

Cadán and Thomas both covered their ears, trying to stop the sound from scraping their souls right out of their bodies.

"Christ, have mercy," Thomas gasped as the horn faded away, his gaze meeting Cadán's. He saw the same horror he felt mirrored in the other Fey's eyes. "He's right outside."

Cadán took a deep breath, steadying himself. "I'll do what I can for ye, but I canna promise he will listen to me." He started to rise.

Thomas grabbed his arm, holding him in place. "Why are you doing this?"

Cadán shrugged slightly, a smile twisting his mouth. "Ye interest me, wildin'. And I suppose I still feel an obligation to yer father." His smile widened. "Besides, I like the thought o' ye in my debt." He rose swiftly to his feet, grabbed a spear that was propped against the wall of the house, and stepped out.

Thomas tried to struggle upright, to help, but a buzzing sound filled his ears, growing louder and louder as his vision darkened, and he had to lie down again before he passed out. As the roaring in his ears faded, silence filled the house. He heard nothing except the faint rattle of the shutters as the night breeze stirred them. There was no sign that anyone was outside.

A slight moan distracted him. Aidan stirred and sat up, his hand pressed to his head. He looked over and his eyes widened. "Thomas! Praise God!" Alarm flared in his eyes as he caught sight of Thomas' bandaged leg. "But you're hurt—-" His gaze flew to Thomas' face. "What has happened? Where is the harper?" He looked around, peering through the darkness, and gave a choked cry as he spotted Odda.

"God, have mercy!" He scrambled over to where the boy lay, scanning his prone form. His face twisted in grief as he made the sign of the Cross. He looked over at Thomas. "God rest his soul. But why is he here? How were ye hurt?"

Thomas swallowed the sorrow and guilt that threatened to choke him. "Odda killed Wulfram. He was afraid Wulfram would take him back. And he knew the *sidhe* meant you harm. He came to stop Wulfram. He must have followed me from Lindisfarne. But Wulfram saw him at the last second." *You will help me.* Odda's voice echoed through his head, bringing a spear of guilt. "It all happened at once. I tried to stop Wulfram, but I was too late."

"Ach, the wee brave lad," Aidan said. "May God rest his soul, and the angels bring him to his rest." He wiped the dripping blood from his wound off his face as he peered around the gloomy house. "But if the lad killed the wicked *sidhe*, where is he? And the harper?"

Blood! Thomas thrust aside Redcap's last scream. How was he to explain that? He answered Aidan's last question instead. "You freed Godric, and he ran out. He turned back at the door." He frowned, remembering. The shock of Odda's sudden appearance and death made everything else fuzzy. "He threw a knife at you. I'm not sure why..." his voice trailed away. Had the Undying come back? Entered Godric again?

Comprehension flooded Aidan's face. "Ah, yes, now I remember. Ye pushed me out of the way, so ye did." The bishop came back and knelt beside Thomas again, his gaze sweeping over his leg. "Ye should not ha' done so, me son." He shook his head, sorrow filling his face. "'Twas the demon that directed the harper's hand, I fear. Perhaps it took him again."

"I don't know. Maybe. But..." He strained at the memory. *Godric stopped in the doorway like he had run into a brick wall. He turned and stooped, letting the knife fly.* Then he had it. The knife. "He hit my leg. But he shouldn't have, not if he was aiming for your heart. I think the demon wanted him to kill you. But Godric aimed low. He didn't want you to die."

Aidan's eyebrows raised. "Ah, I see." He sighed. "He should not ha' fled. But mayhap God will bring him back to us in time." He frowned, looking around again. "But where ha' Wulfram gone? Are ye sure he were dead?"

But before he could think of a reply, a sound of hoofbeats reached them, growing louder and then stopping. Shadows darkened the door, and then Conaire and Nona rushed in.

Thomas let out a shaky breath in relief. Cadán must have dissuaded the Alder King from his task. Or drawn him off. He only hoped the Unseelie had not made a bargain with the fearsome Fey, either with his own or someone else's life. An innocent human, like Deorwald, Oswy's *thegn* who had been taken as a replacement for Matthew.

"Thomas!" Nona's glad cry cut off as she caught sight of the bishop, the blood a black stream on his face. "My lord, you are hurt!" But then she noticed Odda and dropped to her knees beside him, horror filling her face. "Odda!" Her cry came out as a strangled gasp as her gaze flew over the boy, her hands running over him. But her hands stilled as the truth became clear and she stifled a sob, crossing herself as she sat back on her heels.

Conaire went to aid the bishop, handing him a bandage from Nona's bag. "Here, my lord."

Nona got up and joined Thomas. "Are you hurt? The Redcap—"

"He's gone," Thomas said, before she could ask more. Thankfully, she was on the opposite side of him from his leg, and hadn't noticed the bandage yet. "I'm fine. Just need to rest a minute. Are you alright? How did you know where I was?"

"Conaire told me you were to come to Merton's holding. I've been here before, to heal Master Merton. We were not too far away." She glanced over at Aidan, who was being ministered to by her husband, and pitched her voice low so the bishop could not hear. "One the way we met a Fey Conaire knew from Dál Riata. He told us you were here. He also said the Hunt was riding, but we saw no sign of them."

Cádan. Relief touched him. He was glad the Unseelie had escaped. He swallowed, feeling woozy. The blood loss was catching up to him. He forced himself to think. "The Alder King was here. Outside. But he's gone. I don't know why."

Nona's face paled. "Here? But what about Wulfram? Did he go with the Hunt?" She looked around, frowning, but caught sight of Odda again and looked back at Thomas. "What happened?"

"Wulfram's dead," he managed. "Odda killed him."

"Odda killed—" Her voice cut off as she noticed the bandage on Thomas' leg. "Thomas!" She reached for him.

He grabbed her arm before she could touch him. "No. I'm fine. It's just a scratch. But Celyn is out on the road. He killed his brother, but he's badly wounded. You have to go to him."

"Celyn?" Her eyes were round with shock. She gathered herself. "But you—"

"No. I'll be fine," he interrupted, willing himself to sound stronger than he felt. He couldn't let her spend her power on him and have nothing left for Celyn. Thankfully, the darkness hid the pool of blood gathering underneath his leg, despite Cadán's bandage.

Conaire was on the other side of him, closer to his leg, and his keen eyes had seen what Nona's had not. His gaze met Thomas'. His lips thinned, and he frowned.

"I'm fine," he said again, before Conaire could speak. He held the other Fey's gaze, willing him to understand, then looked at Nona. "Go. Celyn needs you."

"I will see to Master Thomas," the bishop said as he fastened the bandage around his head. "Go to your cousin."

Nona let out a breath and stood. "I'll be back as soon as I can. Keep him warm." She grabbed her bag. "Come, we must go," she said to Conaire and hurried out the door.

Conaire followed, but looked back as he reached the door. His gaze met Thomas' eyes, and he nodded once before following his wife.

Aidan knelt beside him. "Thomas, *mo cara*, do not fear. Christ goes with you, even now. I will pray for you."

Relief flooded through him at the sight of Aidan's long face, his eyes filled with compassion. It was over. The bishop was safe, the monastery saved, and Wulfram was gone. But sorrow twisted alongside that relief, clutching at him with shadowy hands. *Odda. I'm sorry.* His thoughts fluttered and broke apart.

He tried to tell the bishop that he wasn't afraid. But blackness overtook him, and he couldn't say a thing.

CHAPTER 65

WHAT WAS NECESSARY

T homas floated in a sea of dreams. Brief snapshots flitted through his mind, one after another, like a slideshow on his laptop. His mother. His father. His brother. Sometimes he saw Aidan, or Celyn, and once, Nona, her face pale, but determined.

But they faded under an onslaught of cold that froze him to the marrow, as if a block of ice encased him. Just when he thought he couldn't stand it any longer, welcome warmth returned. But soon it, too, became too much. From freezing cold, he became roasting hot. Voices whispered through his mind, and nightmare images rippled around him. The Alder King rode after him, Hounds snapping at his heels. Matthew fell away over a cliff, his face contorted in a scream. The Undying reached for him, long claws gripping at his arm as he pelted through a misty landscape, seeking safety but finding none. Odda fell under Wulfram's blade, Thomas screaming his name.

It was a hell he could not escape. Time lost its meaning. But those images also faded, and Thomas came aware of himself. A picture formed in the distance. As he strained at it, the details became clearer.

Nona bent over someone on a bed. Aidan stood nearby, his lips moving in a prayer, he assumed, but he couldn't hear anything, which should have been strange but wasn't, not in that odd dream-like place.

As Nona straightened up, a jolt went through him as he recognized himself lying on the bed, his hair sweat-matted and tangled, his face gaunt and pale. Nona said something to Aidan, her face anguished, and slipped to her knees, tears on her face as she bent her head to pray.

Thomas felt no alarm, only a faint curiosity. The images dissolved into a silvery light, and that curiosity blossomed into an almost painful expectation of something important that was about to happen. Thomas would have held his breath in anticipation if he had had any breath to hold.

He heard a faint, resonant, musical sound, like the distant sounding of a bell on a far-off mountain. As he turned his attention to it, the sound became louder, and he realized it was there all along; he just hadn't heard it before. Two voices in a conversation he finally could hear. The light became brighter, illuminating the indistinct forms of two figures. The light radiated from them, but it came through them, too, bringing with it warmth that scoured away every ragged edge of himself.

But in the scouring, those ragged edges became exposed. All his weaknesses, all his failures, all his pride and anger, all the ways he had rejected the good extended to him and clung instead to the bad, like hugging mouldy garbage that stank of corruption.

Comprehension flared. These were two of the other Undying. Angels. They ignored him as they conversed with each other. Words rippled out of the light.

He is a powerful Nephilim, but ignorant. See what harm he has wrought.

But he is under the Blood. The other Undying's voice was a tone higher than the other. *He belongs to the Almighty. It is not for us to decide.* There was a long pause, and then it spoke again, breaking the meditation. *This Nephilim has done what was necessary.*

But at such cost.

The Almighty has weighed the cost. His grace and mercy are great!

Praise Him!

Praise Him!

Music erupted, enveloping Thomas in a torrent, burning with its passion and love. Just when he thought he could not stand it any longer, it ceased. He felt bereft and relieved all at once.

The angels focussed on him, freezing him in place. He wanted to hide, but there was nowhere to go. His father had told him the angels were not always friends of the Fey. And he was helpless before their burning gazes.

Nephilim, the first one said, the word ringing. *Guard well the children of men. We are watching.*

Their forms dissolved, the bright light fading into silver, which melted into the same scene he had seen before. But this time, an indistinct golden figure stood beside Nona, reaching towards him where he lay on the bed.

The scene tore away and Thomas fell, spinning downwards out of the light. There was time for only a momentary relief from being out from under that all-seeing regard before an odd sensation like breaking up from the ocean's deep into sunlight washed over him in an abrupt transition from one world to another.

A confused jumble of awareness swept over him. Heat, the whisper of a voice, a parched mouth, the weight of gravity, the smell of sweat, blood, and candle smoke. Above all, a throbbing ache of pain that centred in his leg and radiated outwards.

His eyes fluttered open, and he must have stirred, for there was a gasp beside him.

"Thomas!" Nona leaned over him, her green eyes bright with tears. She looked over at Aidan. "He is awake!"

"Praise God for His mercy!" A glad smile lit the bishop's face as he placed a hand on Thomas' shoulder. "Good it is to see ye, me son. I will go tell the others ye have awakened. Rest now. Do not fear. Our prayers will continue." He squeezed Thomas' shoulder and left.

Thomas tried to speak, but his mouth was too dry, his throat too sore. It came out as a croak.

"Shh. The bishop is right. You must rest." Nona's face filled with exasperation as she saw him try to speak again. "Here," she said, picking up a goblet from the table beside the bed and slipping an arm around his head, raising him so he could drink.

The ale tasted sweet and cool, washing out the foul taste in his mouth. Nona helped him lie back, and he closed his eyes with a groan, his head spinning. Darkness tugged at him, but he opened his eyes and forced himself to speak, his voice a rough croak. "Celyn?"

"Recovering." She frowned. "You sent me to him, knowing I would not have any power left to help you after I Healed him. 'Twas very foolish. You nearly died."

Thomas couldn't keep his eyes open. "Not dead yet," he managed, before the dark claimed him again.

Time passed in a jumble of sensations and images. Pain was his constant companion, his leg a dull thunder of agony when he was awake. He escaped in sleep, but only in brief snatches, interspersed with flashes of pain when he moved and woke with a gasp.

He learned in bits and snatches what had transpired after he passed out at Merton's holding. When Nona saw the extent of his injury, she cauterized the wound. But without her Healing power to aid her, infection had set in. Even her attempts to Heal him after her power replenished had not been enough to keep it under control. The infection raged, and they had feared for his life.

But after an all-night prayer vigil, the fever snapped.

Once he was out of danger, Nona moved him and Celyn to Bebbanburg, caring for them both with the help of Brother Eadric from Lindisfarne. She plied him with various foul concoctions that he had no strength to resist. They sent him to sleep, which was a welcome relief from the pain.

But day by day he regained his strength. Eventually, he could be awake for longer than a few moments at a time, giving him the chance to think through all that had happened in those last chaotic moments before Godric's blade hit home.

Godric. Redcap. Odda. Wulfram. The Undying. The images and memories flowed through his mind. *See what harm he has already wrought.* Hallucination or not, those words haunted him.

As did the guilt over Odda's death. Why had the memories of all that had happened when he freed Odda only come until it was too late? He should have paid more attention to those *déjà vu* moments he had kept experiencing, should have realized they meant something.

But would he have done anything differently if he had remembered? Odda knew what would happen when he requested to be free. If Thomas had kept him Bound to keep him safe, the consequences could have been disastrous. He could almost come to terms with it, except for Odda's confidence that Thomas would protect him at the last. Maybe Odda would have chosen differently if he had known that Thomas would fail.

But what else had the angel said? *The Almighty has weighed the cost.* The thought comforted him. Truthfully, it was a mercy that what was going to happen had been hidden. Wulfram's misguided plot had shown him how badly things could go wrong when a Traveller tried to change the future.

But he didn't have the energy to ponder these things for long. Sleep always beckoned and was mostly too hard to resist.

He swam up from blackness and blinked open his eyes to see Celyn sitting beside him. Was this another hallucination?

But then Celyn spoke. "*Periglour.* 'Tis good to see you awake."

Celyn looked pale and drawn, his arm in a sling and a bandage wrapped around his middle. But the Welshman's eyes were steady on his, a glad smile on his face.

"Celyn," Thomas managed, his throat tight. "Nona said you would be in bed for a week more." He eyed the other man. Griffith's blade had slashed his arm, but worse was the injury where his brother's sword had pierced him, just under the ribs. It would have been a fatal blow if Nona had not used her power to Heal him enough to mitigate the harm.

Celyn's mouth twisted in a grimace. "As to that, she would not let me out in a year, if it came to it. But she is seeing to a birthing. Eanflaed is having her babe at last." He shifted on the chair, wincing from the movement. "She would only tell me that Wulfram was dead, and you saved the bishop from Godric's blade. But think you, I would hear it all."

For a moment Thomas was tempted to plead tiredness to avoid answering, but he pushed aside the impulse. Celyn deserved to know, and now was as good a time as any to tell it. He took a deep breath and recounted what had happened from when Conaire had come to him in Lindisfarne. But he left out mentioning Redcap. The less Celyn knew about him, the better.

When he had finished, Celyn shook his head, sorrow filling his face. "Nona told me the boy Odda died, the poor lad. But how had he come to be there at all?"

Thomas' lips twisted. He had told Aidan that Odda must have followed him, but in reviewing all that Odda had said that night, he had worked out the truth. *I heard him. I followed.* "Because he heard Wulfram Calling the other *tylwyth teg* to come to him that night."

"He heard him?" Fear touched Celyn's eyes.

"Through Fey power. Because Odda used to be Bound to him. Odda could still hear his commands to the others. He was afraid Wulfram would make him his slave again. And he knew Wulfram meant harm to Aidan. And to me. So he took a knife and followed Wulfram's voice. He killed him." He forced the next words out. "I tried to stop him. But there wasn't enough time. I was too late. Wulfram saw him, and he—" His voice choked off at the memory, and he shook his head.

Celyn shook his head, seeing his distress. "You must not blame yourself. It happened as God willed." He lapsed into silence. A shadow darkened his face, reminding Thomas that the Welshman, too, had faced his own loss.

"I'm sorry about your brother. It could not have been easy to face him."

Celyn's lips tightened. "He was crazed, raving. A dark hand drove him there, but he went willingly, I fear. Jealousy and anger are fertile soil for the Devil's work."

"Jealousy?"

A sad smile flitted across the Welshman's face. "Aye. He had hoped to marry Murieann, but she chose me. He never forgave me for that, nor for leaving her alone to face the Saxon's madness. For a long time, I could not forgive myself either." His eyes sharpened on Thomas'. "You must not make the same mistake. The ways of God are mysterious. But we must believe His intentions are good. It will all make sense, in the end. Odda is truly free, at last."

Celyn's words brought a small lessening of the guilt that plagued him, but even so, it would not be so easily dismissed. "Yes, I know. But I wish it could have happened differently."

The Welshman sighed. "As to that, so do I." He shifted, wincing at the movement. "Nona said the *tylwyth teg* took Wulfram's body away to the Otherworld."

"Yes."

Celyn looked as if he wanted to ask more, but obviously thought the better of it. "And what of the harper?"

Thomas let out a breath, grateful he would not have to elaborate on the story he and Nona had come up with to explain Wulfram's disappearance. Neither he nor Nona had wanted to guess at what Redcap's motives truly were. "I don't know. No one has seen him."

Conaire appeared at the door. His gaze flickered over Thomas, giving him a slight nod, but he addressed Celyn. "The babe has been born. A healthy boy, praise God and all the saints. Nona will be back here to check on ye both soon, so she will. I had better get ye back to your bed afore she returns, or she will have me hide."

Celyn made little protest as Conaire helped him up. As they left, the bell at Bebbanburg's church rang, tolling the news of the birth. Life continued, as it always did.

Thomas lay back, allowing the sound to sing him to sleep.

CHAPTER 66

ALL WILL BE WELL

A few days later, Thomas awoke from a fitful sleep to the sight of a small crowd of monks gathered around his bed, including Father Gaeth, Lindisfarne's prior; Brother Coerl, and Brother Eadric. Aidan and Nona stood behind the monks.

He squinted at them, wondering if they were real. His fever hallucinations had diminished, but he had learned not to trust his judgement. But then Father Gaeth spoke, dispelling the dream-like nature of the vision. "Praise God and all his angels! 'Tis good to see you awake!" A wide smile creased the prior's face, which faded as he peered more closely at Thomas. "How are you feeling?"

"I'm alive," he managed, unable to find the energy to say more. If he could, he would have said that his mind was foggy from Nona's potions, his leg was on fire, he was as weak as a kitten, and his heart still ached over the loss of Odda.

"Indeed. May God be praised. We have been praying for you, my son." He paused, his gaze roving over Thomas; shaking his head at the sight of his heavily bandaged leg. "The bishop has told us of your sacrifice on his behalf, but now we see the price you have paid."

"The Lady Nona says you are healing well," Brother Eadric interjected. "We were much afraid for you, especially last week. But, praise God, He has answered our prayers!"

"Thank you." As much as Thomas appreciated the visit, he wished they would get on with it. Pain pulsed with every beat of his heart. He just wanted to fall back into the arms of sleep.

Nona must have discerned his thoughts. "Father Gaeth, be quick. He must rest."

"Yes, of course, my lady." The prior nodded at her and turned back to Thomas. "Bishop Aidan vanquished the demon through God's mighty power, but he would not have survived the harper's knife if it were not for you, Master Thomas.

So we have brought you this gift as a sign of the gratitude of the brothers of Lindisfarne. We pray it brings you comfort now, in your time of need."

He nodded at Brother Bram, who held out a small bundle wrapped in worn canvas.

Thomas took it from him, but his fingers fumbled at the wrapping. Coerl saw his difficulty and took it from him. He unwrapped it, holding the gift up for Thomas to see.

A silver cross, strung on a leather cord, dangled from his fingers. It was fashioned in the Celtic style, with a circle surrounding the centre of the cross and etched with swirling designs along every surface.

Father Gaeth took the cross from Eadric and slipped his arm around Thomas' shoulders to raise his head, placing the leather thong around his neck and easing him back on the pillow. He took Thomas' hand and placed it gently over the cross, squeezing his fingers so that Thomas' hand enclosed the cool metal. "Christ be with you, Master Thomas. Do not fear. All will be well."

"Thank you. This means a lot to me. I..." But the words got stuck in his throat and he couldn't continue.

Aidan smiled and stepped forward. "Ach, me son. 'Tis only a small thing. I, especially, am thankful that God brought you to us."

Thomas shook his head. "It wasn't just me. Odda was the one who killed Wulfram. I just got in the way of a knife."

"A knife intended to bring my death. 'Twas brave all the same, so it was." Aidan squeezed his shoulder. "Rest now. Once ye are well enough to travel, we will welcome ye back at Lindisfarne."

Thomas nodded, weariness overtaking him. "I would like that." Sleep took him before he could say any more.

The days passed in a blur, but Thomas felt stronger as time went on. About a week after the monks' visit, Nona came in, her face flushed. The summer heat was waning as dusk approached, but the discomfort in her expression told him it was not just the heat that made her cheeks flame.

His heart sank. She had told him of Conaire's desire to begin their journey home and her wish to stay to oversee his healing. But by the look on her face, her husband's will must have prevailed.

"Thomas," she said, sitting beside the bed. "My lord husband tells me we will leave on the morrow." Distress shadowed her eyes, and she lapsed into silence.

Even though he had expected it, her words pierced Thomas to the core. He managed a nod. "I understand. Conaire's been very patient. I'm sure if it had been up to him, you would have left days ago."

Nona's fine black eyebrows drew downwards in a frown. "As to that, he had no say. I couldn't leave until I knew both you and Celyn were out of danger. And besides, it was good for him to be here, too, to show Oswy his support."

Thomas grunted. "I'm not sure he needs it. The *ealdormen* are happy to keep him on the throne, or so Celyn says. After everything that happened." He hesitated a moment. Questions had percolated through his mind the last few days since he had begun to feel better, questions he could ponder without the relentless pounding of pain to distract him. This might be his last chance to find out the answers. "The story that Aidan and I came up with, about me finding the arm, was pretty weak. I'm surprised everyone swallowed it. Especially since they were all so suspicious of me." The slight tightening of her eyes told him what he wanted to know. "It was the Fey, wasn't it? A few Charms here and there, a little sprinkling of power to help them believe it?"

Nona's eyes sparked at the tone of his voice. "It was best that the humans believed it. For you, and for us. Wulfram's Unseelies had been busy spreading a few Charms of their own. Lies and exaggerations to further their cause. You know that. The true story of the arm's theft and return could not be told. We did what we had to, so that questions would not be asked."

Although Thomas wanted to argue with her, he saw her point. But he didn't want to concede it. "And the reconciliation between Oswy and Oswine? Celyn said it was a near miracle that Aidan's message reached Oswy in time. Was it a miracle? Or did the Fey have something to do with it?"

She shook her head. "As to that, we Fey had no part in it." She cocked an eyebrow. "There was more to this than our own plans. God directed all of us, that I am sure. Do you not think so?"

"Even Odda?" Thomas countered, grief seizing him again. "Why did he have to die? It should have been me."

"And if so, Aidan would even now be dead—or, even worse: Wulfram's slave." She sighed. "I do not understand it all, I confess. But we will not forget Odda's sacrifice. He made the choice freely, or so you said. We must honour it."

Choice. It all came back to that moment in the Otherworld, when he gave Odda the choice, when they both saw what was about to happen. Regret pierced him again. "He thought I would save him. That's why he agreed."

Nona leaned towards him. "You must not blame yourself. You told me you tried to stop the boy. But you could not. None of this was your fault. Wulfram is the cause. And he would have done far worse if Odda had failed, if you had not Called Redcap…" She trailed off, her gaze searching his. "Do not bear this burden. God does not require it."

Her words eased the sting of his guilt, but Thomas knew it would take time for him to believe them. If he ever did. He sighed, wincing as a slight movement of his leg sent a spear of pain through him. Seeing it, Nona drew back, scanning his leg with a frown. Her gaze met his again. "I did what I could, but I fear it will not be enough. Your leg will always pain you. If I Healed you when I first saw you—"

Thomas grabbed her hand, stopping her words. "Celyn would have died. You know it. I knew it then. It's all right. I'm alive. He's alive. That's all that matters."

Nona let out a breath, her eyes softening. "Thomas, I—" He held up his hand to stop her words.

"No," he forced out. "Don't." For one long moment, he swam in the emerald-green depths of her eyes, and then his gaze roved over her, imprinting her face into his memory. He forced himself to break the silence. "Are you happy with him?"

She swallowed, and her cheeks flushed again. "Aye."

He nodded and released her hand, but before he could speak again, Conaire entered the room, as if conjured by their words. He looked between Thomas and Nona, scowling.

Nona looked up at him, and Thomas noted the spark that lit her face. Jealousy twisted its knife, but he ignored it. *Not for you.*

"Wildin'," Conaire said, nodding at him. "I wish ye a safe Crossin' back to your time. We will pray the winds take ye safely home."

Thomas saw he had won some respect from the Ward. *But I almost died to get it.* He squelched the thought. "Thank you. I'll pray for your journey home, too. And for the safe arrival of the baby."

"Aye, God willing," Conaire said, worry shadowing his eyes before resolution filled them again. He turned to Nona. "Come. We must go." He held his hand out to her.

Nona's gaze darted to Thomas, but she pressed her lips together and took her husband's hand, rising gracefully from the stool. "I've left instructions with Brother Eadric for your recovery. He has promised to send word how you fare." Tears sprang to her eyes. "Go with God, Thomas."

"And with you," he managed. Conaire took Nona's arm and led her to the door. She looked over her shoulder at him, their eyes meeting one more time, and then Conaire shut the door behind them.

Thomas shut his eyes. He would miss her. He would miss them all. But he had to let them go. He could not risk staying here too long and being stuck in this time. Doing so would cause many complications, not the least of which would be that his presence here could draw other Travellers, just as Matthew had drawn Godric and Wulfram both. He grimaced. He had to Cross home at Samhain, or at least attempt it.

He stretched his leg, wincing at the pain. Thankfully, he had a few months left before he would attempt the Crossing. He would need them to regain his strength. Both to Cross back home, and to do the few tasks that pressed on him before that day came.

CHAPTER 67

YOUR FATHER'S SON

July 10, AD 643,
Bebbanburg

Thomas leaned against the side of the hut to rest and look over the alehouse. Rain fell steadily, and he pulled the cloak's hood up as a shield. A small pang went through him. His attempt to save Odda's life had ruined his old cloak. This one was a gift from Celyn. A reminder of Celyn's friendship, but also of Odda's loss.

He shook off his melancholy thoughts and focussed on his task. Tonight he sought an answer to one of the lingering questions that plagued him. But he was surprised Raegenold had agreed to the meeting. He would have to tread carefully. The Unseelie King had reasons of his own for agreeing to Thomas' request.

It was after the evening meal, but the waning summer nights still held a couple of hours of light until sundown. Normally, people would still be hard at work in the fields or at home. But tonight, a travelling *scop* had come to Bebbanburg on the heels of Oswy's latest victory and the news of his son's birth. People gathered to celebrate. Music floated through the air, the reedy voice of the *scop* lifting and falling along with the notes of the lyre.

It was not Godric. No one had seen him since the night of Solstice, or had heard of him. Thomas assumed the harper had Crossed back to his own time that same night. At least he hoped he had made it home. Despite all that had happened, he held no ill will towards his fellow Traveller. Godric had been snared into Wulfram's plot. In the end, the harper tried to do the right thing. It wasn't his fault that Thomas had jumped in the way.

But he couldn't stop thinking of the demon's dark form streaking over his head, and of the mysterious disappearance of the Hunt. Had the demon swooped down on Godric once he was far enough from Aidan's powerful presence? Or had the Alder King taken Godric instead of Thomas, perhaps persuaded by Cadán? He came to no answers over the long weeks of healing.

But another question brought him to this meeting with the Unseelie King.

He massaged his leg as he studied the alehouse. Godric's knife had cut through muscle, and the cauterization and subsequent infection had done more damage. He would never walk without a limp. Eadric predicted he would always need a walking stick, but Thomas was determined to build up his leg enough so that he could discard it. But he wasn't there yet. Even this brief excursion from the king's fortress to the village nestled at the foot of the rocky outcrop had already taxed his strength, and his leg ached abominably.

He straightened up, his eyes narrowing. *There.* A young Unseelie, sparkling with Fey power, ambled around the corner of the alehouse and leaned against a fence which enclosed a fat sow and her piglets. He appeared to be admiring the beasts, but Thomas saw he also kept a sharp eye on the alehouse from under his hood.

Just as he suspected, Raegenold hadn't come alone. It gave Thomas a certain grim satisfaction to know the Unseelie King was wary of him. He pushed away from the hut, stepping out so the other Fey could see him.

The sharp-faced Unseelie straightened up and Thomas felt the slight surge of power as the other man Spoke to the king inside. He nodded as Thomas approached.

Thomas ignored him, walking past him and stepping into the alehouse. It took a moment for his eyes to adjust to the dim and smoky interior. But the faint glow of Fey power drew his gaze to Raegenold, who sat at the end of a table in the far corner. His wife was with him, and she gave him a slow smile as she saw him enter. *Great.* Sparring with Eawyn was the last thing he wanted to do, on top of everything else.

He sighed, trying to release his irritation, seeking calm. *God, be my strength.*

As he had hoped, the alehouse was crowded. Which was why Thomas had arranged to meet the Unseelie King there. The more people around, the better.

The performer was a short, wiry man whose enthusiasm made up for his lack of skill. But the people seemed to enjoy the performance. A merry atmosphere permeated the alehouse, a sharp contrast to Thomas' unease at the coming confrontation.

He made his way through the crowd towards Raegenold, greeting those he knew and nodding at others who caught his eye. He saw many familiar faces, including Aethelwin, Oswy's reeve, Father Colm, Framwic the smith, and even the stocky form of Dunn. Badulf, the stable master, looked over as he entered and hoisted a mug at him, a smile on his genial face. Others nodded at him with varying degrees of respect in their eyes. Saving the bishop's life had gone a long way towards persuading the people of Bebbanburg to accept him.

As did the fact that the dark cloud of suspicion, anger, and fear that had hung over them all winter had dissipated with the death of Wulfram and the vanquishing of the demon. The people had even rallied behind Oswy. Of course, victories in his skirmishes this summer had helped. He was poised to become a powerful king who enjoyed the favour of his people.

Thomas slid onto the bench across the table from Raegenold and his queen, trying to control the wince of pain as he did so. But he saw Raegenold's keen regard and knew that the Unseelie had seen it.

Raegenold motioned to a slave. "An ale for him," he said, motioning to Thomas. "And be quick. He has travelled a long way." He glanced at Thomas, amused at the inside joke, and then looked back at the girl and placed a coin on the table. "And another for us."

She nodded, scooping up the coin, and hurried away.

Raegenold's eyes glittered. "Well then, wilding. We are long parted."

Thomas didn't want to exchange pleasantries, but he ignored his irritation, knowing that Raegenold was doing it for precisely that reason. "But never far apart."

A small smile played over Raegenold's lips. He was wearing a dark blue tunic of fine linen, rich embroidery adorning the edges of the sleeves and the neck. A thick gold bracelet around his wrist shimmered in the candlelight. His clear blue eyes, so typical of the Fey, were as bright as glass. His physical appearance was as imposing as his Fey power. The strength of it jangled along Thomas' nerves with a pleasant buzz.

The serving girl appeared again, placing wooden mugs in front of them. He nodded at her in thanks, and she hurried away to serve another man who was gesturing at her.

Eawyn broke the silence. "He looks different, my husband." A slow smile crept over her face. "Older, I think."

Raegenold smiled, enjoying Thomas' discomfort. "I think he has become too much a monk to enjoy what you offer, my love."

Eawyn's eyes raked over him, and Thomas could not stop the blush that accompanied her heavy-lidded look. "Perhaps not."

Raegenold glanced at her, a warning in his eyes. "Enough now, wife. These games are amusing, but the wilding is not interested."

Her throaty laugh caused a man at the table behind her to glance at them. His eyes sharpened in interest as he saw the beautiful Fey, but Raegenold noticed the look he was giving his wife. Fey power surged, and the man turned back, disinterested.

Raegenold looked back at Thomas, one eyebrow raised as he noted his disapproval. "It is best for the human that he not notice us."

"Best for you, you mean."

Raegenold shrugged. "Perhaps. But I think your Seelie sensibilities would protest at Eawyn using him for a toy this night. Am I right?"

Thomas gripped his walking stick. "Yes." He allowed his power to weave through the word.

Raegenold's eyes narrowed. "Why did you ask to meet me? State your purpose."

Thomas allowed a moment to go by to make sure he was ready. "Odda."

A muscle in Raegenold's cheek twitched, and he raised his eyebrows. "The slave? The one who killed Wulfram? What of him?"

The king's eyes were blank, innocent. Thomas might have believed him, if he didn't know better. But Odda's voice intruded in his mind. *An angel told me I could do it.* "You sent him to kill Wulfram. I want to know why."

Raegenold's jaw hardened, and Thomas knew that what he had figured out over the past weeks was correct. He leaned towards the king over the table, pitching his voice low. "I know you did. You came to him in a dream, or used Glamour. Pretending to be an angel. You told him to kill Wulfram."

Anger touched him again at the thought. Odda had made his choice long before that night to do what he did. But Raegenold's interference had only encouraged him. Perhaps there could have been a different outcome if not for that. One that didn't involve Odda's death.

"Have a care, wilding. You are speaking to a king," Eawyn said. Her face was cold and hard, devoid of her usual sensual playfulness.

"I know who I'm speaking to," he shot back. The gleeman's raucous song helped to cover his voice from any who might be listening. "Raegenold. Unseelie. King. Speaker." With each word, he allowed his power to grow until it sang in his blood. He pushed against the Unseelie's mind, just enough to let Raegenold feel his strength. "A Fey who thinks nothing of using a defenceless child to do his dirty work."

Eawyn scowled, her eyes snapping fire at him, power sparkling around her like a nimbus. "How dare you," she hissed. "My husband—"

"Enough," Raegenold said, shooting her a hard look.

Eawyn bristled but remained silent, her eyes simmering with anger.

Raegenold turned back to him. "This is not the time." His voice was as cold as ice.

Thomas' jaw hardened. Raegenold could throw around his weight all he liked. He would not leave without his answer. "This is the only time I'll give you. I want to know why you sent him to kill Wulfram."

Eawyn's silence was short-lived. "My husband, he cannot speak to you this way! He is nothing. He knows nothing!"

Raegenold ignored her, his gaze fixed on Thomas, his eyes narrowing. Finally, he shook his head and looked over at his wife. Wary amusement filled his face. "He knows enough, it seems." He looked back at Thomas, the amusement fading. "The Traveller was dangerous, you said so yourself. He is dead. That is what you wanted. You should be grateful."

Thomas clutched his staff and bit back the first words that sprang to his lips. *Careful.* He couldn't let Raegenold goad him into making a mistake. He knew perfectly well what the Unseelie King was capable of, even with the crowd surrounding them. "We both know you didn't do it for me. Wulfram was stealing your Court, wasn't he? He was a threat to your throne." Raegenold made no comment, and Thomas continued. "But it was too dangerous to get close to him. You couldn't risk it yourself, not with the Undying so near. You needed someone else to do it. I get that. But why Odda? He was just a child."

Raegenold's eyes flashed. "I protect my people. The life of a human child is nothing. They breed like mice, after all. Ten more will take his place." His mouth twisted. "I could not depend on you to destroy the Traveller when the time came. There is too much of the Seelie in you." He leaned back, a smile flashing across his face. "The Calling of Redcap, though. That I did not expect. Not even an Unseelie would have dared that much."

The servant girl went past again, and Raegenold caught her arm. He smiled up at her. "I am hungry. Bring me some of that honey cake, and be quick." Fey power wove through the words as he spoke.

She straightened. "Yes, my lord. Of course." She bobbed a curtsy and hurried off, ignoring the calls for ale from other patrons.

Raegenold gestured at the retreating girl. "Some are easy to Charm. Especially those who have been Charmed before. Your slave had not only been Charmed, but Bound. To two Fey, not just one." He paused to let the barb sink in. "I needed a tool. You provided a handy one. I did not Bind him to me, just gave him the push to do what he wanted to do, given half a chance." The king leaned over the table. Fey power danced along Thomas' skin, questing against the barriers in his mind he had erected to keep the king out. "But in the end, Thomas mac Cadán—Traveller, Speaker—you were your father's son, were you not? Unseelie in your heart and blood. You had the chance to stop the slave boy, but you did not. His blood, and Wulfram's, is on your hands."

The barb stung, but Thomas had expected it. "Yes. Which means you owe me something."

Raegenold drew back, his eyebrows raised, and then a smile played around his lips. He sat back, waving a hand. "Speak."

Gotcha. Thomas hid his relief that his gamble had worked, that Raegenold could not resist the Fey's natural propensity for an exchange of favours. "Celyn ap Wynn. He is a Sensitive and knows the ways of the Fey. He's been Charmed before, too. You and your Court will leave him alone."

The other Fey shrugged. "I have no interest in him. But even if I wanted to use him for my needs, I cannot see how you would stop me. I hear you will Travel again, and soon."

The serving girl returned, carrying a wooden platter with a honey cake on it, which she placed in front of Raegenold. But as she did so, another patron jostled into her, and she had to grab Raegenold's shoulder to steady herself. The king darted a glance at her, anger flashing over his face, and she staggered against the table, her cheeks draining of colour. "Please my lord," she gasped, "I have brought it quickly—"

Thomas touched her arm to steady her, releasing Raegenold's Charm. He had acted on impulse, almost without thought, but Eawyn's sound of disgust suddenly made him realize what he had done. Maybe not the best move, seeing the anger in Raegenold's face, but he didn't regret it.

The girl blinked, frowning slightly as she looked between Thomas and Raegenold. Another patron called to her, and she shook her head as if clearing it and then hurried off to answer the call.

Raegenold eyed him with disdain. "Wulfram was right about one thing. Your concern for the humans is unnatural. If they knew you were Fey, they would kill you without hesitation. And yet you wish to protect them."

Eawyn's face twisted in scorn. "My husband, we must leave. This wilding tries my patience."

Raegenold nodded, but he kept his eyes on Thomas. "Soon. But he has not answered my question. You do not intend to stay here, to be nursemaid to the *wealas*, do you?"

"That won't be necessary." He paused. "You forget. I am friends with the Redcap, he who walks between the worlds."

Raegenold sucked in a breath. Fear flashed through his eyes, followed by anger. "Wilding," he hissed, "I will rejoice when the winds tell me you are gone."

Thomas let out a breath he hadn't known he was holding. The fear that Redcap might intervene at Thomas' behest, along with the obligation of the favour owed, should be enough to keep Celyn safe from the Unseelie Court. *Should be.*

Raegenold stood up, raked his gaze over Thomas, and strode to the door.

Eawyn followed at his heels, but before she stepped outside after her husband, she turned back, her eyes meeting Thomas' across the room.

Tread carefully, wilding. We will be watching you.

He let out a breath as the door shut, relief filling him. It had worked. A wry smile crossed his face. He had just been told for the second time that he would be watched. He took a careful sip of his ale, grimacing. It was a toss-up between which sets of watchers should concern him the most: the angels, or the Unseelies.

He wrestled with the question a moment longer, but as the music swirled around him, he dismissed it. When the *scop* played without singing he was pretty good.

Stretching his leg out with a groan, he abandoned himself to the song, following the story it told. A story both sad and beautiful. One completely human, removed from the world of the Fey.

Chapter 68

Time to Go

Thomas mounted Missy, his leg protesting. As summer turned into fall and the days got shorter, he had been riding for short distances, testing his stamina. The long journey back to the sweet spot would tax his still-healing leg, but it couldn't be helped. The time had come.

Aidan and the monks stood waiting. They insisted on seeing him off, much to Thomas' dismay. He didn't want a long goodbye. Aidan prayed the journeying prayer over him and gave him his blessing.

A lump formed in Thomas' throat as he thought about all that this small community meant to him, and all that they meant for the future. They were not perfect, far from it, but they were faithful. And perhaps that made the difference.

Aidan stepped forward, his hand raised in blessing. "Thomas, me son. Go with God's blessing and the favour of His Son resting on you. Ye have been a friend to us here, and we are grateful, to be sure." He smiled. "And know ye are welcome, if your travels bring ye back."

Thomas managed to smile. "Thank you." Missy danced in place, tossing her head. She was impatient to go. "Thank you for everything," he forced out through the knot in his throat. He held Aidan's gaze for a long moment and then turned Missy's head and urged her to a steady trot, towards the wet sands that sparkled in the early morning sunshine.

Time to go home.

The goodbye he dreaded the most would not come yet. Celyn insisted on accompanying him to the Crossing spot, so Thomas' only task at the king's fortress was locating the Welshman. It surprised him to find Oswy and Eanflaed waiting for him along with Celyn. Their infant son lay in his mother's arms.

"My lord king," he said, going to one knee and bowing his head.

"Rise," Oswy said, gesturing at him, and Thomas stood, using his stick to help him. Oswy's keen gaze swept over him. "The Lord Celyn told me you are leaving Bebbanburg to go back to your home at Byzantium. We wish you a safe journey." He thrust an object at him. "You saved Aidan's life," he said gruffly. "I have not yet given you my thanks. This is a small token of our gratitude."

It was a silver belt buckle, worked with swirling, stylized animal figures and Celtic knotwork. "Thank you, my lord king."

"Go with God, Master Thomas," Eanflaed said. "We will pray for your journey."

"Thank you, my lady."

Oswy nodded at Thomas and then took his wife's arm, leading them away. Thomas watched them go. God had used him to save this king and his kingdom. He prayed all the sacrifices were worth it.

He sighed and turned towards Celyn. "Are you ready to go?"

Celyn nodded. "As to that, I've been ready since sunrise."

Only one last task remained. Thomas went to the graveyard beside the church. First, he visited Odda's grave. He would never forget the boy, not only for his sacrifice, but also because of the empty space within him Odda left behind. Both it and the limp that marked him served as reminders of the danger of his power. And of the limits of it. Even though he thought he would vanquish Wulfram on his own, in the end it was a boy with more courage than he possessed who did what he could not. "Thank you," he whispered to the small mound of dirt. *Too small.* "God give you rest."

He heaved a breath. One more, and he dreaded it. But it had to be done. He found Matthew's grave and looked down on it, his heart aching anew at the loss of his father. The pain had faded, but he knew from experience it would never truly go away. At least he had the hope of seeing his father again, but this time in a place with no goodbyes.

He looked around, committing the landscape to memory. He was determined to come back here in his own time to find it again.

"I'll tend the grave," Celyn said, his face solemn. "He'll not be forgotten."

Thomas' throat tightened. He gripped Celyn's shoulder in thanks before they turned and made their way to the stable.

Arawn was saddled and ready, so there was nothing left to do but to be on their way. Before mounting Missy, Thomas tucked Oswy's gift in with the bundle of other things in his bag. One of those was his father's lyre. He would not leave that behind.

Once past the gates at Bebbanburg village, they headed south. Thomas' spirits lifted as they rode along the familiar path. It was a glorious fall morning, the trees ablaze with crimson and gold. But they didn't far. He pulled on the reins before the last curve in the road that would hide Bebbanburg from sight, turning Missy around to view the fortress perched on its rocky hill, drinking in one last glimpse.

Celyn glanced at him. "Are you sure you wish to leave? There's a place for you here."

It was a tempting thought, here on the brink of leaving. He was comfortable here now, but he couldn't help but think of everything that had happened because Matthew stayed on long past the time when he should have left.

He shook his head. "No, I have to go. Better for all of us."

Celyn grunted in acknowledgement, and they urged their horses into motion again.

This time, he did not look back.

The weather was warmer on this journey than it had been the previous year. The sun shone every day, except for one, when the rain came down in sheets, soaking them to the skin despite their cloaks.

They travelled slowly. Both Thomas' and Celyn's still-healing injuries hampered their ability to ride for long periods of time. But they expected this and gave themselves enough time to compensate for it.

Thomas didn't mind, for the slower pace gave him the chance for a longer goodbye to this time and place. He was going to miss it, even with its dangers and lack of modern conveniences. He savoured the beauty of the thrusting hills and the rushing streams, and the crisp air of dawn. And every night he and Celyn said the *caim* prayer in a slow circuit around their fire, the stars burning in the sky.

Sometimes they stayed overnight in a holding. Thomas played the lyre and earned a coin or two along the way, which he tucked away in his bag, added to the others he had collected.

But even though their pace was slow, it felt as if only a few days had passed when the morning came when a Call to a Gathering shimmered through his mind. *Come, Seelies, Come!*

It was Domech, Calling the Seelies to the Samhain Gathering. Brorda told Thomas before he left Bebbanburg that the king was holding the Gathering near the thin place where he would Cross. They were not far now.

Thomas had not seen the king since they parted at his holding, when Nectan banished him from his Court. Brorda hadn't said so, but Thomas was sure that before he Crossed, the Seelie King would meet up with him. And so he kept himself ready, anticipating the king's Call.

The excitement the Gathering Call left behind added to the nervous tension filling him as the time to Cross grew nearer. He was not sure it was going to work. All he had to go by was the Fey's favourite piece of advice: the wisdom of the Fey comes by doing.

But this time, instead of frustration, the saying brought reassurance, as did the Aidan's advice. *God provides the wind; man must raise the sail.*

He would step into that Crossing spot at dusk and fall into the winds of time, and trust God for the rest.

CHAPTER 69

MOON SHADOW

Thomas woke with a start, alert. Above him, myriads of stars burned on their velvet black backdrop. Even with the light of the nearly full moon dimming their light, it was an impressive sight. But he gave it only a cursory glance as he rolled over and peered at Celyn, who slept across the fire from him, bundled in his cloak.

The stamp of a horse's hoof and an abrupt whinny broke the stillness. Thomas rose to his feet, grimacing as his leg flared with pain. He rubbed it as he straightened up, looking over to where Missy and Arawn were hobbled. Their black shapes moved restlessly. Something had disturbed them. Or someone.

Celyn remained asleep, although normally he was the first one awake when the horses were restless. Thomas frowned, concentrating. A slight glow covered the Welshman like a blanket. A Charm.

He let out a breath. Nectan, likely. But maybe not. He'd have to be careful.

A slight breeze lifted sparks from the coals of the fire. They twirled and coalesced and then broke apart again, dancing past the horses. They snorted and skittered away as the bright embers flitted past and escaped into the darkness.

Thomas clenched his jaw. He grabbed his walking stick, following the sparks and murmuring to the horses as he passed them. Missy's ears swivelled towards him, but she kept her eyes on the humped shape of the bushes lining the small stream next to their campsite. He patted Missy's neck. Beside her Arawn tossed his head up and down. They were nervous. He didn't blame them. He was nervous, too.

The Breastplate prayer ran through his mind as he crossed himself and walked to the bushes, stepping past them to see what lay beyond.

Moonshine illuminated the figure crouching beside the silvery, tumbling water. A long hat swung against his back as he stood and turned to face him.

Thomas gripped his stick more tightly, his heartbeat loud in his ears. He would have much preferred Nectan to Redcap.

The moon was behind the other Fey, shadowing his face. Only the glitter of his eyes and a hint of the sardonic smile playing across his lips were visible. "Not long parted, never parted. Welcome." He spread his hands wide.

Once again, it took a split second for Thomas to realize that Redcap spoke in modern English. *Who are you?* The question sprang to his lips, but he didn't dare ask it. He wasn't certain he wanted to know. He settled on a different question. "Why are you here?"

That was safer. Maybe.

Redcap cocked his head. "Ah, look at you, youngling shepherd. The moonlight becomes you." He swept his hat off his head and bowed. "We are well met again."

"What do you want?" he asked again.

"Redcap does as Redcap wills. But it is what *you* want that brings me here, indeed."

A breeze stirred the brittle leaves once again, and a few fell to the ground, silent as ghosts, as Thomas pondered Redcap's answer.

It was true; there were things he wanted clarified, questions he could ask. He shifted his weight off his aching leg and picked the first that came to mind. "Fine. What did you do with Wulfram?"

A feral smile spread across Redcap's face.

Thomas' blood chilled. He held up a hand before the other Fey answered. "Never mind." Another question came to mind, but he bit it back. How could he trust the other wilding's answer?

Redcap quickly extinguished his answering laugh. Burning hunger flashed through the other Fey's eyes as his hands curled into fists. A brief flash of power shimmered around him and evaporated. He turned abruptly and crouched down, facing the brook, humming under his breath.

It was a song Matthew had loved, about moon shadows, and a sudden ache for his father pierced him.

Redcap leapt up and sang, spinning around and flinging his arms wide, his head tilted up to the sky. "Moon shadow! Can you see it?" He stopped and faced Thomas, the grin fading from his face. "Ask and be quick! The moon calls, and I must be off!"

Suddenly Thomas knew what he wanted to ask, and he blurted it out. "How do I do it? Crossing, I mean?"

Fey power swirled again around Redcap, outlining him in a shiny nimbus. "It is who you are, shepherd and guard, fire-touched Fey. How? By law and by birth, by sun and by moon, by will and by way. None will stop you, none to mind you." He laughed again. "Redcap will show you! Come with me, youngling."

Eager desperation edged his voice, and once again, pity seized Thomas. Redcap was a wilding Traveller who had been thrust into an impossible situation he had no experience to navigate. Just like him. But Thomas had found Celyn, and Aidan, and the monks. Even Nectan had sheltered him when he wasn't even aware of how much he needed the king's protection. He had come to terms with who he was by the grace of God. Redcap had not been so fortunate. He had survived, but it had broken him.

He shook his head. "I can't."

"Can't and won't, can't and won't. Two sides of a spinning coin, a whirly coin, a shining coin!" Redcap danced on the moonlit grass, his movements nimble. But he froze as a wolf's howl lifted above the sound of the burbling brook. "Blood," he whispered. "Blood and blood again."

Thomas swallowed, his skin crawling at the eagerness in the wilding's voice. No matter his pity, he must not forget how dangerous he was.

None of the other Fey forgot. Raegenold's reaction to Thomas' warning was proof of that. Thomas hadn't expected to see Redcap again, and so his warning had been mere bluster. But now the opportunity was right in front of him. He hesitated for a moment longer, not positive it was the right thing to do, but he had no more time to think it over. "Wait. One more thing. Celyn ap Wynn, the Welshman at Oswy's Court. He's a Sensitive. But I don't want the other Fey using him for their own advantage. Watch over him for me."

For a moment there was no response. Redcap stood frozen in the moonlight like a statue, and then the wolves howled again, closer this time. He shuddered. "Blood," he whispered to himself.

He stepped towards the sound and then turned, looking back at Thomas. He tipped his hat, flashing a white grin, and then turned and ran lightly away, humming to himself.

Thomas watched until he disappeared into the shadows. Redcap hadn't answered him, but he sensed the other wilding would do as he asked. In his own way, he would try to help.

Of course, Celyn would not appreciate the gesture, but Thomas did not plan on telling him. He would be safe from the schemes of the Fey. That is what mattered.

The stream burbled on, the liquid tumble of the water the only sound. Although he waited, listening, he heard no other howls. The wolves must have moved further away. He watched the silver stream of water flowing endlessly over the rocks, and then went back to the fire.

CHAPTER 70

SAMHAIN

On the morning of Samhain, Thomas and Celyn awoke shivering under a grey sky, a chilly wind whipping among the trees. Overnight, fall had departed and winter had arrived.

They ate a quick breakfast of hard bread and cheese. But Thomas found it hard to eat. Nervous anticipation only allowed him to take a few bites. He would face the Crossing tonight, and he wasn't sure he was ready.

Missy and Arawn were eager to get moving as well, their breath escaping in great clouds as they snorted and pranced.

"Easy, Arawn," Celyn said, patting the stallion's neck as he settled in the saddle. They touched their heels to the horses' flanks and set off, the icy wind at their backs. A sleety rain pummelled them for an hour, but even when it cleared off, the clouds remained, giving a gloomy cast to the day. But they made good progress, and by mid-afternoon Celyn reined Arawn to a halt.

"This is it," he said, gesturing at a small path that broke away from the main road and led into a small copse. "Look for the forked ash."

A large tree stood nearby, its trunk split half-way down its length from a long-ago lightning strike.

Thomas recognized it. This was the turnoff to Wulfstam, where the *thegn* Siward lived, and where Celyn would stay the night. This was where Godric had waited for Thomas to join him, so they could go to see Wulfram together.

But Celyn had discovered him missing and had come after him. Thankfully. Things would have turned out much differently if he hadn't. If Thomas had met Wulfram then, ignorant as he was of the ways of the Fey, Wulfram would have had no trouble Binding him to his will.

The Welshman had been his protector and his friend, but now the time had come for their parting. Celyn wouldn't go all the way to the Thin Place. He did not wish to be caught outdoors at night on Samhain. Thomas couldn't blame him. Celyn would stay at Siward's holding overnight. If Thomas could not Cross, he would join the Welshman there.

Thomas refused to think of what he would do after that. He couldn't allow himself to plan for failure.

Celyn dismounted and pulled a strip of brightly coloured cloth from his bag and tied it to one of the lower branches. "Look you, this will mark the spot."

Thomas dismounted, ignoring the ache in his leg. His throat tightened, but he forced a word out. "Celyn."

The Welshman held up a hand. Tears shone in his eyes, but his face was composed. "There will be no long goodbye, *periglour*."

Thomas nodded, the lump in his throat making it impossible to speak.

Celyn stepped towards him and gripped his shoulder. "Go with God, and may His Son protect you." His voice was rough. "I will pray for you, wherever your path leads you."

Thomas managed a smile. "The first day I met you, you were praying for me. You're always praying for me." He swallowed. "Don't stop."

Celyn let out a tear-filled chuckle. "As for that, I will not." His smile faded. "God has released you from my care. He will guide you now."

Thomas let out a shaky breath. "I couldn't have made it without you." They embraced. "Thank you. I'll never forget you."

Celyn snorted and pulled away, wiping at his wet cheeks. "As to that, *periglour*, neither will I forget you." He shook his head. "Off with you, now."

Thomas mounted Missy, and without another word, started down the path. But after he had gone a short distance, he turned her around to look back, his heart aching.

Celyn stood, watching him go. He lifted a hand in farewell, and Thomas did the same. Then he wheeled Missy around again and touched his heels to her side.

Time to go.

CHAPTER 71

FEY AT LAST

Wildin'. I am here.

Thomas pulled Missy to a halt, the king's voice fading in his mind. Nectan had come to him at last. He composed himself, and then clucked his tongue, urging Missy into motion.

He rode into the clearing where his journey in this time began one year ago. Where he had woken up, confused and sick, with Celyn bending over him.

Nectan stood by a tall aspen tree whose golden leaves fluttered in the slight breeze, a few spiralling around him as they fell to the ground. The king watched with his arms crossed as Thomas drew Missy to a halt and dismounted. He would leave the mare here when he went to the Crossing. Celyn would fetch her tomorrow.

He tied her to a tree and grabbed his staff. The days in the saddle made it impossible for him to walk without it. He made his halting way over to Nectan and stopped, inclining his head in a slight bow. "We are long parted."

Nectan uncrossed his arms, regarding him solemnly. "But never far apart."

Silence fell, broken by the sharp chittering of a squirrel. Thomas shifted positions, easing the pressure on his leg. "Congratulations. Sounds like you had an easy time of defeating Strang at the Solstice Gathering."

"Not as easy as all that, wildin'. But he will no trouble us again, that is true."

Brorda had told Thomas what happened at the Gathering; how Nectan had turned the tables on Strang that night. "Lucky for you that Wulfram's meeting with Strang was revealed. Brorda told me there were only a few of his supporters left after Eachan and Torht both confirmed it."

Nectan's eyes flashed in amusement. "Oh, aye. The luck o' the Fey can be a great boon, to be sure. And sometimes we make our own luck."

Thomas snorted. He doubted that a meeting between Wulfram and Strang *had* taken place, but Wulfram had been behind the unrest in the Seelie Court, so it wasn't much of a stretch to point to a direct collaboration.

He eyed the king as his amusement faded. Now he could clear up another one of the lingering questions that occupied him during his enforced idleness as he healed. He debated how to bring it up, but decided the direct approach was the best. "Thanks for sending Cadán to me that night. He saved my life."

Nectan stiffened, shock and anger flashing across his face. But then a grudging smile touched his lips, and he shook his head. "Ach, wildin', ye ha' learned to be a Fey at last. How did ye know?"

Bingo. It was an educated guess, but hearing Nectan admit it shocked him even so. He shrugged, schooling his face to nonchalance. "My father said Cadán left the Seelies and joined Raegenold's Court because of his advice. But after Cadán showed up at Solstice, I began to wonder about something my father wondered about, too."

"And what was that?"

"How you found out it was my father's advice that sent Cadán to Raegenold. Only three people knew that: my father, Raegenold, and Cadán. I know my father hadn't told you. I doubted Raegenold did. So that left Cadán. Once I figured that out, the rest fell into place."

Nectan's face remained impassive, but a grudging admiration touched his eyes as he gestured for Thomas to continue.

"Cadán is no Unseelie. He's your eyes and ears in Raegenold's Court. You were the one who sent him to Raegenold. But what I can't figure out is why he agreed to it. He could have been king."

Nectan's lips twisted. "Ach, he didna want the throne. And he weren't fit for it. He knew that as well as I. There is a touch of the Unseelie in him, besides. Enough for him to fit in well in that Court, to enjoy the game we played. But we weren't sure how to do it wi'out Raegenold suspecting. Your father gave us the way. Traveller's words hold weight. A Traveller tellin' someone he should change Courts was something no Fey could ignore or question. Even though it opened the door for us, it gave Cadán cause to worry." He cocked his head. "Why did your father interfere? Not that I weren't grateful, ye understand, but I ha' wondered all the same."

Thomas lifted one shoulder in a half-shrug. The tangles of it made his head ache. "He had his reasons. A Traveller's secrets are his own."

Unease flashed across Nectan's face. "Aye. I suppose I had better not know." He dismissed the subject, fixing him with a steady gaze. "I had no choice but to release ye from your pledge. But I asked Cadán to keep an eye on ye. Raegenold asked him to do the same, so he had no worry someone would discover him being disloyal. The wind blew in your favour that night, wildin'."

"In all of our favour. The Undying controlled Wulfram. It didn't care about the future of the Fey. It just wanted to destroy everything good, here and now. That's what evil always wants."

"Aye, indeed." Nectan shifted on his feet, glancing up at the steadily dimming sky and then back at him. "I must go. The Gathering awaits. But Domech will be watchin' to make sure you Cross." He paused, his amber gaze resting on Thomas. "I will be prayin' that the wind takes ye safely to your home."

Thomas doubted the sincerity in the king's voice sprang from any sentimental reasons. Nectan would be glad to see the back of him, considering the chaos the Travellers had caused. He dismissed the thought. He could hardly blame the king, after all. He drew himself up and dipped his head in acknowledgement. "Thank you. For everything."

Nectan held his gaze for a moment, and then nodded and turned back to the woods. He soon disappeared from sight, leaving Thomas alone.

Thomas let out a breath. Now all he had to do was to wait until sundown.

Thomas paused at the edge of the woods, near the deer path leading to the Crossing spot. Power swirled around him, gaining strength along with the lengthening shadows, making his heart pound faster.

He had not seen Nectan's Speaker, which was fine with him. But a faint tingle told him Domech was nearby. He half-wondered if the Speaker would take matters into his own hands and kill him if the Crossing was unsuccessful, but he dismissed that thought. There was nothing he could do about it, anyway.

Now or never. He set aside thoughts of Domech and plunged into the trees along the path. Memories flitted through his mind of everything that had happened; mingled fear and anticipation jolted through him at the thought of what was to come.

He had spent the past couple of hours in a state of nervous tension interposed with moments of prayer as he waited for sunset. It had seemed an interminable wait, but now time flew, the seconds until sunset rushing by.

The leaves crunching underfoot sounded unnaturally loud. He had forgotten how much noise hard rubber soles made. He wore his old clothes, which he had kept buried in the bottom of the storage chest near his bed in the guest house at Lindisfarne. Although he had scrubbed them as best he could in a bucket of hot water, they were still stained and torn. But better that then showing up in his own time wearing his tunic, breeches, and cloak, which were now tucked in his backpack. Although it was Halloween, after all. He might get away with it.

The clothes felt odd. Too tight in some places and loose in others. His shoulders were broader, his arms more muscular. He was finally past the awkward and lean adolescent frame he had arrived with. Chopping wood will do that for you. And walking everywhere, hauling water, riding a horse. He had matured. And not just physically.

He broke out of the trees and paused, looking over the clearing. Massive oaks stood sentinel, their leaves burnished gold. The last time the sun shone as it set. This time, clouds covered it. The autumnal colours were muted but were no less captivating. A Thin Place.

His heart tripped as the peculiar magic of the Crossing spot swept over him again, as it had a year ago. The same wondrous joy burst upon him like a ray of sunshine, scouring away his anxieties. He walked to the centre of the clearing. The burgeoning power reminded him of Solstice, but this time without the fear that filled him that night. He couldn't help smiling as he spread his arms wide, tipping his head to the sky.

Clouds still scudded above, pushed along by the gusts that blew against him and caused the tree branches to dance. But he didn't feel cold. Far from it. He felt alive, blood-pumping and in-the-moment alive. He dropped onto his knees in the brown grass, thinking of the monks. They would be praying now at Lindisfarne, for him and for Celyn, who said he would do the same. But the thought scattered under the intensifying power.

Last time he tried to Cross he was afraid to surrender. But he had learned much about courage and trust over the past year—from Celyn, from Aidan and the monks, from Nona. And from a young boy who gave everything and rescued them all.

As the sun sank and the power surged, he closed his eyes and allowed his own power to explode into life. It rushed through him in a torrent, merging with the explosion of power as the sun dipped below the horizon. He gripped his cross with one hand and lifted the other to heaven. *Please, God, get me home.*

A rushing noise roared around him. He let go, and everything winked out.

Chapter 72

Halloween

Thomas came to himself as a thundering, whirling blackness faded from his mind, leaving behind a sensation of a vast, timeless, chaotic expanse. A shudder wracked his entire body. Whatever that was, it made him feel as if it turned his skull inside out, and he wanted no more of it. But it had knocked everything else from his head, and for a moment he panicked, reaching for something, anything.

Memories dropped into his mind. A beautiful woman, green eyes glowing. *Nona.* A tall man, stern and gentle all at once. *Aidan.* And another man, a thin scar snaking up his temple, riding a big black stallion. *Celyn.*

The Thin Place. Thomas gasped as it all flooded back. He was alive, God help him. The stabbing agony in every muscle almost made him wish he wasn't. But where was he? Or more importantly, *when?*

He opened his eyes. A white expanse filled his vision. *Snow.* He lay on his side, one arm pressed under him against the ground. It was cold. He closed his eyes again, the effort of working out even those minor details exhausting.

The pain faded after a few more breaths, but the sense of whirling disorientation was harder to shake. It thrummed in his mind like a great white noise, making it hard to stitch his thoughts together. *First things first.* He opened his eyes and forced himself to move, pushing himself to a sitting position, his head whirling. Nausea gripped his guts. He leaned over, retching, and wiped his mouth with a trembling hand as he looked around.

He sucked in a shaking breath as he drank in the sight. Familiar trees met his eyes. The large spruce tree that he had often sat against was right in front of him. *The sweet spot.* He was home. He let out a shaky laugh, which turned into a groan as the nausea returned. If everything would stop spinning, he would feel much better.

The last time he had seen this place... the memory of the demons returned, just as he heard a crashing through the bushes. His heartbeat spiked into overdrive and he tried to rise, but his muscles wouldn't cooperate. His stomach flipped in protest, and he leaned over and retched again just as two teenage boys pushed their way past the faded wild rose bushes and stood blinking at him.

He raised his head and wiped his mouth with a trembling hand. "Don't be afraid," he said, his voice sounding odd through the ringing in his ears.

The boys looked at each other, comical surprise on their faces. One of them spoke to the other, gesturing at Thomas as he did so.

Thomas blinked at them stupidly. One of them wore a Batman costume, the other sported an eye patch and carried a plastic sword, a fake beard hanging on his chin. His scattered brain supplied another bit of information. *Samhain. Halloween.* He realized belatedly why they had looked at him funny when he spoke. *Wrong language, idiot. I doubt they understand Old English.*

Batman asked him a question. For a moment his mind was blank, and then the meaning fell into place.

"Who are you, mister?"

Relief coursed through him. *Thank you, God.* He shook his head to clear the white noise that made it hard to hear, but regretted it as nausea returned and he had to turn aside and heave again.

"Told you. He's just a drunk!" Batman said, disgusted. "Let's go. Mike's waiting for us!"

"Just text him," the pirate said, staring at Thomas in fascination. "Maybe he's hurt or something. Or he's got Covid." He frowned, looking around. "And what was that light? There's no fire."

He stepped closer to Thomas, but not too close. "You want us to call an ambulance, mister?"

Panic spiked through him. That was the last thing he needed. "No, no, I'm all right."

Batman snorted. "You better get a move on. There's lots of cops out tonight." He brought out his phone. Its bright light shed a glow around them in the twilit dusk. He texted, his thumbs flying over the keys. "I told Mike to meet us at the school," he announced to the other boy. "Let's go."

He tugged the pirate's sleeve. But his companion shook him off, staring at Thomas in fascination.

A Sensitive? Maybe. He saw a light when I Crossed. Thomas took a chance. "Look, just tell me something. I need to know what year it is."

The pirate's eyebrows raised, and he looked back at the other boy, who snorted. "Come on, Morgan! He's just a drunk! Leave him alone. We gotta go!"

Thomas tried again, trying to look reasonable. "I just don't remember. What year is it?"

"I'm leaving. I'm gonna call the cops! He's a freak, anyways." Batman crashed off through the bushes, and Morgan turned to follow.

But before he disappeared, he turned back. "2020," he said, and vanished into the trees.

Thomas blinked, and he let out a trembling breath. *One year later.*

He had done it.

He lay back for a moment, gathering his strength, but he couldn't stay long. Batman was right. Cops regularly patrolled this park on Halloween. He had to get going.

His staff lay nearby, and he grabbed it, pushing himself upright with a groan, fighting dizziness. He looked around and spotted his bag lying near his feet. He grabbed it and hoisted it over his shoulder.

He closed his eyes. Aidan's voice came back to him. *Raise your sails, and God will provide the wind.* He opened his eyes. *Okay. Here I am, God. Let's go.*

He pushed through the bushes and emerged into the small grassy area. Faint calls of *Trick or treat* and *Halloween apples* drifted towards him.

The snow fell down lightly, and he looked up, feeling it kiss his face lightly. Triumph surged through him, bringing energy despite his weariness.

Home. He was home.

ACKNOWLEDGMENTS

As always, there are many to thank when completing a project of such scope. I always used to think that writing was a lonely profession. And while it is true that I have spent more hours than I can count alone in my writing space, pounding at the keyboard, it is also true that I have collaborated with many people to bring this book to completion.

Thanks again to the folks at ebooklaunch.com. This cover was a perfect fit for my vision.

My editor, Kristine Buchholtz at Polished Stone Communications, has once again done a stellar job at making the manuscript ready for print. Her insights throughout the entire process, including developmental edits, copyedits, and proofreading, have proven invaluable. Who knew that a random encounter so many years ago at a writers' conference when we were both newbies would blossom into a solid working relationship? Thank you, Kristine!

My beta readers: Cheryl, Lesley, J.L., and Anne-Marie: you are more valuable to me than you likely realize. Your insights and comments have helped me make this book much better. Thank you for spending some of your valuable time helping me in this way!

I have to give a special shout-out to another of my betas, my son, Luke. A stellar writer in his own rights, he provided me with detailed feedback that opened up a whole new dimension in the book (literally and figuratively!) and helped me get to the heart of what I wanted to say. Thank you, THANK YOU.

And another special shout-out to my daughter, Sarah. She has lent some of her considerable artistic skills to create a map for my story world. And more surprises are coming from her brush, so stay tuned!

My readers: To know that you enjoy reading my words is one of my joys. Thank you to all of you who spent some of your hard-earned money on my books and keep coming back for more. Knowing there are people out there who appreciate my work keeps me going on those days when it all seems futile. Thank you!

And, as always, my biggest thanks go to my husband, Mark, and my kids, Joshua, Luke and Sarah. They have picked me up out of the writing doldrums and cheered me on through each new book. My heart belongs to you all.

All to the glory of God.

L.A. Smith
September, 2022

AFTERWORD

With the completion of *Choice*, Thomas' journey into the past has ended. I have been working on these books for almost two decades, from when I got the first idea of the novel until now. I've learned so much about the fascinating world of 7th century England, and about the process of writing and publishing. While it's hard to say goodbye to these characters I have invested so much of myself into, I am also looking forward to what comes next.

And what is that, you ask? Good question! I'm not entirely sure, myself. I will take a bit of a break to think through the answer. I have a couple of ideas for the next book or series, but I need to do some research and make some decisions. Do I continue with the world of *The Traveller's Path*, focussing on different Travellers in different time periods? Should I continue with Thomas' story, with an urban fantasy series on what happens next? We've seen what it is to be Fey back in the 7th century, but what does it look like for him, now? I'm intrigued by that.

Or should I do something completely different?

To be honest, as with any venture one might launch into, to do it right takes a great deal of work and sacrifice, both monetarily and personally. I have learned so much about the writing process since I first began to write *Wilding* that I am eager to write at least one more book and put it all into practice. And I want to write some more short stories, as they are so fun and take much less time.

If you are interested at all in what comes next for me, you can keep up with my writing journey by subscribing to my newsletter, if you haven't already. I try to send out a newsletter once a month, but when I'm facing a deadline and/or deep into a project, that frequency will slow. But in the newsletter you will get the occasional bonus, like a short story, first access to plus be up to date on all my projects. Head over to my website and click on the Sign Up button to subscribe—and you will get a bundle of two short stories featuring characters from *The Traveller's Path* as well!

Thank you for taking this journey down *The Traveller's Path* with me.... I hope you continue to follow along to where the road takes me next!

One last thing... I would really appreciate a review from you at the retailer where you bought Choice. Every review makes a huge difference! It doesn't have to be a long one. Just an honest opinion. Thank you!

WHO'S WHO

<u>THE FEY</u>
Travellers
Thomas McCadden—from the present day
Matthew McCadden—from present day. Thomas' father.
Godric—from 1972. Unseelie Fey and harper who travels around Northumbria
Wulfram—from the present day. Unseelie Fey who lives in Eoforwic
Fey of the Northern Seelie Court
Nectan—king of the Northern Seelie Fey
Eara—Nectan's wife, Queen of the Northern Seelie Fey
Durst—nine-year-old son of Nectan and Eara
Domech—Nectan's nephew and his guard/bowman
Nona ferch Albanwr—cousin of Celyn, visiting Bebbanburg from Gwynedd
Albanwyr ap Bledri—Nona's father, from Gwynedd
Brorda—merchant
Emma—Brorda's wife
Conaire Mac Alpin—Nona's betrothed, from Dál Riata
Torht—bone carver of Bebbanburg
Hilda—wife of Torht
Strang ap Siric—*thegn* of Oswy, Nectan's rival for the throne of the Unseelie Fey of the North
Eachan mac Flann—Horseclan Fey of Dál Riata, cousin to Fidelma
Binne—Eachan's wife
Fey of the Northern Unseelie Court

Raegenold—king of the Northern Unseelie Fey
Eawyn—Raegenold's wife and queen of the Northern Unseelie Fey
Cadán Longshanks—guard, and Raegenold's confidant
Grith ap Ethernan—also called Ulchabhán (the Owl).
Solitary Fey
Jack Redcap
The Huntsman/The Alder King

BEBBANBURG FORTRESS

Oswy—king of Bernicia, newly crowned in August, AD 642
Eanflaed—wife of Oswy and daughter of King Edwin of Deira
Aethelwin—reeve
Father Paulus—Roman priest who accompanied Eanflaed to Oswy's court
Celyn ap Wynn—exiled warrior from Gwynedd
Father Colm—Irish priest from the monastery at Hii. King Oswy's advisor and scribe
Baldulf—stable master
Uthred—warrior/guard

BEBBANBURG VILLAGE AND AREA

Dunn—coerl, formerly of Stowham
Framric—smith
Eappa & Eadmund—brothers; nephews to Framric
Bronwyn—Nona's maidservant
Raedmund—thegn
Odda—ten-year-old boy who is Thomas' Bound slave

LINDISFARNE

Aidan—Bishop/Abbot
Father Gaeth—Prior
Brother Barach—Guestmaster
Father Donal—head of scriptorium
Brother Iobhar—head of the monastery school
Brother Eadgar—cellarer, in charge of supplies

Brother Eadric—chief healer in charge of Infirmary
Brother Seamas—chief shepherd
Brother Frithlac—herbalist
Brother Bram—metalworker and artisan, maker of silver implements for the monastery
Brother Jarlath—one of the monks
Father Eata—one of the monks

DAL RIATA

Conaire mac Alpin—newly appointed lord of the holding on Loch Glashan
Elatha—step-mother to Conaire
Tynan—Conaire's friend and trusted warrior
Albanwyr ap Bledri—Nona's father, visiting from Gwynedd
Fidelma (Fee)—widow of Matthew McCadden
Eachan mac Flann—Fee's uncle
Binne—Eachan's wife

DUN ADD FORTRESS

Ferchar mac Connaid—newly crowned king of Dál Riata
Grith ap Ethernan—Ferchar's trusted advisor. Also called *Ulchabhán* (the Owl).

EOFORWIC / KINGDOM OF DEIRA

Oswine—half-cousin of Oswy and king of Deira
Griffith ap Wynn—warrior of Gwynedd, brother to Celyn
Wulfram—Unseelie Traveller

About Author

L.A Smith lives in a small town in Alberta, Canada. She loves drinking tea, walking her dog, knitting, and writing. Not necessarily in that order, and not necessarily all at once.

You can catch up with L.A. Smith on:

Facebook— https://www.facebook.com/lasmithwriter

Twitter—@las_writer

Instagram—https://www.instagram.com/lasmithwriter

Goodreads—https://www.goodreads.com/author/show/19196383.L_A_S mith

For all the latest on her books, sign up for the newsletter at lasmithwriter.com and get a FREE book as a thank-you (scan QR code at the beginning of the book!)

Also By L. A. Smith

Rare, Prized and Feared: Tales from The Traveller's Path
Bound: Book Two of The Traveller's Path
Wilding: Book One of The Traveller's Path

www.ingramcontent.com/pod-product-compliance
Lightning Source LLC
Chambersburg PA
CBHW032150190726
48290CB00005BB/1494